All rights reserved.
ISBN-10: 1517114098
ISBN-13: 978-1517114091

AUTHOR'S FOREWORD

Diamonds For The Wolf is the third in the Jack Renouf series and follows immediately on from the second which ended in October 1940.

This is a stand-alone adventure and, though it is not necessary for you to have read either of the first two novels, you might find the list of principal characters and my notes on separating fact from fiction at the end of this novel of help.

The two previous stories are:

Against The Tide (1939)

The Last Boat (1940)

Please visit my website www.johnfhanley.co.uk if you wish to peruse the more detailed historical information which underpins them.

If you enjoy **Diamonds For The Wolf** please leave a rating or a short review on Amazon.

John F Hanley
September 2015

Prologue

Transcription of a document in the British National Archives, ADM 223/463

TOP SECRET.
For Your Eyes Only.
12 September 1940.
To: Director Naval Intelligence
From: Ian Fleming

Operation Ruthless
I suggest we obtain the loot by the following means:

1. Obtain from Air Ministry an air-worthy German bomber.
2. Pick a tough crew of five, including a pilot, W/T operator and word-perfect German speaker. Dress them in German Air Force Uniform, add blood and bandages to suit.
3. Crash Plane in the Channel after making SOS to rescue service.
4. Once aboard rescue boat, shoot German crew, dump overboard, bring rescue boat back to English port.

In order to increase the chances of capturing an R or M [Räumboot – a small minesweeper; Minensuchboot – a large minesweeper] with its richer booty, the crash might be staged in mid-Channel. The Germans would presumably employ one of this type for the longer and more hazardous journey.

NB. Since attackers will be wearing enemy uniform, they will be liable to be shot as franc-tireurs if captured, and incident might be fruitful field for propaganda. Attackers' story will therefore be that it was done for a lark by a group of young hot-heads who thought the war was too tame and wanted to have a go at the Germans. They had stolen the plane and equipment and had expected to get into trouble when they got back. This will prevent suspicions that party was after more valuable booty than a rescue boat.

This memo is authentic.

What follows is largely fictional.

DIAMONDS FOR THE WOLF

JOHN F HANLEY

1

1940: Tuesday 22nd October

It should have been a short journey – less than four miles Saul reckoned. Even in the blackout the cabbie had promised no more than thirty minutes but then he hadn't expected to hit an elephant on the Harrow Road. The elephant's keeper was out of breath following her chase, as was the cabbie after his tirade at her stupidity. Saul intervened. He'd grown up in South Africa – he understood elephants. Only, because of its small ears, I thought this one was Indian and probably didn't comprehend Afrikaans so I shoved him into the taxi before he upset the pachyderm.

This delayed us further and, after squealing to a halt outside the Soviet Embassy at 13A Kensington Palace Gardens, the cabbie was shouting again – at us this time. He wanted the five-pound note that Saul had waved at him at the beginning of the trip as an incentive to drive during the blackout. It was probably too early for the Luftwaffe to make its nightly visit so the capital was still and waiting in quiet anticipation. Without the wail of sirens and the thunderous explosions of bombs there was little to disguise the vocal irritation of the poor cabbie and this drew the attention of the two policemen protecting the embassy from unwelcome visitors.

'Now then — we'll have less of that noise.' There was still sufficient ambient light to make out the expression on the sergeant's sour face as he leant on the taxi's roof. 'What's the problem?'

'This bloody shyster,' howled the cabbie stabbing his finger at Saul's head. 'He promised a fiver for this fare and now he's welching on it!'

'A fiver? I don't earn that in a week. How far have you come, for God's sake?'

'Canfield Gardens,' Saul responded.

The sergeant shook his head. 'That's nonsense; it's not worth—'

'But he promised, and just look at my bumper – it's his fault. I told him that—'

'You can't blame me for your driving into that elephant, you stupid *kaffir*!'

I grabbed Saul's arm. 'Give me the fiver.'

He opened his wallet and extracted a crisp white note.

I hadn't seen many of these and, even with the extra pay for special duties, it would take me a month to earn that much.

I approached the cabbie. 'Here, you know where he lives. We'll need transport back there when this bash is over.' I tore the note in half and offered one to him. 'Wait here for a couple of hours and I'll give you the other bit after you drive us home.'

'Well eff, you and your effing elephant. If you think I'm going to effing wait for you to finish your effing party in that effing place you've got another effing fink coming. Stuff your effing money up your effing arse and keep the effing change!'

'That's enough. Give me both halves.' The sergeant held out his hand and I surrendered the two bits of paper. He reached into the cab and removed the key. 'Now, you rude little man, do as the gentlemen suggest and wait like a good person until they finish their business then you can drive them back and earn this money which is far more than you deserve in a month of Sundays. And if you offer any more abuse I will take your taxi and shove it up a part of your anatomy where it will fester and itch for some time. Do we understand each other?'

The cabbie opened and closed his mouth a few times then nodded silently.

I sensed Saul about to open his and start the argument again so pushed him towards the gates.

'Just a moment, young gentlemen.' The sergeant rounded on us. 'You can't just waltz into the Soviet Embassy without an invitation. I'd like to see yours.'

'We don't have invitations. I'm meeting my boss in there. He'll vouch for us.'

'And who might that be?'

'I can't reveal information like that. Here, check this.' Saul fished in his pocket and held out his ID.

The policeman switched on his hooded torch and examined the card. 'Sub-Lieutenant Marcks, RNVR. Wavy Navy, eh? What about your mate or is he your batman?'

'Renouf, 5514027, Hampshire Regiment,' I answered

He shook his head. 'No. You need an invitation or your names on the list.' He looked at the other policeman. These on your list, constable?'

'No, sarge, 'fraid not.'

'That's it then. Best get back in your taxi and find some more stray animals to play dodgems with.'

Saul fiddled in his pocket again and brought out another card which he held out to the sergeant who examined it then sucked some air in through his teeth.

'I see — NID, eh? Naval Intelligence Division. So you're a couple more of the "funnies" for the party with the Commies. Well, I won't stand in your way but, if you'll take my advice, I wouldn't show that to Boris and Doris over there.' He pointed to two dark figures staring at us from inside the wrought iron gates. 'They might send you to a different party in the basement to see if you actually have any intelligence.' His acidic expression stretched into a broad smile as he stood back and threw a casual salute in our direction.

Close up, the two Russian guards were even more intimidating and as soon as the larger of the pair, whom I assumed was Boris, closed the gate on us, his partner Doris pulled Saul towards her and frisked him in a less than gentle manner. Rather than start a diplomatic incident I allowed Boris to maul me without retaliation while rehearsing a couple of moves I'd recently learnt which should have brought him to his knees though quite what I would have done after that eluded me. Fortunately, I didn't need to contemplate further action as Saul spoke softly in another of his foreign languages, pulled out his wallet and passed over a couple of ten shilling notes in place of the missing invitation cards. Not for the first time I wondered what he was getting me into.

Doris, who looked as though she could have picked the elephant off the taxi with one hand, opened one of the double doors and ushered us into a gloomy interior. The lobby was deserted but the building echoed to the noise of geese squabbling on the floor above. We were confronted by acres of red carpet and a twin staircase fenced in with oak balustrades. Dim overhead lights revealed two large urns atop the stairs standing guard on either side of a rounded archway which framed an entry to the farmyard of cackling birds above. We took a staircase each and paused to salute each other half way up. I couldn't resist touching the gigantic urn on my side. Perhaps it held Poland's ashes. It seemed appropriate as a massive portrait of Comrade Stalin leered down at us.

We followed the sound into a room which seemed to be furnished in gold – not quite what I expected from the dour Soviets. There was plenty of glitter from the guests who turned out to be human rather than geese. A white coated giant from the same litter as Boris lumbered over with a tray of drinks. There seemed to be a choice between something bubbling in crystal and something deathly still in squat glasses. I never feel the need for alcohol until the first drink and I've become steadily weaker at refusing that so I lifted the former and slurped it so quickly that the bubbles attacked my nose and made me sneeze all over my neatly pressed khaki uniform. Saul selected the alternative which I assumed was vodka and tipped it down his throat in one. It wouldn't matter if he spilled any on his uniform. Even though it was tailored for him and the Royal Navy would always win in the inter-service style stakes, he could ruin any uniform as soon as he shrugged into it. At his best he looked like a sack of spuds and tonight he hadn't even reached the bottom rung of the smartness ladder. With his red hair, freckled face and relaxed figure he looked very much like a Guy Fawkes dummy ready for the bonfire. Casting another glance around the room I realised two things — that I was also on the bottom rung of the rank structure as all those in uniform seemed to be officers and there didn't seem to be any food — caviar or otherwise.

Saul spotted someone, seized my elbow and negotiated us through the throng until we reached a small group that was listening to a tall naval officer, also sporting the wavy rank stripes of the Royal Naval Volunteer Reserve. His were the two and a half rings denoting a lieutenant-commander with additional emerald green stripes inside the gold. Between drags on his cigarette, he was speaking in a lethargic yet compelling manner. His broad forehead promised intelligence and the arched eyebrows suggested wit but his eyes were cold and his lips, while full, seemed cruel when he paused to listen to a question. There was danger in this man and an aura which suggested total confidence beyond the borders of arrogance. If this was Saul's boss, I didn't think I was going to like or impress him very much.

'Ah, Marcks; about bloody time. You really are a shambolic little monkey. Get lost did you?'

'Apologies, sir, we had an unexpected meeting with an elephant.'

The group turned their heads to examine Saul. One of them was a striking looking woman with frizzy hair, a full mouth and warm brown eyes. She was wearing a bright green gown which clung enticingly to her slender figure. She laughed. 'Really, Ian, is this your new secret weapon — the elephant brigade?'

'No, Litzi, this is Sub-Lieutenant Saul Marcks, a South African Jew with excellent connections to those who pay my wages. He has his uses though I'm at a loss to recall any at this precise moment.' He exhaled a plume of smoke in my direction. 'And, unless I am mistaken, this is Jack Renouf, one of his chums from that island of Jersey which is currently under occupation by Hitler's legions—'

A tall distinguished yet dissipated looking man standing next to Litzi interrupted. 'Fleming, are you really trying to sound like Churchill or are you just becoming more self-important by the minute?'

Litzi elbowed the interloper out of her way and pushed him towards a nearby waiter. 'Piss off Kim and send that waiter over. There's no need to hurry back. Ian and I want to talk to these two.'

I waited for a retort from Kim but he smiled and slipped away. The other two men followed him.

I was about to speak when Saul nudged me and addressed his boss. "You would have been quite amused by the elephant, sir. One of those farmed out by Regent's Park Zoo for safe keeping. He even had white stripes—'

'So you thought he was a zebra, I suppose and tried to converse with him in one of your tribal languages?'

There was an underlying amusement in his tone which suggested that their relationship wasn't as fraught as I'd first thought so I chimed in. 'Yes, sir. He did try but it was an Indian elephant and she didn't understand—'

Fleming chopped me off with a string of French in the polished hauteur of a Parisian accent enquiring about my recent experiences in Scotland. This was clearly a man with little patience for small talk. I am cursed with the inability to show appropriate respect for rude superiors so I responded in my very worst Breton and told him what I thought of Parisians.

'Marcks assured me you were fluent in the language but neglected to tell me that you sounded like a Norman peasant.'

I laughed then replied, in an exact copy of his accent, that, should he feel the need to insult a Norman next time he was in France by suggesting that he sounded like a Breton, he might need to seek refuge with the Germans.

Saul didn't understand French and, judging by Litzi's expression she wasn't familiar with the language either.

Fleming's lip curled as he blew more smoke towards me. 'Touché, though my little monkey did warn me that you love playing with fire and don't know when you've burnt your fingers.'

Of course he was correct though my latest specialty seemed to be burning my own bridges.

'Perhaps he also told you that most of the fires I play with were started by him?'

'Enough of this.' Litzi grabbed my elbow and steered me away. 'Jack has just invited me to dance with him so we'll leave you two to your office chat.'

Her English accent was near perfect but I detected some German inflections and she certainly looked more Eastern European than English. I followed her without resistance grabbing another glass of bubbly on the way. We traced the sound of an orchestra to a rather austere room where the carpet had been rolled up to reveal an intricate parquet floor. Litzi looked at my boots and, though she could see her reflection in their polished toes, I suspected she was wondering what the metal studs might do to the floor. Before I could voice the thought she called over the man she'd shoved away earlier and who was now sitting and smoking with an attractive woman. He got up and moved reluctantly towards us.

'Jack, what size shoes do you wear?' Litzi asked.

'Size ten normally though I don't know what the *European* equivalent might be.'

She smiled, revealing perfect white teeth and looked at me with her golden eyes. 'Yes, I'm no English rose. I'm Austrian, Jewish and a Communist. I'll tell you more later, but now I want you to dance with me as I've been told that you are rather accomplished.'

'Not as skillful as Saul. He'd be a better bet for whatever you are scheming.'

'You have no idea what I might want you for but there is no way I am going to be seen dancing with someone who looks like a scarecrow however nimble he might be on his feet.'

Kim stood quietly listening to our discussion before Litzi noticed him. 'Jack, allow me to introduce my husband, Harold Philby known to friends and enemies alike as Kim — he was born in the Punjab in India and his parents read a lot of Kipling if you're interested. Now, Kim, dear man, give Jack your shoes so he can dance with me without ruining the ambassador's floor!'

In Kim's place I would have smacked her rather attractive bottom with one of my shoes but he pulled them off and surrendered them without comment. I struggled out of my boots, undid my gaiters and squeezed into his handmade patent leather shoes. They were not the best fit but I sensed that further protests would be futile and that if Litzi really wanted me to dance with her then I could hardly refuse.

We joined in a waltz and she followed well though her tight fitting strapless gown wasn't best suited to ballroom dancing. She was a bit stiff and seemed reluctant to extend her line in the turns. Her body was more lithe than sensuous but she eventually moulded well into mine and we swept around the floor in close harmony. I couldn't place her scent though once I had been an expert in such things. Unlike Hélène, the other Communist agent I'd met, she didn't use perfume to disguise poor hygiene. Litzi was scrubbed, vivacious and unusually attractive. I guessed she was about thirty which made her ten years older than me but suspected that those extra years had been filled with far more drama and scheming than mine.

Dancing at this level leaves little energy or desire for talking so she obviously wasn't in a hurry to question me. It had been many months since I'd been this close to a woman and with the champagne, music and dim lights I wasn't in a rush to stop either. Three quicksteps, two foxtrots and another waltz later the orchestra called a break and Litzi pulled me out of the temporary ballroom and into what looked like a library. Before I could protest she kissed me on the lips and pulled me into her. But I couldn't respond. She was such a strange amalgam of Caroline and Rachel that even my *little* brain was confused as it flooded with blood. I uncoupled my lips but held her tight while whispering a quick excuse in her ear. 'Sorry, I can't. You're married.'

She released herself then placed her hands on my shoulders and looked into my eyes. 'Pity, but please understand that Kim and I have been separated for years.' She ran her fingers over my cheek. 'I know about Caroline, Rachel and Taynia though.'

Her words were like a punch in the guts. How the hell could she know such things? It must be Saul but why would he reveal my closest secrets to a Communist? He hated them.

Before I could ask she spoke again. 'Your uncle told me and Malita's right — you are a puzzle but probably one worth solving — though not tonight. Thank you for the dancing though, I loved it.' She took my hand. 'We should return the shoes to the poor man. He's confused enough without making him stumble around in army boots. What would his friends think?' She giggled. 'Come on let's —'

She was interrupted by the sound of an unusual stringed

instrument. 'Ah, the balalaika – the entertainment is about to begin.'

I was beginning to wonder if there were any Russians other than Boris and Doris here but when we re-entered the ballroom some musicians, wearing what I took to be traditional costumes, were tuning triangular three-stringed instruments on the small stage. In addition to the four men there was a drummer and a woman with a normal guitar. Kim strolled over with my boots and gaiters and I returned his shoes.

He leant over as I was tying my boots and whispered. 'Be careful; test the water before she persuades you to dive in!'

Litzi hissed at him then asked me what he'd said.

'Nothing much; just thanked me for showing his shoes how to dance and hoped they teach his feet.'

She pinched my cheek. 'Liar.'

Before I could test the water any further the troupe set fire to the air with their balalaikas and I sat down to listen.

Litzi whispered in my ear again. 'This is a traditional gypsy song called "*Marusia*" — haunting isn't it?'

The tempo increased and the musicians swayed with their instruments filling the room with something more than haunting. It was magical. The applause was riotous. As it died away, a slender girl dressed in a figure-hugging black dress stepped onto the stage holding a violin. There were shouts from the audience and she bowed shyly before nestling the instrument into her neck. She nodded and the balalaikas began again.

Litzi nudged me. 'You'll love this — it's called "*Kalinka*".'

The troupe built the tempo slowly then paused as the violin began with the most haunting sound yet. The girl looked severe but leant into the melody and her whole body seemed to tremble with the emotion. I was transfixed.

'Close your mouth, you might catch something.' Litzi laughed in my ear.

It was too late. I'd caught it.

We all stood and clapped enthusiastically. There were shouts of appreciation in Russian and the angel holding the violin obliged with a solo encore. I felt the salty tears running down my cheeks as images of Caroline teasing the same level of emotion out of her grand piano flooded back.

'I think I've lost you, Jack. Would you like to meet her?'

Of course I didn't. I couldn't cope with the memories she'd already ushered in. Why would I risk her dragging me out from the fortress I'd built for my own emotional protection? 'Yes,' I answered.

Saul beat me to it so I held back while he spoke with her. Up close she was nothing like Caroline or Rachel but stunning in a very different way. She seemed delicate, almost vulnerable with high cheekbones underlining dark, almost blueberry, eyes. The milky white skin of her shoulders seemed like porcelain as though she avoided the sun at all cost. Her black hair was squeezed into a severe bun but her mouth was sensitive and full. She wore no jewellery apart from a gold five-pointed star dangling beneath a deep red ribbon pinned to her right breast. She smiled coyly at Saul's compliments though I sensed that it was only politeness that kept her within range of his clumsy charm.

Litzi pulled me forward and brushed Saul aside. 'Masha, allow me to introduce Jack Renouf. Your playing has affected him greatly.' Before I could open my mouth she continued. 'Jack, this is Mrs. Mariya Dobruskina, the Ambassador's niece. Please say hello.'

I'd been too focused on her breasts to spot the ring on her finger. Litzi was teasing me with another married woman.

Mariya, who seemed to be called Masha, held out her hand which felt tiny and cool in my large paw. 'A pleasure, Mr Renouf; I hope you did not find the music too distressing. Perhaps you have a cold?' Her voice was husky and almost without accent though her tone teased. Her eyes seemed to absorb the light and betrayed an inner sadness. Something passed between us which made me shiver but Saul, insensitive as ever, managed to spoil the moment.

'Don't waste your time with this poor soul, Masha; he's exhausted his capacity for love and is but an empty husk, devoid of anything other than self-pity. He's not even an officer!'

There were many disadvantages in not having a commission, principal of which was wearing hobnailed boots, though I turned this into an advantage causing my officer friend to hop across the room cursing in Afrikaans.

Masha gave me a pitying look before turning away and leaving the room.

Litzi poked me in the ribs. 'She's a widow, Jack. That medal she's wearing – Hero of the Soviet Union — was awarded to her husband. It's all that's left of him. Really, she's in just as big an emotional mess as you are. Go after her. Be kind and listen.'

This was wrong. What could I do to help? Nothing. So I went.

I'd almost caught up with her when Fleming appeared by my side. 'Come with me, Renouf. The Soviet Ambassador wants to meet you.'

2

'Why, sir? I'm only an army private and here because of my friend. Why would the Ambassador want to waste time on me?' I hurried to keep up with him as we descended the twin staircase.

Fleming grimaced but carried on talking. 'Marcks is right again. You are in a bit of a muddle. However, I'm sure that he will explain and don't worry he's not going to ask about your obvious interest in his niece!'

Was everybody observing me? 'Really sir, is this necessary?'

'Well, Renouf you're not under my command at present so let's say it's a request that you would be unwise to refuse. Now, before the introductions, you are to understand two things. One, the ambassador is a great friend of Great Britain and two, every conversation he has in this building is almost certainly recorded and reported on to Moscow so be very careful and do not compromise him with any careless remarks or thoughtless questions. However, you will need to be honest with him as he already knows a great deal about you.'

'My uncle I suppose?'

'Let us say that he gains his information from a wide variety of sources and perhaps your uncle is one of those. I've never met this Fredrick Le Brun but, from what Marcks tells me, he has led quite a remarkable life and is held in high regard by the Soviets. Now, do you understand what is required of you?'

'Yes, sir. Listen, learn and control my tongue.'

'Don't be flippant. This could be very important. The Soviets may not be our allies at the moment, may have hopped into bed with Hitler, but they had very good reasons. If only our own politicians had possessed a similar level of concern for this country they shouldn't have let that happen and would have had more time to prepare for the Nazi onslaught.'

He walked on until we reached a large oak door. He knocked. A gruff voice invited us in. It was a large square office with a massive desk behind which sat a rotund cheerful looking man of middle age wearing a dinner suit. He studied us with warm brown eyes, stroked his walrus-like moustache and indicated two chairs in front of the desk before delving into a drawer and brandishing three large cigars.

Fleming remained standing. 'Ambassador Mayskiy, may I introduce

Jack Renouf. I believe you wished to meet him.'

I stood beside him feeling very uncertain. I'd faced my headmaster, senior politicians and policemen from this position before but there was something most unsettling about being propelled into this situation with the Soviet Ambassador. What next — Churchill?

'Thank you Commander, you are most kind.' He stood up, stretched across his desk and offered me his hand. It was warm and his grip was strong. 'Please sit and join me in one of these excellent cigars given to me only last week by your Prime Minister.'

'Thank you, your excellency, most kind.' Fleming took his, sniffed it, fumbled in his pocket, pulled out a cigar cutter and started to prepare his smoke.

'Good, take it with you. I'm sure you'll enjoy it later.'

Fleming responded in Russian and, though I had no idea what he said, it was clear that he had expected to stay. Mayskiy responded with more Russian while smiling apologetically. Fleming shrugged his shoulders and left closing the door quietly behind his disapproving back. I was now alone with Stalin's representative who could very well press a hidden button and summon Boris and Doris to take me somewhere less comfortable for further questioning should I fail to take heed of Fleming's words.

Mayskiy held out the cigar.

'Thank you, sir, but I don't smoke. I know someone who would appreciate it though if you wish to—'

'That would be Fleming's aide; your friend Saul Marcks wouldn't it?'

I nodded while trying to frame a response which wouldn't appear flippant but it was too much for my brain. 'Yes, given its provenance he would certainly treasure it though I'm not sure he's man enough to smoke it.'

He laughed. 'And you're too much of an athlete to try yourself! Good for you.'

He settled back in his chair and went through the pantomime of cutting and lighting the beast. My eyes kept being drawn to the massive portrait of Stalin hanging like the sword of Damocles over the fireplace and above Mayskiy's head. If Fleming was right then the ambassador had to be even more careful with his utterings than I did.

Eventually he had it alight and blew some thick clouds in my direction. The aroma was certainly less obnoxious than cigarette smoke and probably not as intimidating as Stalin's pipe.

I waited.

He drew on his cigar again and prodded some papers on his desk with his free hand. 'As you are no doubt aware we know quite a lot about you but I'm interested in what makes you tick, as you English say, so I want to hear your story from the horse's mouth so to speak. You will excuse my idiomatic usage but English is my third language. I've improved my accent but your construction occasionally trips me up.'

I was about to compliment him but realised that I would be wasting our time. Just answering his questions would be the safest bet. So I waited for one.

'Please, don't be shy. Tell me about last year and how you got involved with the industrial diamonds first.'

I should have guessed. He wouldn't be wasting his time discussing Marxism with a private soldier. Prevaricate, lie or tell the truth? I chose the simple option. 'Through my mother's brother, Fredrick Le Brun, known to the police in Jersey as "*Red* Fred". Not very original but we Jersey folk have a deep suspicion of *socialists* who want to dictate our way of life.' He showed no reaction to that dig and continued to enjoy his cigar. It struck me then that he knew all about the bloody diamonds – probably more than I did and this was just an opportunity to discover more about me. 'What do you really want to know? Ask me and I'll tell you the truth without any diplomatic flannel.'

He smiled, placed his cigar in an ashtray, opened a cupboard in his desk and pulled out a bottle and two small crystal glasses. He filled them with the clear liquid then pushed one towards me. 'I've heard much about you, Jack and believe that you can be very candid after a drink or two so please join me.' He lifted the glass and swallowed the contents in one swift movement then refilled it.

'Aren't you going to smash the glass against the fireplace?'

He laughed. 'You mustn't believe everything you see in the movies. These are expensive glasses and throwing them towards Comrade Stalin would be disrespectful.'

And probably fatal so I picked up my glass had a quick sip and then downed it. My bravado with alcohol had caused me much misery in the past and I was sure I couldn't match him but I had to be polite. The liquid was cool and smooth and only exploded when it hit my stomach. I felt my face glowing with a new fire so pushed the glass to the side out of his reach. 'If you want to get any sense out of me don't refill my glass.'

He picked up his cigar and sucked deeply on it. 'Carry on with your story. I'm especially interested in why you risked so much to get involved.'

'It wasn't about diamonds initially. It started when I discovered that the man who was paying too much attention to my girlfriend wasn't whom he claimed to be and was probably a spy. This Rudi Kempler, I later discovered, was a German officer who was involved with my girlfriend's father in smuggling industrial diamonds stolen from De Beers in the Belgian Congo to Germany. I was just angry that, even though I reported him to the Jersey authorities for travelling under a false passport, they took no notice and refused to act. I even caught the bastard taking photographs of—'

'This is the gentleman who beat you in a swimming race?'

'That didn't mean anything and he did drag my best performance out of me. Good enough to get me selected for the Helsinki Olympics — only Hitler sabotaged that event when he invaded Poland.' I was going to mention Stalin stabbing Poland in the back but managed to bite my tongue in time. 'Kempler, who was masquerading as a Dutchman, had already swum for the Germans in the Berlin Games of 1936 but I could have beaten him with the right training.'

'Yes, the training. You had a very special coach didn't you? What was his name? Dr. Pavas wasn't it?'

Skillful interrogators didn't need to use thumbscrews.

'Yes, like my uncle, Miko hated the fascists – they'd tortured him and murdered his wife.'

'As they had abused your uncle and mutilated Malita in Spain. These were the Romanian Iron Guards who burnt his books and wanted to crucify him just because he was a Jew.'

He was too well informed. I remembered the shock when Rachel and I had dragged Miko's story out of him. That was the moment I'd lost my innocence and all sense of caution. 'Yes, after that I wanted to share his burden and become a Jew myself.'

'That would have been most unwise. This is not the time to become Jewish – indeed many, including Sir Ernest Oppenheimer, who runs De Beers, have become   Christians instead. More sensible Jews have deserted religion altogether and embraced the future without that curse.'

'Didn't one of your Communist prophets declare that religion is the opium of the people?'

'"*Die Religion ist das Opium des Volkes*" is what the *German* Karl Marx wrote and the literal translation is "religion is the opiate of the masses."' He sounded like my old headmaster. 'Marx was correct. Slavish acceptance of these illogical concepts inhibits revolution.'

I wondered if he had renounced his religion as well because, unlike Saul, he certainly looked Jewish. Before the army had shaved off my curls, many had mistaken me for a Jew and, playing Shylock in my school's production of Shakespeare's *Merchant of Venice*, had reinforced that. My church-going father had not been amused and had stormed out of the Great Hall when Shylock had started fighting back and being rude about the Christians who were bullying him.

'I think I agree with Marx. After witnessing those horrors off St. Nazaire I find it difficult to believe in a just God. That doesn't and never will make me a Communist though.'

He shrugged. 'Perhaps some more vodka might help?'

I shook my head.

'You were there at the sinking of the *Lancastria*? You saw the Nazis at their worst?'

I felt the heat rising and it wasn't alcohol. 'Yes, I saw the bombing, the thousands struggling in a sea of oil and the Nazis returning to drop incendiaries to burn them to death. Fortunately, they didn't explode but who knows how many were lost in those dreadful twenty minutes.'

'At least 8,000, or so your Prime Minister believes, though he judged it prudent to prevent publishing that at the time.'

I must have looked puzzled for he continued. 'Mr Churchill has often sat in this study and shared his concerns.'

So Stalin would be well aware of our current plight. Now I felt very uneasy. If Churchill was that close to the Russians and I was now in the bear's lair what was the real purpose of this meeting?

Mayskiy broke into my brooding. 'I understand that Dr Pavas was with you in St Nazaire and that you ended up as part of an elaborate deception plan to smuggle out the world's entire supply of heavy water under the Germans' noses.'

'We didn't know that it was a ruse until they got the stuff to England. The real supply came out through Bordeaux. I don't know where it is now.'

'Neither do we but I suspect that Dr. Miklos Pavas isn't too far away from it!'

I shook my head. 'I don't really understand what all the fuss is. It's only water for goodness sake.'

He blew some more smoke in my direction. 'It's obvious that you're not a scientist and neither am I but developments in the splitting of the atom are naturally of interest to us. Do you happen to know where your Miko might be at present?'

I stepped around the open trap door. 'Sorry, I haven't seen him since he escaped from Jersey. Let's hope he's safe somewhere.'

'Well your Caroline is safe in occupied Jersey looking after her father, the man who was instrumental in trying to smuggle those diamonds to Germany. England is also riddled with fascist Capitalists – let's hope your authorities know where they are.'

He would have got that information from my uncle and, from what he'd told me, the Communists had infiltrated our intelligence services so would be well informed about the Nazi sympathisers rooted in the establishment.

'Perhaps they're not really Nazis but anti-Communists. I suspect that the vast majority of the Germans didn't become fascists after reading "*Mein Kampf*" nor the Russian population become Communists after reading Marx's and Engel's manifesto. Ordinary people react to unpleasant circumstances rather than embrace ideologies.'

'An interesting theory, young man — probably one you've tested on your uncle but I don't think we have the time for a dialectical discussion. Besides, Churchill once told me that democracy is the worst form of government known to man — except for those other forms that have been tried from time to time.'

'So why am I here?'

'Tell me about Caroline and Rachel.'

'Caroline was an alluring spoilt brat and I didn't know whether I was in love or in lust with her. Rachel was a friend who ended up being trapped between us—'

'And bore your child, Taynia?'

He'd caught me again. I swallowed the bile as the vodka kicked upwards from my stomach. 'Yes, and your agent, Hélène, prevented me from getting both of them to safety.'

'You said you were going to tell me the truth and we both know you are being rather economical with it!'

I grabbed the glass and pushed it towards him. He topped it up giving me some time to think. He already knew so much there wasn't any point in avoiding the truth. I replaced the bile with the smoother alcoholic acid, wiped my mouth with my hand and responded. 'It was Rachel's decision but she was under Hélène's influence. She persuaded Rachel to stay because—'

'You couldn't answer her simple question about where you would go if Caroline beckoned.'

'Simple? It was far from simple. It cost my brother his life!'

'And several Germans, I believe.'

'That wasn't my doing. Hélène and her agents did that. I just dumped their bodies at sea.'

'And who helped you kill the two French fascists in Jersey?'

'No one — I had no choice. It was them or my friends and what I then believed was this bloody *heavy* water we had to stop the Germans grabbing.'

'And those friends would include the Jewish legionnaires who helped you escape?'

'As well as my uncle, Malita and Commander Brewster.'

He considered me for a long moment. 'Killing is never easy and I don't envy you the nightmares you—'

'No, I have no conscience about those two nor the German officer I shot in France. I would have killed Kempler the year before but Caroline stopped me. I didn't know he was her half-brother and had been playing her game to make me jealous and force me to choose between her and Rachel. She was misguided over that and Kempler revealed his true feelings when he was prepared to drown her to prevent me escaping from Jersey. You see…' my lip was beginning to tremble so I swallowed, desperate to complete the sentence.

'I've found the answer. I'm not in *lust* with Caroline just completely in *love*.' My throat constricted but it wasn't reflux from the vodka just the agony of separation. I blinked furiously to contain the tears but felt a warm trickle down my cheek.

Mayskiy gave me a curious look but waited until I had composed myself. 'So tell me what happened to the diamonds.'

Thankfully, I could answer that but would have been very confused if he'd asked about my interest in his niece.

'You know as much as me as I'm sure my uncle has briefed you. I haven't seen them; only a small sample back in July 1939. We gave them to Hélène to dispose of and she took them back to France. For all I know she dumped them in the sea to prevent the Germans getting them. This happened before you signed your pact with Hitler

and started trading with him. Perhaps, the diamonds were part of the deal. You've been selling him oil and food so why not let him have enough industrial diamonds to keep his factories busy for three months or so?'
'You tell me you're in love with Caroline but what do you feel for Rachel?'
That was another sucker punch but I could only be honest. 'I love her and Taynia.'
'Would you risk your life for them?'
'I've done that twice already so of course, but now I'm wearing this uniform, I'm not likely to get the chance.'
Mayskiy glanced over his shoulder at Stalin's portrait, sighed and turned back to stare at me. 'There are two reasons we wouldn't have sold or exchanged those diamonds with the Nazis. One; we never had them and two; we need them ourselves. There's also another more pressing problem — we've lost contact with Hélène and need you to help us find her.'
'But how? She's in Normandy. Surely, your own agents are better placed than I am? What can I know that they don't?'
'Rachel will know.'
'But she's with Hélène!'
'No, Hélène smuggled her out. She's in Jersey.'
'What, with her parents? They wouldn't let her in the house especially not with my child.'
'They didn't. She and Taynia are living with your mother and father.'

3

For once Saul was stuck for words. He stared open-mouthed as I told him what Mayskiy had said about Rachel and Taynia.

'Are you just pretending to be surprised or did you really know all along?'

He shook his head. 'I had no idea. Your uncle told me they were all in France.'

'When?'

'A month ago — this is crazy.'

'Only if Mayskiy is lying and why would he do that?'

'I don't know. Let's see what Fleming says when he returns.'

'Did you tell Fleming about Taynia?'

He bristled and brushed his hand through his hair. A sure sign that he was about to deliver a big fib. 'I didn't tell him as such. He asked me to confirm a few facts that's all.'

'You treacherous little shit. What the hell is this all about?'

'The diamonds probably, though the Russians must be worried about Hélène and if their network has been compromised. They don't want the Germans to know, that's clear.'

'At least Rachel and Taynia are out of it; they should be safer in Jersey—'

'Unless, our dear friend Kempler finds out. You know how much he loves Jews — especially ones who throw wine over him.'

'Were we mad to let Hélène have that shipment? Would the Jersey authorities really have returned them to Caroline's father and his crooked investors?'

'You know they would. And we would have been taken into protective custody. No, we did the right thing.'

'Only the right thing looks like it might now turn around and bite us on our backsides.'

'Hey, it's not our fault that Hélène didn't send the shipment to her comrades in Russia. We didn't know she was going to hide it.'

'Do the Russians really need it? Didn't you tell me that they had massive reserves of their own?'

He shrugged. 'Who knows with the Russians – their planned economy is a fairy tale at best. Perhaps they've underestimated what their industries need. Even Stalin isn't stupid enough to think that this agreement with Hitler is worth more than the paper on which it's typed. Hitler's made no secret of his ultimate aim to spread east for *Lebensraum* .'

'What?'

'Living space for the Aryan supermen which is currently occupied by the '*untermenschen*' Slavs – it's in black and white in *Mein Kampf* after all.'

'So, let's assume that these three million carats are still accessible and not at the bottom of the sea. How can we get them through Occupied France, across half of Europe, and into Russia?' I asked.

'They were in twenty-two hardwood crates each weighing about eighty lbs. If they'd fit into one cabin cruiser then a cargo plane would be the easiest though it would have to fly an unusual route.'

'That's the Ruskie's problem. We don't need the bloody things – just prevent the Germans getting them.'

'The bottom of the sea is probably the best place then!'

I shook my head. 'From what Mayskiy was saying I suspect that he's looking for an opportunity to get us to help Moscow now as a positive gesture because he knows that Hitler is building up for the next stage of his world domination.'

'You're right. Stalin must be delighted that we're still in the war and keeping the Germans on their toes in the West. If we'd lost, the Nazis would be at the gates of Moscow by now. Or, perhaps Stalin lives in a fool's paradise and trusts Hitler.'

'Well, there's bugger all we can do about it. I'm still a private in this scratchy uniform and you're a bag carrier for an even bigger chocolate sailor than yourself.'

'He's a monkey – not a sailor and you need to control your tongue, young man.' Fleming wandered into the ante-room. 'I suppose you two have been working out a devious and unworkable plan.'

'We've—'

'Forget it. I have the plan. We'll work out the details tomorrow. Marcks, you can shift your desk from Baker Street to my office in the Admiralty and bring your mouthy chum with you. I have some special work for him.'

'But, I'm due in Scotland tomorrow. I'll be posted AWOL if I don't get back.'

Fleming laughed. 'You amuse me, Renouf. There you are the diamond thief and Nazi slayer worrying about some petty military bureaucracy.' He waved his hand. 'I'll fix all that with one phone call, or if you cease to be of use, another call will have you confined to the Tower of London!'

'But—'

'Enough. This has been a most successful evening so far. Now it's time to celebrate. Let's get out of this dreary place and make a night of it in Soho. First though, we need to get you dressed properly. You're about my size so we'll stop off at my apartment and I'll lend you some proper clothes and *shoes*.' He smirked. 'Don't want you swapping with the maître d' at the Café de Paris. Marcks, be a good chap and toddle off and find Litzi. Tell her the plan then we'll sneak out of here and grab that taxi you've got waiting. Oh, and tell her to bring a female friend for Renouf.'

'What about one for me, sir?'

'Don't be silly. You're the bag carrier now go — fetch!'

Fortunately or unfortunately — I wasn't yet sure — our friendly cabbie was still there. Saul retrieved the two halves of the five pound note from the policeman and waved them in the cabbie's face.

'These are yours but we have an extra journey up West and I'll give you these when we get there. There might even be another fiver if you're prepared to wait.'

'Alright, mate. We'll talk about that when we arrive. Jerry will be here soon and I'm not going anywhere near his effing bombs.'

Saul turned back and pointed out Fleming escorting Litzi and Masha, now wearing matching black overcoats, out of the embassy gates. She smiled at me and I felt a fear compounded of that odd mixture of lust and guilt. After what I'd just learned about Rachel and confessed to her uncle about Caroline how could I even contemplate…? Saul nudged me with his elbow. 'Be careful, Jack – you're heading for the rocks again!' Before I could respond he called out. 'Where to, sir?'

Fleming ignored him until he had both ladies safely on the rear seat then gave me a playful shove into the taxi. I tripped over the door sill and sprawled onto the floor which made Litzi snort and Masha giggle.

Saul helped me up as Fleming scrambled in. He opened the hatch and yelled at the driver. '22 Ebury Street, Belgravia and then onto the Café de Paris.' He sat down between Litzi and Masha leaving me with the jump seat and Saul with the floor.

I'd enjoyed calmer moments training with the legionnaires up in Scotland and, other than wild ewes, hadn't had to face the dangerous hazards of female company afterwards.

The driver engaged gear and started to pull away but the cab sank on its springs and stalled. Had the elephant returned? No, it was only Doris whose considerable presence had compressed the suspension when she jumped onto the running board. She yelled something at the driver and he switched off the engine. Then the passenger door was almost hauled off its hinges as she yanked it open. She peered in and directed a stream of Russian at Masha who spat back some vitriol of her own.

Litzi shrieked with laughter. 'You won't believe this but Masha's not allowed out without her two bears to protect her. I believe she thought she could get away with it.'

Fleming hosed a languid stream of Russian towards Doris which provoked the bear into trying to force her way into the cab. Saul was still on the floor and blocking her path so she grabbed his uniform collar, dragged him out and dropped him on the pavement. I was aware that a large limousine had pulled up alongside us and spotted Saul being hoisted in the air and thrown into the rear seat by Boris.

Masha spoke calmly. 'My apologies. My uncle insists that I am not to be left alone in this dangerous city. I am to be accompanied by the servants or I will have to decline your invitation and return to my prison.'

Litzi chipped in. 'Well, Ian, what do you think? Would our two bears enjoy some swing dancing at the club or should we let them put Masha back in her cage? Actually, I think the regulars would be hugely entertained by these two trying the Lindy Hop!'

Fleming raised his hands in surrender. 'There's not room for everyone so let the man bear follow in their car. I suppose they can keep Marcks as a hostage — he might learn a few new words.' He spoke in Russian to the woman bear including what sounded like the addresses he had given our driver.

Fortunately, Doris was too large for my jump seat so settled herself on the floor and rested one massive shoulder against my knee. I just hoped Fleming wouldn't find it "oh so amusing" to get me to teach her how to dance.

Saul and I had played this game at school when, whatever the surprise we cooked up for each other, we had to appear completely calm and nerveless. We were both quite good at this but this evening's turn of events stretched my self-control to its limits. In truth I was scared of Litzi and what her kiss had provoked but I was really frightened of Masha and wondered why she had allowed herself to be pulled into this daft adventure. I should be in bed preparing for the frustrations of travelling through a war battered country instead of gallivanting around London to satisfy Fleming's sense of fun. The French had a word which described him more than adequately – a flâneur - someone who strolled or sauntered through life — I suspected that he was easily bored, loved gambling and needed to assert himself in every social situation so that he was always in control. He was a chain smoker and had another one of his Morland Specials going now. He also seemed to have an abiding love affair with alcohol and would probably react violently to anyone who suggested he call it a night. Yet, according to Saul, this was the man to whom Admiral Godfrey had entrusted the planning for Churchill's demand to set Europe ablaze. God help us.

  Litzi and Doris were also smoking leaving Masha and me to choke on their fumes. We arrived at Fleming's flat soon enough and disembarked. The other limo pulled up and Boris and Saul were left with instructions to ensure that our driver didn't escape

4

Somehow, the façade of his accommodation and Fleming seemed a total mismatch. Even in the dim light I could make out double-height fluted columns which supported a shallow pitched roof. On either side were three storied rectangular towers each framing three windows. Fleming opened the left hand door and ushered us into a large windowless meeting hall lit by the flickering glow from a well stoked fire place. He switched on a series of lights which shone on grey walls. It reminded me of an old chapel.

'Lavatory over there if needed.' He pointed to an alcove. 'Renouf, come with me.'

I followed him across the floor and past a large black sofa positioned in the middle of the room. We squeezed around a small dining table in what seemed like a gallery. The whole room was surrounded with empty shelves underneath which were stacked a collection of shiny black boxes. He paused to switch on a radiogram and tuned into some dance music. 'Here, entertain yourselves while I tidy up this lost soul.'

Litzi pulled Masha to her and whispered something which caused both of them to cackle with nervous laughter. Doris stood perplexed in the centre of the room and crossed herself. There was certainly an air of mystery in this sombre place, a hint of darkness and strange arts. Perhaps she'd spotted a sign of the devil. So much for Communism cleansing its followers of the *opium of the people*.

Fleming ushered me into a bedroom equally as austere as the hall and switched on two low-level lamps. Their dim light barely reflected off more grey painted walls but at least this room had a window although it was shuttered from the inside. I wondered what strange parties he hosted in this odd refuge. As I was getting my bearings he picked a dinner suit from a rail in the corner and dropped it on the bed which was draped in a black counterpane. He pulled open the top drawer of a black chest of drawers and handed me a shirt still wrapped in laundry cellophane. 'Take your pick, collars, ties and socks in the second drawer. I'll be in the bathroom. If you need any help call for Litzi.' Chuckling to himself, he disappeared through a door painted the same colour as the walls.

I spotted myself in the full length mirror next to the clothes rail.

The image glared accusingly at me as if to say. *What are you doing? Get out now — this man is deranged.* But I was intrigued rather than disconcerted by his odd behaviour so I shrugged at myself then started to undress.

'Very nice. There's something about a younger man isn't there Masha? So unspoiled and refreshing.'

Army underwear is practical rather than fashionable but doesn't leave much to the imagination and I could sense that at least one of these two was letting hers work overtime. I turned and found myself face to face with Doris and shivered.

'Oh dear, we've frightened him. Call her off, Masha, the poor boy's trembling.'

Masha spoke quickly to Doris. The huge bear smiled and advanced towards me. I retreated behind the bed holding up the suit trousers in defence.

Fleming came to my rescue. 'That's enough ladies. Litzi, help the poor lad. Fetch a pair of shoes from the rack and see if you can make him look respectable enough for polite company.

I didn't need any help. During my abortive year reading English at Oxford I'd attended enough formal dinners to manage my own dressing but two could play this game. 'Thank you, Commander, that won't be necessary. Masha can stay if she likes but I'd prefer it if Litzi took the bear next door for a dance.'

'There's no doubting your bravery, Renouf but I'm beginning to worry about your judgement! Come on Litzi let's leave these two to establish diplomatic relations.'

Masha said something else to Doris who made a fist with her right hand, stuck her thumb through the top two fingers and thrust it in and out while licking her lips. The room was too dark to see much detail but I could feel the heat from Masha's cheeks as she coloured up. She glared at me then turned and led everyone out of the room.

I took my time and examined Fleming's inner sanctum carefully looking for more clues to his character. I doubted I would be able to escape from his clutches now as he held such tremendous power so any little bit of information would be valuable. I couldn't find anything other than a framed obituary, hanging over the bed, for Major Valentine Fleming MP, written by Winston Churchill in 1917.

This must be Fleming's father and clearly a man much valued by the Prime Minister. It was a fulsome tribute to a friend killed, after three years fighting in the trenches, by a stray shell in Picardy.

Fleming could only have been nine or ten when his father was killed and it was really telling that he kept this tribute so close to him. I read the final paragraph aloud: "As the war lengthens and intensifies and the extending lists appear, it seems as if one watched at night a well-loved city whose lights, which burn so bright, which burn so true, are extinguished in the distance in the darkness one by one." My voice caught on the last line and I felt an overwhelming sadness.

'It's alright, old chap. It's just another corner of a foreign field that is forever England and all that. Come on, we know what we're fighting for but not tonight. Tonight's for dancing and drinking and forgetting.'

5

We left Fleming's creepy temple in the taxi. I was clutching an old kitbag holding my uniform and boots. I was tempted to appoint Saul as my batman and hand it to him but he was still trapped in the Soviet limousine face pressed up against the rear window as Boris leant against the door.

The two Russian bears exchanged a few words before Fleming sauntered over and opened the door to speak to Saul. 'Café de Paris, Marcks. Show them the way.'

We arranged ourselves in the same position in our cab though Masha avoided eye contact with me and peered out of the window as we negotiated the blackout.

We all heard the high pitched wailing but the driver reacted first and slammed on the brakes.

'That's it. I'm not going any further and you can stuff your fivers—'

'Fine, if that's what you want. We'll requisition your cab. Renouf, you can drive. Toss this erk out and follow the road to Piccadilly Circus then—'

'Bleeding 'ell — you can't do that. I'll have the law on you.'

'And we'll explain how you abandoned your fares and ran away leaving us no choice but to drive your vehicle to safety. Probably lose your licence as a result. Show some guts man; there aren't any bombs yet.'

Defeated, the driver cursed, thumped his steering wheel then drove on.

We arrived to the distant sound of bombs and anti-aircraft fire.

Fleming sniffed the air. 'The East End — probably the docks again. They won't venture up West.'

'Are there bomb shelters here?'

'My God, Renouf you sound like that snivelling driver. The Café de Paris is one of the safest spots in London. It's twenty feet underground — that's why it's so popular. Why sit in a dingy shelter when you can be enjoying a reasonable steak and dancing with half decent women?'

'I'm sorry, sir but I don't have any money on me.'

Litzi laughed. 'Don't worry, Jack, it's free. They can't charge for off-ration food but the drinks cost a fortune. Besides, Ian's like royalty and never carries any either. He says his face is his currency. He'll treat you for now but you can be sure he'll extract payment one way or another later.'

But Fleming was already arranging payment with the driver. He'd removed his keys and was holding them out. 'Now, my man, you have a choice. You can wait here or join us for a meal though no drinking as I want you sober when you take us home.'

He beckoned Saul over. 'Give the man another five pounds as a token of our good faith.'

Saul had never experienced any difficulty in spending his father's money so extracted another note and thrust it at the bemused cabby. The Russian driver, a Boris look-a-like, locked his limo and sauntered over — both seemed keen to join the party.

We breezed past the doorman who saluted Fleming. He thanked him by grabbing my kitbag and thrusting it into his arms. We passed through double blackout curtains and descended a broad flight of stairs onto an upper gallery which circled a ballroom below. An orchestra was nestled between two broad staircases that swept down to an oval dance floor shrouded in what looked like sea mist but smelt like cigarette smoke blended with expensive perfume. This haze swirled around disturbed by gyrating couples so close to each other that there was no room for proper dancing. Most of the men were in uniform from all the services especially RAF blue. There were few army officers and certainly no private soldiers.

The maître d' intercepted us, bowed to Fleming and escorted us to two tables on the balcony. It was almost as though we were expected. I noticed Saul slip something to the maître d'. Had he been appointed to the role of Fleming's banker? Fleming arranged the seating and placed the hired help on one table though the poor cabby looked completely out of his depth. He had removed his cloth cap though and his bald head glistened in the theatrical lighting. He was in for an interesting time with the Russians and I doubted he'd be effing and blinding with them.

Fleming placed Litzi on his right and Masha on his left. Saul beat me to the seat next to her which left me prey to Litzi once more. A waiter appeared with a menu but Fleming waved it away and, without asking, ordered steaks for all of us.

He beckoned to the sommelier and asked for martinis for our table followed by Tattinger '28 champagne and a bottle of vodka for the help. Perhaps that would mellow the cabby but with those three for company it might very well kill him if he ignored Fleming's instruction about alcohol. Saul couldn't drive; it would probably be beneath the Commander which left me and I could drive anything but found extreme difficulty walking after a few drinks.

Saul interrupted my thoughts with a dig in the ribs. 'Is that Fleming's penguin suit?'

'Yes.'

'Bit tight across the shoulders. Fix the bow tie yourself, did you?'

'What are you — my batman?'

He smiled expansively, lit another cigarette and gestured towards the floor. 'What do you think of this?'

'Spectacular; you'd hardly believe there's a war going on.'

'If you ask some of those RAF types you'll probably find they were up before dawn dancing with German fighters and will be back looking for new partners tomorrow.'

'I'm trying to find words to describe this. Decadent springs to mind as does delusional. The British upper crust whistling in the dark – orchestra playing while the Titanic sinks.' I shook my head in mock despair.

Saul blew smoke in my direction. 'Quite apposite, Renouf, as Grumpy used to say; but then you didn't know that all of this is modelled on the grand staircase and ballroom on that ill-fated ship. However, the danger isn't below us this time. Anyway, cheer up — this could be your last meal.'

I felt fingers creeping up my back and Litzi whispered in my ear. 'Time to dance, Jack. Do you think Ian's shoes can cope?'

Looking at the circulating mass below I doubted they would be given a chance. However, I stood up, helped her out of her chair and led her down the stairs. Saul glared at me, probably wondering how to get Masha to dance without offending Fleming by leaving him alone.

I needn't have worried. Before Litzi and I had reached the top stair, an attractive brunette was kissing Fleming's cheek and he'd waved at the waiter for another chair.

Litzi growled. '*Scheisse*, that bitch again. Always ruining my evenings.'

I waited until we were in hold. 'Who is she? How will she ruin your evening?'

She trod on my toe and pulled herself up so that her lips were touching my ear. 'Are you really as innocent as you look, Jack? That's

Lady Ann O'Neill, another married woman who should know better. Her husband, the Baron, is in the army training abroad.'

'You're a married woman, Litzi so what's different? Does she see you as a bitch?'

This time I was rewarded by an attempted knee to the groin but I'd expected it and blocked it with my thigh.

'*Bastard;* if she does snare him later, you'd better be more on your guard than that!' She hissed in my ear and then bit it.

I started to protest but she smothered my mouth with a kiss full of my own blood. My sensible-self wanted to haul her off the floor but sense in this atmosphere was as absent as the lookout on the Titanic. She couldn't be as dangerous as the flights of Messerschmitts the men around me would be facing in a few hours' time, so I kissed her back and wrapped her so tight she struggled to breathe.

If anyone noticed our behaviour they must have been too polite to react apart from Saul who swept Masha alongside and proclaimed, 'There, what did I tell you. He's more than a bit muddled.'

Masha disengaged from Saul and tapped Litzi on the shoulder. 'Excuse me, my dance I believe.'

Startled, Litzi released me and turned on Masha but there was something in the Russian's eyes which must have given her pause as she curtsied graciously and reached for Saul.

Masha offered herself for hold and I accepted; the blood which had been rushing to my second *little* brain had now diverted to my cheeks. I looked sheepishly around but the other dancers were ignoring our little pantomime and still moving to the rhythm of the slow foxtrot.

Memory of another occasion when I tried to excuse Rudi as he was dancing with Caroline flooded back. That had ended badly, with the German on the floor tasting his own blood and Rachel fleeing in humiliation. I blamed Saul for plying me with drink that evening but everyone else held me responsible for acting like an idiot. I'd fled to the beach then and fallen into a deep pool.

This time there was nowhere to run and I held a beautiful Russian in my arms who had just rescued me from my own stupidity. I had the grace to thank her and did my best to move us around the room without bumping into Saul and Litzi. Suddenly everyone was clapping and it wasn't for our performance. The band leader was taking a bow and a Negro had assumed his place to even more enthusiastic applause. More Negroes followed him and settled themselves in the places vacated by the white musicians. I didn't know what to expect but spotted the other dancers clearing some space around them and then, with a blare of brass, the band launched into a high tempo swing number and the genteel gyrations were replaced by energetic whirling. Masha seemed delighted and threw herself about as I held her hand and swung with the exciting rhythm. One advantage of this type of dancing was there was no time or enough breath for talking but our eyes occasionally met and I sensed that there was more curiosity than disapproval in her brief glances.

After a trio of exhausting numbers the floor started thinning as dancers returned to their tables and much needed drinks. As space appeared Saul started showing off and Litzi kept up with him. He was completely unathletic normally but set him loose on a dance floor and he came to life and seemed inexhaustible. Litzi seemed equal to it so perhaps it was a Jewish thing.

Masha broke hold and applauded, as did many of the other patrons; even the RAF officers seemed happy to praise a Wavy Navy show-off. Possibly, Saul had saved my bacon for the evening. I was feeling very hungry now and looked up to see Fleming tucking into a steak. I led Masha up the grand staircase and back to our table. The help were gobbling theirs up and roaring with laughter between mouthfuls. Even our cabby seemed to be enjoying himself.

Fleming wiped his mouth with a serviette and stood up as Masha arrived. 'Allow me to introduce Lady Ann O'Neill. Mrs. Mariya Dobruskina, Ambassador Mayskiy's niece and....' He hesitated struggling for my name.

'Jack Renouf.' I offered then didn't know whether to bow or not but Lady Ann anticipated and held out a slender gloved hand. She held mine briefly before gently pushing it away. Up close she was truly stunning with grey-green eyes and gorgeous dark hair. A satin off-the-shoulder gown hugged her svelte figure and there was something almost majestic about her presence.

Breeding, my father would have called it. After all, the aristocracy probably didn't marry without consulting the stock book first. She was probably in her late twenties so a bit younger than Fleming. They made a striking pair almost as though they were holding court.

She wasn't eating but smiled benignly as the waiters delivered our steaks though the smile froze as Saul approached with Litzi.

Fleming was casual. 'You already know Marcks and Litzi, of course, needs no introduction.'

Saul, well-schooled in social niceties kissed Ann's hand while Litzi managed a curt nod. 'Hello, Ann. I trust you're well; and your husband?'

Fleming snapped. 'Enough, Litzi or perhaps you'd like to sit with the help?'

Masha giggled. Saul slurped his martini and I studied my steak.

Ann laughed. 'Thank you Litzi, he's very well and I'm sure would send his regards if he knew about your interest in his health. How's Kim, still pining for you?'

Litzi picked up her evening bag and started towards the other table. 'No need, dear. I'm just leaving. I'm here with the Coopers. Do pop over to say hello to Diana; you know how fond of you she is. Pleasure to meet you Jack, enjoy your meal. Goodbye.'

Fleming stood, anger stencilled into his back as she left. But when he turned he was all smiles. 'Please sit, Litzi. Champagne everyone?'

While the waiter poured the bubbly I attacked my steak uncomfortably aware that this was some less fortunate individual's ration for the week. Masha dallied with hers leaving most for the kitchen staff. The waiters delivered two more but Litzi was too busy glaring at Fleming to pay much attention to hers and Saul wolfed his down so he could light another *du Maurier*. A giant shadow loomed over our table but it was only Boris and he spoke in Russian to Masha.

She smiled. 'Nicolai has asked me to dance with him. I hope no one *minds*.' Even Communists seem to enjoy irony. I watched them glide down the stairs with Nicolai looking surprisingly nimble for his size. They were quickly into the rhythm of a lively swing number and I couldn't help but admire his footwork.

Masha was laughing and really seemed to be enjoying the attentions of her bodyguard.

Litzi leant over. 'It's not quite what you think. Nicolai was with Masha's husband when he was shot down in Spain. He was a heavyweight boxing champion before he joined the air force.'

'So he was a pilot as well?'

'No, he was his, how you say, batman — he's related to the Ambassador.'

'What about the one who looks like a weightlifter?'

Litzi laughed. 'You mean Yuliya. She was indeed a champion weightlifter. She's also Nicolai's sister so be careful what you say.'

So not Doris and Boris after all. 'They're very good at this type of dance. Is it popular in Russia?'

'In spite of the Nazis it's even popular in Berlin. "*Snakehips*" wouldn't be though!'
'Who?'
'Ken Johnson – the band leader.'
'Why snake—'
'Watch and you'll see.'

As if on cue the black man started to swivel his hips and thrust his pelvis at the dancers as he conducted the band. He was so unrestrained that the dancers gradually slowed to a standstill and began to applaud. It drove him to even more wild exertions until many of the diners were on their feet showing their appreciation. Saul even whistled and started mimicking him. Yuliya spotted this, thrust her chair back, grabbed Saul's hand in her giant mitt, dragged him down the stairs and started to throw him around to the beat.

It was so funny I spilt my champagne and had to fumble with a serviette to mop up the liquid from Fleming's dinner jacket. When I'd finished, with a little help from Litzi, Fleming had disappeared.

Litzi snorted. 'Typical. He's sneaked off to that woman. Look,' she pointed to a table directly opposite on the other balcony, 'he's socialising with the Coopers.'

'Who are they?'

She shook her head. 'You don't know? You've been spending too much time with the sheep and too little with the cows, Jack. Duff Cooper, Viscount Norwich, and his wife Diana, the Viscountess. She was quite a famous actress but he's another old Etonian like that viper Ann's husband and Ian of course.

Cooper is a great friend of Churchill's and is Minister for Information though I can never get more than a polite nod out of him.'

'Might that be because you're a Communist snake and Diana and Ann see you as a threat?'

While she choked on her champagne I tried to examine them through the haze. The Minister looked like my old history teacher – large square head and impressive moustache slightly wider than Hitler's. His wife, however, was quite striking — even though she must be my mother's age. Fleming was holding her hand but she draped herself over him and kissed both his cheeks. Ann seemed to enjoy this and darted a glance in our direction.

Litzi leant in close again and I was fearful for my other ear. 'I'm beginning to like you even more. I wonder if you're better in bed than Saul.'

It was my turn to choke. 'I don't believe you!'

'Ask him if you must but he has a lovely apartment in his parents' house in Canfield Gardens. I spent a week there recently. It was fun but I don't stay anywhere for too long these days.'

'Where do you live?'

'Since Kim rescued me from Paris I don't have a home of my own. They keep a room for me at the embassy but I have many friends in London including Ian though his house is an abomination — you know he bought it from that fascist pig Oswald Mosley. Ann won't go there so that's the last we'll see of him again this evening. She has a town house in Mayfair — that's where he'll spend the night.'

'What about—'

'Don't worry; I'll make sure you have somewhere to rest your weary body after I've exhausted it.' She paused. 'And I don't mean through dancing!'

But that was all she was going to get. She might remind me of Caroline in one of her wilder moods but she really was a dangerous snake and, tempted though my *little* brain was by her rather obvious desire to get me into a bed, I knew I had sufficient moral resolve to resist her. So I dragged her back to the dance floor and used "*Snakehips*" energy to drain enough from her that I wouldn't need to apply my latest training techniques to defend what was left of my honour. During our leaping about I spotted Fleming leading the cabby away.

I glanced over at the Cooper's table but it was empty so Litzi was probably right. Claiming thirst I took her back to our table and spotted a folded note in Saul's place. It was from Fleming. *'Marcks, follow your desk to Room 39 tomorrow at14:00. Bring Renouf. Have my clothes cleaned first.'*

She wanted to read it but I put it in my pocket. 'Sorry, it's personal.' She probably knew where Room 39 was but I thought it best to pass it to Saul first.

He'd been rescued from Yuliya by the limo driver and it took me some time to find him at the bar. I handed him the note.

He cursed. 'Just like Fleming. Off with the fragrant Ann is he?'

I nodded. 'So Litzi says. Tell me, has she really had her wicked way with you?'

It was his turn to choke on his brandy. It might have been the dancing but his face was bright red.

He shrugged. 'A gentleman never talks about his conquests.'

I laughed. 'Especially if he's the one who's been conquered!'

'Not jealous are you, Jack?'

'Hardly, she's too hot for me and her teeth are rather sharp.' He finished his drink. 'I suppose we had better scarper then before someone presents us with Fleming's bill.'

'How are we going to get back to Canfield Gardens?'

He rubbed his chin. 'I know. I'll invite our Russian friends to sample some of my father's vodka collection. They'll give us a lift.'

'Careful, Doris has her eye on you. Her name's Yuliya actually but I'm sure she can teach you a few tricks Litzi doesn't know.' I imagined her bouncing him off the walls of his bedroom and wandered what would break first – Saul or his bed.

Litzi approached with Masha. 'Naughty boys abandoning us like that. I've been telling Nicolai about your lovely house and he's agreed to drive us all there if you provide the entertainment.'

I looked at Masha but couldn't read her expression. 'Won't your uncle worry if you are late?'

'He has far greater things to worry about and he knows that Nicolai and Yuliya will keep me safe from anything and *anyone*.'

Was that a message for Saul or me? 'Well, ladies it seems we're in your hands.'

Litzi smirked. 'So you have seen sense, Jack. I accept your surrender.'

6

Fortunately, the Germans saved me. We were driving along Oxford Street when the air raid sirens started wailing again. Saul was between Nicolai and the driver on the front bench seat of the massive ZIS limo providing directions. I was squashed in with the three women behind. It wasn't as unpleasant as it might have been as Masha was on my lap. Saul suggested we carry on but we were waved down by two policemen, near Madame Tussauds, just south of Regent's Park.

'Don't you know there's a raid on?' The sergeant enquired of Nicolai not realising that the driver was on the other side. The other policeman inspected the car with his hooded torch.

Saul responded. 'Sorry, officer, we don't have far to go.'

'That's correct, sir, as this is the end of your journey. You know what happened in there last month, don't you?' He pointed to the distinctive rotunda of the waxworks museum silhouetted by the searchlights bouncing off the cloud cover.

'No, but I'm sure you're going to tell me.' Saul was barely succeeding in keep his sarcasm at bay.

'Jerry dropped a couple of large eggs, sir. They destroyed nearly 400 waxwork figures. Apparently, the only one to survive was Hitler's. Now, we don't want any more heads blown off do we especially as you seem to have more in this vehicle than it was designed for.'

He jerked Nicolai's door open and didn't seem intimidated when the giant hauled himself out. The other policeman opened my door and helped Masha onto the pavement while we followed. I sensed she was about to claim diplomatic status when the sky screamed in protest as a bomb sliced into the ground only a few hundred yards away. We all grabbed our ears and ducked down as it exploded and punched a pressure wave over us as we cowered behind the heavy limousine which rocked with the blast.

Without flinching, the sergeant continued in his almost conversational tone. 'You'll find Baker Street Underground just up the road. I suggest you get there as quickly as your legs can carry you and find one of the lower platforms.'

As we scrambled over the road there were more bright flashes from detonations followed quickly by massive crumps from the east.

Masha's evening shoes were not really suitable for running so I swept her up in a fireman's lift and ran ahead. Nicolai spotted my action and did the same for Litzi saving Saul from a dilemma. It was only a hundred yards or so and she weighed far less and was a lot softer and warmer than the rock-filled backpack I'd had to haul over the Scottish highlands. I got there first but didn't know where to go and had to wait for Saul. Reluctantly, I lowered her to the ground. Eventually he trudged up panting and led us in. Fortunately there were ARP wardens holding lanterns to guide us down the several flights of concrete stairs to the Bakerloo Line. The station lighting was dim but sufficient to illuminate the white arrows pointing the way to the escalators and the lower concourse which was at least fifty feet underground.

It was heaving with people many of whom, trusting the live rails were switched off, had settled down on the track for the night. I'd heard that the network of tube tunnels was considered the safest place and many Londoners set up overnight homes in their protective depths. The smell of so much humanity crammed in together was not pleasant but, with Nicolai and the driver's help, we secured a small corner for ourselves. In the surprisingly quiet atmosphere we huddled down to wait for the "all clear" to sound. It seemed as though everyone was listening for the howling descent of the bomb which held his or her name. With his usual foresight Saul had acquired a bottle of cognac – on Fleming's account no doubt – and passed this around. Nicolai produced a pack of playing cards and was joined by his sister and the driver leaving the four of us to find a safe seating arrangement behind them. Safe in my case meant keeping Litzi at a distance so I snuggled down next to Masha and manoeuvred Saul towards our friendly snake. I would have preferred just to talk with Masha but we were all too close to have private conversations.

However, Litzi started in her usual brash way. 'How many lovers have you had, Jack?'

The combination of vodka, martini, Champagne and now cognac had loosened my tongue so, instead of snapping back with a smart remark, I told the truth.

'One; I've only had one lover.'

'But you have a child and two girl-friends. Is the lover the mother or—'

'I love all three of them but only Caroline is my lover. Rachel and I had a moment of madness and Taynia is the result. Now all three would seem to be out of reach, trapped in Jersey and surrounded by thousands of Germans.'

They absorbed this then Masha asked. 'But how many of them love you?'

Saul responded before me. 'Only two of them – the third doesn't even know who he is.'

Litzi slapped his head. 'We're being serious here, Saul.'

'That's a first for you then. We won't ask about your *love* or should I say *sex* life as the air raid won't last that long.'

He was rewarded with another slap. 'You don't know enough about me to make that comment. You have no idea about what I've experienced. Even if I was prepared to tell, you wouldn't understand.'

'But you did tell me about some of your mad moments – married at eighteen to young Karl but that only lasted months then you found your Stalin. What was his name – Peter?

'Gabor, his name was Gabor and he was a true revolutionary – a real man. And he taught me that looks are not important but passion is. Something you and your friend Jack do not understand. Life is just one big joke to you. Call it English understatement if you wish but it reveals you as shallow.'

But Saul wouldn't leave it alone. 'So how did you come to marry such a typical Englishman as Philby then? Isn't he just another *shallow* public school boy like Fleming and Jack and me?'

She sighed. 'You won't believe me but I did love Kim. It's just that…shall we say events conspired against us…forced us apart. Now he has someone else, Aileen, she's a nurse and not much of a challenge. He took other lovers when we were together but that's not what…anyway, enough about me. It's your turn under the spotlight, Saul—'

I interrupted. 'You'd need a searchlight to dig out his secrets, Litzi. I actually believed that he was in love with me for a while!'

'Bastard — that was just Rachel's joke. He knows I'm very fond of her.'

'And terrified of Caroline—'

'With good cause. She's even more…bohemian than Litzi!'

'Well, I've never met these two though your uncle has spoken about them but I can tell you one thing for certain – Saul was no virgin when I shared his bed.'

'I suppose that's one advantage of meeting him during the

blackout.'

Masha touched my arm. 'Litzi is right – you English can't take anything seriously.'

'But I'm not English – I'm a Jerseyman with lots of French blood in my veins and Saul is really South African with Boer blood in his – so your theory is wide of the mark.'

'Not really. Blood means little. The Jesuits say, "Give me the boy for his first seven years and I will deliver you the man". You both had an English education so you belong to them.'

'Tell that to Hitler and his henchmen. They don't believe in nurture – just blood and even if I only had one Jewish grandparent I'm still an enemy of his Aryan Reich.'

'Saul's right. Rachel didn't even know she was half-Jewish until last year but if the Nazis catch her she'll be taken into *protective custody* and sent to a concentration camp along with our daughter who is a quarter-Jewish.'

'Well, probably more than that as Jack's always wanted to be Jewish anyway – though I've never understood why. Playing the Jew in a Shakespearean play is not sufficient qualification as I keep telling him.'

Masha spoke softly. 'I have Jewish blood as well, as does my uncle — that's why we hate the Nazis.'

'Even though they're still your allies?'

'They are *not* our allies. We just have an agreement not to attack them and I hate that as well. The fascists in the Condor Legion killed my husband in Spain. They're trying to kill us now.' She pointed to the roof. 'I just want the chance to pay them back.' There was fire in her tone now. 'Just give me the weapon — any weapon — and I'll…' Her voice caught and she started to sob.

I put my arm around her and Litzi leant over Saul to rub her back and say some soothing words in her own tongue. He looked at me. We'd been here before. The Germans had killed my brother, tortured my uncle, bombed my island and we'd witnessed them murdering 8,000 helpless souls on the *Lancastria*.

Masha was right. Thousands of feet above us, they were dropping bombs on women and children, trying to destroy our civilisation and, as Churchill claimed, drag us into a new dark age. I just hoped that Fleming would be able to fashion a weapon for us to gain some revenge.

After the "all clear" was relayed below and we emerged from the station it was obvious that the Germans had got their revenge in first. The searchlights bouncing off the scattered clouds cast an eerie flickering glow over us. Towards the east the horizon pulsed with waves of red and orange as we picked our way over broken glass and tried to ignore the pungent smell of burning possessions and probably something worse. The air was full of dust though it wasn't thick enough to obscure the smouldering corpse of the ZIS lying in one of several new craters on the Marylebone Road. Nicolai tried to approach it but another policeman blocked his path.

'Sorry, sir but it's too dangerous. If it's yours I'll take the details. It'll be cleared away soon. If there is anything of value left please visit your nearest police station in the morning to make a claim.'

Nicolai raised a threatening arm but Masha pushed between them. 'I must report, officer; that this is a diplomatic car, the property of the Union of Soviet Socialist Republics and you cannot remove it without permission. My embassy will instruct your superiors in the correct procedure. For the moment I request that you guard it carefully.'

Apart from Fleming's burnt kitbag and my barbecued uniform, I wondered what of any value might still be left in the wreck but the policeman wasn't going to argue. He shrugged and walked away.

Saul looked at his watch. 'One o'clock in the morning and another four hours at least before dawn. We have some choices. We can go back to the underground and try to sleep or we can take a three mile hike around Hyde Park to your embassy. Or we can trudge about the same distance to my house around Regent's Park and up to Finchley. I'm fairly certain there won't be any buses for a while and I'm sure all the cabbies are tucked up in bed or hiding in their —.'

I interrupted him. 'We can't ask Litzi and Masha to walk that distance in those shoes and—'

'You can carry me if you like, Jack,' said Litzi.

Despite all the explosions my brain was still ticking. 'I know, let's find a telephone. The embassy will have another car they can send to collect our Russian friends...and Litzi — then you and I can walk to your house.'

Litzi sulked while Masha explained to the others. They agreed so we returned to the station where there were several telephone boxes and amazingly the first one worked. When Masha emerged she explained to the Russians then turned to Litzi. 'They'll be here in about thirty minutes but there won't be room for everyone. You are welcome to come with us but I won't be offended if you prefer to spend the night with Saul and Jack. It is your choice and—'

'There is no choice,' I interrupted. 'Litzi, you should go with them. Saul and I have a meeting tomorrow and—'

Litzi laughed. 'You need your sleep. I understand but there will be other times, my Jack when you will not be so tired.'

Masha came up to me, hesitated, then reached up and kissed me on the lips. Hers were soft and cool and sent a shiver through my body. Before I could respond, she pulled away then leant in and whispered in my ear. 'Thank you for a most interesting evening, Jack. We'll meet again soon. There are many things I want to discuss with you.' She turned to Saul and kissed him on both cheeks. 'Take care, both of you.'

We watched them leave to wait outside for the limo then Saul, who always struggled with silence, turned on me. 'What are you playing at, don't you—'

'Not now. You told me that your office is near here. Can you get into it at this time of night?'

'I suppose so; it's only a couple of minutes' walk. There's a new hush-hush organisation moving in so they're doubling the size of the place — workmen there at all hours.'

'Didn't Fleming say he was moving your desk tomorrow to a room 39?'

'Yes, but only figuratively; the desk isn't travelling to his lair which is in the Admiralty Building off Horse Guards Parade. That's where we're meeting.'

'I can't turn up like this.'

He laughed. 'You could but he'd probably kick you out. Besides he wants his clothes back, nicely laundered. Double buggeration, as you like to say. That means we'll have to go to my place and you know how much I hate walking.'

'So why didn't you mention your office to the others?'

'We share a lot with the Russians but Fleming would have my guts eviscerated if I showed them what was going on there!'

'Don't worry. I'll carry you if necessary but you're going to have to talk – I want to know everything about Mrs. Philby and Mrs. Mariya Dobruskina.'

'What if I don't want to talk?'

'Won't talk and can't walk? I'll have to drag you then. Come here you little monkey!'

'Jack, you remember when you were talking about Caroline when we left my house?'

'Well?'

'Why did you ask me about Berkeley Square?'

'Because...' my pulse quickened and I shivered, 'on our last night together, she played something on the piano for me — *A Nightingale Sang In*—'

'Then, you need to know that last month, the Germans bombed Berkeley Square and those nightingales don't sing anymore.'

7

Room 39 must be Saul's idea of Heaven. The air was so thick with cigarette smoke that he didn't need to light his own. Through the haze I could make out an army of metal filing cabinets jammed up against oak panelled walls and a flotilla of desks competing for the limited central space. Everyone was in naval uniform and buzzing about probably trying to impress the queen bee who sat majestically in the far corner behind a battleship of a desk. We approached through the clatter and chatter and came to attention in front of Fleming. He was holding a green Bakelite phone at arm's length and rolling his eyes in exasperation. He waved the instrument at two chairs and we sat. Eventually, he tired of the one-sided conversation, dropped the phone onto its cradle, and studied us.

'Good of you to turn up. Need to synchronise watches, Marcks. Yours seems to be running about thirty minutes late!'

'Sorry, sir, we had problems getting Renouf through security. They didn't like his ID card. It seems the army is almost as welcome here as civilians.'

'Has Renouf mislaid his uniform? Is that why he's wearing that appalling suit?'

I held out my package which had been neatly tied up before the security section had got to work. 'Your dinner suit and other articles, sir; all dry cleaned and laundered as requested. My uniform fought a Jerry bomb and lost I'm afraid.'

'Well, never mind all that; stop fumbling and put it down, man. We're not here to socialise now. You won't need it for a while. You've been seconded to Naval Intelligence, if such a concept is not self-contradictory, and my clerk is cutting orders to make you an acting sub-lieutenant in the RNVR, like our little monkey. You'll have to take the course at Greenwich but we'll hang fire on that for a moment. Now we—'

He was interrupted by another phone call and whipped the receiver off its cradle, listened briefly then spun his chair around and turned his back on us.

I already knew about the secondment as Saul had managed to contact my HQ in Scotland where the admin clerk had confirmed it but warned that my CO was very unhappy about the way normal channels had been bypassed. I didn't blame him but Saul told me that protesting was not an option as Fleming wielded enormous power.

We daren't speak while he was engaged in his conversation so I peered through the haze and caught glimpses of sunshine glinting off the rain speckled surface of Horse Guards Parade outside. The back garden to No 10 Downing Street was just beyond and I wondered if Churchill was at his desk. From the deferential sounds emanating from Fleming he might very well be on the other end of the line.

Conversation over, Fleming seem more jaunty. 'You recall I mentioned a plan yesterday; well…oh do grab a pen, Marcks and take notes as it will need some polishing.' He thrust a pad across the desk. 'Make it legible this time and in English, please.' He pulled a folded sheet from a pile beside him, opened it out and turned it to face us. It was the1935 Ordnance Survey map of Jersey. 'Well, Renouf, you're going home for a while — first class travel at his Majesty's expense. Pleased?'

My heart was hammering and I felt clammy though that was probably after last night's excesses. 'Of course, sir, though I suspect it's not a holiday you have in mind.'

Saul piped up. 'Am I going as well, sir?'

'Don't be an imbecile. This isn't work for a desk monkey. You'd be more hindrance than help. Now listen; this is what I have so far. We need to insert Renouf clandestinely onto the island — I understand that you locals prefer to live *in* rather than *on* the island but we'll strive for grammatical exactitude if nothing else. Your task is to find out if Rachel knows where we can find Hélène. You can also swan about a bit and take a deco at what the Germans are up to but we need you back as soon as possible. Have a look at the map and point out the best ways of accomplishing this without getting caught. For example, could we drop you in by parachute?'

That suggestion held no appeal at all and my face must have revealed it. He chortled. 'Only a thought but not very practical given the size of the island and the preponderance of Germans. Can't fly you in either as all your fields seem to be cultivated and the beaches are well guarded.'

He produced a series of high altitude photo reconnaissance shots. 'No, the only option is by sea. So, how? From the stories Marcks has told me both of you seem to know the coastline very well.'

'Landing by launch would be suicidal, sir unless we take the route the French used in 1781 around where Seymour Tower now stands; a mile off the coast, but the Jerries would have thought of that and probably have guards out there. I think the best bet is to drop Jack off a couple of miles out and let him swim in. We can work out the tides and pick a good spot around the north coast.'

Saul seemed keen to feed me to the fishes so I said. 'There is a better way, sir. I've been training in two man kayaks. We call them folboats as they fold up from about fifteen foot in length to about four foot and can be stored in a bag so are easy to hide. We could be dropped off by submarine and—'

'I'm not risking a submarine just to buy some Russian friendship!'

'How about an MGB? We know a commander with local knowledge who—'

'No, Marcks. I'm not endangering one of those either. But we are developing something new down in Cornwall. One of the reasons you've sailed your desk over here is to make room for the ISRB in Baker Street. They've got a scheme using French fishing boats which arrived with evacuated troops last year. The Helford River in Cornwall will be their base from where they will be inserting agents into France but I could persuade them to drop you off the coast of the island and pick you up again. Not sure about the kayak – swimming is probably easier especially as you would need another paddler—'

'That's it, sir; another man and I know the perfect person. He's German and mad enough to volunteer. He could infiltrate the garrison and pick up all sorts of information while I talk to Rachel.'

Fleming found another piece of paper and traced his finger down it. 'Do you mean Willie Grun by any chance?'

'Yes, he's in the French Foreign Legion, hates the Nazis and is Jewish. Like all of us up there, he's keen for some action.'

He opened a red bordered file and pulled out some documents.

'Pseudonym of course — according to this SIS "scarlet pimpernel" file, he's really Wilhelm Karl von Gersdoff. Jewish on his mother's side only – she's Polish, a doctor. Father is a baron – Hitler hates the aristocracy. Father was a catholic until his marriage. Now he's a colonel in army intelligence. Mother was arrested in 1938 – present whereabouts unknown.' He scanned what looked like a service record. 'Seems a good choice – speaks more languages than me and beats you in all categories apart from vehicle maintenance.'

'I think you'll find we're equal in swimming.'

'Competitive, eh? How would you fare against him in unarmed combat?'

'Find a gun, sir!'

He rubbed his chin then lit another of his Morland Specials and offered one to Saul who declined, pulled out his silver case and extracted a du Maurier. I tried not to cough but my eyes were already red from the fug in the room and my lungs were desperate for fresh air. I'd never tried and would never understand how sane individuals could willingly suck smoke into their lungs. Perhaps they only ever used them for talking and not pushing their bodies to the limit. That said; many of the commandos were smokers. I shook my head.

'What's wrong, Renouf. Don't like the plan?'

'Sorry, sir, just thinking about details such as land mines and barbed wire. Otherwise, it should be a piece of cake. I stabbed my finger at a point on the north coast. 'Egypt is a possible. Come ashore at Petit Port and climb up into the woods. Only problem is the old fort which the Germans might be using as a guard post.' I moved my finger further east. 'There's Saie harbour which is just a small concrete slipway – easy to land but possibly guarded. Or there's La Coupe Point at the north end of Fliquet Bay. It's treacherous at certain stages of the tide but I know it well and it's only three quarters of a mile from my farm.'

'They might be guarding the beacon though and Brayes Rock could take a big bite out of you!'

'Thanks, Saul. Do you have any suggestions?'

'I'm quite fond of the parachute idea.'

'That's enough, Marcks. It's Renouf's neck so let him choose. Your new desk is over there.' He pointed to the far corner.

'Find tide tables and whatever else you need and work out the best time in the next week or so. Bring me the plan when you have it and I'll put you in touch with the officer in charge down in Cornwall to arrange the next stage. See my clerk and get the German transferred then—'

'Fleming. I must speak with you.' A tall scruffily dressed civilian was striding across the room with Fleming in his sights. He brushed aside a couple of officers who were in his way and arrived, red faced and very angry. 'What in blazes are you doing cancelling *Ruthless*. Don't you realise how important it is. I must have those codes. Explain yourself man!'

Fleming regarded the interloper coolly. 'Doctor Turing, how

pleasant to see you again so soon. All well in Hut 8 is it?'

'Don't be so stupid, Fleming. You know very well that you've set us back months.' He fished a piece of paper out of his jacket. 'Don't pretend you don't know about this memo. You promised me the codes and I helped you with the plan and now you've abandoned it!'

'Do calm down, old chap. How about some tea? Marcks, don't just sit there, go and fill the kettle for Doctor Turing .'

'I do *not* have time for your social niceties. If you are not going to cooperate I want to see Admiral Godfrey.'

'I'm afraid he's rather busy at the moment but do take a seat and I'll attempt an explanation.' The room had fallen silent during this rather striking man's assault but Fleming stood up and flapped his hand at the officers and they returned to their tasks.

'By the way, this is one of our new recruits.' He indicated me. 'He's from Jersey and—'

Ignoring me, Turing cut him off. 'I have no interest in him or where he's from. I need answers now.'

Fleming glared at him, withdrew another cigarette from his silver case, lit it, blew some smoke in our direction and pulled another sheet from the pile on his right.

Turing coughed. 'You know I can't abide that filthy habit. You told me you used to be an athlete so you should know better.'

Fleming considered this for a moment. 'I was never in the same league as you either on the track or in the classroom but I see no harm in this simple pleasure and,' he gestured around the room, 'neither do my colleagues.'

I was with Turing on this but kept quiet and stole a glance at him. His hair was short and badly combed but in profile he looked quite handsome. I assumed he wasn't a proper doctor but some sort of scientist who was more than a little disappointed in Fleming.

Turing smacked his hand on the table revealing nails bitten down to the quick. 'Well, I'm waiting. Why have you cancelled the operation? — and none of your waffle — just the facts.'

He reminded me of my physics master who used to lose his rag at us if he smelt gas in the lab and demanded to know who had turned on the Bunsen burner taps. Turing was a lot younger of course and looked about Fleming's age.

Fleming blew another stream of smoke but this time towards the window. 'Just the facts? Very well. The crew was training in the Heinkel off the coast and was shot up by one of our own fighters.

The aircraft survived and can be repaired. The crew are all in hospital.'
'That's not what it says in the memo!'
'Of course not. We're very careful what we commit to paper.'
'If the aircraft survived why don't you find another crew?'
'What, another group of German speaking Englishmen? Do you have any idea how hard it was to find the first one? Of course not — codes and machines are what interest you — not people.'
Turing leapt to his feet. 'You're impossible. I gave you the idea and you got it passed. Now you've got cold feet – just like the thousands of sailors we're losing in the Atlantic. I need those codes now before Hitler starves us into submission.'
'Steady on. You can't win the war by yourself!'
'Perhaps not but if you don't listen to me, we'll probably lose it.' He kicked Fleming's desk, stomped over to the green baize door and thrust it open. 'Let's see what Godfrey's got to say.'
Fleming hurried after him into what I assumed was the Admiral's office and closed the door.
Saul returned with a tray bearing a teapot and four cups. 'Where've they gone?'
I pointed towards the door.
'Room 38? *Kak*, luckily it's soundproofed. The Admiral has a volcanic temper. I suppose we'd better wait; sugar and milk?'
I tried to quiz Saul about this operation *Ruthless* but he refused to tell me anything. I guessed he didn't know and was trying to suggest that he had inside knowledge that he wasn't allowed to share.
It wasn't long before Turing left the office with a hint of a smile on his handsome face and marched out of the room. Minutes later Fleming appeared and resumed his seat. He seemed unperturbed. 'Slight change of plan, chaps. The Jersey op is on hold. *Ruthless* is back on with your "yellow peril" variation, Marcks. You're fluent in German and so is this Willie Grun. Renouf, you can swim and are supposedly a commando. We just need another killer and a pilot. Any ideas?'

8

Friday 8th November 1940, 06:30 St Eval RAF base, Cornwall

'Commander Fleming's compliments, sir and it's time to get your arses off the ground.' The RAF sergeant's face cracked into a smile before he clambered down from the cockpit. As his boots hit the concrete he started to salute, hesitated and turned the hand gesture into a V for Victory sign.

Flight Lieutenant Cassons laughed. 'Poor sod doesn't know what to make of us. Shouldn't really salute a German officer should he?'

'I thought he got it about right! The Commander is still seething that he wasn't allowed to join us.' I replied.

'Well, he's welcome to my seat if he's really that keen. Claims he can fly but I'd like to see him manage this lump of Luftwaffe *scheisse*.'

'It was a perfectly fine aircraft until your RAF boys brought it down. I hope they patched it up with the same level of enthusiasm.'

Saul's voice crackled through my headphones, his excitement overriding the static. 'That's it, confirmation from the tower. Let's go and pinch something.'

Cassons' tone was more soothing. 'Follow correct procedure, Marcks, old chap and do keep calm.'

I joined in. 'Yes, Saul, you'll have enough excitement when we ditch this crate. You've got the forecast; a moderate sea is tough enough in a boat so I'm not looking forward to smacking into it at sixty mph. Now, check your message and confirm the exact heading.'

'*Petseleh*, you listen to Renouf. Make sure you are correct or I give you lesson in lifesaving you never forget!' The legionnaire I'd known as Willie Grun, but who was really Wilhelm Karl von Gersdoff, the son of a German baron spoke near perfect English with a slight German accent, flawless French, Spanish, Italian and Russian. According to Saul, he was also fluent in Yiddish and Hebrew. However, we'd agreed to keep his real identity to ourselves.

'I agree, Willie, but let the '*little prick*' do his job.'

'Grun, check on Buesnal please. He's probably asleep. Don't want him waking up and shooting at our escort!' Cassons cut across our nervous chatter. 'We're winding up the engines now so prepare for take-off.'

We'd only performed this manoeuvre a couple of times in rehearsal

and, with a gusty wind blowing across the barely visible runway, it promised to be another hairy experience. Cassons switched off his throat mike and turned to his right to look down at me from his pilot's seat now elevated for take-off. 'You're the Shakespearean scholar. Is this right, "*Once more unto the breach, dear friends, once more—*"' '"*Or close the wall up with our English dead.*" Seems appropriate but later in the speech Henry V mentions stiffening the sinews and summoning up the blood!'
Cassons laughed. 'Well we've done that already – we look a right sight.'
Even in the dim hanger lights our "blood" stained bandages seemed rather overdone but once they were soaked in the briny Fleming believed they would add authenticity to our story.
We trundled out of the hanger and taxied along the runway. I knew little about flying but something about engines so I'd been given the bomb aimer/navigator/co-pilot's and engineer's role. In this Heinkel, that didn't involve too much as there was only one control column though it had an arm that could be swung over to my side to give access to the ailerons and elevators. There were no engine or rudder controls though I could reach some of the trimmers and the radiator coolant handles and read the main engine instrument cluster in the panel above our heads. At best I could keep it airborne and engage the autopilot but landing or, in our case, ditching was way beyond me. The two Spitfires detailed to escort us and keep other friendlies from shooting us down whilst in Cornish airspace were already circling above in the faint pre-dawn light.
Cassons finished his check-list, set the superchargers for the two Jumo engines to 1.35 atmospheres before opening the throttles and releasing the brakes. The take-off was surprisingly smooth and, after raising the undercarriage and flaps, he reduced the pressure and engine revs for the climb. Fleming had decided that to avoid alerting the anti-aircraft defences we would head for the closest coast which was only a few miles to our north-west and climb out sixteen miles to 15,000 feet over the sea. Even without a bomb load this would take about thirty minutes, as we didn't want to overstress the engines.
As we headed towards the setting moon we passed over Porthcothan Bay and caught up with our escorts. The large circular compass dial above me was still displaying 305 degrees when I calculated from my stopwatch that we'd finally reached point Alpha. 'Skipper, if you're happy you can turn onto 152 now and head south-

east.'

From this altitude the sun was clearly visible as Cornwall crept towards it with only the occasional cloud masking its glow. Despite the wind over the ground it was a beautiful morning; ideal in some respects for our purpose though more cloud cover would have helped. However, it did make my navigational task easier. Within minutes, with the airspeed indicator registering just over 300 kilometres per hour in the following wind, we passed back over Newquay and across the centre of the county. Off to port, the China Clay pits around St Austell looked like the lunar surface as we cruised past Truro and out to sea again near Portscatho.

I looked over Cassons' shoulder at the Heinkel's main chronometer in the centre of his control yoke which we'd set on Day Light Saving time. It read 07:10 as we headed out into the English Channel. 'Another twenty-four minutes at this speed to point Bravo, skipper. Throttle back perhaps? Don't want to arrive too early.'

'Right, the Spits will leave us soon. I'll reduce the revs and start the descent when they've gone. I'll try to reach there in forty minutes then aim to arrive at point Charlie on the hour.' He reactivated his throat mike.

'Okay, chaps, ETA 08:00 with the Jerries. Give a polite two fingers to our escort, enjoy the flight and prepare for a refreshing swim.'

We flew on in our captured Heinkel 111, painted with a few new bullet holes and other scars and wearing the correct insignia for *II./KG 27* which was based in Dinard. We were all wearing Luftwaffe flight overalls and soft leather helmets. According to Cassons this was far superior and much more comfortable than the usual RAF kit. He wasn't so impressed with the flying characteristics of the hastily repaired German medium bomber which he'd been working on at Farnborough before he'd been detached for a special operation. He didn't know but could thank Saul for bringing his name to Fleming's attention. Even though he didn't speak German, I'd persuaded the Commander to select Joe Buesnal, who had escaped with me from Jersey back in July, because of his other special skills.

As the twin Junkers Jumo engines droned on there was little to do so, rather than reflect on the odd circumstances which had induced us to "volunteer" for what had all the hallmarks of a suicide mission, I retreated to my day dream world where Caroline, Rachel and now my mystery Russian girl, Masha might offer a temporary diversion.

9

Her cold fingers clawed at my wrist desperately clinging on to her only means of escape but, as the boat gathered speed, it was useless. I tried to release my hold on the rope streaming from the stern as it jerked me through the choppy wake but for the umpteenth time I failed, trapped in a time bubble, unable to release myself to save her from Kempler who had anchored himself around her waist and was dragging her back to the island. Her eyes pleaded and she screamed something as the inevitable laws of physics ripped her from my grasp. I screamed, 'I'll come back. I love you.'

'I love you too, Renouf but wake up and pull yourself together, man!' Cassons whacked my shoulder and jolted me sideways.

It was always the same dream, the boat speeding away and Caroline disappearing into the misty sea but sometimes she wore Rachel's face. Today, the two had merged; the image swirling into the plump innocent features of a baby girl — my daughter, Taynia.

I shook my head. 'Sorry, just the usual nightmare.'

'A day mare, surely — Rachel again?'

He'd met Rachel; escaped with her from France but knew nothing of Caroline unless Saul had told him. I nodded. 'Yes, but I'm awake now. What's the time?'

'07:40; descending to 500 feet and turning towards point Bravo. You'd better get into the nose and start spotting.'

I released my harness and climbed down into the bomb aimer's position though the additional Perspex the RAF engineers had wrapped around the lower half of the nose to protect us during ditching distorted the peripheral view.

We'd been waiting at St Eval for several days for the weather to improve and now there was a ridge of high pressure over the South West but the barometer was falling as a trough edged in behind it. Below me the sea looked rather wrinkled with long waves pressing in from the Atlantic. Fortunately there were no white horses yet but ditching was going to be marginal at best. I used the captured Zeiss binoculars to scan ahead looking for any flash of yellow against the grey sea.

A Coastal Command flying boat had been shadowing the

Rettungsboje – Saul's "yellow peril" rescue buoy — since a Royal Navy MGB released it into the channel stream the day before. It was one of several which had been washed up on the south coast during the violent weather earlier in the week. The last report sent just before we took off confirmed that it had been taken in tow by a Kriegsmarine *schnellboote* and was heading towards the French coast. In the two hours since it was last sighted it couldn't have travelled more than thirty miles in the prevailing sea conditions so we'd crept in behind its track and were now approaching from the south as though we had taken off from Dinard.

The German *Rettungsboje* was quite substantial and had room for a bomber's crew in its hexagonal cabin which was eight feet deep topped by a six foot oval turret complete with signal mast and wireless antenna though the transceiver was limited to marine channels and not capable of communicating with aircraft. We'd had a chance to try this one out and it was quite comfortable for five airmen who didn't suffer from seasickness and certainly better than a rubber dinghy for whiling away the hours before rescue.

The odds of spotting it were slightly better than finding a needle in the proverbial haystack but not much and the expanse of troubled sea below me seemed without end from this height. Ironically, the buoy was painted brightly to attract attention while the E-boat which was towing it was camouflaged to avoid detection. I was surprised by Joe's deep voice in my earphones. 'There's the bugger, off to port!'

I twisted around and spotted the "yellow peril"; focused the binoculars and saw he was right. I traced the tow line and the stern of a grey painted *schnellboote* bounced into view. *Schnell* meant 'fast' but for some obscure reason the Royal Navy called them E-boats. Whatever it was called, it was highly dangerous and, with a crew of about twenty-five, wasn't going to be easy to take as a prize. We had surprise on our side but only three of us were trained in this type of warfare. Saul had to be protected and Cassons was no commando.

His voice crackled over the intercom. 'Marcks send the Morse code for sighting the buggers. Cornish for "ship" isn't it?'

'Roger, skipper sending "*gorhel*" now but no position right?'

'Correct, who knows who might be listening.'

We'd learnt a series of codes based on the almost extinct Cornish language so didn't need to carry any notes just in case we were bagged by the Germans.

'Wilco, skip.' I couldn't be sure if Saul was extracting the Michael with his jargon or just doing his job but Cassons gave him the benefit of the doubt.

'Right, chaps, here we go. I'm banking towards the E-boat and starting the smoke. I'll have to cut one engine so belt in and brace for impact when I shout. Good luck.'

I scrambled back to my seat and belted up as Cassons fired the electrical circuit which set off the smoke bomb under the port engine. The aircraft lurched and shuddered as he shut it off and raised the revs on the starboard side.

'They're trying to hail us on the emergency channel.' Saul's voice struggled over the screaming engine.

'You've got the story – tell it to them. If they get suspicious end the transmission — and pray.' Cassons wrestled with the controls as the plane wriggled alarmingly. 'Now, I'm dropping the flaps — we've got to lose more speed. I'll take her in on her belly parallel to the waves.'

He was grunting with the effort as all trim was lost and the plane began to drop like the 20,000 lb rock it was once lift disappeared.

'Send the ditching code now!'

Appropriately that would be "*mor*" — the Cornish for "sea"

At least the E-boat had spotted us now and should rush to our rescue. We couldn't take more than our side arms and knives with us but would those be enough?

When Caroline and I had watched helplessly as three of these Heinkels had strafed and bombed Jersey just a few months before I'd wished with all my being that they would crash into the sea. Now I was in one, I wasn't so sure I relished that particular outcome but there was no more time for daydreams — just prayers.

'Brace, Brace', Cassons shouted then cut the remaining engine and the Heinkel gave a final sigh then smacked its belly onto the sea.

10

We bounced once then recoiled a few feet into the air. I was in a folding seat with little back support so I clung on to the radio compass assembly with my right hand and braced my left against the back of the pilot's seat. As the airframe stopped rebounding and hit the solid wall of water my trunk continued at over forty mph almost ripping my arms from their sockets. Fortunately, years of swimming training and farming had overdeveloped my shoulder muscles and they didn't give. Ditching in a fold down seat is not something I would recommend for anyone of slighter build but we'd survived for the moment. The aircraft was settling now, kept afloat only by the surface area of its large wings. It was the matter of only a short time before gravity overcame surface friction and the weight of the engines dragged it under.

Without the roar of those engines it was quiet enough for Cassons to shout out to the rest of the crew who were in the waist of the plane. 'Roll call. Sound out!'

A stream of German exploded from Willie followed by what I was sure was Saul's entire vocabulary of Afrikaans curses.

There was a slight pause then Joe called out. 'Piece of cake. I've had harder belly flops than that from the ten-metre diving board.' I'd witnessed most of his dives and it struck me that he might be exaggerating. 'Want me to rescue the machine gun, skipper?'

Joe was quite capable of holding the MG 15 and its double ammo drum over his head in the water and "walking" it over to the German boat which was about 800 yards away and altering course towards us. I'd watched him carry a galvanised bucket full of seawater over his head for one hundred yards in deep water so this would be one of his "pieces of cake". However, it would not appear to be the normal behaviour of a Luftwaffe crewman and might alarm our Kriegsmarine rescuers.

'Get out first and get the dinghy deployed.' I shouted back.

Cassons had slid the overhead panel back and was clambering out onto the fuselage. I released my harness, shrugged out of the parachute pack and stretched my arms which felt like I'd just sprinted one hundred yards wearing a lead belt, then followed him.

We were moving up and down with the swell now and, as I looked back, I could see that the Perspex had finally cracked and water was surging into the cockpit.

Behind us, the other three had exited from the dorsal position and were easing themselves onto the port wing. Willie had inflated the dinghy but it was going to be a tight squeeze for five of us and we had to keep our weapons dry.

Saul was first in, looking paler than I'd ever seen him. Joe eased his massive bulk in carefully and dragged his machine gun after him. Cassons slid in while Willie kept the rubber craft steady for me as I followed. He held on to the painter then clambered onto the fuselage again.

'*Scheisse*, they come very fast — too fast.'

He was right. We needed time for the plane to sink. We couldn't afford for them to look too closely but short of jumping up and down on the wings there wasn't anything we could do.

Willie called out again. 'Can you hear that?'

'What?'

'Aircraft engines!'

'Where?'

Willie twisted and turned trying to locate the sound direction.

I could hear it now. That pulsing desynchronised roar of powerful radial engines.

'Beaufighters.' Cassons called out. 'Get in the dinghy, Grun, Quick now. The buggers are going to attack us and try to claim a kill.'

Willie scrambled down, slid into the dinghy and pushed off. Joe and I grabbed paddles and started to pull away as fast as we could.

Off to our right, we heard the rattle of machine guns as the *schnellboote* spotted the danger and started to blast away at the two twin-engined fighter-bombers. They were wasting their ammo but stirring up a real hornets' nest. Two giant shadows zoomed over us and split either side of the German boat climbing rapidly so that they could coordinate their attack.

'Well, there it is, as Fleming would say— one monumental cock up.' Saul shook his head. 'We're not going to pinch anything today. They're not going to stop for us!'

'Too bloody true. They'll be lucky to survive if those two have any bombs on board.' Cassons sounded envious and I didn't blame him — that was proper RAF work not skulking around in stolen uniforms living out one of Fleming's fantasies.

'So where does that leave us apart from the bloody obvious', I asked.

Joe picked up his machine gun. 'I could shoot at them if that helps.' He offered.

'No, but you can ditch that over the side. We need to lose some weight. Keep your life vests on though. We're going to need them.' Cassons stared up at the two Beaufighters as they reached the apogee of their climbs and flipped over to dive from opposite directions on the *schnellboote* as it opened its throttles and weaved away at top speed.

'Perhaps not, skip.' Joe pointed. 'Look, they've abandoned the rescue float.'

He was right. They'd cut their tow and it was drifting towards us. At least we wouldn't drown and, with the large red crosses painted on its side, we should be safe from the RAF if their current prey eluded them. We'd also be safe from Fleming for a while.

We'd left this captured buoy in original condition with all its supplies intact just in case it was checked before being taken in tow. Clambering aboard was far more difficult than it had been when it was moored up the creek near Helford in Cornwall. The sea was moving from moderate to rough and there was no sign now of the Heinkel which had sunk before we were halfway to this strange vessel.

The steel double doors on the deck opened outwards allowing access down a ladder into the hexagonal space most of which was below the surface. There were hand rails all around the deck. Inside was a communal area with a table above which hung an oil lamp which Willie lit. There were four bunk beds and a food preparation area. Apart from not being equipped with a transceiver capable of communicating with aircraft it was the perfect example of thorough German planning and could keep a crew safe and secure for up to a week if it wasn't drifting towards a rocky coast.

Before we'd belly flopped I'd estimated that we were about thirty miles from the west coast of Guernsey. It wasn't too difficult to estimate tidal flow but, factoring in wind speed and sea state, meant that we could end up as guests on my sister island within the next twelve hours or, if we missed its rocky embrace, crash into the French coast by this time tomorrow. Of course we could miss everything and bob about in circles indefinitely. These things were meant to be anchored and not wander about at the mercy of wind and tide.

However, we were dry and safe for the moment and Willie

celebrated by lighting the stove and making us all some excellent coffee. Apart from food and other survival stores secured in the many compartments there were playing cards and chess sets to keep us amused in our lobster pot.

We agreed a lookout rota and I volunteered for the first two hour slot but Cassons beat me up the ladder and was retching over the side when I finally scrambled up. In between heaves he muttered that air sickness and sea sickness were two very different afflictions. I didn't argue but thought that if he didn't get his stomach under control I might have to lash him to the handrail to prevent the sea claiming him.

Soon Saul joined us. He was immune to sea sickness but the others had sent him topsides as he wanted to smoke and they weren't immune to his fumes. We watched Cassons for a while without comment while Saul finished his cigarette.

He tossed the butt into the sea and grimaced. 'It was the same when we escaped from France. None of the airmen could cope with the motion.'

'Neither could Willie but he's learned how to control his stomach while we've been training up in Scotland.'

Saul laughed. 'What, garrotting deer and shagging sheep?'

I sighed. Saul's idea of stiff exercise was moving his backside from his chair in the corner of Room 39 to the one in front of Fleming's desk outside the Admiral's office. Willie, Joe and I had been paddling canoes, swimming underwater and scaling cliffs on the rocky shores near Achnacarry before breakfast each day. It was a good cure for seasickness and certainly drove laziness out of the body.

'Cassons is looking all in. We'd best get him below, Saul. It's just dry heaving now. Don't want him to freeze out here.'

The pilot was reluctant to be confined again but, under Saul's supervision, I managed to manhandle him below.

I grabbed a fresh mug of coffee and resumed my shift on deck. Only another ninety minutes before I could put my head down. From this low elevation there was nothing but the grey and white claws of an agitated sea slapping our yellow sides and propelling us steadily eastwards so I braced my legs against the bucking motion and scanned the horizon again.

Joe joined me on deck with a pair of binoculars though I doubted he would be able to keep them steady enough to see anything.

'How long do you reckon, Jack... before the Jerries are back?'

'Don't know but the E boat will have sent a distress message and the Luftwaffe have fighters on the airfield in Guernsey. Depends on whether they had to scare off the Beaufighters first. They'll probably try to spot us from the air and then send out another vessel if the E-boat needs repairs.'

'It would have been tough taking that boat with only three of us against twenty-five.'

'Don't forget Saul and Cassons.'

He laughed. 'You did your best but Saul will never make a fighter. He's a brain box. He'll know how to do it but, if there's a problem, he'll freeze. He's not much of a shot either, is he?'

'No, I'd rather he was in front of me than behind if he starts shooting.'

'Might be best to empty his magazine so he can just wave the pistol around.'

'That's a thought but he might surprise us, you know.'

In between training on the Heinkel Joe, Willie and I had spent a few hours in the hangar with Cassons and Saul trying to prepare them for an attack on a German boat. However, we knew from bruising experience it takes months to hone action and reaction to become really effective. By the time our two pupils had remembered what to do next they'd be dead. Of course, the German sailors wouldn't have any training in unarmed combat and we should have an element of surprise. But would that be enough?

I'd shown Saul how to garrotte a sentry, stick a sharpened steel knitting needle in behind his ear, break his neck by tugging his helmet backwards and other devious tricks. But these were aimed at killing without second thought and only useful on dry land and not on the heaving deck of a boat at sea. In close quarter fighting, knives were best and we commandos had practised on tethered rafts. Now, disguised as Luftwaffe flight crew we all carried captured 9mm Luger pistols in side holsters but, even on solid ground, they were hopelessly inaccurate beyond a few feet. Those Parabellum rounds weren't man stoppers either. Probably the best weapons for fighting on deck were cutlasses and dirks but carrying those would certainly remove the element of surprise.

Joe sighed. 'We'll just have to wait and see but we must get to their radio first.'

'Let's just hope that there isn't a Jerry plane circling overhead.' I shook my head. 'This really is a crazy plan. It's a shame Fleming isn't

here to show us how he ever imagined it could work.'
'I'd pay good money to see—'
'Listen!'
'Aircraft engines?'
We scanned the sky in all directions but couldn't spot anything though the growl of distant aero engines continued.
'I'll get Cassons back up. He'll be able to tell us what they are.'
When I'd finished hauling the seasick pilot back on deck Joe had identified a black speck making lazy spirals in the distance. Cassons tried the binoculars but couldn't keep them steady. He listened intensely. 'Only one — twin engines about 1,000 feet up — probably a Ju 88.'
I hadn't felt nervous up to that point but the mention of the bombers which had sunk the *Lancastria* in front of us made my stomach lurch.
Willie had clambered up and had a flare pistol in his hand. He looked at me. 'Your decision.'
For some unknown reason Fleming had placed me in charge of the action phase. If we didn't draw the plane's attention now and they spotted us later it might arouse suspicion, as a genuine Luftwaffe crew in our position wouldn't hesitate. My stomach was somersaulting now but I nodded my assent and he fired. The flare burst into red flame about 200 feet up.
The distant engine note changed. Cassons clutched the rail and muttered 'He's seen us...' before convulsing over the side again.
I had an idea. 'Let's pretend Cassons is seriously wounded and unconscious. Take him below and when they come to rescue us we can pass him up and keep their hands full…and Willie, bring up the signal lamp in case they try to communicate.'
Minutes later the Ju 88 flew overhead while we gesticulated wildly at our "saviour". The pilot gained altitude and started a lazy circle. Soon a lamp was blinking at us. Saul knew the German codes and translated. They were asking for our aircraft number. If we responded they might seek more information via radio from their HQ. Our number was genuine but a call to Dinard would reveal that the plane was probably still on the ground unless we were lucky and it was out on a flight somewhere. Would they bother? They had no reason to be suspicious so it was probably just standard operating procedure. I told Willie to give it and he flashed the signal lamp and we all held our breath but almost immediately the aircraft operator

responded with a cheery message that help was on its way within thirty minutes and they would hold above us until it was in sight.

That was a bloody nuisance because we would not be able to storm whatever vessel arrived with the plane still overhead. We'd have to get on board quietly and keep our act going until it left which meant that Joe, Cassons and I would have to keep dumb. Being "unconscious" would help Cassons but what could Joe and I do to maintain the fiction? The Luftwaffe wouldn't have non-German speaking air crew. Another flaw in Fleming's plan though he had originally demanded German speakers. Unfortunately, they were still in hospital. What a buggering mess and I still didn't know what Saul was meant to be "pinching" and he wouldn't tell me.

Fortunately the circling plane didn't send any more signals so we waited apprehensively for the next stage of Operation *Ruthless* to unfold.

11

When it finally arrived it was a considerable disappointment. Rescuing downed airmen had been delegated to an armed fishing boat no more than seventy feet long. As it drew closer we could read its bow number; FK14. It had a canon on its foredeck though it was covered in canvas and pointing skywards — not much of a challenge at all. But it was Saul who was most annoyed as such a plodding vessel would be unlikely to contain anything worth pinching.

Working backwards Saul calculated that it must already have been at sea when it received the call for assistance, as it would have taken well over two hours for it to transit from St Peter Port. We waited until it was within hailing range and Willie started shouting abuse at the crew. Saul explained that the rivalry between airmen and sailors was as strong in Germany as it was in England. From what I could judge FK14's crew gave as good as they got and the atmosphere was fairly relaxed as they threw us a line. The top of our rescue float was level with the fishing boat's prow so Joe pulled on the rope until we were alongside its deckhouse. Cassons was still feigning injury so one of the sailors dropped down to help manoeuvre him on board. I counted five crewmen on deck and spotted one man at the wheel. There might be an engineer below as well.

As soon as we were on board and had the float in tow the aircraft waggled its wings and flew off. I didn't know how long I would have to keep up the dumb show as the sailors seemed curious and wanted to talk. So far Saul and Willie had kept the conversation and joking going but we would have to make a move soon. One of the sailors ventured down the ladder into the bowels of our "yellow peril" and I nodded to Joe to follow him. Any noises from there should be sufficiently muffled. Willie spotted what was happening and moved towards the deckhouse leaving me to tend to Cassons while Saul distracted the remaining crew by pointing at the covered gun and asking questions. As soon as Willie secured the radio I would act. Saul had two of them laughing with him by the gun so I knelt down, moved Cassons' hand to his holstered Luger and prepared my move.

Joe emerged from the float and gave me the thumbs up. There was a smothered shout from the wheelhouse so I rose up and drew my pistol. There was no need to kill any of these hapless sailors so I released the safety and fired a shot into the air. Cassons sat up with his gun drawn and Saul backed away and withdrew his. He yelled something in German and the crew raised their hands and fell to their knees.

Willie shoved the captain out of the wheelhouse and forced him to the deck. There was sufficient rope coiled on hooks to secure all the sailors before we dragged them below to the surprisingly large day cabin. Joe retrieved the last one from the depths of the rescue float, shovelled his unconscious body over the boat's gunnels and hauled him below.

It had taken less than five minutes; no one had died but, according to Saul, we had failed, as we had nothing to show for our mission apart from an old French fishing boat and six prisoners. None of which would impress Fleming.

At least we were all alive but now we had to make a choice. First we needed to know where we were. Saul retrieved a chart from the wheelhouse but, without a fix on our current position and surrounded only by a grey expanse of sea, it was guesswork. The skipper would have a good idea but he'd be unlikely to volunteer anything other than his name rank and number. Unless…

Willie took FK14's captain, who arrogantly kept repeating his chant of 'Fedder, *Oberbootsmann,* 15931/45K', over to the bowels of the "yellow peril" for a chat. I'd remembered his remarkable skill in extracting information from reluctant sources from our time in France. Sure enough, he returned minutes later dragging Fedder who, displaying Willie's interrogation trademark, was still chewing on his own socks. Once he was secured below Willie huddled with Saul over the chart for a while.

'From information received,' Saul chuckled, 'it appears that we are here.' He stabbed his finger at a spot about twenty nautical miles to the north-west of Guernsey. 'Our nearest port would be Dartmouth – about fifty miles but that takes us a bit too far north and close to Guernsey for my liking. I think we need to head out west and then turn to Plymouth—'

'What about Helford? They could make use of this boat. Could even be our transport to Jersey,' I suggested.

'It's possible. Let me check the engines and fuel.'

He returned with a big grin on his face. She's not quite what she seems. There's a massive Petter Atomic four cylinder diesel engine with at least 250 BHP — made in Somerset of all places. I'm guessing that she's good for twenty knots in a sprint and should cruise happily at fourteen. That's a suspiciously powerful radio setup as well. I think Willie should make further enquiries of the captain about the true role of this boat.' He measured the chart again. 'If we steer 290 degrees it's about one hundred miles.' He rubbed his chin. 'Assuming this tub can average thirteen knots in these sea conditions then we could be there before dark. Sunset's at about 18:00 and we'll have nautical twilight for another hour. Towing the float would slow us down by a few knots so we'll have to abandon —'

'But not just yet. Let's give Willie a few minutes alone with each of the crew in the "yellow peril" to see how much info he can squeeze out of them — Saul, you can make notes if you have the stomach for it — then cut it adrift.

Willie removed his knife. 'I like that, Jack. They probably don't know much anyway and certainly won't reveal anything over a cup of tea and a chat under the rules of your British fair play. Bring their radio man here and I'll *ask* for his cooperation.'

He didn't need the knife or a visit to the rescue float. Perhaps the sorry state of their captain had already loosened tongues as the radio man powered up the transceiver and attached the Morse key while I removed the microphone. Asked nicely he even produced a booklet with the catchy title of *"Seeverteidigung Orne-Mont St Michel"* which Saul pocketed without comment.

I tied up the rating again while Saul selected the correct frequency, donned the headphones and started keying. An expert might have been able to follow his fingers and work out the letters but he was too quick for me. I guessed he was sending "*melen – cok – lun – eth.*" which would translate as "yellow – fishing boat – Monday – eight." This would decode as "No pinch – fishing boat (instead of E-boat) – Helford – ETA eight hours." We had other memorised code words. Successful pinch would be *glas* (for blue), Dartmouth was *Mergher* (Wednesday) and a range of numbers in Cornish from five to fifteen for time in hours.

Fleming would be waiting for these at St Eval and I imagined him stomping about in frustration at the failure to *pinch* what I now suspected was the sort of code book a larger Kriegsmarine vessel would carry.

I also pictured Fleming explaining the failure to Turing who seemed desperate for this information.

Willie interrupted my thoughts. 'Do we need this cargo?' He

pointed below to where the crew were tied up.

'What do you mean?'

'They are surplus. Let us deliver them to Neptune.'

'No! Not in cold blood – they're no threat and they might still have valuable information.' To Willie, all Germans were now Nazis and the only good Nazi was a dead one. I indicated the bow gun. 'If you're desperate to shoot something then use that to sink the float. There's no—'

'Willie's right, Jack. We're better off without them.'

'Saul, stick to sailing a desk. You're not a killer!'

'So far; but look at this.' He took my arm and led me to the port side of the wheel house. There were two paintings of RAF Beaufighters tumbling towards the sea in flames as well as another three of small boats sinking.

'These Nazis have been quite busy showing compassion at sea. I think we should put them in the float and sink it.'

What had happened to Saul? He'd never seen action and as far as I knew had never hit anyone in anger. I'd rescued him from school bullies enough times to know he preferred his tongue to his fists.

I shook my head firmly. 'No. If they'd fought us it would be different. Are they a threat now?'

Cassons had followed us and was staring at the paintings. 'Remember the *Lancastria*.'

'Of course and I'll never forget. You've shot down enemy pilots but that's impersonal. I've killed from this distance.' I prodded him in the chest. 'But that was a matter of survival. This isn't.'

Willie joined us. 'It would seem three to one. I'll take them to the float.'

'Wait. This isn't a democracy. For better or worse, Fleming put me in charge but I'd like to hear Joe's opinion. Willie, please send him up here.'

I was a private in the Hampshire Regiment with the comedy rank of acting sub-lieutenant in the Royal Naval Volunteer Reserve. In a fair fight I could overpower Saul and Cassons but would struggle against either of the other two.

I had official but could I establish personal or moral authority? Suddenly, this had become very important to me and I wasn't sure why.

Joe emerged and contemplated the trophy paintings. He rubbed his chin thoughtfully. 'Willie's told me about this. I'm not sure. We've just spent months training to kill without thinking about it. Now, I've got too much time and I'm puzzled.'

It was probably the longest speech Joe had ever made but he was a policeman and trained to uphold the law not take it into his own hands.

'Take your time.' I looked at Saul then Cassons. 'We have to live with this decision.'

Cassons was older and outranked me but, in this instance, didn't have the authority. I sensed that he might be reconsidering so I waited, hoping that his humanity would prevail.

Saul broke the spell. 'You've always wanted to be Jewish, Jack but you've never understood what that really means.' He sighed. 'I doubt you ever will. Have it your way.' He stalked off to the prow and started to untie the canvas cover over the gun.

Cassons nodded. 'I'll relieve Willie.'

Before he could reveal his thoughts I tugged at Joe's arm. 'Go and help Saul. Get the gun ready. I'll cut the line.'

A sense of relief flooded through me as I sawed at the hemp and watched the float drift away. It was a 2cm flak gun, standard issue to the German Army and adapted for Kriegsmarine use. We'd trained on a variety of captured German weapons and this was one of them. Willie brushed past me without comment and selected some boat-tailed HE tracer rounds from the ammo locker and loaded the magazine. These would self-destruct after a mile or so but should have sufficient velocity to puncture our "yellow peril".

Saul returned to the wheel house, engaged the propeller then manoeuvred us away from the pitching float. Joe harnessed his massive shoulders into the long-barrelled gun and rotated the platform until the target was in his sights. When we were a hundred yards away he opened fire and emptied the magazine without missing a single shot.

The rescue float's red-cross signs were obliterated and the superstructure blown apart. The rounds wouldn't penetrate under water so the *Rettungsboje* would drift about until it was swamped and eventually sank.

If it was found first it would leave the Germans with a puzzle even bigger than the one Joe had yet to resolve. We moved the crew into the old fish hold one at a time and Willie interrogated them while Saul made notes. Nothing further was said about my leadership as we fought our way over the Atlantic swells towards the Cornish coast.

12

'Bloody RAF fools. When I find them I'll wrap their idiot propellers round their stupid necks or, better still, stick their thick heads into those propellers while the engines are running. Wait until I—'

'Excuse me, sir, but they were only doing their job. They didn't know about our mission, surely.'

'Shut up, Renouf, and drink your pint of whatever watered down rubbish that is. I'll let off steam if I want to.' He tipped the brandy down his throat and glared at us individually — daring anyone to speak. I sensed Willie about to accept the challenge but Saul interceded first. 'Another one of those, sir?'

'No, I need to have a word with the chaps running this show before I push off. Marcks, you'd better stay here and help with the navigation plan. Cassons you come with me and work out a suitable punishment for those Beaufighter crews before I set Turing on them. Buesnal, you can help crew the boat that takes Renouf and Grun to Jersey. Contact me once everything is in order.' He tossed the Kriegsmarine booklet to Saul. 'You might as well keep this. I can't see any use for it and Turing would only turn it into confetti and shower me with it. I'll pass your interrogation notes over to our specialists. I must say, the Germans seem to have been surprisingly cooperative.' He smiled.

It was late evening in the Ferry Boat Inn inside the Helford Passage and FK14 was moored a few hundred yards up the creek leading to Port Navas. We'd been intercepted by a motor gun boat a few miles short of Falmouth and escorted around the treacherous coast and up the tidal Helford River. Our fortunate prisoners had been unloaded and taken into custody by the Military Police who would doubtless deal with any complaints they might have about rough treatment with their usual brand of sympathy.

The inn was quite busy with locals as well as the few sailors who were just beginning to establish a base around the network of creeks. We'd met its commander, Lieutenant Holdsworth RN who had just set up his HQ in Ridifarne, a rather splendid house overlooking the Passage.

A local had told us there was a far better pub called the Shipwrights Arms on the other side though we'd need to pay the ferryman to get us over there. But I'd had enough travelling for one day and was looking forward to a comfortable bed in Holdsworth's new acquisition.

The home-made pasties were so wonderful, Joe had munched his way through two before Fleming arrived. The Commander had brought our kit down from St Eval and after debriefing us was being driven to Truro to catch the sleeper train to London. We watched as he moved over to Holdsworth's table where an elderly gentleman, wearing the same number of RNVR stripes as Fleming but without the green inserts, had previously been introduced to us as Lieutenant-Commander Smyth, Resident Naval Officer of the Helford River.

Two locals, one in Home Guard uniform and the other in a suit with an ARP armband, both smoking pipes and about Fleming's age, wandered over with their pints of beer and asked if they could join us as the pub was now crowded. We shuffled up and made polite conversation. Fortunately, Fleming had brought our uniforms otherwise we'd have had the Home Guard detachment sticking bayonets in our faces rather than offering pints. I still felt uncomfortable in my RNVR rig as I had yet to undergo any officer training though Willie had pointedly refused to salute me until I did.

We were guarded in our responses but we could sense they suspected that we had just returned from some clandestine mission. Loose lips sink ships but, in this quiet corner of Cornwall, it was unlikely there were any German spies to report our conversations. However, it would be just like Saul to stir things up by lapsing into German! Fortunately, he seemed too sleepy to make the effort.

The two men, Frank and Jim, were quite forthcoming though. The former was a quantity surveyor working on a new airfield on the other side of the Lizard Peninsula and the latter worked on his family's farm at Trewothack. They didn't usually frequent this pub but had been on exercise that evening. They both recommended the pub in Manaccan which was very friendly and offered excellent ale. So there were a few places to fortify our spirits while Saul worked up a plan to smash Willie and me into the granite cliffs of my island home.

This part of Cornwall is very different to Jersey where the cliffs are twice as high and almost vertical in places. Around my island, with a range of over forty feet, the tides are far larger and the currents much more challenging. We tried though and paddled our folding kayak to the mouth of the river and practised landing at Toll

Point. During daylight it was feasible though trying to hide the folded canoes was almost impossible in such rocky terrain. There were several suitable sea caves around Jersey's north coast but at this time of the year it would be suicidal to try to navigate into them at night, with any sort of sea running. The south and east coasts were far more accessible but likely to be patrolled for that very reason. The west with its very long surf beach would have left us far too exposed. It had to be north but the small harbours would also be guarded. In reality we had no information about German defences which might even include minefields along the cliffs. Struggling with a sixteen foot long wooden framed canvas boat through breaking waves and tidal surges would have been a nightmare. Saul suggested we use a small dinghy instead so I bundled him into one in the sheltered creek and sculled it in the single handed French manner up to Dennis Head and invited him to scramble ashore. Already moaning about the cold he declined the opportunity to hop out and secure the craft against the rocky outcrops and suggested we might use large rubber inner tubes instead.

Back in the Shipwrights Arms, which was now our favoured local, and still shivering from his *accidental* fall into the sea, he conceded that we needed a different plan and that he should travel to London to see Fleming as he'd heard about some experimental diving suits made of rubberised twill that were being used, along with rebreathers, by the submarine service.

During his absence we focused on refitting FK14. The engine was in excellent condition and after some fiddling I thought I might have squeezed another ten horsepower out of it. We needed to make her look more like a fishing boat so the gun had to be removed and replaced by a mast and sail. Other special bases had been set up for insertions into mainland France and we were in touch with the groups in Newlyn and Mylor. Holdsworth introduced us to **Daniel Lagadec**, a Breton fisherman, who had just joined his unit. Initially he was a bit sniffy when he realised that we weren't French though he warmed up when I spoke to him in Breton and told him he was lucky we weren't Parisians.

Daniel had escaped from Concarneau and been back a couple of times since so was familiar with not only the coastline but also German procedures and documentation. He helped us disguise the boat by painting her in a mixture of the green and blue favoured by the Breton fishermen. We added a false registration number — SM

2683. We'd debated which port to use as her home base and discarded the smaller Norman ones closer to Jersey. Even though she looked like a Concarneau vessel from further down the Brittany coast, we decided on St Malo, as it was sufficiently large to hold a wide range of vessels. Once Fleming had released the boat to him, Holdsworth's plan was to repaint it and change registration numbers after every trip. Our clever shipwright constructed a false wall between the fish hold and the foc'sle where we stored a variety of captured German weapons including two MG 34 rapid fire machine guns and five MP 38 submachine guns along with several cases of 7.92mm and 9mm ammunition. We also requisitioned two Lee Enfield .303 rifles with telescopic sights as Joe and I were already expert in their use. Along with a dozen Walther P38 automatic 9mm pistols we stored a couple of flare guns and several one and a half pound blocks of plastic explosive with time pencil detonators. We also carried three cases of German stick grenades which we could throw much further than our own 36M "Mills Bombs". This hoard would only be used in a dire emergency but we had to service the weapons on a regular basis.

During this time Joe fell in love. While a product of pure chance, it seemed to the rest of us that Leading Wren Dorothy Collins, who'd been assigned as one of the drivers who delivered stores to us on a daily basis, was the perfect match. Statuesque or even Amazonian was the first impression Dot created when alighting from her truck's cab. Though she was a couple of inches shorter than Joe she looked as though she could change a tyre without needing a jack. The naval overalls she wore didn't flatter her but she seemed to bulge and narrow in the right places. She was also rather pretty and sweet natured though I did decline the invitation to arm wrestle with her after one pint too many. Having seen her frolicking about with Joe in the cold waters of the creek and ducking him mercilessly I didn't really want her marking me in a water polo match either.

After a particularly heavy night in the pub we'd agreed to Saul's request that we name the boat after *Jacob's Star* which had been sunk under us at St Nazaire in June. He'd told us that his father was still trying to discover the right pen pusher at the Admiralty with whom to pursue his insurance claim. So FK14 became *Étoile de Jacob* and we all prayed she would have a luckier life.

I wondered if *Maia*, the thirty foot crabber Joe and I had stolen during our escape from Jersey and which was still in Falmouth, could be used. We might pretend to be checking crab and lobster pots and sneak in that way but I felt sure the Germans would have thought of that and introduced some systems as they had in France where coded flags were used on a daily basis. We'd still need to be landed at night but it was feasible even though the crabber was seriously underpowered. Still, it would be preferable to parachuting in. After another brutal day kayaking up and down the creeks at times without a paddle we returned to **Ridifarne** to discover that Saul had left a message that he was on his way back, had good news, and was bringing an Italian frog.

13

Joe regaled us with stories of Luigi's restaurant in Colomberie where he'd enjoyed complimentary food when on the beat and how much he enjoyed Italian cooking. Sadly, Luigi had been interned in Oxendens Holiday Camp in Fauvic along with all Italian nationals when Mussolini declared war on us in June. To ensure a decent supply of ice cream, if nothing else, the occupying Germans would probably have released them. Joe wasn't too sure whether he would like frog pasta but thought it might be better than Mrs Holdsworth's cooking. To his disappointment we discovered that Saul's message had been truncated in transmission and he arrived with a real Italian *frogman*, along with two underwater suits and a military policeman.

The Italian looked tired and despondent but soon perked up when Holdsworth opened a bottle of cognac and dispensed drinks all round. Willie seemed unimpressed and questioned the man in Italian but he responded in perfect English and seemed quite willing to discuss his capture in Gibraltar harbour. This disappointed Willie who probably had been hoping to loosen his tongue without wasting good alcohol.

He was obviously a good swimmer so I asked him about his stroke, best times and competitions to loosen him up a bit more. As this was more about him than military secrets, he told us that he was a champion freestyle swimmer and had played water polo for his country. When Joe and I revealed that we played the game and that I had trained for the aborted 1940 Olympic One Hundred Metres Freestyle he relaxed even more. Willie had been part of the German swimming team in 1936 though he'd been dismissed before the finals when it was discovered that his mother was Jewish so he quizzed our captive about his experiences in Berlin. After much shrugging and sighing he had to confess what Willie and I already knew that the Italians had only entered high divers as their swimmers and water polo players had failed to meet Olympic standards. The Japanese, another of Hitler's allies, had dominated the swimming that year so perhaps our Italian friend was prone to envy as well as exaggeration.

Holdsworth winked at me and left us with the bottle. While Willie and the Italian, whose first name was Damos, reminisced about training programmes, I took the opportunity to visit the outside lavatory.

Saul followed me. 'It's all very entertaining but we don't need to interrogate him. Fleming's experts had him for a week and he's been most forthcoming.'

'Why? He's an elite commando isn't he — surely he wouldn't betray his country?'

Saul laughed. 'He's Italian so claims to be peace loving. He says he hates this war even though he's being paid 1,000 lire a month with an extra bonus of 700 for time spent underwater. Now he's a POW, his mother will receive half of his pay. He was selected because of his swimming ability and Mussolini doesn't take kindly to those who refuse his requests. I've been with him for a couple of days now and, if he's in any way typical of the Italian attitude to war, we have little to worry about.'

'But he was trying to blow up the battleship HMS *Barham* wasn't he?'

'Yes, so the Italian navy must have their own version of Commander Fleming sitting behind a desk in Rome.'

'Another ill-thought out plan then?'

'No. It was well conceived and they trained hard but the key piece of equipment, which would seem to be a torpedo fashioned into underwater transport for two divers is, in his own words, a "*maiale*" — a pig. I suppose, as a farm boy, you must have tried riding one of those for fun.'

I had and it wasn't. 'So why have you brought him down here if the Italians' efforts are such a joke?'

'We've captured one of their submersibles now and Fleming thinks we can improve on it so be careful or you might end up as a porcine jockey! No, the reason he's here is to show you and Willie how to use the rubber suits and rebreathers.'

'And he's doing this willingly?'

Saul shrugged. "There's nothing secret about the suits. Pirelli have been making them for underwater sports for several years only our naval intelligence boys hadn't bothered to read the diving magazines.'

'So this is the new plan. No kayaks, — we're going to swim in?'

'As you keep reminding us, Jack, anything is better than parachuting. Now, let's get back and help him finish the brandy. I believe it's quite cold underwater this time of the year.'

It was — even wearing woollen underclothes beneath the rubberised fabric. The two suits were large enough for Willie and me though very tight. They'd been designed to keep the water out and were quite a struggle to put on. French chalk was essential to lubricate the inside of the rubber pants and there was a ten stage process to ensure a snug fit of the vest and sealing collar. There wasn't a hood but we had a choice of rubber shoes or swim fins. Disrobing was equally difficult but we were comfortable enough walking around in the black suits. The rebreathers used pure oxygen and Damos warned us that this could be very dangerous if used for too long. As we weren't planning a long underwater swim, we decided to dispense with them and use goggles and snorkels instead. We were familiar with those and I'd used foot fins in swimming training.

The main problem was buoyancy, as we might need to go deep to avoid detection, so we experimented with diving belts until we had the right balance. We harnessed water-proofed bags to our backs and practised dressing and undressing in the dark. Despite the risks of capture and being classified as spies we decided not to carry uniforms but civilian clothes instead. Once dressed in these we would squeeze the diving equipment into the backpacks and carry them with us to a suitable hiding place. The Pirelli suits would need to be thoroughly dried out before we could use them again so we would have to find some cover. We included a good supply of French chalk as well as water and some basic food rations though our intention was to reach my farm as soon as possible.

Apart from avoiding detection as *Étoile de Jacob* delivered us to a point where tide and wind would be in our favour, swimming through waves and surging swells, scrambling over rocks, keeping our feet off mines and eluding German patrols, it should be, as Joe suggested, a piece of cake.

14

It might well have been if the weather boys had been a bit more accurate. On Wednesday 13th November we motored out of the Helford, under Daniel's command, aiming to transit between Guernsey and Alderney after dusk and reach the Écréhous reef just before midnight. The forecast was for variable winds from the southwest backing north-west, fresh at times locally with cloud and occasional rain. What we got was quite different.

Although, at the time, it was unexpected and frightening, if we'd known the full extent of their omission we would have turned back. As we discovered later, Jersey was hit by the fringe of a cyclone and battered by one hundred mph winds as we anchored off Marmotière on the rising tide. The reef was five miles from Jersey and the same distance from Portbail on the Normandy coast. Saul and Joe knew it well and Daniel had sheltered there in the past though it was well to the east of the normal route from Cornwall to Brittany. We planned to use it as a base while Willie and I took our brief holiday on the island. Marmotière, which is only a couple of hundred yards of rocky outcrop at high tide, holds a tiny cluster of stone walled cottages — one of which belonged to my cousin and was occasionally inhabited during the summers of peace.

Because we were east of Jersey we enjoyed a degree of protection from its high cliffs and the remnants of the cyclone, sweeping in from the other side of the island, lost much of its force before it struck us. It would have been a living hell for Cassons and it tested my stomach to vomit point. Too close to the rocks, we daren't try to manoeuvre into the lagoon. Fortunately, our enormous diesel engine produced enough power to enable us to keep our head into the storm but we wouldn't be able to approach the island until the winds dropped and the massive swell subsided.

On the plus side, no sane fisherman would be at sea and the German sentries on the island would be sheltering and not worrying about invading British forces. We were pretty sure that there weren't any Germans on the reef so we decided to hold station until dawn and then motor into the lagoon and feign engine problems should anyone pass by to investigate.

As dawn crept over us from the French coast we were battered by heavy rain squalls which did little to placate the raging waves bursting over the rocks surrounding us. Saul persuaded Daniel to take the risk of the falling tide and edged us past Le Fou Rock and into the lagoon. It wasn't a spring tide so there was sufficient water for us to avoid grounding. Joe and I took the dinghy ashore and I found the key to the cottage in its usual hiding place. I left Joe with a pair of binoculars and he agreed to stand watch from the highest rock and wave a French flag at us should he spy any boats heading our way. We would hear aircraft and had agreed to ignore them unless they approached to investigate when we would hold up a crab pot and mime fishing.

Fortunately, no one approached and Saul and I went out on a pot raid. We discovered two decent sized male spider crabs and two lobsters and took them ashore to cook in the cottage, as Saul didn't want us stinking out the cabin. Crab pots meant that fishermen would be regular visitors so we prayed that the sea would ease before nightfall then *Étoile* could move to within a thousand yards of the spot we'd chosen on Jersey's north-east coast to drop us in our new fashionable Italian suits.

Before Hitler embarked on his world conquest Jersey had been one of the most popular holiday destinations in the UK — near to France but close to home —promising something exotic yet safe. I'd travelled back and forth on potato boats, mail boats, cabin cruisers and had last left being dragged behind a fishing boat. I'd never flown and though I'd swum ashore before after escaping from Port Bail I'd never travelled in a rubber suit wearing goggles, which constantly misted up, while trying to breathe through a short rubber tube. I'd surfed on wooden boards at St Ouens catching breaking waves and often been tumbled head over breakfast and dumped onto the sand. Fighting a receding storm surge at night over and around the irregular shaped conglomerate which passed as rocks in this part of the coast while at the mercy of capricious swells alternately pitching me up then dropping me down six feet at a time began to seem far worse than throwing myself out of an aeroplane attached to a bundle of silk hopefully packed correctly in some far away hangar.

Without swim fins it would have been impossible and, minus the pale moonlight peeking through the scudding clouds, suicidal; but I wasn't cold — just wet, miserable and very frightened. So far Willie and I had managed to keep together but now we were caught in the currents swirling round the rocks it was proving too difficult and I stopped trying to communicate with him and focused on finding a way through their dangerous embrace.

Even in broad daylight this would have been challenging but now, with only brief glimpse of our surroundings, we were completely at the mercy of forces way beyond our control. We had calculated our swim from *Étoile de Jacob* to coincide with the rising tide and hoped that its forward surge would neutralise any wayward undertows and cross currents. We both had captured Italian watches which had been specially made for Damos and his undersea warriors and sported luminous hands. We'd synchronised them with the boat's chronometer before dropping over the side and, from the occasional glances at my wrist, I realised that we'd been in the water for over an hour and didn't seem to be getting any closer to the massive bulk of the cliffs silhouetted against the fleeting moon glow of the western sky.

My mouth was raw from salt water and, despite the goggles, my eyes burned from the spray. My face and hands had passed through cold and were now delightfully numb and immune to the scratches from limpet shells and the rough kelp we called vraic which still clung to the battered rocks. Yet somewhere in the riot of iodine assaulting my nose I sensed the smell of land and fields richly layered with well-rotted manure.

A sudden break in the clouds allowed the moon to cast a beam of hope over us and at last I could see where we were. On my left was La Coupe Point and over to the right was Le Couperon. We were only a hundred yards from safety and the blessed smoothness of La Saie slipway. I tried to shout to Willie but caught a mouthful of spray which scorched my throat. Instead I raised my arm, pointed north and kicked my fins into action hoping he would follow.

He did and we slithered up the slipway together until we could roll over and pull off our fins. We crawled over the shingle and kept bumping into large branches with jagged edges which littered the shoreline. These must have been blown over the cliffs by the storm. They made our passage more difficult but provided cover from any inquisitive eyes. Eventually we reached the foot of the steep grassy pathway. This led up to the old guardhouse overlooking the Neolithic burial chamber which had only been discovered when the British garrison started to build a gun battery on the headland to deter the French in the late Seventeenth Century. How times had changed. The stone and brick built guard house was still there but deserted and didn't show any sign of recent occupation. The very large stones, which had supported the earthen roof of the burial chamber, were covered in lichen and in the eerie light of the moon made me shiver. Was it the ghostly presence of those early humans who had perished and been placed with due ceremony in this shallow grave over 5,000 years before or was it just the wind whipping over my numb body?

We sheltered in the doorless guard house and struggled out of our rubber suits, dressed ourselves in what we hoped would pass as farmworkers' clothes and crammed our swimming equipment into our backpacks. We decided to move on in case any Germans had been ordered to brave the elements and patrol the area. We were conscious that they might have placed anti-personnel mines as an added defence but even Willie doubted the Nazis would have desecrated such a well-known prehistoric site. I wasn't so sure so kept us to the hedgerows and led the way to my home with some trepidation not entirely sure whether this was borne of fear of discovery or disquiet at what I might discover when we arrived. If Rachel and Taynia were really there how would they react? She'd ordered me out of her life in June yet, apparently, she'd now sought the protection of my parents. Had she changed her mind? If so I would have to do everything in my power to help her and my little daughter. With those thoughts dominant I hardly noticed the destruction as we stumbled over fallen trees and uprooted bushes in our circuitous route but one image I couldn't suppress was that of Caroline's hand slipping from my grasp as her Nazi brother dragged her away. Was she still here? If so, would I risk the mission in an attempt to see her?

15

At this time of the year I would have expected our potato fields to be covered in a blanket of vraic to both fertilise the soil and protect it from pests before planting began in January. The vraic was there but, when I dug my fingers in, they came up with wheat seeds. It made sense as our special Jersey Royal potatoes were a lucrative cash crop when exported to the UK but the local population would need flour above all else. I guessed that my father had been persuaded by the authorities to abandon our little kidney shaped golden nuggets for next season. I wondered what else had changed.

The chickens wouldn't recognise me; neither would the cows but Victor, our prize bull, whose irascible nature forced everyone, apart from my mother, to steer well clear of him, might bellow a challenge to me. Of course, my father might have finally lost patience and sent him to the abattoir though I doubted it. Who knew how long this war would last and the island remain occupied? Best to keep a couple of months supply of food on the hoof rather than cash it in now, though my mother's argument would have been more personal — she loved the dangerous brute.

To avoid any confrontation I took Willie around the outer boundaries and we crept up on the barn. The cockerel was shouting the odds as the pre-dawn light filtered in from France so we slipped in very quietly. Only one of our lorries was there; supported on bricks – there was no sign of the wheels or tyres. The tractor looked unused so I assumed that Dad had been ploughing with our two old horses. It was inevitable that fuel would be rationed but he would have needed extra labour to carry out that heavy work. I hissed to Willie to hide while I checked to see if anyone was living in our farmworkers' accommodation which hadn't been used since Loïc, his wife Katell and her brother Corentin returned to Brittany in June.

The cottage was deserted so he must be using inexperienced day labour, as genuine farm workers would be as rare as hen's teeth. We'd tried using townies before the Germans arrived in July but I'd had to send them away before my father, who could be even more destructive than Victor, carried out his threat to literally whip them into a semblance of useful shape. I returned to Willie and told him to get some rest while I checked on my parents and Rachel — if she was indeed there.

It wouldn't be long before my mother emerged from the farmhouse for the morning chore, crossed the yard and went into the cowshed to relieve our herd of its overnight bounty. Her usual routine would start at 07:00 but the hands on my Italian watch were creeping past the half hour before the front door opened and she stepped out. I froze, suddenly aware that what I was seeing wasn't a dream but my mother in the flesh and only a few yards away. Tears pricked my eyes but I fought the overpowering urge to rush to her and sweep her up in my arms. Impatiently, I swept them away with the back of my hand and refocused on her. She looked cold but healthy and full of her usual morning purpose. The door opened again and my father shuffled out — for a farmer he was surprisingly uncomfortable with early mornings and not to be trifled with before breakfast or any other time until he had read the Evening Post at the end of the day. He seemed uninjured for a change — no obvious bandaging or plaster casts — so Mum must have been able to keep him away from people who displeased him. He stretched and yawned then trudged after his wife. I waited in case anyone else appeared but, though there was a flickering light from the kitchen, the front door stayed firmly shut. If we still had fifteen cows it would take them over an hour to milk, filter the precious liquid into churns, add the bicarbonate of soda to stop it souring, then herd them out to pasture.

Should I investigate the house before revealing myself to my parents? What if Rachel really was there? Indecision gripped me but I couldn't hide here forever. I strode out, heading for the cowshed but almost tripped over my own feet as my mind redirected me to the house. I sneaked around the outside and peered through the windows but the ground floor was deserted. The backdoor was unlocked so I eased in and tiptoed through the hallway to the foot of the stairs. The kitchen was empty with only an oil lamp for illumination. I tried the light switch but it clicked without exciting the bulb. The storm must have brought down the power cables. The range was glowing a deep red and though and I was tempted to stay and bask in its warmth I carried on. I'd stolen up these stairs in the past, after arriving home too late to provide any sensible explanation for my father, so avoided the fourth step, which acted as the house's burglar alarm, and reached the landing in silence. My parents' bedroom door was open and a quick glance confirmed they were still sharing the same bed.

I moved on to Alan's old room pinioned to the spot by a spear of sadness as the image of his broken body overwhelmed me. I shut my eyes to banish it but let out a muted sob and clutched at the door frame to steady myself.

'Jack! What are you—'

I spun round and there was Rachel in a dressing gown, hair long once again, staring at me, opened mouthed. We held our respective poses for a couple of seconds then she lept forward and threw herself into my arms.

We'd been friends for over five years but lovers for less than five minutes. Under a box-shaped raft, constructed of scrap timber from the old liner RMS *Mauretania*, supported by half a dozen empty oil drums and tethered by a line which allowed it to float between five and twenty feet above the sand, I'd made the biggest mistake of my life. On the evening of the day after Rachel discovered that not only was she adopted but half-Jewish and had confessed her terrible secret to me — the one person she felt she could trust — I'd taken advantage of her vulnerability.

We'd talked about this since and she always claimed that it was her fault and not mine. I wanted to believe her but had always failed to convince myself and knew I should have been more responsible and suppressed my desire or at least withdrawn it before it exploded and ruined her life. In the darkness, under wooden planks and with only our heads above water, it was a manoeuvre I'd failed to accomplish in time. It was only by another accident, twelve months later, that she allowed me to discover the consequences. These were the thoughts that occupied my brain now as my friend and the mother of my child hugged the breath out of me. It was a desperate embrace, full of relief and a strange tenderness and we clung together in silence. I kissed the top of her head and fought back more tears feeling both bereft and helpless waiting for her to pull away yet resisting any attempt she might make. This wasn't a Litzi or a Masha and certainly not Caroline but I loved Rachel and, though it broke my heart, I knew I was not in love with her.

Though slender and bonier than I remembered, she was physically and mentally strong. She recovered before me then pulled away. 'What are you doing here? Why have you come?' She fixed her eyes on mine shaking her head in confusion then alarm. 'Are you alone?'

I'd determined to stick to the story we'd worked out and not tell her the real reason but try to find out about Hélène more subtly but

this meant lying to her and I realised she did not deserve that. 'I'm not alone. Willie is in the barn and probably asleep by now. Saul and Joe are anchored out in the Écréhous reef and will come back for us in two days. We need to—'
'What's the time?' She interrupted; worry etched on her face.
I looked at my watch. '7:45, why?'
'Quick, you need to alert him.'
'To what?'
She shook her head. 'Franz.'
'Who?'
'He's a German soldier stationed at the outpost at this end of the breakwater. He comes here every day to collect a small churn of milk. He sometimes brings us crabs or fish in exchange.' She smiled shyly. 'I think there's probably another reason for his visits but he's very polite and never comes into the house — but he will wait in the barn.'
'Christ, if he stumbles into Willie, he's going to be one very dead milkman and we can't afford that. I'll go—'
'No, I will — in case Franz is early. You stay here,' she smiled again, 'you can keep Taynia company – she's seven months old tomorrow. Try not to make her cry.' She ushered me into my old bedroom where a cot lay beside the bed and my young daughter paused in playing with a rag doll and focused her beautiful blue eyes on the stranger standing alongside her mother. She smiled though it was probably wind as I perched on the bed beside her and held out my finger which she grabbed and pulled into her precious little mouth and bit with two small teeth.

16

Later, when Franz had strolled down the hill to his comrades, and Dad had trundled the milk churns up the lane for collection, we all sat around the table in the kitchen while Mum cooked us breakfast. My father was still trying to come to terms with my reappearance and seemed confused by Willie's presence. Rachel unscrewed a jam jar which seemed to hold mashed vegetables and began to feed Taynia with a small spoon. Mother handed me a double handled cup full of warm milk from our own cows. When my little daughter pushed the spoon away and reached for the cup Rachel placed her on my lap and asked me to help her drink. Much to my father's amusement, I struggled to prevent Taynia splashing me with milk. Though the air was pregnant with questions, once Taynia had finished and was allowed to play with some stuffed toys on the floor, we scoffed our breakfasts with only the occasional comment from my unusually patient parents.

Unable to contain himself any longer, my father leant across the table. 'Well, I suppose you're not here for a holiday and you want information so go ahead and then we'll ask our questions, won't we, Mary?'

'Yes, Aubin, but mine will be first, won't they?'

He sighed and settled back in his chair. 'Bugger me, but alright, just keep it brief.'

Where to start with a farmer? 'I noticed that you've planted wheat instead of spuds any—'

'Bloody interfering *Boche*. There aren't many of them but they're like bloody horseflies. One officious bastard turns up, speaks perfect English, and tells me that the Kommandant wants full details of the farm and, get this, needs to know my qualifications!'

Mum and Rachel had heard this before but Willie and I laughed. 'So you told him to bugger off did you?'

'No, Jack. Your father was perfectly polite and replied in *Jèrriais* pretending he didn't understand English. This flummoxed the German who tried French but all he got in return was a load of tosh about the price of Royals and a few rude references to the '"new order". The Jerry left us a pile of forms in English to complete then escaped without a scratch. He was—'

'Bloody lucky,' my father continued, 'I took them to the Constable but—'

Willie looked puzzled so I interrupted to explain. 'Our friend, Ken Gallichan, is the Constable of this parish – the role's similar to a mayor but with all the powers of a police chief thrown in as well. He even has a seat in our local parliament.'

Willie shook his head. 'English democracy married to French feudalism and conducted in an ancient language – explains a lot.'

'Not that the *Boche* will ever understand it. Anyway, Ken said I had to fill in the forms as they'd been approved by the nobs who have appointment themselves to our Superior Council. Seems that this lump of lard, Oberst Schumacher, who's the Feldkommandant and sits on his lazy arse in College House all day, has this bee in his bonnet about efficiency and responsible farming. Next thing, the Jerry returns with a couple of soldiers and informs me that I can't plant any seed potatoes and have to plough up the fields and scatter wheat—'

'By this time, your father has learned to speak English and gives the Jerry a piece of his mind and rants on about the lack of labour, petrol and wheat seeds—'

'I was just about to demand some German labour when Mary interrupts and offers the Jerry a cup of tea. Well, blow me, but I'm not having that in this house — then the penny drops and I remember that the last thing we need is Germans digging up parts of this farm.' He looked at me. 'And you know why.'

He was right. There was much under our rich soil which couldn't be sold in the market. Three bodies, scattered rifle parts and my uncle's motorcycle for a start. 'So, what happened?' I asked.

'Father stormed off and left it to me.' Mum shook her head. 'It's strange but the Germans have been doing their very best to be polite and helpful and, of course, they have no sense of humour so I took out the bottle and offered them the last of our Camp coffee. They looked horrified, declined, saluted and marched their jackboots out of the yard. The next day, a lorry delivered several sacks of seed and a brown bag of freshly ground coffee.'

'So there hasn't been any trouble with the German garrison?'

Father laughed. 'Garrison? They've barely enough troops to police all the harbours let alone guard the countryside. They expected to conquer England in the summer and haven't really prepared for this standoff. They even let us keep our wireless sets so we can listen to the BBC news.'

'That won't last, Aubin. I heard from Marjorie—'

'The Rector's wife – he sits in the States parliament as well.' I told Willie.

'Colonial democracy supporting feudalism and sanctioned by the Church. No wonder the Fuhrer claims to have liberated you!' Willie grinned.

'Well, yes. It's true they do believe they are liberators but Marjorie told me that Edgar's heard that there's been some trouble in Guernsey and they've confiscated their wirelesses. So I don't think it will be long before we have to surrender ours. They already censor the Evening Post and—'

'It's only useful for one thing now—'

'That's enough, Aubin. There's no need to be crude.'

Before my parents got into a real niggling match. I needed another line of questioning. 'We know their navy is pretty active around the islands and the Luftwaffe has squadrons on both islands but are you saying that they haven't dug in and fortified?'

'A battalion could land and take the island in less than a day it's that weakly defended.' My father shrugged. 'But what would be the point? We're over a hundred miles from England and now come under the *Department de la Manche*. The Germans have what they call a *Feldkommandantur* based here for all the islands and we draw supplies from Granville. Without that we would starve. All orders are issued from France and implemented here even if they apply or not which does produce some comic moments as they have to look for things like subways and light emissions from blast furnaces which don't exist here. The military command seems more concerned with escapees than invaders. So, unless we take Normandy and Brittany, there is no way we could hold the islands without massive civilian casualties. Nothing's changed since you left. I'm surprised the Germans bother with us at all — we're only a drain on their resources.'

'Propaganda. That's the reason and the fact that this is the only British territory that Hitler has conquered.' Willie sighed. 'I know the Nazi mentality. They're like cockroaches — they'll breed until the only way to remove them is to burn them out...or starve them but you'd die with them.'

I was beginning to worry about our report should we manage to deliver it to Fleming. If he thought there was an opportunity to retake the islands and strike a propaganda blow of his own, he'd have us working on another cunning plan which would end in disaster. Short of removing the entire population of the islands by sea while trying to prevent the Kriegsmarine and Luftwaffe bombing the ships to smithereens there wasn't a sensible plan until we held the west coast of France again. Not that Fleming or Churchill were great fans of "sensible" in their planning. We might have to exaggerate the German strength to dissuade them from planning a disaster.

My mother placed her hand on my arm. 'Is this the only reason you've come here?' She glanced over at Rachel, 'just to report on German strength?'

17

Time for honesty. 'No, we've been sent to speak to Rachel because Hélène is missing. I won't go into the politics behind this but we've been tasked to find her and those at the highest levels believe that Rachel might have the key.'

'Who are you working for?' Rachel asked.

'I'm afraid I can't tell you that but —'

'Then you've had a wasted journey,' she snapped.

I studied her face. Her cheeks were flushed; but was it with anger or embarrassment? 'Don't you know where she is or don't you want to tell us?'

'Both. Look, our group was compromised but Hélène didn't know if it was Vichy's intelligence service, one of de Gaulle's groups, or on orders from Moscow. It might even have been the Gestapo chasing Jews. She also received an important message from a Spanish source that she wanted to investigate.'

I sensed that she might be holding something back but didn't want to challenge her. 'So you split up and went into hiding?'

'Yes, but in my case, in plain sight. I used my Jersey ID to come home with Taynia but my "parents" wouldn't have me in their house with my "bastard" child!'

Taynia must have sensed her mother's distress and started wailing. My mother picked her up and soothed her while Rachel glared at me. 'How did you know I was here?'

'I didn't know for certain. I can only guess that my uncle still has contacts here who managed to get a message out but—'

'Yes, that would be it.' My father interrupted. He wasn't much of an actor and I suspected from his face that he knew more than he was prepared to tell. He would have had to feel desperate before he contacted someone he believed was a Communist though.

'Well, I can tell you that we were given the information by the Russians and they are very keen to find Hélène.'

Rachel shook her head slowly. 'That might not be a good thing for Hélène. Whatever she might have told you, Jack, she's first and foremost an anti-fascist rather than a true Communist. She appears to be one of Stalin's obedient servants but she was greatly troubled by his decision to join Hitler in devouring Poland.'

'Is that why she hid the diamonds rather than send them on to Russia?'
'Not those fucking diamonds again!' She spat out the words.
My mother flinched and drew Taynia into her almost for protection from the unexpected profanity.'
'I'm sorry, Mrs Renouf. That shipment we stole has caused no end of trouble for Hélène and threatened to split her group. That's why she's hidden it where no one will find it – especially the Germans who are the only ones who need it!'
'Do you know where it is?'
She glared at me. 'Is it me and Taynia or just the diamonds you've come for?'
'I've been asking myself that question since I sat in the Soviet Ambassador's office and he dropped the bombshell that you were living here.'
Her face froze.
My father started to speak then thought better of it and muttered some curse to himself. Willie gave me a pitying look and shook his head in disbelief at my indiscretion.
Rachel reached over and plucked Taynia from my mother, sat her on her lap, and turned her face towards me. 'So, tell us, Jack. What's your answer?'
I stared back at her and, without considering the consequences, replied. 'I'm taking you and Taynia back to England—'
'But—'
'Where, if you'll have me, we'll get married and give Taynia a name other than "bastard".'
My parent's faces mirrored instant relief. Willie rolled his eyes.
'How — how on earth, are you going to do that?' Rachel demanded.
'I need to find out some more information and then we're going on a fishing trip. Now tell me about Franz and his outpost down the hill…'
But my father did far more than that. He retrieved the Ordnance Survey map of the whole island which he spread out on the dining room table. He also produced one of my old school jotters in which he had made a series of coded notes which he now related to various locations on the map. Apparently, Franz had been rather loose-tongued. Because he came from a farming family near Hanover, he'd relaxed in my father's company and revealed rather too much about

the organisation of the German forces in the east of the island. Father had carried out his own reconnaissance from the corner of our farm which overlooked St Catherine's breakwater and made a note of how it was patrolled by the Germans. Lovers of routine, the few troops had organised a circular route to cover both sides of the half-mile long granite breakwater with one patrolling from the eastern tip along the top promenade overlooking Fliquet Bay while the other started from their hut on the land side and walked the lower level checking the sweep of St Catherine's Bay and the Martello Tower at Archirondel. Their leisurely pace meant that each length took twenty minutes. They would meet in the middle for a brief exchange then continue to either end until they met again. This left the rounded tip where a field telephone was secured to a box on the wall, unguarded for at least ten minutes three times each hour. They changed personnel every two hours from dawn to dusk and stayed in their temporary wooden guardhouse overnight. Franz had let slip that there was a plan to construct a more permanent outpost out of reinforced concrete and install a canon and machine guns to cover the anchorage but at present they were armed only with rifles and one squad machine gun. The next outpost was on the other side of Anne Port to the south and Rozel Harbour to the north. My father had observed both and the routine and accommodation was broadly the same.

He had also observed the fishing boats which the Germans allowed out during the day in fair weather but not during rain or fog in case they were tempted to escape. There were two moored in St Catherine's which always had deep water and boats could land their catch on the slipway. Rozel dried out at low tide and the short slipways at Anne Port and La Maison near Gibraltar weren't really suitable for boats and only used by farmers to collect vraic. What I found particularly interesting was the boat kept at St Catherine's which was used exclusively for crabbing. He'd spotted that occasionally a German solider, sometimes Franz, who appeared to be the senior NCO, would join the two young men who worked it. He also told me that the two were employed by my old enemy Surcouf whose family now owned another fishmonger's shop in town as well as the main wholesaler that supplied the market. He was sure they were the two who had been recruited by Surcouf to assist me when I had agreed to skipper *Maia* before Joe and I stole it for our escape in July. He even knew their names and where to find them and that one of them had been in trouble with the Constable for drunken behaviour and the other had fallen out with his own parents. It didn't take long for us to piece together a plan to persuade these two to join us in an escape but we would need to fool the German patrols if we wanted to put to sea without an alarm being raised. Willie suggested that we steal a German uniform and he play the part of a soldier overseeing the fishing. This might work but whatever we did we had to ensure nothing could be traced back to my parents and that no Germans were harmed.

I had no conscience about stealing another of Surcouf's boats as father told us that he had turned up at the farm after Joe and I had escaped in *Maia* and demanded compensation for my theft. He'd driven up in his green Lagonda drophead coupe but left without it when my father had offered to compensate him with his pitchfork on the spot. Unfortunately, my father had then "forgotten" to close Victor's gate and he had taken a liking to the sleek British sports car which must have reminded him of a particularly attractive cow and given it one of his more robust servicings. Father had reported this to the Constable who arranged for it to be collected and delivered to St Helier where it was impounded by the Germans. After the dents had been repaired it was shipped to France like all the other quality automobiles, with the exception of a certain red Bugatti, the occupiers had selected to improve the transport stock of officers of the Reich.

I needed to see for myself so we left Willie to help Mum and tramped up to the spot where Alan and Uncle Fred had set up their sniping nest the evening Kempler had tried to kill me nearly eighteen months before. I hadn't asked Dad about the aftermath of our escape on *Maia* but he volunteered it when we settled down to observe. He'd not been able to see that much that evening though, through occasional gaps in the swirling sea mist, he'd spotted Joe manoeuvring *Maia* towards the shore. He'd even got brief glimpses of Kempler, Caroline and me struggling in the water. Fortunately, I'd taken all his guns otherwise he would have started shooting at the two boatloads of German soldiers trying to capture us before we were swallowed by the thickening mist. However, he'd heard the changes in the fishing boat's engine note and worked out that it had managed to escape into the fog. Mysteriously, no Germans had subsequently appeared to search the farm or make any arrests. I filled him in on the details of our escape, told him about the letter Saul had received via Switzerland from Caroline and that she'd mentioned our farm and given the impression that all was well. I asked him if he had he seen her or heard anything about her.

He bit his lip. 'Of course you want to know but, after what you've just promised Rachel, shouldn't you be putting her out of your mind?'

He'd never taken to Caroline though it was Mum who had more cause to dislike her family. Caroline's mother had almost stolen my father from her before I was born yet I thought they'd both accepted her when she stayed with us before I tried to escape with her back in July. Kempler had thwarted that attempt and I'd lost her but I shouldn't have been too surprised as Mum and Dad had always liked Rachel and, now she'd produced a granddaughter, they were bound to favour her over Caroline.

'Well, shouldn't you?' he prompted.

Mum had told me the evening I brought Alan's broken body home that the only thing that had stopped my father leaving her for Caroline's mother was when she revealed she was pregnant with me. I didn't know if my father was aware of what I had been told and perhaps now wasn't the time to bring it up though he was probably the only person I knew who should understand. The irony was that Rudi Kempler would have become my father's stepson if he'd followed his heart and Caroline would never have been born. It was amazing how unexpected pregnancies could twist a knife in time and alter fate for so many people. But he needed an answer.

'No. I can't wipe her from my mind. I can't stop being in love with her even though I might never see her again. But, I have a duty to Rachel even though she refused to let me help before. I'm not sure if she really will marry me if we do get back to England but I will make sure she and Taynia are safe.'

He grinned. 'You're planning to get them to Uncle Fred and Malita aren't you? She'd love to have a child to look after.'

'Is that wrong?'

'No. No, it's probably one of the most sensible things you've ever planned. She can't stay here. Even with Caroline's protection, it's far too—'

'What do you mean "Caroline's protection"? Does she know Rachel's here?'

'Of course. She's made a point of driving out to see us in that swanky Bugatti several times since Rachel arrived two months ago. It beats me but the two of them seem to get on well enough, considering.'

'What about Rudi Kempler, that Nazi half-brother of hers?'

'Oh, he's long gone. She told us what happened after he "saved" her from you. He didn't stay after that embarrassment. Apparently, he's using his economic skills to help the *SS* reduce their running costs. Himmler thinks very highly of him.' He spat into the grass. 'He'll probably get the Knights Cross for extracting riches from the Reich's enemies to pay for that lunatic Fuhrer's wars.'

'What about her father?'

'That piece of shit. He's not even good for manure though our little flies, Philips and Surcouf, swarm all over him. He'd like to run to Switzerland but his stepson wants him to stay here. Caroline thinks he's being used as a safe harbour for some of the profits he's creaming off for himself.'

'Do you think she'd like to escape to England with us?'

He looked confused as though he was debating an answer with himself. He studied at the ground. 'No, I don't think she will. Why take that risk when she has all the wealth and privilege right here. No curfew or food shortages for her and plenty of attention from our new masters. She even plays the piano for them at the Forum. Why would she give that up to be bombed in England?'

'For me?'

His eyes clouded over. Distant memories of his own perhaps. He shrugged. 'I don't know, but you're going to take the risk and find out, aren't you?'

'Yes, I am.'

18

'Well that's that then. I know you're as stubborn as me. Together we might even give Victor a run for his money in those stakes. But, are you as patient?'

'Why?'

He looked at his watch. Tide's coming in, but it seems a bit rough for crabbing. I bet you a pound to a blood orange that greedy tyke, Surcouf, will turn up with his crew and send them out to his pots.'

'Even he's not that stupid. Look at the swell out there.'

'We'll see.' He raised his binoculars again. 'Go home and put your feet up if you find it too cold.'

So we took turns and at midday an old two-ton Bedford lorry chugged up to the head of the slipway and Surcouf hopped out followed by the two boys.

'I see you're still driving on the left then.'

He chuckled. 'But not for much longer. The Jerries keep getting confused and crashing. There was something in the Evening Post about it. For safety reasons the bastards are considering making us all switch to the right. Mind you, there's not much petrol about even though the buses are still running.'

A German approached Surcouf and cigarettes were exchanged. The boys, George Le Bihan and Brian Le Masurier — according to my father — unloaded some wicker crab and lobster pots as well as three petrol cans. There were a couple of medium sized wooden fishing boats moored in the shelter of the breakwater though sensible fishermen would have hauled them ashore for the winter a month ago. I watched, rather amused, as Surcouf seemed to be arguing with the boys. There was much gesturing out to sea and I saw the German guard shrug his shoulders and shake his head. Eventually the boys seemed to be persuaded to carry a rowing boat down the slip and lower it into the unsettled sea. One held on to it while the other struggled down with the pots. Surcouf stayed with the guard smoking until everything was loaded then wandered down and issued instructions to the boys. By their body language it was clear that they were very reluctant but he seemed to be shouting at them. They were all wearing rubber boots and I rather hoped that the waves now surging up the slipway as the tide gathered momentum would unbalance Surcouf and tip him into the water. Those boots would quickly fill and drag him under. We'd been classmates for years and I knew he was no swimmer. The boys were but I doubted they would leap in to rescue their employer in these conditions. But, sensing the danger, he stepped back to the safety of the high granite wall and left them to it.

One of them, George I thought, grabbed an oar and pushed away from the slip while the other, Brian, started to scull. It looked very precarious for a while but they managed to reach the nearer of the two boats which seemed to be about forty foot long with an enclosed wheelhouse and a sturdy winch for hauling in pots. Its name was picked out in white paint on the prow of the dirty blue hull but was difficulty to read because of the wallowing motion. I made out *Astakós*— with an acute accent over the "o". Surcouf had specialised in both bullying and being pretentious but it didn't sound French or Latin so was probably his attempt at Greek though I had no idea what it signified. They unloaded and fiddled about for a while then clambered down into the dinghy and rowed back to the slip. Surcouf stubbed out his cigarette and hurried down to meet them. There was much gesticulating from him but the boys landed the dinghy and, ignoring him, carried it up the slip. He followed, shouting at them and cuffed George around the ear. The German seemed to find this amusing and called into the hut. Two more came out, one of whom Dad assured me was Franz, and watched while Surcouf kicked and cuffed his employees towards them. Eventually he tired of this and hurried off to his lorry. Without a backward glance he drove off leaving the two boys stranded. I knew they lived near St Martin's Church so they'd have a good two mile walk in rubber boots even if they cut across the fields. I handed Dad the binoculars and told him I was going to intercept them and explain that there was an alternative to life under their current employer.

I spotted them in the middle of the woods and remembered their playground nicknames from junior school. Brian, whose father owned a garage, had an obsession with farm machinery and used to chug around changing imaginary gears whilst ploughing a make-believe field. George followed him everywhere so they became "Tractor" and "Trailer". Unbelievably, Brian seemed to be holding an invisible steering wheel now as they climbed the narrow path with George trailing behind him. I wiped the smile from my face and sat calmly as they drove upwards. George recognised me immediately and his mouth worked like a hungry fish while he tried to find words to express his surprise. Brian got his tongue working first.

'Jack! I never expected to see you again. What the hell are you doing here?'

I stood up and shook hands with them. Three years younger than me, they'd just left Victoria College last time we met and I'd always treated them with more sympathy than some of my fellow prefects. They weren't the brightest birds in the garden but I'd taught them lifesaving, helped them improve their swimming strokes and thought they had been somewhat in awe of my prowess in the pool.

'I've come to rescue you from that shit Surcouf and recruit you to serve the King. Are you interested?'

Brian, whose brain was marginally larger than his friend's, responded first. 'Are you here to blow up the Germans? We'll help, won't we, George.'

'Yeah, we can spy as well if you like. You got any guns?'

Lord help us; but I knew they could handle a boat and would prefer positive leadership to the abuse they'd received from Surcouf. From what Dad had told me, their parents would be pleased if they escaped before they did something stupid and dropped their families well and truly in the manure.

'Yes, but not with me. Have you heard about the British Commandos?'

They nodded but Brian spoke again. 'On the BBC news. Churchill said he wanted to set Europe alight or something like that. Count us in.'

Apart from looking bemused George also seemed worried. 'But how are you going to get us off the island?'

'Did Surcouf tell you when he'd be back to collect your catch?'

'How did you know...you've been spying on us haven't you?' Brian challenged.

'Yes, we have and my friends were impressed by the way you handled that dinghy just now.'

'Friends?'

I put my finger over my lips. 'Yes, but I can't tell you more at the moment. Do you know what the weather forecast is for tomorrow morning?'

'Surcouf said it would be much better but, without a Jerry on-board, we're only allowed to go a mile off shore.'

'Good. My friends and I still have some work to do but I need you to bring *Astakós* around to La Maison slipway tomorrow at 08:00. Can you manage that?'
'But we won't be able to reach the slip. The tide won't be right until later.'
'Forget the dinghy and borrow that larger rowing boat to get out to *Astakós*. What does that mean, by the way?'
'Surcouf says it's Ancient Greek and means *lobster*. We call it *lollipop* though.' Brian said.
'Well, motor over and catch a buoy as close as you can then row in to pick us up. You'll have three passengers and some equipment to transport. Don't worry about the guards, leave them to us. Any questions?'
George was first. 'What should we bring?'
'Warm clothes and whatever personal possessions you can row out there without making the Germans suspicious.'
'What should we tell our parents?'
'I wouldn't but that's up to you, Brian — just make sure you don't mention *my* family.'
'Don't they know you're here?' Brian asked.
'Of course not — I wouldn't want to endanger them. Now, are you really ready for this? After all, this island is no place for strong, fighting men like you to be trapped until the war is over, is it?'
They nodded again but George spoke up. 'But how are we going to get to England. We've barely got enough petrol to reach the Écréhous.'
I smiled at them. 'Relax. We're not alone. We've got the Royal Navy waiting.'
Brian's jaw dropped. 'You mean a submarine?'
'Wow,' said George.

19

It was a big risk but, as they were known to the German guards, shouldn't arouse the same level of suspicion that we might if we just stole the fishing boat. If we could disguise Willie as a German we would have another edge and should be able to get out beyond the bay before anyone could make a fuss. The main problem would be if Surcouf decided to turn up before midday which was why I'd chosen an earlier start despite the unfavourable tide. The other difficulty might be if the boys decided to confide in their parents or even started boasting to friends that the Royal Navy was shipping them out by submarine. I couldn't discount the last but hoped it would be treated with disbelief.

On the way back I stopped by my brother's unmarked grave and spent a few minutes in quiet contemplation.

I suppose all mothers have the same attitude to feeding their offspring but, now she only had the one son left, it seemed as though she wanted me to have Alan's share of lunch as well as my own. One advantage of living on a farm was easy access to vegetables though the Germans had taken note of all livestock and my parents would have had to rely on the black-market to provide a roast beef meal if they hadn't set up their own local bartering group. The smell of those cooking juices had me salivating like Pavlov's dog long before I reached the farmhouse. Whether it was wise to let those aromas escape with Germans sniffing the air only a few hundred yards away was another matter.

Fortunately, the wind stayed onshore and we weren't interrupted. We couldn't explore further beyond the farm during the day but needed to work off that lunch so Willie and I joined my father to carry out some maintenance. Like the remaining lorry, our old Standard Ten car was up on blocks but I was able to finish the job of repairing the carburettor I'd started back in June. We pumped up the tyres and hid them but kept the car on the blocks just in case any Germans came looting or, as they called it, requisitioning for military purposes. Dad had hidden some cans of petrol and diesel in a safe place but he offered the former for our trip. From what the boys had told me, between the Germans' concerns about escapees and Surcouf's parsimony, they never had enough to travel beyond the reef and we would need a healthy reserve in case we had to start looking for *Étoile de Jacob*.

The electricity supply hadn't been reconnected so Dad had attached the battery pack to the wireless and, before lunch, we had listened to an ENSA concert for munition-workers with Doris Mann and Alfred Van Dam and his State Orchestra on the BBC Home Service which was all very jolly. The One o'clock news headline was more sombre and gave a brief report on a heavy bombing raid on a midlands city. On a cheerier note it seemed the Greeks were giving Mussolini a bloody nose and repulsing his invasion along the whole front. There was some crowing about the Royal Navy's recent devastating air attack on the Italian fleet in Taranto with an exaggerated claim that it was the turning point of the war. Beating the Italians to a pulp wouldn't make any difference but I suspected Hitler would have to divert resources to pluck *Il Duce's* chestnuts out of a fire he shouldn't have started. There was also a report about how the courts were now dealing very harshly with those who were caught looting bombed properties in London. I hoped that meant a firing squad.

After work we settled down to prepare our stomachs for more food and Rachel turned on the wireless again to listen to Children's Hour. This featured "songs that help you along by Dr. Thomas Wood". The example played, much to our amusement, was "Boots, boots, boots, boots!". Willie and I got up and marched around the house which reduced Taynia to a fit of giggles and we played with her until Mum called us for dinner while we listened to the Six o'clock news. This ruined our appetites as the brief headline we had heard earlier was expanded into something quite devastating. Even the announcer seemed to have difficulty as he revealed the identity of the midlands town. Apparently the Luftwaffe had made a maximum effort employing over 500 aircraft in waves of indiscriminate bombing which lasted more than ten hours. The city was Coventry and it had been flattened. Its cathedral was a blackened skeleton and there were nearly 1,000 casualties. It was the sheer barbarity of the continuous bombing which seemed focused on punishing the civilian population rather than attacking any industrial centres which made his voice catch. We listened in silence, our food cooling in front of us, as he told us of reports on German radio which presented this as a triumphant retaliation for an earlier RAF raid on Munich, the birthplace of the Nazi party.

I couldn't even imagine the horror the people of Coventry must have endured, defenceless, cowering in their underground shelters for what must have seemed like an eternity before those fortunate to survive emerged to a vision of hell beyond the imagination of even the most fire and brimstone preacher. Willie and I exchanged looks because we knew that the reality behind the BBC news would be far worse. Our Ministry of Information had learned from Goebbels, Germany's minister for propaganda, the importance of suppressing the truth through manipulating the news to maintain public morale. Cassons had told us the BBC always exaggerated our successes and downplayed our failures in the air. According to him, if one believed the press reports, the RAF had shot down more planes than the Germans had ever built. So, once the ruins of Coventry had been cleansed, the final butcher's bill would be far greater than the one presented now. There couldn't have been a family in that benighted city left untouched by this cruel and inhuman act.

Only Taynia ate her food that evening while Willie and I waited for darkness to fall in the hope that we might be able to exact some retaliation of our own.

20

We were going to bypass the village to the south but on a hunch I took us over the fields and approached the Royal public house. Some parishioners believed the heart of the tiny village was conducted to the beat of our friend the Rector from his pulpit in our ancient church; others that it pulsed from Ken Gallichan's pen as he presided over the parish from his Constable's desk. St Martin was different from all the other parishes in that its administration centre from where the elected Constable managed his unpaid honorary police force was the only one of the twelve parishes to have a public rather than parish hall. Apparently, money had run out during its construction and the "public" had come to the rescue. Both factions were correct but I knew that the real brains of the parish could be found dispensing wisdom on a nightly basis in the public bar of the Royal.

Dad had mentioned that curfew, which ran from 23:00 to 06:00, was strictly enforced by the paid and uniformed police in St Helier but the centeniers and constable's officers in the country parishes used a lighter touch if they bothered at all. Technically, I was still a constable's officer, having been sworn in by Ken Gallichan in June though my position had not been ratified in the Royal Court. I'd dug out the warrant card from my bedroom and brought it along. I wouldn't show it or myself in St Martin but it might come in useful if we stumbled into some nosey bugger checking on the blackout in St Saviour or the outskirts of St Helier as we made our way to Grands Vaux.

Electricity had been restored in the pub at least as some of the village brains revealed when they stumbled out of the back door on their way to the outside lavatory. Each time the door opened or closed it released a wave of that peculiar noise associated with raucous public debate well lubricated by alcohol. Dad had mentioned that the Germans had banned all spirits in public houses and that only beer and wine were still available. He also told us that every publican still maintained a stock under the counter for urgent "medicinal" purposes. Black-market goods and bartering arrangements were also available to those in the know. Fortunately, there weren't as many Irish labourers in St Martin as in the more populated parishes as, being neutrals, they were exempt from most of the German regulations; including curfew. But it didn't take many to create a party and Dad told us that, even though the pub was meant to close before 23:00, the Irish usually insisted on a lock in — especially on a Friday evening.

Although it was still early it seemed that there was a celebration going on. The Irish had no love for the British so perhaps they were toasting the Luftwaffe's destruction of Coventry. There were probably some off duty Germans and a few silly Jersey girls in there as well but I wanted to see if our two potentially stupid boys were preparing for their great "submarine" adventure in the wrong way.

I couldn't enter without being recognised so I described the pair of them to Willie and he slipped into the lavatory to wait for an opportunity to enter the pub with someone rather than go in alone and arouse suspicion. He took the few shillings and some overvalued Occupation Reichsmarks my father had given us in case he had to buy a drink. I wasn't too worried about him as, with one of my father's caps and old coats, he didn't look too out of place. He was reasonably fluent in at least six languages and might even pick up some useful information though I doubted his Hebrew or Yiddish would be of much use. We did need a German uniform but I advised him not to take one off a soldier while he was still awake. I also asked him politely not to kill any Irishmen he found too offensive. While waiting, I tried to peep through the windows but the blackout was too effective so I settled down and rehearsed in my head the route to Caroline's house thankful that the clouds were thin enough to allow some moonlight to filter through.

Willie returned within twenty minutes, reeking of cigarette smoke and beer. He burped. 'How can anyone get drunk on that slop?'

'It's a Randall's pub. Some say they brew their beer from piss collected from drinkers of Mary Ann. They're both brewed in town and I wouldn't touch either, but forget the warm urine, were they there?'

'No young boys who fit your description just half a dozen soldiers with two old tarts; a few farmer types keeping to themselves, a few Frenchmen and another six or so noisy Irishmen who seemed to be annoying everyone else.'

'That's why Dad never employed any of them. No discipline and they seem to live for what they call the "craic". Learn anything?'

'Not much. I couldn't understand the farmers' language. The Germans seemed to be betting on which of them was going to be stuck with walking the tarts home. The Irish were celebrating someone's birthday and they weren't drinking beer. No mention of Coventry. There was a group of Frenchmen who seemed to be making arrangements with the barman. I saw some packages changing hands. So, where to now?'

'I'm still concerned about those boys. Brian lives across the main road on his parents' farm. George's father has his own garage and farm machinery business in Maufant. 'We'll have a look at the farm first.'

It didn't take long and we managed not to alert any livestock or dogs though I was surprised to discover a shabby Austin Twelve whose bonnet was still warm. They must have visitors. Willie waited while I circled round the house which, like ours, had been built in a natural depression in the ground. It was nearly 23:00 now and all was quiet. But there was a faint glow emanating from a gap in the curtains of one window on the ground floor. I crept along and looked in. Brian and George were sitting at the kitchen table talking to two women I presumed were their mothers. One seemed more upset than the other. Two men appeared from the passageway and joined them. It looked like the boys had not heeded my advice though I hoped they hadn't mentioned my name. There didn't seem to be any anger and all four were embracing as I slid away. Should I go in and explain to their parents or would that lead to arguments? I'm sure they wouldn't believe that their sons were going to be picked up by submarine so would want some realistic details. No; I could handle the boys but their parents were bound to be more inquisitive. Best leave well alone. The boys had found the courage to tell them and perhaps that was a lot better than finding out from a note.

I told Willie that we needn't worry about the boys and he told me he was looking forward to meeting Caroline. Suddenly, I wasn't so sure. Perhaps my father was right. What good would come of it?

21

We made good time across country to the south of Maufant Manor. Having a compass was a godsend because the moon kept playing hide and seek and we were constantly changing direction to avoid fallen trees and uprooted bushes. Soon we reached the head of the valley and started our descent. My plan was to traverse the escarpment above Paul Mill and edge towards Les Routeurs, Hayden-Brown's expensively converted farmhouse, by following the ridge line from the east.

They hadn't kept any pets in the past so I hoped Caroline's miserable father hadn't suddenly become an animal lover. The island authorities had to destroy over 5,000 abandoned dogs and cats in June. In my role as a constable's officer I'd had to round up many of them for delivery to the Animal Shelter and had told Caroline how difficult that was. From her reaction then I didn't think she'd be forming any new relationships with four-legged beasts now though I did feel a tingle of jealousy mixed with guilt that she might have adopted a two-legged specimen as an image of Masha briefly flashed across my mind.

A dark coloured Hillman Hawk was parked outside but there was no sign of her red Bugatti. I knew the house very well and led Willie through the garden and around the conservatory to the back door. It was also unlocked and we slid in to the warmth of a centrally heated house. Electric lights were on in the passageway and front hall as well as on the walls leading upstairs. No shortages of fuel or power in this household. We listened intently.

Silence, though Willie tapped my shoulder and pointed above. There was something faint — a rhythmical metallic sound. Dreading what I would discover but desperate to know, I motioned him to follow me up the thickly carpeted treads. It wasn't coming from Caroline's room but she might have moved. We crept along the gallery and stopped outside a room where the heavy door was slightly ajar. I hoped it wouldn't creak as I eased it open a few more inches but the hinges were well oiled.

The curtains were drawn and the room was dimly lit from two low-level lamps. The bed was side on and I almost burst out laughing as I spotted Caroline's father lying on his back straddled by a naked woman I recognised as the pert Frenchwoman, Christine, who'd been his maid the year before. Whatever she was doing now couldn't be classified as dusting — more like polishing the family silver perhaps. I stepped backwards and beckoned to Willie to follow me along the corridor.

I had to keep biting my lip to suppress the bubble of laughter building inside but as soon as we were in Caroline's bedroom and the door was shut I had to let it out. Willie looked bemused as I giggled and choked before sprawling on the bed. Not that there was much room as it was strewn with discarded dresses as though Caroline had been holding an audition of her evening gowns. The air was heavenly with her combination of perfumes though *Joy* was the dominant scent. It had enveloped me for nearly a whole week when we had almost lived in this bed while waiting for the Germans to invade the island. She had so many talents; was a concert pianist, an Olympic standard diver but, in any competition for household chores, she would always win the wooden spoon. Her room was a complete mess and I started to giggle again as Willie picked up an assortment of underwear and cleared a space to sit on the cushioned stool in front of her vanity mirror. He watched me and waited.

I told him what I'd seen and he smiled and asked. 'Should I kill them now or let them finish?'

'Neither. They mustn't see me so go and introduce yourself. Pretend you're a French burglar with accomplices outside and have come to steal what you can before buggering off to France. She's French and he understands but isn't fluent. He is in German though. He's also an arrogant bastard so you might have to ask your questions more than once if—'

'You can leave that to me. Is she attractive?'

I laughed quietly. Willie had established a reputation amongst the commandos as something of a swordsman and always bagged a catch when we had a weekend pass into the town though I sometimes wondered about the effects of alcohol on his eyesight. 'She likes them young and even tried to seduce Kempler but he's too fastidious and won't plant his seed anywhere than in a perfect Aryan. Until I discovered he was Caroline's half-brother, I believed he had selected her to help breed the master race.' I shrugged. 'But, if you are in the mood for a middle aged Frenchwoman, be my guest. Only there's work to do first. We need the combination to his safe and any other hiding places he might have for his valuables. This must look like a robbery. You also need to find out where Caroline is and when she's coming back. Christine will tell you. They hate each other.'

After I explained a bit more about the layout and the secure wine cellar he went to work while I investigated the other bedrooms. The one across the corridor from Caroline's was interesting as it was exceptional tidy but contained several Kriegsmarine officer's uniforms in the wardrobe. There were civilian suits as well as a trunk full of casual clothes. I couldn't find any identification but, from the stripes on the uniform sleeve, it seemed that Hayden-Brown was hosting a sailor with the same rank as Fleming though this one didn't seem to be a volunteer. There were no photographs but several novels in English. I tried on the dark blue double-breasted reefer jacket which seemed to be made of woollen doeskin. It was a good fit though the sleeves were a bit long — perfect for Willie though. I looked in the mirror on the inside of the wardrobe. The double rows of gilt metal anchor buttons and the gold embroidered eagle and swastika on the right breast made it more impressive than my acting sub-lieutenant's RNVR uniform. I also tried on a pale grey leather jacket which would be sea going rig. It came with leather trousers and canvas shoes. All were a good fit so Willie could look smart and I would look practical. If we could find some deck overalls we might be able to disguise Rachel as a sailor.

The next bedroom was obviously Christine's and a model of order which was probably another bone of contention between her and Caroline. She must hate living with her father and his mistress but, if I had my way, she wouldn't have to for much longer.

I heard some noise from the adjacent room and hoped that it wasn't the sound of her father's bones breaking. I waited until all the bumps and muffled shouts of bodies bouncing down the stairs had subsided then entered Hayden-Brown's bedroom. The mixture of sweat, sickly sweet perfume and fear wasn't an intoxicating smell but I held my nose while giving the room a good examination. The wardrobes were built-in and full of well-tailored suits and highly polished shoes. Another task for Christine when she wasn't rubbing the silver I supposed. The drawers held nothing of particular interest apart from a couple of framed photographs of Caroline's mother who I assumed was back in her sanatorium in Switzerland. I wondered if Rudi realised what his stepfather and the hired help were up to or if Caroline had taken any delight in telling him. She could be spiteful and I knew Rudi was very attached to his mother but, as

Caroline had explained before, his only real passion was making money for the Reich and himself.

Next was the office and I bumped into Willie on his way out of the kitchen. He was rubbing his hands and smiling.

'What do you want to know first?'

'Where's Caroline?'

'That was easy. She's playing the piano at a private party at Kriegsmarine headquarters in a hotel called the *Pomme d'Or* near the harbour. I suppose you've discovered the guest's room?'

'Yes, and through the powers invested in me by the Prime Minister, I hereby appoint you to the rank of Korvettenkapitän in the Kriegsmarine.'

'That means I now outrank you so I hope there are some boots for you to polish.'

'Christine's probably been seeing to those on the quiet.'

'Or Caroline!' He chuckled. 'Only joking. Her father claims he was only escorting her and the old tart didn't contradict him.'

'You didn't—'

He pulled a face. 'I'd need several litres of that Randall's piss or a bottle of decent cognac like this before I'd rust my sword in that scabbard.' He produced a bottle from behind his back. 'There's a treasure trove down there.'

'Never mind the looting. When's she due back?'

He looked at his watch. 'Any time now. Best get prepared.'

'Agreed; we'll deal with the safe later. Let them get in then put sailor boy to sleep before he sees me. I'll jump in and save you from Caroline then we can sit down, have a swig from that bottle, and work out our plan.'

Unfortunately, Caroline, never one to follow someone else's plan, nearly created disaster for ours. We heard the distinctive exhaust note of the Bugatti and Willie hid in the hallway while I stepped into the office and peered out through the large keyhole. The front door opened and Caroline came in chattering in German with the sailor. I'd expected them to go to the kitchen, the lounge or upstairs but she shrugged out of her overcoat, started cursing in Italian and disappeared in the direction of the conservatory. Soon her curses were drowned by the sound of a piano being hammered into submission. The officer turned to close the door, spotted Willie and shouted a warning. Fortunately, Caroline was crashing out chords at full volume and wouldn't have heard the struggle, which in fairness to

Willie, was very brief. After he'd gagged him with his own socks, we carried the unconscious man into the office, rolled him up in the large Persian rug, tied it up with the curtain sash and jammed it into the kneehole of the massive desk.

I asked Willie what they had been discussing as they came in and he told me that Caroline was fuming about a mistake she had made in one of the pieces she'd played at the hotel. Her companion had tried to reassure her that no one had noticed but she'd kicked him before hurrying to the piano to replay the section. For someone so personally untidy this perfectionism with her music had always amazed me.

My heart was thrashing away and it wasn't from the exertion of wrapping up her escort as I approached the conservatory where we'd shared so much together. I watched and listened for a while sensing that Willie was standing behind me. He'd always wanted to meet Caroline though he'd never understood my obsession with her. I watched entranced as her bare shoulders swayed with the rhythmical energy. She was wearing a low cut royal blue dress pinched in at the waist and her golden hair was bundled on her head exposing a long and elegant neck adorned with a double string of pearls. But Willie wasn't as spellbound and prodded me in the back pitching me forward though she continued to pound away at the keys oblivious of my presence.

Joy, in its literal as well as perfumed sense, enveloped me. I desperately wanted to reach out and fold her into my arms but, as long as she was playing, I was frozen. Finally, she stopped, letting the last chords echo into silence then shouted a stream of German over her shoulder to the man she assumed was standing behind. Willie replied in German. She leapt off the stool, saw me, and fainted.

I lifted her gently, relishing her warmth and softness, carried her into the lounge and laid her on the largest sofa. Willie followed with the cognac and three glasses. I held her left hand until her eyelids fluttered and her striking blue eyes focused on mine. She searched my face, squeezed my hand, sat up and slapped me so hard that my head whipped back in surprise.

Willie exploded with laughter and threw some more German at her. She spotted the bottle, grabbed it from him, raised it to her lips and swallowed a large mouthful.

'Some woman; what you call a minx, no?' He retrieved the bottle. 'I understand now. With this one you will always be on the edge of

Heaven or Hell. Congratulations or commiserations; I'm not sure if—'

'Shut the fuck up you big ape. Who is this monster, Jack, and what is he doing here and why are you here and why—'

Self-restraint evaporated and I kissed her, sucking in the brandy fumes, pressing my lips hard into hers until they softened and she responded shifting us into a different world; one a long way from reality and far beyond any temporal reach.

Eventually, Willie coughed and, as we drifted apart, spoke. 'We need to talk, Jack. Then you might wish to help the lady tidy her bedroom.' He handed me the bottle which now seemed less than half full.

Caroline slumped back onto the sofa, closed her eyes and shook her head. 'Have you killed him?'

'Who? Your father?'

'No, Karl...our guest.'

'Just a guest?'

Her eyes opened and she snarled at me. 'Yes, you dope. Stop acting like Othello. He isn't Rudi and he's very sweet and kind; I do—'

Willie answered for me. 'Relax, your sailor is having a sleep and your father and his tart are alive and enjoying each other's company in the cellar.'

She grimaced. 'That's a shame then. Did you catch them—'

'We did but, before you ask, neither of them saw me. Willie is pretending to be a French burglar so we need to steal some valuables.' I turned to him. 'Did you get the combination?'

She laughed. 'Not again. He's only just recovered from the last theft. You won't find much in there, a few trinkets, and bundles of currency though there are some documents which might mean something to whoever sent you.'

'Come on, let's have a look. Willie, can you manage to lay the carpet in the cellar?'

'Naturally, that's what big apes are for isn't it?'

Caroline eyed him more closely. 'Umm, Rachel did tell me about you though she might have omitted a couple of interesting details.'

'Stop flirting with him. He's got a date with a sailor. You and I need to talk—'

'Jack, take her upstairs before I do!'

Caroline levered herself up from the sofa and flounced towards him with an evil glint in her eye. 'Rachel also told me about your attempt to kiss her and how that ended. I told her that she was far too polite. You want to have another go?'

Willie stepped forward, ducked down and had her in a fireman's lift before she could react. He swung around and headed for the stairs while she beat her free fist on his back. I followed, intrigued and a little concerned. I'd witnessed Rachel humiliating him in front of his legionnaires and been surprised at how well he'd taken it. Now that I knew him so much better I wondered if I'd need to assume a less passive role this time. He kicked the bedroom door open, dumped her face down on the bed, pulled her arms behind her back and pinned her wrists so she couldn't move. 'You can stay if you like, Jack. You might learn something.'

He was stronger and quicker than me but he'd left himself vulnerable. In three swift moves I could chop his kidneys, place my knee in his back and break his neck. I sucked in a breath, felt the adrenaline surge and prepared to launch myself then it struck me that if he'd wanted to take this any further he wouldn't have presented such an easy target so I stood my ground.

He bent his mouth to her ear and muttered something in German, released her hands, slapped her bottom hard then stood back. 'I like Rachel a lot. You — not so much. You don't deserve Jack's juvenile devotion but then I've given up on love so I'll leave you two to discuss what just happened while I do the dirty work.'

He thrust past me, face reddened with something far deeper than physical exertion. Quivering with the suppressed adrenaline rush I watched as Caroline rolled over, rubbed her wrists and stared at me. An honest military assessment of me might conclude that though I was physically strong, extremely fit and mentally stubborn, I was emotionally frail. She beckoned me to her and, validating my own report, I shuffled towards the edge of either Hell or Heaven.

Self-deluded or not, I was convinced that, if what followed was indeed an hour in Hell, Hitler and his cohorts would be smiling when we delivered them to the Devil. It would take far longer than an hour to understand her erratic social behaviour so I didn't waste a minute of it trying. She was Caroline and I accepted her for what she was. That's love I suppose — the mystery which seemed to have eluded Willie.

Later he knocked on the door and peeked in. 'Time to work out how we are going to get back to the farm and what we're going to do with our friends in the cellar. I've tried the safe but can't get in. Sailor boy tells me he's off duty for the weekend so won't be missed. So rouse yourselves and let's start burgling.'

Caroline slipped into one of the discarded dresses without bothering with underwear and followed us into the office. She opened the safe without difficulty and extracted some gems, bundles of sterling and Reichsmarks, a handful of gold coins and some keys which she said belonged to properties around the island her father had acquired very cheaply. She scanned a file of documents which were in German. 'You'll find these very interesting – there's even a letter from Rudi with instructions about setting up companies here. Some notes about Swiss banks and more correspondence with Rudi's uncle at the Reichsbank.' She whistled and waved a worn red leather notebook. 'Here's a list of his contacts in the island government and details of their proclivities. Wow, who'd have thought it? This is priceless — perfect for blackmail. He's even got dirt on the Feldkommandant and some of his staff.' She got up and placed everything on the desk. 'When he finds that these are missing, he'll probably have a heart attack.'

'Is there anything else obvious we should pinch?' I asked.

'After that last episode he doesn't keep much of value here though you could swipe some of the jewellery he's given Christine for her services. I'll show you. You'd better take some of mine as well.' She paused and looked at Willie. 'Are you going to put me in the cellar with them or beat me and tie me up in my bedroom?'

'Neither,' I answered, 'you're coming with us.'

She looked stunned. 'But I can't. Surely, you know that. I told your father—'

'How? Why?' My heart was hammering again. I really believed she would want to escape. She had in July and only been stopped when Rudi tugged her from my grasp. Why wouldn't she want to now, when we had a good chance? What hadn't my father told me?

She came to me and held my face in her hands. 'I thought you knew.'

'I don't understand.' But my heart must have because my pulse was racing and my stomach sinking.

'After you escaped, Rudi dragged me along to see your parents. He made it very clear that if I ever left the island through force or choice or even if I was killed by enemy action he would ensure that your parents and all their relations and close friends were arrested and deported to Germany for re-education in a concentration camp.'

22

'Gleiches muß durch Gleiches geheilt werden.' Willie spoke first though it made no sense to me.

'He says "fight fire with fire" but it's hopeless. Rudi's father is dead, our mother is in Switzerland and he's in Berlin along with his uncle. He's out of reach but your family is hostage here.' She leant back against the desk. 'I really thought you would understand. I've worried about this since July. He's keeping me here to control my father and believe me, Jack, he *will* carry out his threat. It happens every day in Germany and the occupied territories. If you displease the regime or its servants you are removed. It's been going on since 1933. There are camps everywhere and no one returns.' She pleaded with her eyes. 'You have to leave me behind. I can cover for you; convince my father that it was just a burglary carried out by Frenchmen. I might even be able to point the finger at Christine. You must take the valuables and go.'

I remembered my father's reaction when I told him I was going for Caroline. He'd seemed confused when I asked him if she would want to leave with me and didn't answer straight away. He knew then that, should I persuade her, the consequences would be catastrophic for all our family. Yet, he hadn't told me. Had he hoped she would dissuade me or had he been prepared to sacrifice everything so that I might enjoy the love he'd been denied?

'Does my mother know about this?'

Caroline nodded.

'And Rachel?'

'Yes, I told her.' She stepped away from the desk and grabbed my hands, eyes piercing mine. 'You must take her with you, marry her if she will have you, and give Taynia her father back. I know it's ironic. Your father and my mother and how the wheel has turned almost a full circle but the fates are against us. We have to accept that and—'

'First we have to kill to make time for love.' Willie interrupted.

I glared at him. 'Since when have you become the philosopher king?'

Caroline laughed. 'You've studied literature; you know all about theatrical tragedy but you're not a member of the audience this time. So don't turn it into melodrama. I'll be fine. I'll survive and when this bloody war is over, if we still feel the same for each other, fate will bring us together again. So stiffen your sinews, my love and get the bloody hell out of here before we all end up in one of Hitler's holiday camps!'

Trapped within my racing heart and sinking stomach, hiding behind the adrenaline and trembling muscle, somewhere in the overwhelming emptiness, did I detect a glimmer of hope — or was it just relief?

I pulled her into me and kissed her for as long as she would allow ignoring Willie who was collecting the documents and stuffing them into a leather briefcase. Eventually, like in a staring contest, one of us would have to surrender and release their lips but it wasn't going to be me.

Willie decided for me and pulled us apart. 'Time is not on our side. We have to rob some more, then change and hope that car outside works.'

'But first you have to make it look convincing. I'll help.' Caroline started pulling books off shelves, and dragging drawers out of the desk. 'Come on, let's ransack the place — starting with my bedroom.'

We followed her upstairs and while she selected some items of jewellery she claimed were guilty gifts from her father, we endeavoured to make the room look even less tidy than it had been before we started. The other rooms were easier, especially the sailor's, though we took all the clothes we needed before wreaking havoc on his possessions. I rescued a pair of seaman's overalls for Rachel along with a military overcoat. It would be cold at sea.

Caroline was like a whirling demon laying waste to her father's bedroom and went berserk in Christine's pristine chamber. Finally we had a bag of valuables Caroline assured us would be missed along with the briefcase crammed full of papers, notebooks and currency. I wondered if her father would report the crime to the States Police or the Germans first though I doubted Karl, the shipwrecked sailor, would give him a choice

We found a full German army jerrycan of petrol in the garage and used an empty one to syphon another four gallons from Caroline's Bugatti. It was nearly three o'clock by the time we finished and Willie was getting anxious. There was a final act which I had been dreading but Caroline insisted. 'You have to hit me hard enough to make it look real. Bruise my arms then slap my face. Wait...' She hurried off to the kitchen and returned with a bottle of tomato ketchup then stood in front of me.

'I can't.' I stuttered.

'It'll have to be Willie then. She held out her arms and turned her face towards him. 'Be careful with my fingers, please.'

'Two hours ago I would have enjoyed this. Now, I like you more, but not enough to refuse.' He grabbed her left wrist in both hands and twisted them in opposite directions. She shrieked with pain and then he slapped her open handed across her left cheek. If he'd used his backhand, she wouldn't have needed ketchup but an ambulance. As it was, she fell to the floor, before crawling up and taking a mouthful of the tomato sauce and swilling it around. She hadn't thought this through and didn't know what to do with the residue. She could hardly spit it onto the floor as even the dumbest investigator would find that suspicious so she returned to the kitchen, hurled the bottle against the antique clock she hated and spat the mouthful after it.

She certainly looked battered and the bruises would spread in a few hours but there was something wrong. After we'd spent that heavenly time in her bed she'd changed into a different dress. Sailor boy would find that surprising so we all went back to her room and she was about to step into the original gown when Willie grabbed it from her and ripped the bodice and waist band. Despite the pain from the slap and wrist burn she laughed as I helped her into it. She'd shaken her hair loose earlier and now fussed it so that she looked like she'd been dragged through a hedge. I had no doubts that she had the acting skills to carry out the charade effectively but we agreed the details and even the names the three supposed French burglars had called each other. Of course we'd left fingerprints all over the place but I'd never had mine taken and Willie's were probably in Germany so had we committed the perfect crime?

I went outside to check the Hawk and found it in perfect condition with almost a full tank of petrol. The ransacking had used up the surplus adrenaline but I was feeling bereft as we made the final arrangements. I changed into the officer's deck uniform and bundled my clothes up ready for the car while Willie checked Caroline over. He shook his head. 'One more tweak is needed but you should say goodbye first.'

She reached out and hugged me tight. No kissing this time as her cheek was already swelling up and I'd never liked the taste of tomato ketchup. I drank in her perfume and kissed her hair, her ear and her enflamed cheek but couldn't get control of my tongue for any last words. I released her.

Willie dragged her into the kitchen and the door to the cellar then tied her hands behind her back. I followed almost in a trance. He unlocked the door but before opening it he turned her to face him and spoke softly. *'Es tut mir wirklich leid.'* pulled her left breast loose from the remains of her gown and pinched her nipple hard. She screamed and I flinched — then he opened the door and pushed her gently inside before slamming and locking it.

After he'd ripped the telephone from its socket and changed into the Kriegsmarine uniform we grabbed our bundles and, like clever French thieves, stole into what remained of the night.

23

'Buggeration! That's all we need.'

'It's only rain.' Willie shoved the packages into the boot. 'It'll pass.'

'It had better because the guards won't let us out fishing when it's raining or poor visibility. They don't want any more locals fleeing their model occupation.'

We settled into the well-worn seats and I started the engine. The Hawk had a local registration but there was a stiff piece of card inside the driver's side of the windscreen with the symbol of the Kriegsmarine and some bold writing in German.

Willie examined it and sniffed. 'Parking permit. We Germans do love order. I think sailor boy has borrowed this from the car pool.'

'Good. I've an idea that my father can return it so any search will start in the wrong place.'

'That's a risk isn't it?'

'No greater than the one we're taking. I think you'll need to concoct some story in case the sentries try to stop us. Why would a senior Kriegsmarine officer be in a crabber with two local boys setting out in poor conditions?'

While he thought about it I manoeuvred out of the driveway on to the hill leading into the valley below. The headlights had blackout slits and in the rain forward visibility was minimal. I kept on the main roads to avoid any fallen trees and had just passed Five Oaks when Willie answered my question. 'Mines. We're surveying the fishing area before we lay mines. We had to wait for the storm to pass through and now we've arranged with your friend Surcouf to be taken there by his two young helpers. If any sentry queries that I'll give him a good German dressing down. We must make sure that Rachel and Taynia are well hidden.'

'Good. If we're lucky they won't see us loading up anyway. I'm still worried about the rain though. Even those lumbering sentries will be suspicious about sailors surveying something they might not be able to see very well.'

'Let us hope it stops then.'

We rolled into the farmyard without incident just before four o'clock and I parked in the barn. The rain squall had passed but the air felt like more were due. Father was awake but the others were asleep. Once roused, Mum insisted we all eat breakfast and busied herself with the range while I explained what had happened and warned them that George's and Brian's parents might pay them a visit. Dad didn't seem too perturbed by this and assured us that both fathers were solid and reliable. That probably meant that one of both of them were members of his Freemasons' lodge. But it was a relief; for the Germans were bound to investigate the disappearance of *Astakós* as the Surcoufs would be making an almighty fuss. The St Martin's community was small and close knit and, apart from the beer sodden intelligentsia propping up the bar in the Royal, unlikely to open their mouths without counting their change first.

Rachel tried on the deck overalls which were far too large. Even wearing two dresses and an overcoat she looked ridiculous so she fished out Mum's sewing machine and got to work. For an expert seamstress it wasn't difficult to refashion the garment and, after breakfast, she paraded in front of us again. I now felt confident that, from fifty yards or so, she would pass as a slightly built crewman. Her hair was the main problem but a fisherman's woollen cap solved that. While she had the machine out I asked her to run up something else which I thought might come in useful.

Once we'd secured our frogmen's suits and other swimming equipment into old feed sacks along with our civilian clothes and loaded them into the boot we still had an hour or so to kill. Franz, the German corporal, would be here on the stroke of 08:00 so we needed to be well gone and waiting in hiding near the slipway before then.

Dad asked me to join him in the barn. I knew he'd been biding his time and expected he wanted to talk about Caroline. His first question surprised me as sensitivity to others had never been one of his strengths.

'How do you feel?'

It was a good question but I wasn't sure I had an answer for myself let alone anyone else. I considered for a moment then tried to rationalise what I did feel at that moment. 'Frightened — for you and Mum. I think Caroline will be alright. She's a survivor. I'm also worried about the next few hours. Rachel is very brave but we are taking an enormous risk in daylight. I don't see any other choice though we—'

He placed his hands on my shoulders. 'You know that's not what I meant. How do you feel about Caroline?'

The only light came from a hurricane lantern hanging above the car so it was difficult to read his expression. His voice was soft though and oozed a concern I'd never heard before. I had to be honest with him even though it meant uncapping the emotions I'd been bottling up for the past few hours. I lifted his hands, wrapped my arms around him and rested my head on his shoulder and tried to find the words as my mouth tightened and my lips trembled. 'Empty, heartbroken, helpless, angry. My insides are churning, I feel tearful but mustn't show it.' I swallowed desperately, fighting my reluctant tongue. 'It's this bloody war, Dad. It is so fucking unfair!'

And then I let it go and sobbed like a child into his neck. Great heaving sobs which made me tremble but he squeezed me even tighter trying to transfer his massive strength. I found some more words which had to fight their way out. 'I want to stay and be with her, look after her, protect her...'

He didn't interrupt but waited for my final convulsion. '...I love her so much.'

He patted my back and gently pushed me away until we were facing each other. It felt like the tears had ripped my cheeks; my nose was blocked and my mouth quivered like a fish drowning in the air.

'I understand everything you say. This is what I went through twenty years ago but—'

'Don't tell me I'll get over it!' Anger suddenly surged through me. '*You* never did!'

'I know, I know. But I love Mary, always have and always will. What you and I have shared is something beyond normal love. I can't analyse it, don't have the words. I know it's special but it's also dangerous when you fall in love with a beautiful woman.' He seemed to be struggling. 'There's the insecurity and jealousy, when you seem to have what most men desire...it's not something...but...there it is...being in love is a... *burden.*' He wiped something from his cheek. 'You have a hope to cling on to because it wasn't your decision. I had to kill my own hope and, by God, I know I made the right decision.' He shook my shoulders hard. 'But there is something else you feel isn't there?'

He was right but it felt like a betrayal. I nodded.

'It's *relief*, isn't it?'

I nodded again and looked up at him through misted eyes. 'How did you know?'

'Because you're my son.'

24

Before we listened to the wireless at 07:00 we agreed the story my mother would provide for Franz should he enquire about Rachel and Taynia. He already believed that Rachel was a local girl who had come to help on the farm. Mother believed the German suspected that she had fallen out with her own parents because of Taynia. We decided that she should tell him that two gentlemen in a car had called for Rachel the previous afternoon and told her that her mother was very ill. She had packed and she and Taynia had left with them. They hadn't volunteered any more information and mother didn't know where they'd taken her. If Franz wanted to follow it up he might be able to discover where her parents lived but we doubted he'd make the effort.

Dad was going to drive us down to the lane opposite La Maison slipway where we'd stay hidden until George and Brian arrived. We'd unload the car and take two trips out to the boat if there wasn't sufficient water for it to get close to the slip. Once we were safely aboard and underway he would drive the Hawk to town and park it as close to the harbour as he could to give the impression that our imaginary French burglars had caught the morning boat to Granville. He'd then join the queue at the Town Hall to register his wireless set as the Feldkommandant had now ordered. After that he would walk to the Snow Hill station and catch the SCS bus back to St Catherine's. The plan wasn't without risk but he assured us he would be alright. In comparison with ours it was almost sensible. At the moment he was making a copy of Hayden-Brown's red notebook with the names of his contacts amongst the Germans and local collaborators. He reckoned this could prove very useful in the future.

The BBC news was mainly about the aftermath of the Coventry bombing and some triumphant nonsense about the Greeks continuing to bloody Mussolini's nose. Weather forecasts had been suspended some months before so that the Luftwaffe had as little information as possible about conditions over the UK.

At 07:15 the BBC cheered us up with Leon Cortez and his Coster band. He produced a new twist on the old favourite and introduced "My Old Dutch" in a strong cockney accent before launching into a powerful up tempo piece which brought back memories of the Café de Paris and… but I stopped myself thinking about another woman and turned it off. Our goodbyes were muted and I determined to put on a braver face than I had in the barn. It was all very English and stiff upper lip. Even Willie managed to be formal and clicked his heels in mock imitation of the Kriegsmarine officer in whose uniform he now stood.

I sat alongside Rachel in the rear with Taynia on my lap. She didn't seem to mind the German uniform and fiddled with the piping on my jacket. We had a picnic basket in which to put her for the journey out to *Astakós* and hoped she wouldn't start screeching in the chilly air and unusual motion. Mum didn't wait outside waving goodbye as she insisted she had cows to milk but I suspected she didn't want us to see her concern.

The day was clearing up but there were still scattered showers though visibility was good. At eight o'clock on the dot I spotted George anxiously looking up and down the road which led to the breakwater. I called him over and Dad drove onto the slipway. We were hidden from most of the breakwater and, while Brian held *Astakós* as close as he could on the rising tide, we managed to transfer everything and everyone without incident. As we headed out to sea I looked back. All that remained was a puff of exhaust as Dad drove the Hillman Hawk away.

The wheelhouse was large enough to accommodate Rachel and Taynia below screen level and I stood with Brian while Willie and George manned the deck. We headed due east hoping to pass no closer than 400 yards from the end of the breakwater before turning north-east for the Écréhous. I used the binoculars and focussed on the two soldiers as they reached the mid-point of the breakwater and exchanged their usual pleasantries. They were both carrying rifles. The one on the higher level must have spotted us as he was facing in our direction. He pointed and the other turned around and raised his own pair of binoculars. I lowered mine and pointed as well. We were officers so it would be suspicious if we waved so we just ignored them. The one on the lower level gesticulated to the one above then picked up his pace and hurried along to the rounded end where we knew they kept the field telephone. If we accelerated or steered away from the breakwater it would rouse his suspicions. Their corporal would be talking to my mother at the moment and she might have persuaded him to help her with the milking. The Germans would have a standard operating procedure which would inevitably involve reporting to a higher authority if they were concerned. On the plus side, the guard would recognise the boat and Brian and George but might wonder about the passengers.

I nudged Willie. 'Looks like you get to play the officer after all.'

'Or finally get to do some killing!'

I assumed he was joking as the only weapons we had were knives but the Germans would be watching us through binoculars from their shed so we had little choice but to try Willie's plan before starting a fight and endangering Rachel and Taynia. Fortunately, my little daughter appeared to be asleep in her basket.

As we approached I could see that the guard seemed a bit agitated and was leaning over the railing waiting for us to come within hailing distance. He would have noted the Kriegsmarine uniforms and ranks so would probably be polite though he would certainly have given Brian and George a rollicking if they'd not had our protection as they were supposed to report to the Germans before making any trip beyond the bay.

When we were about fifty yards out the soldier saluted and shouted something in German. Willie gestured to Brian to bring us in closer. Officers wouldn't engage in shouting matches and if we did have to silence the guard and his telephone we'd need to be close anyway. Because of the tide he was at least twenty feet above us and couldn't see into the wheelhouse. I glanced through the window and held my breath praying that Taynia wouldn't wake up. Rachel was ready with a comforter just in case but Brian looked scared. George was on the prow with a boat hook ready to fend off from the granite walls. Willie was calmness personified and waited until we were mere feet away from the iron ladder before speaking in rapid German. I was trying to see it from the guard's perspective and just hoped that the two boys didn't panic. Willie finished speaking and the guard asked a question.

Willie replied with an edge to his voice. The guard snapped to attention and saluted again. Willie turned his back on him and gestured to Brian to proceed.

I let my breath out as George fended us off. He called up to the guard in English. 'Hey, Stefan, if the officer gives us time, I'll bring some crabs back for you.'

The soldier smiled and I instantly revised my opinion of George's mental capacity. The Écréhous reef was another five miles away so there was still time for the Germans to become suspicious especially when we sailed beyond the designated fishing area.

'What did you tell him?'

Willie grinned. 'Our story, of course. He seemed a bit confused so I told him to telephone Kriegsmarine HQ and ask to speak to Kapitän zur See von Nostitz if he needed any more explanation. Naturally, he declined. He seemed satisfied and that was a clever move by George. They won't worry about us now unless there's an escape from Caroline's house or we don't return this afternoon. We might be spotted from further along the coast though.'

If Saul was still hiding *Étoile de Jacob* around the reef he wouldn't be expecting a fishing boat with Kriegsmarine officers on board. We could remove them but if there were other boats nosing around the uniforms might give us an edge. From the lookout spot I'd used above my cousin's cottage I knew *Astakós* would be spotted long before we could see them but our faces wouldn't be recognisable until we were much closer.

Rather than risk confrontation they might just speed away. *Étoile*, with her powerful engine, could run at over twenty knots if necessary. The best *Astakós* could manage was ten so we'd never be able to catch up.

We didn't have enough petrol to get all the way to Cornwall so we'd just have to moor in the lagoon until dark and hope they returned. If they didn't we'd have to make a run for the south coast of England, over ninety miles away. According to Brian, our forty horse power engine would consume four gallons per hour even with the wind and tide with us. That meant we'd run out of petrol well short of the English coast and we'd still have to pass between German controlled Guernsey and Alderney where there might be minefields.

I took the binoculars and headed for the prow but, as we caught the tidal surge off La Coupe Point, the spray was too relentless for me to focus. I retreated to the wheelhouse and waited to see if the fates would be with us or not.

25

But I didn't believe in them and had asked Rachel to fashion something to help us just in case any or all of the three mythological goddesses commonly known as the "fates" were really against us. When we were still a mile short of the reef I ran it up the mast and tugged on the halyard until our improvised black and white Cornish flag of St Piran, made from a length of blackout curtain and some white tape, was unfurled. I'd thought about the Union flag but, if any Germans were still watching through powerful telescopes from the island, the bright splash of colours might alert them. The Breton flag was also black and white but we had spent enough time amongst the proud Cornish for Joe and Saul to recognise St Piran's and know that the Germans would never fly it by accident.

As we transited Bigorne rock I could see that *Étoile* was in the lagoon and Saul, Joe and Daniel were on deck observing us closely. Brian manoeuvred us alongside while George threw a line to the much bigger boat. Willie saluted then tossed his cap up to Saul who caught it, slapped it on his head and threw back a string of German. He stopped, mouth gaping wide, when Rachel came out of the wheel house and waved. I retrieved Taynia and stood proudly on deck just as he had composed himself and was about to say something intelligible. The sight of me holding a baby was too much and he pretended to faint while Joe jumped down to give Rachel a bear hug then slap me on the back so hard I almost toppled into the lagoon, baby and all.

Once all the introductions had been managed and our kit transferred to *Étoile* Rachel took Taynia into the cabin and we had a conference. I started. 'Luck, or the fates, have been with us so far but I don't think we should wait here much longer—'

'You're not suggesting we travel in broad daylight are you?' Saul interrupted.

'I don't think we have a choice. I'll fill you in on the details later but our absence could be discovered at any moment.'

'But, it will take some time for them to mount a sea search.' Saul persisted.

'Of course; but what about the Luftwaffe?'

'They already know we're here but don't seem too fussed. We've been overflown twice and mimed engine breakdown each time. There's been no follow up since yesterday. When Joe reported your boat with Kriegsmarine officers on board we thought you'd been sent to investigate. That Cornish flag was a peach of an idea.'

Daniel coughed. 'Saul is right. It would be too dangerous to travel between the islands now. We must wait for poor weather or darkness.' As he spoke a squall moved in from the west and rain slashed the side of the boat. We—'

Willie interrupted. 'They will be looking for our fishing boat so we need to get rid of it.'

Brian spoke up. 'We could sink it – serve that bastard Surcouf right.'

I thought for a moment but Rachel was the next to speak. 'Why not use it as a diversion. I'm no sailor but can't you lash the steering wheel, set the throttle thing to full speed and send it off to France by itself?'

We all looked at her.

'Genius,' was Saul's response. 'If we take it out to clear the reef and set the wheel for 190 degrees it should avoid all the rocks and keep going until it runs aground near St Malo.'

I looked at my watch. 'It's nearly 09:30. The guards at St Catherine's won't start worrying until this afternoon. We just don't know how long it will take before the prisoners escape from Les Routeurs or are rescued. They've been in that cellar now for eight hours or so. They could be there for the rest of the day or they could be out already.'

'It's a shame you wouldn't let me kill the lot of them – especially that minx you seem so fond of.'

Saul looked alarmed. 'Is Caroline with them?'

'I'll tell you all about it later. I think Willie's joking but we have to make a decision.'

'Not *we* — *you* have to make the decision. Fleming put you in charge, remember?'

Rachel came to my rescue. 'How long will it take the fishing boat to reach St Malo?'

Saul, always very quick with mental arithmetic, answered. 'If we set the throttle for about six knots it should take about six hours. On that course it will pass within four miles of Gorey and might be spotted in the first hour which shouldn't cause them any concern. It'll be dark by 17:00 so, if we set it off at 11:00 that might buy us enough time. We need to get it out of here though.'

Brian spoke. 'George and I will do it. I know how to set the course and the engine.' He hesitated. 'You will pick us up though?'

'I'll join them. I need some exercise.' Joe volunteered. 'Give me a chance for some fishing. Don't worry, boys — they won't leave me behind.'

And we didn't. Saul replaced the Cornish with the Breton flag before Joe and the boys took *Astakós* off to the south to potter about for a couple of hours with our dinghy in tow. It had a small outboard motor which they would use to get back to us after they set the fishing boat off on its ghost trip. Willie wanted to use some of our plastic explosives to set a booby trap on it should any Germans be unwary enough to board her. I knew he was disappointed that, after all our training, he still hadn't been able to reduce the German forces by a single casualty. I told him there would be plenty of time for his version of pest control once Fleming had us back under his wing. So, rather than listen to me filling in Saul about our holiday on Jersey he went down to our armoury to clean some weapons and polish his knife.

By the time Joe, George and Brian returned Saul was up to date, Daniel thoroughly bemused, and Rachel impatient to get away. Only Taynia seemed composed and content with her lot.

As dusk was creeping up on us a Dornier 17 dropped down and started a lazy circle about one hundred feet above. While the rest of us stayed out of sight in the cabin, Saul and Daniel went on deck to wave and mime that they were still working on the engine. Someone in the plane flashed a message in Morse code which Saul spelled out but it was in French which he didn't understand. Daniel translated that the Germans were asking if we had seen a fishing boat named *Astakós*. After some play acting on deck Saul bustled into the cabin, grabbed a torch and told me what the Germans wanted. Should he reply or not?

Would a Breton fisherman understand Morse code? I asked him to find out if Daniel did and, if so, to send "*non*". If he didn't then he should ignore them. I warned him not to get into a Morse conversation with the Germans. I watched anxiously as he discussed it with Daniel who seized the initiative, snatched the torch, examined it then smacked Saul around the ear, shrugged up at the plane in apology and sent him back to the cabin. He then waved to the plane and pointed towards Granville. The Dornier waggled its wings and banked away to follow the false lead while we prepared for sea.

Finally, darkness settled over us and we left the lagoon heading north-west for a point nearly fifty miles away between Guernsey and Alderney. Daniel steered while George kept a lookout and Brian manned the compass. Gauging wind, tide and currents was a complex task but one which came naturally to our French skipper. He planned to run at around sixteen knots until turning after three hours to a new course which would take us in a straight line WNW to Helford. All being well, that leg of 160 miles would take about ten hours and we should arrive in time for breakfast in the creek. We would make a brief coded radio transmission at midnight to alert coastal forces of our presence and intentions.

Saul helped Rachel settle Taynia in one of the bunks and sat with her while they exchanged stories. I tried not to listen but she was quizzing him on her future. Apart from getting her and Taynia to my uncle and Malita I hadn't thought much more about what would be best for them. I'd offered marriage but she had yet to give a response. We'd need to have that conversation and I'd have to prepare her for the interrogation she was likely to receive about Hélène.

For the moment I tuned them out and focused on Willie and Joe and the other bottle of Napoleon brandy we had requisitioned from Hayden-Brown's cellar for medicinal purposes. After a couple of swigs the anger I had been supressing about Kempler's threat to my family bubbled to the surface. 'You know, there's only one way I can rescue Caroline and protect my parents…' I took another swig.

Willie smirked. 'This should be interesting—'

'I'm going to suggest to Fleming that he lets me loose to track down Kempler and kill him. It shouldn't—'

Willie laughed. 'He's in Berlin. Do you realise how far that is?'

'That doesn't matter. Fleming will come up with a plan.'

'It might involve you jumping out of a plane though,' suggested Joe.

I grabbed the bottle again. 'So what? I can do that…if necessary.'

They both laughed this time then Willie launched a stream of German at me.

'What did you say?'

'I said that as you don't understand German you will have no luck!'

'I can pretend to be a French worker. From what I hear there are lots of them in Germany.'

Willie sighed. 'Very well. This is an excellent idea and I'm sure Fleming will approve. He might even suggest that for efficiency, as this will be an expensive trip, you might like to assassinate Hitler while you're there.'

'I'll sign up for that.' Joe volunteered.

'Well, on the positive side, you are both highly trained and resourceful killers. On the negative, neither of you speak German nor have the faintest idea about how to find and kill Kempler let alone Hitler.' He swallowed another mouthful of the fifty year old cognac. 'Of course, I could come along and show you how to accomplish this noble mission—'

'Would you?'

'As you English say, don't be so bloody daft. I wish you well though and there's one small favour, or two really, that I would beg of you before you leave.'

'Well?'

'As this will be a one way ticket and you will either be killed very quickly or very slowly, do either of you have any objection if I take Dot as my mistress before rescuing Caroline and turning her into a good and obedient German wife?'

26

In many ways the Helford area of Cornwall was very similar to Jersey but the major difference was tangible when we moored up in the creek just after dawn — the smell of freedom. Even though I'd spent long periods away from Jersey, I'd always relished opportunities to return. Now, I felt relieved that the air here wasn't weighed down with the blanket of helplessness which seemed to be smothering my home.

I mentioned this to Joe but he poked me in the ribs with one of his massive fingers. 'Don't be daft. It's not the air — it's the bloody Germans. Just give us the chance and we'll kick the boxheads out — might have to kill some of the fuckers first though.' He wrapped a paw around my shoulder. 'Only a matter of time, Jack….' He released me and waved his arm. 'Look, there's Dot. I'm going to take her back to Jersey after this. You watch, she'll win everything at the club—'

'Careful, she might replace you as our first team goalie!'

'That's the spirit. Come on, I bet Mrs H will have a decent breakfast for us.'

She did and afterwards she cleared Joe out of his room to make space for Rachel and Taynia. He moved in with me and I wondered if it was a favourable exchange — his elephantine snoring for my daughter's night time wailing.

Rachel had made it clear that I didn't have a choice in the matter. We'd spent an hour or so during the voyage talking about the future and she was adamant that she would not accept my offer of marriage. She didn't want me sacrificing myself but we both knew that the real reason was her fear that I could never commit more than half of myself as the other would still belong to another woman. Saul had spent even more time with her and I didn't think it was on my behalf. He'd been smitten with her for years but never been brave enough to risk rejection by declaring himself so I doubted the impartiality of any advice he might have volunteered.

Before I had a chance to discuss the matter with him he was called away to the telephone. While he was thus engaged I wandered down to the Ferry Boat Inn with Joe who had arranged to meet with Dot for a swim. Despite his heavy breakfast Joe quickly stripped to his trunks and plunged in after her. They splashed about for a bit then set off in a steady front crawl across the tidal stream following the ferry route to the village about 700 yards away. Having to adjust for currents and the incoming tide, it would be over a mile round trip. Dot would have to slow down for Joe so it would take them at least forty minutes. I left them to it, guessing that they'd probably stop for a cuddle midstream, and strolled over to an upturned dinghy on the beach.

I was perched on its hull trying to fathom out the problems Rachel had presented when I noticed Saul shuffling, in what passed as a sprint for him, down the path towards me. Out of breath, he was reaching for a cigarette to calm his racing heart when I heard a female voice shouting from across the creek. I stood up and peered towards Helford and spotted Dot's arm raised vertically in the air. Alongside her seemed to be a monster thrashing about in the water. A variety of sharks explored these waters but only in the summer, or so I'd been told, and none of them were dangerous to humans. Seals and porpoises can be a bit frisky but hardly a threat to someone as strong as Joe but he seemed to be wrestling with something. Dot lowered her arm to point at Joe then raised it again urgently. It was the standard signal for a swimmer in trouble. I'd taught life-saving and passed enough blind initiative tests to have recognised it earlier. I cursed and shouted at Saul. 'Get this bloody thing in the water quickly!'

He looked confused as I flipped it over and started to drag it across the sand. 'What's happening?'

'It's Joe. I think he's got cramp and it looks serious.' I'd had it once in both legs and knew how painful and debilitating it was and bloody frightening in deep water. I just hoped that Dot had the sense to keep away from him and not attempt a rescue for he would drag her under. I pulled off my boots before clambering aboard while Saul grabbed a pair of oars which were resting against the low sea wall.

'*Kak*, there aren't any rowlocks.'

'You'll just have to scull then. Can you manage?' He already looked fit to explode after his jog down to the beach.

'It's all I'm going to do. I'm not jumping in again. You sort him out.'

He could scull a lot faster than he could run and we were soon close enough to see what had happened. I'd guessed correctly and Joe was rolling around in agony unable to stretch his legs against anything solid. Dot was keeping her distance wary of his flailing arms. He was close to panic and we needed to calm him so he could at least reach for an oar. One trick we'd practised in simulated life-saving to avoid the patient grabbing the rescuer was to take off your trunks and offer one end and hold on to the other. I was about to suggest that to Dot and hope she'd take it in the right spirit when Joe disappeared beneath the surface. Saul spun us around, released his oar and reached out to position it in the water where Joe had sunk. Dot had duck-dived and was probably going to attempt to pull Joe to the surface. That would be the end of both of them so I pulled off my jumper and leapt in between them.

It probably wasn't deeper than fifteen feet in this part of the channel and I spotted movement against the lighter sand of the sea bed. If Dot and I could get an arm each we might stand a chance of dragging him to the surface. I took a deep breath, ducked under and forced myself deep with strong arm pulls. More by luck than judgement I arrived at the same time as Dot and managed to secure a grip on one of his wrists. I had to make sure his massive hands didn't grab any part of me. Fortunately, Dot seemed to have done the same with his other arm.

Our natural buoyancy was lifting us upwards but, in his panic, Joe was still struggling and holding us down. Even if I'd dared release my grip there was no way I could apply enough energy to knock him unconscious and stop the manic squirming. He must have experienced a moment of clarity or perhaps lost his last breath as he suddenly ceased moving. Using our free arms Dot and I struggled for the surface.

Joe's great head emerged face up and he floated briefly while we tried to tug him to the boat. Saul's oar was within reach so I grabbed it with one hand and pulled Joe towards me. We needed to get him on his front in the boat to attempt resuscitation but I'd heard about a new method being employed by life-guards in America. It would mean suppressing my sensibilities and coping with a male taboo so I steeled myself. Pulling him into the oar and resting his neck over the blade I opened his mouth, made a seal with my lips and blew a lungful of air into it. Dot joined me and while Saul held him steady we took turns in giving him what I supposed we could call the kiss of life. She seemed to enjoy it far more than me.

But I couldn't tell if we were having any effect. While she continued I tried to find the carotid pulse on his exposed neck without success. If his lungs were full of water we needed to pump it out but that would mean either towing him to the beach or hauling his dead weight into the boat. One would take too long; the other might prove impossible. I cast around but no one else was in sight so I clambered aboard and told Saul what we had to do. He untied the painter and threw one end to Dot who threaded it around Joe's chest and under his armpits. It wasn't the thickest of ropes but would give us more purchase than his wet and slippery skin. Dot hoisted herself over the gunwale and joined us. Saul used the oar as a lever sliding it down Joe's back while we tugged on the rope. As we got his shoulders aboard Joe's dead weight threatened to drag the dinghy over and it started to swing like a pendulum. Saul kept levering but he was stuck. We had to move him to the transom and haul him in from the stern. We dragged him round and I jumped in again and holding the transom with my left hand placed my right arm under his knees then heaved. Fortunately, Saul anticipated the motion and counterbalanced it by shifting his weight backwards. It suddenly struck me that we didn't need to get all of him in the boat, just get his stomach over the side and use gravity to pump the water out. The narrow wooden transom would act like a rifle butt punch in the guts and expel the air or, in this case, water out of his lungs. It was a desperate measure but there was no alternative. I shouted up what we should do and Dot and Saul manoeuvred him into position. I scrambled aboard, forced his shoulders over the thwart and jerked his arms towards me using the transom as a pivot on his stomach. It felt hopeless but I had to keep pumping even though it might break his ribs. I exchanged a helpless look with Dot whose face seemed frozen in despair. For once Saul was silent with nothing witty or annoying to say.

27

'Ahoy. Are you in trouble?'

I glanced up. It was Holdsworth and another man in a kayak paddling furiously towards us.

I called out. 'Yes. We need to get him ashore and find some oxygen.'

'Is his heart beating?' the stranger asked.

Dot felt for his pulse and shook her head.

'No.'

'Damn. You need to restart it. Oxygen is no use unless you can pump it round his system.'

'Who are you? A doctor?'

'Yes, and I'm coming aboard.' While Holdsworth held the kayak steady, he climbed over the gunwale. 'Tremayne, Surgeon-Commander. We need to get him in and roll him onto his back.'

He supervised while we dragged Joe across the centre thwart. He checked his pulse, opened his mouth, rooted inside with his fingers and extracted a clump of seaweed.

If I hadn't been so cold I would have blushed — I'd forgotten that most basic of checks. Dot and I had been wasting our breath if his windpipe was blocked.

Tremayne looked across at me with a quizzical expression. 'Never mind, young man, you did everything else right.' He rolled Joe onto his side and thumped him between his shoulders. Water spurted out in a steady stream. Satisfied, he put him on his back again and started pressing down in a rhythmical way on his chest. 'Heart massage — difficult through this massive chest but I think we might have caught him in time.' He paused, blew some quick breaths into Joe's mouth then returned to the chest presses. After a minute or so, he stopped to check his pulse and smiled. 'Now, let's get ashore and see if we can't rustle up a bottle of oxygen from your diving stores. He should be stable now but we've got to keep him warm.' He pulled off his own jacket and indicated that Saul should do the same then grabbed my discarded top and wrapped the clothing around Joe's cold body.

We put him into bed and Tremayne took a syringe out of a black doctor's bag he'd retrieved from his car and injected something into Joe. He was wrapped in blankets and we'd found some hot water bottles to place in with him. Tremayne listened to Joe's heart with a stethoscope, nodding as he moved it about. 'I think he'll be fine. You think he had cramp in both legs?'

'On top of a heavy breakfast. He should—'

'Have been more careful but it wasn't just that. Muscle spasms can be caused by a variety of factors but, judging from his breath, I'd guess that an excess of alcohol was more than likely the cause as it would have made him very dehydrated. Before you swim in cold water though, you should warm your muscles up first.' He looked at Willie who had joined us. 'I suspect your trainers have already told you this but I accept that there isn't always the time when you're in action. On this occasion there was no excuse so I hope you will explain that to him when he comes round.' He smiled at Dot. 'Perhaps he'll listen to you, my dear.'

'I hope they'll listen to you as well, James.' Holdsworth spoke from the doorway. 'Dr Tremayne is the new area medic for our various flotillas. Luckily he was on the water this morning trying to convince me that he's fit enough for more...active service. I think you'll agree he passed the first test!'

He certainly looked fit enough but, as he was about the same age as Holdsworth who had two grown up sons, I wouldn't like to subject him to a real test, though now wasn't the time for flippant comments. We left Joe to sleep it off and, in the absence of a nurse, Dot agreed to monitor him as Tremayne was concerned that there might still be water in his lungs. He'd come across a couple of cases where survivors from immersion had come around only to succumb hours later to dry drowning.

With this new worry and Tremayne's advice on our minds we went in search of something non-alcoholic to warm us up. Mrs H provided it in the form of mugs of sweet Horlicks. We supped in silence before Holdsworth took the doctor off to show him *Etoile* and asked Willie to join them.

Well trained by a busy mother I offered to wash up the mugs and shoved Saul towards the sink. 'So, what were you in such a hurry about earlier? You looked fit to burst.'

He looked at his watch. '*Kak*! Fleming was on the telephone. He wants us in London, pronto. We need to catch the train from Penzance or Truro.'

I sighed. 'Well, we'd better get packed and on our way. Can Willie borrow Dot's lorry and drive us do you think?'

'I hope so but it will be a bit of a squeeze.'

'Why?'

'Because he wants us to bring Rachel and Taynia as well.'

We caught up with Holdsworth and Saul told him that we had received orders to get to Truro as soon as possible and asked if Willie could be detailed to drive us in Dot's lorry. He didn't seem too happy but couldn't think of an alternative driver. Saul went off to find Rachel and I went to pack and change into civvies as Fleming had stipulated no uniforms. While I waited for them I copied out more names and details from Hayden-Brown's notebook. Saul would give Fleming the bundle of documents written in German as well as other letters we had purloined. I'd already decided to give Rachel all the jewellery as she was not only homeless but penniless as well. I felt sure Caroline would approve. We'd already shared out the English currency much like privateers from a previous century. I hoped the boys wouldn't spend too much of it in the local pubs.

Though Willie might have made an excellent tank driver, the Cornish lanes would have defeated him within the first hundred yards. None of us had navigated this route alone before and a compass and small scale road map is of little use when to go north-east you often have to travel south-west first along narrow tracks where even from the cab of a truck you couldn't see over the hedges. It would be a nightmare in summer when the vegetation was rampant. I drew the short straw which I suspected had been fiddled by Saul and had to sit in the load bay while Rachel and Taynia squeezed in between him and Willie up front.

Rachel hadn't complained to me about the move and Saul didn't give any indication that she might have resisted but her expression was so cool that I kept the gifts for a more opportune moment. Road signs had been removed to confuse any German invaders which made Willie's task even more difficult and I was treated to several reversing moments when Dot's lorry planted kisses on Cornish walls and shrubbery. Eventually the road seemed to widen behind me and we passed through a largish village with a quaint pub called The Red Lion quite close to a square with a community notice board listing forthcoming events in Mawnan Smith. It probably wouldn't be of much help to German troops as only a Methodist group and the W.I. had posted anything.

Making better speed now we soon bypassed Falmouth, crawled through Penryn and joined the main road which I recognised as leading to Truro. It was nearly midday when Willie stopped in the car park adjacent to the railway station. I stretched my legs while Saul enquired about the next London train.

He returned, looking rather frustrated. 'The Paddington train will be here at 16:06 but that's the down-line service terminating at Penzance. It will be returning up-line and stopping here, but not until tomorrow at 11:30. I'd better telephone Fleming. Say a prayer for me.'

28

When he returned, his face was flushed and he looked like he needed medical care rather than prayers. Unusually for him, his speech seemed disjointed and he even stuttered in places. Behind the flâneur I knew that Fleming was not only a bully but could be incredibly rude. From Saul's demeanour it would seem that he had endured more than the usual bollocking and was suffering the after effects of a stream of acid spat into his ear.

The upshot of the telephone conversation was that we were to proceed to St Eval where a plane would be waiting to take us to London. Willie confirmed that we had enough petrol but, before we left, I went into the station and secured a train timetable determined to offer it to Fleming when we next met as an aid to his future planning. Saul had always been reluctant to stand up to bullies — I'd always been too stubborn not to.

While not as circuitous nor fringed with so many high hedges, the journey was not without incident as Willie embraced a Cornish stone hedge too intimately and we had to stop to change a tyre. I suggested we find somewhere for a bite to eat but that spooked Saul and he demanded that we get to the airfield without any further delay. So hungry, dusty and more than a little irritated, we rolled up to the airfield's perimeter and discovered two Redcaps armed with Lee Enfield rifles manning the barrier outside the guard hut. During our previous short stay the base had been guarded by RAF personnel so I wondered about the increase in security.

If civilian police could be officious and patronising, the military version could add violence and positive hatred in their dealings with soldiers who displeased them. Appearing out of uniform, unannounced, without official papers and claiming we were expected by senior staff was grist to their mill and, while Rachel and Taynia were escorted into the guard hut by a Royal Air Force corporal, we were forced out of the lorry at gun point and made to kneel outside.

Saul started berating them in what was probably a very watered down version of the language Fleming had injected into his ear. This was not a sensible idea as one of them rammed the butt of his rifle into Saul's back and flattened him to the ground. While that was probably standard procedure for a trained MP dealing with an unruly soldier, booting him while he was down was even less sensible because, without, forethought but plenty of malice, Willie and I rolled over and kicked the MPs behind their knees. Before Saul had lifted his head to protest about his treatment, his two attackers were pinned alongside him with the business end of their Lee Enfield rifles in the nape of their necks.

The problem with the sort of intense combat training we had received was that time for reflection before, and consideration of consequences after, rapid reaction had been deliberately sublimated to ensure success. Though we held sway we were now in a perilous position. The RAF man's mouth was hanging open in shock and the telephone receiver dangled by its cable from his hand. We'd disposed of the guards but were we really going to storm the base? I looked at Willie and he shrugged then nodded his approval as I ejected the rifle's magazine and removed its bolt. He did the same and we allowed the two MPs to get up then presented them with their bolts while holding on to the rifles. Saul scrambled to his feet, grabbed the telephone and demanded that the corporal put him through to the base commander's office.

Saul wasn't having much luck on the telephone today for, within minutes, a truck roared up and disgorged a squad of armed airmen. After processing by even more Redcaps which involved us exchanging our ID cards for some well-placed body punches we thanked them for their consideration and were delivered in handcuffs to the base commander's office. Rachel had been spared the formal welcome by the MPs but was marched in behind us. There was a flicker of recognition in the base commander's eyes as he looked at us over his half-moon spectacles. I noted his name: Group Captain Pascoe – another pasty muncher. He instructed our guardians to remove the handcuffs and leave.

Once the door was closed, he exploded. 'What, in the name of the Almighty, were you thinking? Assaulting Redcaps? I remember you three so I understand that you have a collective death wish but not on my bloody base! And why has this young lady brought a child into my office?'

Before Saul could add to our woes I answered. 'Please accept our apologies, sir but the two MPs exceeded their authority and we reacted instinctively. No one was hurt apart from Sub-Lieutenant Marcks.' I waited for his reaction.

A grin crept across his face making his fine specimen of a moustache twitch. 'You might well believe that but the Redcaps have your names now and their definition of "hurt" might not be the same as ours. For your own safety I suggest you stay well clear of them in future.'

Willie muttered something in German and Pascoe snapped. 'What did he say?'

Saul beat me this time. 'He says that it is the same in all armies and—'

I interrupted Saul. I'd ask Willie what he really said later. 'Have you received a message from Lieutenant-Commander Fleming about us, sir?'

He shook his head. 'No, I haven't seen or heard from that…officer… since that debacle with the Heinkel.' He hesitated. 'I understand that he is not entirely welcome on any air station in this area after touring them to find a couple of pilots to eviscerate…but never mind that. I want to know what is going on and why this woman is with you.'

Before I could answer Rachel handed Taynia to me, stepped forward and spoke in French with a heavy Breton accent.

Pascoe looked puzzled and searched our faces for a translation.

I sensed Willie was about to provide one with his own interpretation and spoke first. 'She says she is an agent and that we've just rescued her from the Gestapo in France. This is her daughter, Taynia. She is very alarmed at the behaviour of your soldiers and feels like she has been pulled from the frying pan and thrown into the fire. She would like some water, something to eat and a place to sit and feed her daughter.'

'Of course, please forgive me. Do sit down…all of you.' He picked up the telephone and issued instructions. 'Before your refreshments arrive perhaps you'll be kind enough to explain what is really going on and why you are here.'

'Before we do that, sir, could you tell us why you have Redcaps crawling all over the place?' Saul rubbed his back as he spoke.

Pascoe removed his glasses, reached for a cloth and started to polish them. 'That's a good question and normally I wouldn't bother to explain but, in a way it's all very embarrassing and Fleming's fault. You see, your German bomber was spotted by several locals and reported to the police and other authorities. The whole escapade was meant to be on the QT and, as you know, we tried to avoid alerting anyone. It was relatively easy to quash the local enquiries but last week there was a small explosion on the other side of the church. Someone further up the chain of command put two and two together and came up with six. They suspected that the IRA might be up to their old tricks again and despatched a platoon of MPs to guard the place. Truth be told, the Redcaps have precious little to do at present and have been using this as an exercise. We're training our own airmen in security but at the moment there's a command gap—'

Willie made a longer remark in German.

'What did he say? He's German isn't he?'

Willie responded in perfect English. 'Yes, I am but I'm also Jewish and I said that I fear for my people as our only potential saviours seem to have their heads so far up—'

'He's rather tired and irritable at the moment, sir. You'll have to excuse him. We've been sent here by Commander Fleming to meet a plane to take us to London. Are you sure he hasn't sent a message?'

He picked up the telephone again. 'When did you last speak with Fleming?'

'About two hours ago, sir.' Saul answered.

'What's his number?'

Saul told him and he asked the exchange to put him through.

From his end of the conversation it was obvious that he hadn't been able to speak to our boss. He replaced the receiver and smiled at us. 'They say he isn't there. He's out and about looking for an aircraft.'

29

That information seemed to have a negative effect on Saul's appetite but the rest of us, especially Taynia, quickly disposed of the swill, which passed as lunch. From one of the producers of Britain's favourite early potato I was now a consumer of some form of rehydrated potato powder purchased by an insane RAF quartermaster as the fields surrounding the airbase were bursting with real ones. He must be on a very tight budget as the animal slaughtered for the meat lurking beneath the thin gravy must have led a very unhealthy life. Whatever colour and flavour the other vegetables had once displayed had been boiled away by a disinterested cook. However, this was the officers' mess and perhaps the quartermaster was an NCO and looked after his chums first. We were contemplating a choice of pudding carelessly described by the mess steward when Cassons marched into the room.

Saul's face split into an explosive smile as he jumped up and thrust out his hand. 'Peter, have you come to get us?'

'That's right. No time for grub though. Got to get a move on. Let's—'

'Thank God. I thought it was going to be Fleming.'

But Cassons ignored him and embraced Rachel whom he hadn't seen since we all escaped from France back in June. She introduced Taynia and Cassons contrived to show no surprise even when she mentioned that I was her father. Instead, he clapped me on the shoulder and offered congratulations.

Willie threw him a casual salute. 'From the additional half stripe it would seem that congratulations are in order for you also, Squadron Leader.'

I hadn't spotted the promotion but shook his hand. 'I suppose if we'd been successful you would have been made a wing commander or group captain.'

He laughed. 'Never mind all that nonsense. Grab your possessions and let's get out of here.'

Willie watched us get up. 'I'll see if any of the desserts are better than the swill we've just eaten before I take the truck back. That's if I can find the way.'

Cassons shook his head. 'No, you're wanted as well. Leave your vehicle. You're coming with us.'

A truck was waiting outside the mess and we scrambled aboard for the short drive to dispersal. As we approached the holding end of the main runway I spotted an unusual looking bomber. It had a shark like Perspex nose leading to a mid-wing over which sat an elongated cockpit sloping to an empty gun turret and a long tapering tail terminating in twin fins. The wings supported two large radial engines and the aircraft was supported on a tricycle undercarriage. It was painted silver like a commercial airliner but had no squadron markings; just the usual RAF rondels.

A ladder was propped up against the lip of a large loading door in the port fuselage side and Cassons helped us up into a gloomy interior with two small windows at the tail end though you'd have to crouch to see through them. From the outside it looked like a bomber but this one seemed to have continuous ribbed flooring over what should have been the bomb bay. There were no seats just netting and harnesses. As Rachel settled Taynia next to her the engines burst into life and the aircraft shuddered with their rhythm. Hurriedly, she pulled some cotton wool from her bag and plugged Taynia's ears. Cassons indicated that Saul and I should follow him up to the cockpit.

Saul trembled like the engines as we saw who was in the pilot's seat.

Fleming glanced over his shoulder at us. 'Ah, the monkey and his chimp. Find a seat and brace yourselves. This flying pig can be a bit awkward on take-off.'

My heart started to race with the engines. Surely he wasn't going to fly this plane but Cassons tapped him on the shoulder. 'You can try if you like, sir but I suggest that the rest of us disembark first.'

'Spoil sport.' He laughed in his hyena fashion and vacated the seat.

Cassons slid in while Fleming pulled down the folding second pilot's seat and buckled up. Below him was an arched entrance to what seemed to be the bomb aimer's lair. I settled for the navigator/radio operator's seat leaving the other fold down one for Saul.

Fleming had been joking but he wasn't wrong. The "pig" wobbled along to the runway's threshold where Cassons wound up the engines to full throttle then released the brakes. It was unusual; speeding along on the level rather than nose up but, after what seemed an eternity, the wheels unglued themselves and we lurched into the air. I watched the altimeter patiently over Cassons' shoulder until it read 5,000 feet then the plane levelled off.

Fleming removed his headset. 'Right, Cassons carry on, I'm going back to speak to Renouf's girlfriend. I hope that child doesn't bite.'

He scrambled past me and descended into the main fuselage. I unbuckled and got up to follow him but Saul grabbed my arm. 'Best leave him to it. You don't want a scene in front of Rachel.'

I didn't really care about Fleming shouting at me but I didn't want him bullying her or upsetting Taynia but Saul was right — she'd have to put up with lots of questioning after we landed and Willie was there as a witness.

Despite the growl of the two engines I could hear Cassons clearly as he asked Saul about our latest escapade. He provided some terse answers but I tuned them out and slipped into Fleming's seat to get a better view of the English countryside creeping along below. There were few clouds and the sun splintered off greenhouses and vehicle windscreens, winking at us in a random code.

'What is this thing?' I asked Cassons.

'The plane? It's an Albemarle. This is one of the prototypes. It was meant to be a light bomber but it's too late, too heavy and too slow. The Ministry insisted that Armstrong Whitworth made it of non-strategic materials—'

'What do you mean?' Saul interrupted.

'Steel and wood with a plywood covering — no aluminium — so it's rather heavy for its size. It's got twice as much power as a Blenheim but it's slower.'

'What's Fleming planning for it then?'

Cassons laughed. 'He's going to paint it matt black, canopies and all, and use it to parachute commandos into France. There's a hatch in the floor they can drop through. It can carry ten fully armed at a time and—'

'I suppose we'll be the mugs who have to sail over and rescue them.' Saul interrupted again.

'You might have to rescue him as well. He's determined to see some action but the admiral won't let him.' He shook his head. 'Problem is that he's not a team player. My cousin was at Eton with him and told me that he was brilliant at athletics and probably the best they'd ever seen. He won the Victor Ludorum twice but always seemed to prefer his own company. Apparently, he had to live in the shadow of his older brother Peter who was an absolute star at Eton.

He seems driven — desperate to prove something to his family. Do you think that makes him dangerous company?'

Saul and I answered together. 'Yes!'

I picked up a clipboard which held what looked like a flight plan from Hendon via several waypoints including Salisbury to St Eval and back. According to the final ETA we should be landing back at Hendon in less than an hour. I wondered if Rachel and Taynia might like to ride up front and take in the view. We could lie down together in the bomb aimer's position and watch our not so green but still free England scroll below us. That would mean interrupting Fleming though so I let my mind meander imagining Caroline and her sensuous perfume competing with the military odours seeping from the airframe and engine exhausts. Locked into my rather pleasant daydream I didn't realise that Willie had joined us, carrying Taynia in his arms, until I felt a hand on my shoulder. I turned towards them amused to see my little daughter rubbing Willie's bald head while staring at the sun reflecting off its smooth surface. I reached out for her but she clung to Willie who seemed unusually cheerful.

'What's tickling you apart from this little cherub?' I asked.

He started to chortle which amused Taynia and she squeezed his nose. Surprisingly, Saul reached out and she almost jumped into his arms.

Willie rubbed his nose and laughed. 'I wish I had a camera. This is such a picture of domestic bliss only the child doesn't seem to know which one is her father. Whoever wishes to claim that honour needs to get back there to the rescue *de suite.*'

'Is Rachel having a tough time?'

He smirked. 'No, it's Fleming who needs rescuing, Jack. You do seem to choose formidable women.' He shook his head. 'He started questioning her about Hélène in French but it's so noisy back there that they're shouting at each other. She gave the same answers we've heard before. He accused her of lying and she spat back at him using language I last heard from a whore in Marseille. He mounted his high horse and gave her a lecture in English along with some less than subtle threats.

'She switched to Spanish and, though I'm not fluent, I've heard enough from my time in the Legion to realise that it might have made even that whore blush. Perhaps Fleming doesn't understand the language because he didn't slap her face or her bottom as I would have done if she'd spoken to me like that. Instead, he pulled out his silver cigarette case and offered one to her. They're creating their own smoke screen back there so I've brought the little girl up for some fresh air…where are we?'

Cassons twisted in his seat and answered. 'About forty minutes out from Hendon in North London. We'll be starting our descent soon.' He smiled at me. 'Willie might be right. I've not had the pleasure of meeting your Caroline but Rachel isn't to be trifled with is she? How did you—'

Saul pulled Taynia's finger out of his nostril and interrupted. 'The sad irony is that Jack didn't choose them — for reasons beyond comprehension, they chose him and he's trifled with both of them. He's welcome to Caroline but Rachel deserves so much better and—'

'I suppose you're offering your services as lover, step-father and protector then?' I shot back.

He turned his golden-eyed stare on me. 'Yes, if she'll have me.'

'You'll need to learn how to tie your own shoelaces first!'

Willie chortled. 'This is almost as amusing as watching her shredding Fleming but you two are about as ready for marriage as he is for flying this plane.'

'Does that mean I qualify? Because she is rather lovely.'

We all stared at Cassons in disbelief.

Saul was quickest. 'No, you'd be better suited to Caroline. You look and sound like a gentleman but you'd have to let her fly…all the time and everywhere. Isn't that right, Jack?'

'Let me get this straight. You've always lusted after Rachel and now you think you're man enough to marry her. Willie, you think you can tame Caroline and would like a shot at Rachel and our newly promoted squadron leader believes he has enough hours on his log book to beat the three of us. So where does that leave me?'

It was a silly question and I should have anticipated the answer but Saul pierced me with it. 'It leaves you with the only one who hasn't chosen you yet — Masha!'

Before I could protest, Fleming appeared. 'That bloody woman is impossible. Renouf, get back there and sort her out.'

At first I couldn't see her through the fug then realised she was kneeling in the tail peering out of the window. I crawled alongside her and waited for her to acknowledge me. She took her time then sighed heavily, stretched out like a cat and rolled onto her side to look up at me. I mirrored her position and we lay staring at each other for a few moments daring each other to speak first.

I lost. 'You've upset Fleming.'

She shook her head and raised her voice. 'I can't hear you.'

I moved closer until our heads were almost touching. The stale aroma of second hand tobacco smoke almost overwhelmed her floral scent but her closeness was comforting and made me tingle especially as she didn't pull away. 'I said that you've upset Fleming.'

She laughed and placed her mouth close to my ear. 'I know. It wasn't difficult. He's a bit full of himself — likes women to know their place. But there's something about him. It's his eyes I think. They look cruel but they are so fascinating. I imagine that he's driven a lot of women crazy.'

'Not you though?'

'Oh, I could be tempted. It's not just the power or the challenge but he has a special quality. It's not just strength…he just seems so sure…about everything.' She sighed again. 'I think he quite likes you and Saul but wouldn't hesitate for a moment to sacrifice you for what he would see as the greater good…so you be careful…don't let him *volunteer* you for anything without questioning it first.'

It was my turn to sigh. 'That's not how it works. Yes, I could ask for a transfer and just risk my neck in raiding parties but, as you say, he has something special and it's not just with women. He's at the very heart of this war and…without him, you'd still be a hostage in Jersey…hang on a minute…this new concern for my health…does this mean you are considering accepting my offer?'

She ran her fingers over my face touching my eyes then my lips. 'That's tempting as well but I'm sorry. It's not just Caroline though Saul did tell me about the little Russian girl — what's her name?'

'The bastard; just wait until I—'

'What?'

What could I do? Bully him? I had nothing to hide. 'Her name's Masha.'

'Yes, Masha. But it's not about her either. The trouble is that we're too much alike, you and I. We were so close because we were more like brother and sister until that…stupid moment. But…we can't regret that because look at the result. You must never blame yourself either…but we wouldn't be right…together.'

'Is there someone who would be right?'

She caressed my cheek. 'Apart from that brief encounter under the raft I've never touched or been touched by another man. I've had plenty of offers and opportunities but I wasn't saving myself for you.

The truth is that I don't think I'm looking for anyone; not with Taynia in tow. Once this war is over, perhaps the right man will find me.' She pulled her hand away and looked into my eyes though I was sure she'd closed the shutters behind hers for what she said next chilled me to the bone. 'You'll always be Taynia's father and I'll never stop you seeing her but I don't need a husband. When I do I'll be looking for a man and not…I'm sorry…a boy.'

30

I crawled away trying desperately to make sense of what I felt. Anger? Yes. Frustration? Sort of. Humiliation? Of course. Disappointment? Naturally. But underneath, gnawing at me, was the same feeling I'd experienced after leaving Caroline — a burgeoning sense of relief. I couldn't be sure. Perhaps she was right — a man would know but I was only a boy! Yes, that did make me feel anger towards her but doesn't the truth always sting? I looked back. She was peering out of the window again; a sunbeam sweeping across her as the plane changed course and my stomach provided the only internal feeling I could rely on as it started to descend.

Back in our original positions with Willie possibly staking his claim back in the fuselage Cassons ordered us to buckle up as Hendon was a small enclosed airfield surrounded by houses and he had to approach at a steep angle. Four bumps too many on the grass runway followed by harsh braking and we taxied up to an imposing redbrick building. Fleming was first off, dragging Willie and Saul with him. He told Rachel and me to wait for transport but wouldn't answer any questions. We watched from the steps as the three of them marched off to a Humber parked outside the building. Without a backward glance Fleming lowered himself into the driver's seat and was off before the passenger doors had fully closed.

Cassons found us and suggested that we walk over to a white painted low slung building a couple of hundred yards away and wait inside as he had to take the Albemarle back to Farnborough before dark. He passed me a note which Fleming had scrawled while Rachel was knocking sense into me. "Call the office, Whitehall 1450 and tell them you're at Hendon. You will be picked up within the hour. Report to me in Room 39 tomorrow at 14:00."

Taynia was hungry again and becoming irritable. I carried her across the grass, found an orderly and asked if there was a telephone and a canteen we could use. He couldn't take his eyes off Rachel who smiled willingly at him but spoke in French. English to the core, he raised his voice and spoke slowly enough for even Taynia to understand then led us to an office where he arranged for a clerk to provide a telephone. I got through to the Admiralty and relayed Fleming's terse message and was told to hold. Five minutes later, the female voice informed me that a car would be waiting at entrance number six just off the Watford Way in one hour precisely then hung up before I could ask any questions. We were guided to a canteen where Rachel managed to find some warm milk and a few biscuits for Taynia. My stomach wasn't ready for food or any more kicks from Rachel so I sat in silence wondering what Fleming had arranged for us.

She focused on Taynia though I didn't feel she was ignoring me and the atmosphere between us seemed surprisingly relaxed. I sensed that she'd finally said what she'd wanted to for a long time and there was no further need for discussion of anything other than practical details. After forty minutes I suggested we gather our bags and find the pickup point. She let me carry Taynia who was more cheerful now but a little tired and she snuggled her soft cheek into my shoulder, her hair tickling my chin.

It was colder now and we huddled together outside in what I hoped was the right spot, wandering why we couldn't be picked up from inside the airfield. On the dot, my question was answered as a massive Russian ZIS 101 limo pulled up and, to my consternation, Nicolai levered himself out of the driver's door. My pulse hammered in my temples. Fleming had sold us to the Russians. He may not have extracted much information from Rachel but I was damn sure the Reds would squeeze every last ounce about Hélène out of her. I hoped I could bring Nicolai down but there was the driver to contend with and how could we run with Taynia to protect?

Nicolai approached with the beaming smile of a Russian assassin and held out his hand. I passed Taynia to Rachel and I reached out for it, mentally rehearsing a quick knee jab to his privates followed by a hip throw and stranglehold when I heard the unmistakeable voice of Uncle Fred shouting a greeting in *Jèrriais* and I breathed out in relief. He alighted from the passenger door and limped to Rachel before folding her in his arms. They hugged like father and daughter and he fussed over Taynia like a grandfather. Nicolai and I watched the scene and suddenly I understood what Fleming had planned. My uncle and I embraced but I managed to prevent the tears from forming as he muttered to me in *Jèrriais* that everything was going to be fine and that Malita would be so happy to see us.

Nicolai picked up our bags as Fred led us to the car. He opened the door and my heart skipped several more beats. 'Rachel,' he said, 'allow me to introduce Mrs Maryia Dobruskina though I know she prefers to be called Masha.'

From the depths of the car a small hand appeared and reached out to shake Rachel's. As she handed Taynia in, she turned to look at me with a knowing smile.

The ZIS is a copy of the American Buick but is built like a tank. It should seat seven in relative comfort and Rachel chose to sit up front between Nicolai and my uncle leaving me with Taynia and more than enough space in the rear. My little daughter was really tired now and I placed her between myself and Masha. She snuggled in and dropped her head onto my lap. Masha looked amused and stroked her back. I called out across the divide which was longer than my legs at full stretch. 'Where are we going?'

My uncle twisted in his seat to look at me. 'Dunstable — it'll take about forty minutes.'

'What's in Dunstable for goodness sake?'

'A little surprise but we'll chat more when we get there so just relax. You can tell Masha all about your latest adventure while Rachel and I catch up.'

So, my uncle was to be the velvet fist in the Soviets' iron glove. Masha smiled at me and I just hoped that the Russians would see the light and dump Hitler. I realised that I wanted them to be on our side for more reasons than just winning a war though I did wonder what, if anything my friendly widow, might find attractive in a mere boy when she had loved and lost a man.

31

But Masha didn't seem particularly interested in my "adventures" and, apart from a few desultory questions, contented herself with comforting Taynia who soon abandoned mine for her more comfortable lap. It was probably embarrassment, brought into focus through Rachel's proximity that harnessed my tongue. After her cruel personal assessment of me I still felt uncomfortable and every bit the *boy* sitting so close to Masha. She must have sensed my unease so we stayed in our separate worlds listening to Rachel and my uncle chattering away up front.

It was just after five p.m. when we passed through an impressive gated entrance and followed a winding tree-lined road which finally opened out into what must have once been a magnificent lawn. Normally, at this time in November there'd be little light left but since we'd stayed on Daylight Saving Time there was still another thirty minutes or so before sunset so I could see that the lawn had been carved up into a series of allotments each dedicated to winter crops. Beyond the scarred earth was a building which took my breath away.

Sliced in half horizontally by the sinking sun was a grand house which must be several hundred years old. On the left was a Romanesque temple façade pierced by two rows of three double-height windows. Set back from this by several feet were another two rows of four similar windows all surrounded by rampant ivy clinging to the red bricks. In the centre stood another temple-like structure extending outwards but with three even larger windows accessed by a full width platform of grey steps. To its right was a mirror image of the other side. At ground level there was an equal number of much smaller windows and even more in the roof line. Above the centre was a turret with a balustrade edged with chimney pots. The entire façade of red bricks was edged with flat off-white plaster columns. As we drove around the vegetable garden I realised that this was probably only the tradesmen's entrance and whoever lived here would need dozens of servants and a substantial bank balance to keep it warm.

Nicolai, either out of disdain for such aristocratic splendour or mere tiredness, braked rather late. The monstrous limousine lost traction on the gravel and skidded before side swiping one of a pair of statues guarding the steps. Much like the Tsar before it, the statue succumbed to the Soviet hammer and toppled to the ground. We alighted from the tank while Nicolai fussed around his victim attempting to resuscitate it. As we gathered our luggage we were treated to a round of applause from a tall woman standing at the top of the granite steps leading up to the manor.

'Bravo, I've always disliked that particular ancestor of my husband's — wanted to assassinate him myself many times.' Her voice was like cut glass but flavoured with a strong Scottish accent. She shaded her eyes to see us but the sun picked her out like a theatrical spotlight. She was well dressed in the manner of the upper classes — sensible shoes, tweed skirt and woollen cardigan. Though her greying hair was in a tight bun, she looked completely relaxed.

Uncle Fred grabbed my elbow and dragged me up the steps. 'Kitty, allow me to present my nephew, Jack Renouf.'

She held out a slender hand and took mine in a very firm grip. 'Pleased to meet you. I've heard a lot from your uncle. I'm sure you won't disappoint.'

In what way I wondered but said. 'I'm sorry but—'

'Jack, this is Katherine Stewart-Murray, Duchess of Atholl.'

It was out before I could stop myself. 'Oh — one of your class enemies then, Uncle?'

He laughed. 'Not at all, Jack. In fact, she's known as the *Red* Duchess.'

'But you may address me as "your Grace" though I'd be happier if you called me Kitty, like your reprobate of an uncle whom I believe you call *Red* Fred behind his back!'

Before I could think of anything more stupid to say I heard a scream from behind the Duchess. 'Yak, it is you. I no believe Fred. He tell many porkies.' Malita hurried forward, wrapped herself around me and ran her hands over my head. 'Your curls; where your curls?'

'I had to—'

'No, they are lost. Ah, but someone is found. Rachel and...' She let out a torrent of Spanish and rushed down the steps to sweep Taynia from Masha's arms. She smothered her in kisses building up a head of steam which threatened to explode her boiler of happiness.

The Duchess seemed to know Masha and Nicolai and we followed her into an impressive drawing room which overlooked what had been the lawn. She rang a bell and two men wearing British Pioneer

Corps badges on their battledress uniforms arrived to collect our baggage. They looked swarthy and I suspected from their accents they were Spanish. As they left, a gaggle of young children peered in before Kitty shooed them away. Was this place an orphanage? But Rachel was ahead of me and asked the question.

'In a way, my dear. We have about one hundred children here. They are mostly Basques from Northern Spain but we have other refugees from Franco as well.'

'Is this your palace, your…um…Grace?' Rachel asked.

Her Grace was amused but before she could answer two women appeared with trays bearing the ritual machinery of an English tea ceremony. I studied Kitty as she collected our preferences and poured the brown liquid into bone china cups from what looked like an antique silver tea pot. She had a strong face, full lips and a pronounced nose but the really striking feature was her hooded eyes. They sparkled under heavy eyebrows giving her a perpetual air of knowing amusement which I guessed some people would find challenging or encouraging depending on how they felt she viewed them. Her poise and easy manner placed her somewhere between the English "formidable" and the French *formidable*. A good person to have on your side as I was sure she would be a redoubtable opponent.

Fred wasn't in awe of anyone and while Kitty poured he answered for her. 'Kinsale House belonged to one of her Grace's husband's cousins. It was requisitioned as a hospital during the last war then bought by a Jewish American couple who spent a little bit of their fortune restoring it to a stately home. They sniffed the wind blowing from Europe when Hitler annexed Czechoslovakia in '38, didn't like the smell and buggered off back to New York. Kitty was at a loose end—'

'Your uncle means I had just resigned from Parliament over our government's craven appeasement of Hitler and stood as an independent in my old constituency—'

'Jack has some experience of duplicitous politicians, Kitty, so he won't be surprised to learn that your former Tory colleagues turned against you and threw all their weight behind their official candidate and—'

'I lost.' She laughed. 'Good thing too — I was fed up of that spotty boys' debating club and—'

It was like a tennis match with Kitty serving and Fred volleying her story. They reminded me of an old married couple but she seemed to be in her mid-sixties and Fred was at least fifteen years her junior though, thanks to the attention of his Nazi interrogators in Spain, he looked about the same age. They continued in the same vein outlining their meeting in the ruins of Guernica in 1937 where she was conducting an unofficial investigation into the Spanish Civil War. In short, she returned to England to persuade her government to support the Republicans against Franco's fascist Nationalist movement. Despite publishing a book about her experiences few people seemed to want to listen. Appeasement was the policy the majority of the British people seemed to favour if the press reports were to be believed.

At one stage I dared to interrupt the flow of their match and asked if she lived here. She didn't as her committee work extended to supervising accommodation around the country for nearly 4,000 children who had been evacuated to Britain three years previously. I suspected there was other work which was less transparent especially as Masha seemed to have some involvement and my uncle would need more than childcare to satisfy his hunger for revenge on the fascists who had tortured Malita to the edge of insanity.

I must have exposed a raw nerve when I enquired about funding for her work as she railed about the short-sightedness of politicians and praised the efforts of the Russians who had been so helpful. Masha beamed but this turned to a scowl when the "*Red* Duchess" explained that she was also less than delighted with many aspects of Communist rule and, even with her serious misgivings about democracy, could never support such an oppressive form of government. Trying to avoid a storm in our teacups, Fred snatched the bouncing ball from us and suggested that we be shown to our rooms before supper as he and Malita wanted to have a private word with Rachel and thought that Masha might like to show me around.

32

A night at sea in a near hurricane or one on dry land in an English stately home trapped in the cross-currents of intrigue, emotional explosions and drowning in self-doubt? A simple choice but, as there wasn't a boat in sight, I had to endure it on land while keeping my head into the wind and maintaining a stiff upper lip. Malita was distraught over Rachel's rejection of my offer and cried for Taynia. Fred tried to calm her but, as usual, failed and she turned on him, then me and finally fled the room screeching about that *puta* Caroline.

Masha's tour of the house was frustrating as Nicolai trailed us everywhere. At one point she shouted at him in Russian but he just smiled, wagged his finger, and kept following. After inspecting ornate bedrooms turned into dormitories, reception rooms converted to classrooms, and an enormous basement kitchen redolent with the smells of olive oil and garlic she lost interest. Defying Nicolai, she leant in close to me and whispered that, if I wanted to talk, to find her later in the bedroom she had been allocated. That moment was the eye of the storm and my spirits lifted though it might just provide another woman with the opportunity to slap me down. I needed to talk to someone but Fred and Rachel were ensconced in a room by themselves, Malita was fussing over Taynia in hers which left the Duchess in the drawing room. I had no idea how she could help as I opened the door but discovered her chairing a meeting of adults in Spanish and retreated before she spotted me.

There were children everywhere; their chatter in a mixture of English, Spanish and what I assumed was Basque, providing a background buzz rather like crickets on a summer's evening. Masha had told me that the British newspapers called them the "Basque Babies". In 1937 they'd travelled from Santurce, Bilbao's seaport, on the SS *Habana* an old steamship — more than 4,000 children and adults crammed into spaces designed for less than 400 — across the Bay of Biscay to Southampton. That must have been a pitiless voyage and I chastised myself for comparing emotional turmoil with the real dangers of tempestuous seas.

During our tour Masha had taken me into a large room in the corner of the ground floor with a highly polished black grand piano displayed on a dais. Several rows of chairs were lined up in front of it and she told me it was used by the Duchess for performances. Apparently she had attended the Royal College of Music in London and was an accomplished pianist. I experienced a sense of déjà vu as an image of Caroline caressing then pounding her own keyboard flitted across my mind. I mounted the platform and lifted the hinged seat of the piano stool. There were several books of classical pieces and a few sheets of more popular music. During my time at Oxford I'd taken piano lessons in a juvenile attempt to impress Caroline but my tutor had suggested I would be better playing drums as I had no real ear for music. I could read a top line though and I placed one of my favourites on the stand.

This was a Steinway concert grand and Caroline would have swapped it for her own in a heart-beat. I settled on the double-width stool and experimented with some scales. The depth of sound it produced was amazing as was the resonance even in the heavily curtained and thickly carpeted room. Tentatively, because there were three flats in the key, I picked out the top line from *A Nightingale Sang in Berkeley Square*. Last time I'd tried to play her piano Caroline had laughed dismissively before throwing me off and playing that tune with the full majesty of a trained artist. She'd stolen my heart back then. Would I ever see her alive again? I hesitated before the chorus then tried to play the single melody with some expression while singing the words. I'd finished the first phrase "That certain night, the night we met, there was magic abroad in the air" when I sensed that I was no longer alone. The Duchess was watching me. I stopped. 'I'm sorry, I couldn't resist.'

'No, stay where you are. I'll join you.'

She nudged in on my left and shuffled along until our hips were touching. Her perfume was very different from Caroline's; less intense but with more floral tones and it had an immediate effect. She was old enough to be my grandmother, was hardly a beauty but had such a powerful and almost hypnotic presence that my hand trembled on the notes.

'Shall we start from the beginning? Don't worry, I'll follow you.'

She played the bottom line with her left hand and filled in harmonising with her right. Concentrating intensely, I struggled through to the end and let out a great sigh as she finished with a flourish.

She patted my knee and half turned to fix my eyes with hers. 'I've heard about Caroline from your uncle. Why don't you tell me some things I don't know about her.'

Under that soulful gaze I unburdened myself and spilled out all my worries, fears and hopes. She didn't interrupt and when I'd finally run out of words, didn't offer any observations or advice. She asked two questions; who was Caroline's favourite composer and what was the most memorable piece I'd heard her play. I knew that she had a special affinity with Beethoven but the most memorable piece had been her fierce rendition of Chopin's "Revolutionary" Etude at the Palace Hotel the night I almost killed her brother. I was torn but plumped for Beethoven and his "Appassionata" sonata which I'd helped Caroline with when she was struggling to get the sound she'd wanted.

Kitty got up and I followed as she opened the stool and rooted around until she found a music book. 'Tell me, was it the third movement, the *allegro*?'

That sounded right. 'Yes, that's the final dramatic section isn't it?

She flicked through the pages then placed the book on the stand. 'When I nod you turn the page, please.'

There were so many notes that I hoped I could keep up. 'I'll try.'

'You'll do better than that, young man.' She smiled then started to play.

Her version was more stately and deliberate, but it hit me so hard that it was some minutes before I realised that we had gained an audience. I couldn't take my eyes off her, waiting for the nod but sensed more and more people filtering in. Wondering if one of them was Rachel I almost missed the nod but recovered just in time.

Just like Caroline, she came alive with the music, bursting with energy, swaying with the intensity of the climax until, the final notes enveloped the audience and they roared their approval.

My eyes misted over but I felt cleansed. I wanted to kiss her cheek and whisper my thanks but, in front of all these people, lacked the courage. Before I could summon any she stood, bowed then closed the lid and walked out of the room. Entertainment over, the children and adults followed her until I was left alone with my uncle. There was no sign of Rachel or Masha.

He approached holding a book in his hands. 'For the complete Kitty experience I think you need to read this.' He handed over a cream and orange Penguin edition of *Searchlight On Spain* written by the Duchess of Atholl MP, and led me to a comfy looking leather chair in the corner. I sat while he turned on a standard lamp then left.

Hours later, feeling sheepish, idiotic and even more in awe of Kitty, I retired to the impressive bedroom I'd been assigned with a much more adult perspective of my petty concerns measured against the reality of what she, my uncle and Malita had witnessed in a country torn asunder by political and religious fanaticism.

It had been a long and tiring day but I really wanted to talk with Masha now especially about what I'd read and what her husband had died for in the skies above Madrid. But it wasn't even ten p.m. yet. One benefit of this bedroom, apart from a private bathroom, was a wireless set. I'd give it another hour before venturing forth so twiddled with the tuning dial until I found the BBC Home Service. The announcer explained that for the next fifty minutes we would be treated to a piece of music written by Vaughan Williams and played by the BBC Orchestra conducted by Sir Adrian Boult. It was entitled the *London Symphony* but, try as I might, I couldn't hear the sound of one bomb dropping.

I awoke suddenly to the sound of hissing static. It was well past midnight and much too late to bother Masha but I washed my face and brushed my teeth anyway and then with a frisson of excitement stepped out into the corridor.

33

But clever Nicolai wasn't guarding Masha — he was guarding me! My room was near the north end of the west façade. Masha had casually pointed out hers during the tour and it was around the corner in the south wing. Nicolai had positioned himself at the junction of the two corridors and was sitting in a chair facing my room. I walked towards him but he held up his hand in a stop gesture. Only in extremis would I attempt to fight Nicolai, so I waved back, turned right and descended the stairs to the ground floor. Now what?

I'd just wanted to talk to her but now I was annoyed and started to see this as a mission rather than an opportunity. The entrance hall was dimly lit. I listened but all was quiet so I slipped through the blackout curtain and eased opened the double height glazed door. Moonlight filtered through the clouds and I paused until my eyes adjusted then counted the windows as I stole along the walls to the protruding south wing. If I was correct Masha's room was the second one in from the corner. Sadly, no one had left a ladder lying around but nature had provided ivy. I estimated that it was about thirty feet to the window ledge of her room — no problem for a *boy* who'd spent months with commandos scaling cliffs in full battle order. But what was I going to do when I reached the ledge. I could hardly smash the window and throw in a Mk 3 concussion grenade to stun my victim. I'd have to pry it open and struggle through the heavy blackout curtain then hope Masha didn't raise the alarm. Knowing that Nicolai was guarding the corridor would she expect me to arrive in such a flamboyant manner and be prepared? Might she even have removed the curtain and be peeking out waiting for me?

It was cold in the thin moonlight and I was only wearing a jacket over my shirt. My civilian trousers were thin and my shoes not really suited to climbing. I stood back and tried to calculate the odds of failure against the prospect of a success which could easily result in humiliation if I'd misread her signals. Smart money would be on my falling and ending up on my arse in a rhododendron bush anyway.

Sod it — I'd come this far so I might as well have a go. I grabbed two fistfuls of ivy and started to climb. It was easier than expected and I soon reached the window ledge. My feet were secure either side of the main ivy stem which ran up between two of the windows so I was able to stretch across and test the wood frame. There was a slight gap between the bottom of the box sash and the sill and I managed to insert the fingers of my right hand and lever upwards. I'd tested the window in my room and the sash cord and weights had been maintained and didn't require much effort to open. The blackout curtain was in place so Masha hadn't been waiting for me. Perhaps she'd given up. Once I'd created about a foot of space I plucked at the heavy material looking for a corner to nudge aside. There was a dim light glowing from where I expected to find the bed — perhaps she was reading. No, she was talking. To herself? I listened carefully. I wasn't that familiar with her voice but there was another one I knew only too well — Rachel's! I couldn't make out the words through the curtain, wasn't even sure what language they were using but it didn't matter. I could hardly surge into the room now so I stopped being a *boy*, swallowed my disappointment like a man, closed the window and clambered down. There'd be another day.

But it wasn't that one. I'd overslept and when I pulled aside the curtain spotted that the ZIS had disappeared and a khaki painted Humber was parked in its place. I hurried down to the drawing room where Kitty had informed us breakfast would be provided. There was no sign of Masha but I was greeted by a faceful of Saul in full uniform.

'About bloody time, Sleeping Beauty. I was about to come and get you.' He glanced at his watch. 'Get cracking. We're meeting Fleming in two hours.'

'I thought that wasn't until this afternoon.'

'Plans change especially when the Commander's making them. New time, new place; probably new plan but he hasn't told me.'

'Is Rachel still coming with us?'

'Yes, and Red Fred as well.'

'Do I have time for some food?'

'Not really but there's some cold toast you can munch in the car so get your kit, change into your uniform, and I'll make you a sandwich.'

'Where's Masha and—'

He sighed. 'Don't know, don't care. Now get a bloody move on.'

He'd never learned to drive as his father believed him to be a total liability on the road so I wasn't surprised to find an ATS girl at the wheel. Rachel made a point of sitting up front with her leaving the rear for the three of us. I made sure that Saul was on my right so I could use my hand to squeeze some much needed information out of him as we drove.

We didn't get very far as the Duchess wobbled around the corner and started chasing us on a bicycle. Our driver stopped the car and waited until Her Grace, ringing her bell vigorously, pulled up alongside. She dismounted, propped the bike against our rear bumper, and beckoned to me. I opened the door and slid out. It was a chilly morning yet she was still wearing the same cardigan, even more pearls and a straw bonnet on her head. Not quite sure how to greet her but now wearing my naval uniform, I saluted.

She waved my gesture away. 'Follow me, young man. I'd like a word with you.'

I trotted after her forceful stride trying to keep up until she rounded the south wing and stopped out of sight of the car. Her deep-set eyes seemed to shine on me like the searchlight she had applied in Spain. 'A few words of advice, Jack. I know you are not innocent in the ways of war which, like all before, is being fought by young men of your age. This might confer an advantage as you are better trained than most and…from what I hear…can be quite ruthless. But, you won't just be fighting your peers and there are some truly evil men abroad; many hiding in the shadows…' She stopped, removed her hat and wiped some beads of sweat from her brow. 'God, I do sound like a pompous politician at times! Look, you're not a fool. Just…don't believe everything you're told. I don't know who you can really trust but it shouldn't be the Bolsheviks.' Her eyes shaded over. 'They want to destroy Capitalism especially the fascist version but seem to preserve a special hatred for each other if they choose the wrong strain of Communism.'

I must have looked puzzled as she reached for my hand. 'Stalin is a frightful monster — possibly worse than Hitler — who cares nothing for his people and is obsessed with fighting off invisible enemies. His brand of Communism is based on terror and demands absolute obedience.' She sighed. 'There are those who support him at present in the futile belief that once the revolution is secured he will soften. There are others who oppose him secretly and take a more worldly view. They want to create revolution from within by inspiring the workers to overthrow their masters in every Capitalist democracy. Stalin despises these as he believes world domination can only be achieved through *his* leadership.' She paused and squeezed my hand. 'He will do everything he can to destroy these and *anyone* who assists them.'

She released my hand and glanced towards the corner of the building as if she expected someone to appear at any moment. 'Please keep this to yourself and don't discuss it with your uncle but I believe Stalin lost the war in Spain through incompetence. The Republican government was democratically elected and the people had great passion for their cause but he despised their version of Communism because there was too much debate and belief in freedom. Fascists usually stick out like sore thumbs. Take away their uniforms and they seem impotent. Stalin's followers don't need uniforms and are experts in disguise. Believe me when I tell you that they have infiltrated all the Western Democracies. The infuriating thing is that most of them are highly intelligent yet extremely foolish — some might say naïve — but they are far more dangerous than a mob of armed fascists. I'm sorry; I must sound like an eccentric aunt worried about 'reds' under her bed. I think I've said enough but you also need to be careful of that flâneur Fleming — he lives in a very different world and sees all this…' she waved her arm in an almost helpless gesture. '…as an opportunity to make a name for himself. Your uncle still has divided loyalties and I'm afraid that our little Russian widow might not be quite what she seems. '

I waited; expecting her to provide an opinion on Rachel and Saul, though she could only have met him briefly, but instead she replaced her hat then reached into one of the voluminous pockets in her full skirt and extracted a copy of her book. 'I hope you found this of use. Please take it with you. I suspect you would like to discuss it with me but I've taken up enough of your time and they're waiting for you. They will want to know what I said…so show them this.'

I recognised the small cut in the top corner of the cover; it was the same book so she must have retrieved it from my bedroom. I didn't know what to say. She radiated such genuine concern but, apart from what Fred had told her and what I'd confessed to her about Caroline, she barely knew me. He'd mentioned that she was childless and her playing had moved me as deeply as Caroline's, but she was of a different generation. Yet there was a strange connection between us made even stronger after I'd absorbed her warnings about the Communists. So, in the absence of any sensible words, I stepped forward and hugged her. She was rigid, seemingly without softness and didn't respond. She didn't shove me away either, just waited patiently until I'd come to my senses. I felt a flush in my cheeks then she patted my back and I released her.

Her face was expressionless but I thought her eyes held the hint of a smile. The aristocracy are trained from birth not to show excess emotion or surprise but to remain calm and in control at all times and deflect when necessary so she pointed at the ivy creeping up towards Masha's window. I followed her gaze and realised that several branches were broken and hanging down.

'I'm a very light sleeper and, despite the children, this is a very quiet house. I don't suppose you know anything about this do you?'

I was only self-trained in retaining poise under all circumstances but I did manage an immediate reply. 'Yes, it's ivy and can be a real pest.'

She took my arm and led me back to the car.

34

The book seemed to satisfy their curiosity especially when Saul opened it to discover the she had signed the fly cover "For Jack — *Veritas vos liberabit* , Kitty." She'd added another phrase in Spanish. "*Un diente es mucho más que ser apreciado que un diamante.*"
'Truth will free you, eh?' Saul shook his head. 'Bit late for that.' He whispered. 'It might have freed Rachel though.'
Then he shrieked as I dug my fingers into the nerves above his knee. Rachel put a stop to it by leaning over the back of her seat and telling us to stop acting like children, so I wasn't even a boy anymore in her grown up eyes. Fred tutted and pointed to the driver's back and shook his head. I asked him what the second inscription meant and he whispered. 'You'll find that out soon enough.'
While Saul rubbed his knee I alternated between glaring at Rachel's head and staring out of the window as we progressed towards London. We stopped long before the Admiralty and drew up outside a nondescript grey building several stories high in Baker Street.
I couldn't resist. 'So, you've been relegated to your old office. Tough luck, old chap.'
'Don't be daft. Fleming's busy and is going to fit us in between other meetings here today.' Saul bridled at my comment.
He led us through a maze of freshly painted corridors past uncompleted offices where the smell of sawdust dominated until he parked us outside a large room somewhere on, what I guessed was, the third floor. We settled into uncomfortable arm chairs while Saul went in search of Fleming.
Apart from the sound of hammering and sawing the building was very quiet as if its occupants might be talking in whispers. I tried speaking to Rachel but she ignored me and turned to talk with my uncle instead. Her behaviour was beginning to irritate me now and I was about to challenge her when Saul reappeared and, like a dental receptionist, announced that the Commander would see Miss Vibert now. He followed her leaving me alone with Fred.
'What the hell is going on? Why is Rachel being so…' I struggled for the word.
He patted my arm. 'This isn't about you, Jack. She's worried about Hélène. She feels helpless and is just putting on a brave face.'

'But why is she—'

'Punishing you? She isn't and this is not about Caroline or…' he laughed, '…Masha! She's frightened that she might put Hélène in more danger if she says too much. Your boss seems very cosy with the Russians and Rachel believes that they might want to find Hélène for the wrong reasons.'

'So, this isn't about the diamonds?'

'Those cursed things! Not directly but they might have a role to play. I don't know what Fleming's game is but you can be sure your welfare is not his main priority.' He pulled a pipe out of his pocket and fiddled with it. 'I'm not sure what Saul is up to either.' He searched another pocket. 'Bugger, none left. Just as well. Malita hates it. Look, I suggest we wait until we have a better idea of what's afoot before jumping to any conclusions. Can I have that book?'

I handed it over and he flipped through a few pages until he found what he wanted. He started to read. '"*First of all, small parties of 'planes threw hand-grenades and bombs at people who, terrified rushed to shelter….monster bombs tore buildings vertically from top to bottom…..those who were not trapped in them streamed out of the town and were machine-gunned as they ran by the fighting 'planes working in line*—'

I interrupted him. 'That's the attack on Guernica she's describing though she spells it differently. I read it last night. She wasn't there was she?'

'Not at the time…I was though and met her there some months later and tried to open her eyes to that particular Nazi atrocity.' He sighed. 'It appears that we might be here for some time so let me tell you a bit more about Kitty and what she saw and wrote about but didn't get published.'

By the time Saul returned I was feeling quite sick from the stomach churning detail of the cruelty inflicted on civilians by both sides and was more than pleased to escape with him from my uncle's stories. He led me into a small recently completed office where the Commander was seated behind a new desk smoking one of his Specials. Rachel sat opposite smoking as well. To my surprise, the man whose shoes I'd taught to dance was standing by the window.

'Ah, Renouf. Good. You know Philby don't you? He's just taken over the Iberian Desk here. Now, we seem to have made some progress. Rachel has been reluctantly helpful but I now understand why. Philby and Marcks will fill you in on the details but I'm going to have to ask you to go on a journey—'

'Back to France, sir?'

He shook his head. 'Not this time. Portugal first, then Spain.'

My heart skipped a few beats. 'Why?'

He looked like he was going to snap at me but instead inhaled deeply and blew twin streams of smoke out of his nostrils while considering my question. 'Very well. I don't need to tell you how confidential this is. I should really ask Miss Vibert to leave the room but as her information has been key to the plan and she is going to join what we are pleased to call the Inter Services Research Bureau she is also subject to the Official Secrets Act, so may remain.' He removed another cigarette from his case and lit it with the stub of the previous one before continuing.

'Less than a month ago, Hitler travelled to Hendaye, just over the Spanish border in the German Occupied region of France, to meet Franco. It's a little town on the Atlantic coast far too pretty to host those two monsters. We have little information about what transpired but the two of them were in discussions for over twelve hours. Hitler planned to persuade Franco to join in the war against Britain. They'd never met before and, fortunately, it seems that they didn't get on too well. Spain is struggling in every area and only has two things of use to Germany. The first is a continuing supply of wolfram or tungsten which is essential for his war machine. He gets a lot from Portugal but it has to travel through Spain —'

'Tungsten, that's Norwegian for "heavy stone" isn't it sir?' Saul interrupted.

Fleming flicked some ash at him. 'Yes but it's not like that "heavy water" farce you were involved in, Marcks. However, that's not our main concern. Hitler really wants Gibraltar which, as you know, is absolutely vital to our interests in the Mediterranean and beyond. We believe that if the Italians hadn't had their arses so comprehensively kicked in North Africa, Franco might have been persuaded. Now that we've given their navy such a bloody nose in Taranto as well, he'll want to be hedging his bets. But he is dependent on Hitler for a whole range of imports especially weapons and food so we have to exert pressure to stop him caving in and letting the Germans seize Gibraltar.'

'I'm sorry, sir. I don't see how I can help—'

'Of course you don't — that's my job. We've been bribing Franco's supporters with gold for some time and making promises they can drip in his ear but we believe he might find three million carats of industrial diamonds attractive especially as the Germans will pay an outrageous price for them.'

'Didn't they secure their own supplies when they invaded Amsterdam though?' Saul asked.

Fleming shrugged. 'How much is enough? We have more than we can ever use but I'm not in a position to raid those supplies. But, thanks to Rachel, we now have a means of finding that horde your friend Hélène had the *PERSPICACITY* to hide from her masters. If we can persuade her to hand those over we can keep the whole business off the books and away from interfering politicians. Isn't that so, Philby?'

'Yes, Ian. Spot on.'

I looked at Rachel who was peering at Fleming intently. 'Is this true? Will she help? That would be a complete betrayal over everything the Russians fought for in Spain.' I paused trying to frame my next words carefully. 'It would mean a death sentence for her, wouldn't it?'

'Yes,' she looked at me, her eyes misty. 'You remember that people sometimes promise to do anything to save the person they love.'

That hurt. I nodded dumbly.

'Well, Hélène has discovered that her husband isn't dead. He's still alive in one of Franco's hell camps and his freedom can be bought.'

35

Thursday Nov 21st
British Overseas Airways Corporation Terminal,
Poole Harbour.

Saul pointed out to sea. 'That's Brownsea Island. Runway 3a is over there; heading West. It's over a mile long so you shouldn't have any problems.'

'What — even in this sea state?'

'It's only a small chop — nothing to that beast.' He indicated the massive flying boat moored about one hundred yards out from our observation window.

Willie peered at it. 'American, I think. They make everything so big. It dwarfs your Empire boat. It seems too heavy to fly.'

'So, you'd prefer your Heinkel on floats would you?' But, before he could answer, Saul carried on. 'Fleming seems to think I'm a bloody travel agent. I don't know why he didn't use Thomas Cook. If you knew just how—'

'Yes, you've told us but, you're just annoyed because he wouldn't let you go with us. Not that you would have been much use as you don't speak Portuguese, Spanish or French and I've got Willie to manage any Germans.'

'And hold your hand. You're not exactly a world traveller are you? You've only been to France. I've—'

'Alright, you've flown this route before with your father and mother and can find your way from Durban to Lagos and points onward with your eyes shut…and before you tell us how pleased you are with yourself for arranging his trip this time just remember you haven't seen him since *Jacob's Star* sank under you in St Nazaire.'

'We've discussed it…in letters.'

'What's he flying all this way for anyway – surely not to make his claim in person at the Admiralty for its loss?'

He sighed. 'Probably, but he does have important government business as well.'

'So, he will be delighted that you got a free travel warrant for him for the Lagos Poole link then?'

'Okay, he can be a bit of a caricature at times and yes he does fit your joke quite well.'

'What, the one my father and other St Martinese tell about it taking two Jews to make a Jerseyman — especially one who farms in Trinity?'

Willie smacked both our heads. 'Enough with the Jewish jokes, already.'

Saul looked at his watch 'Nearly quarter past seven. They're cutting it a bit fine?'

'Who is? Who's joining us?'

'Not Rachel, if that's what you're hoping. Fleming wouldn't allow it.'

'Because of Taynia?'

'No.' He shook his head. 'He doesn't worry about domestic details but he says she has to undergo training first—'

'With that research bureau?'

'The ISRB? That's just the cover name for S.O.E – Special Operations Executive.'

The thought of Rachel, tough as she was, becoming a British spy made me feel weak at the knees but there was little I could do to stop her though I did wish she was with us now. She was almost fluent in Spanish and would have been a great help in finding Hélène especially as she was the one who had provided the information about where she might be in hiding on the Spanish border with Portugal. Though her information was months out of date and this could all be an expensive and dangerous snipe hunt and Fleming had plans within plans, I did feel a frisson of excitement at the prospect of spending a few days in a neutral country playing hide and seek with all the agents he and Philby had told us would be interested in our presence.

'So, if it's not Rachel we're expecting who is it?'

'I don't know — Philby's made those arrangements. Here are your courier passports. They're valid for a one way trip to Madrid via Lisbon and expire on the 28th which gives you a week to get there. These are the tickets for the first leg. You'll be flying out into the Atlantic before turning south for Lisbon. Should take about seven hours. They're normally really luxurious but now the Brits are running them don't expect too much in the way of hospitality.'

I looked over Poole Harbour. 'I'm surprised that Jerry doesn't attack the flying boats here. They seem an easy target.'

'You don't want another lesson in international diplomacy do you? Suffice to say. It suits everyone to allow travel between neutral countries. We use this route to send agents to Portugal the Germans send theirs to Ireland. We all need channels of communication though don't expect to be offered tea if you end up having a private conversation with the Gestapo in a back room in Lisbon.'

Other passengers were gathering in the departure area before being led to the tenders for the brief sea trip to the mooring. Saul had a copy of the manifest which showed thirty-two named, and two unnamed passengers. Some of these were en route to Durban but the majority, including businessmen from Sweden, Ireland and England, were only going to Lisbon. The military men were also split with some on their way to Madrid. The largest group was composed of American diplomats and businessmen all terminating their journeys in Lisbon.

The majority wore better fitting suits than us but Saul seemed sure that wouldn't arouse suspicion as British civil servants weren't renowned for sartorial elegance. Fleming had insisted that we try to remain inconspicuous and Saul had been given funds to kit us out at a branch of the Fifty Shilling Tailors. My navy blue three piece suit fitted reasonably well and the black brogue shoes would be comfortable enough for dancing should the opportunity arise. Willie's slightly baggy grey suit was topped off with a cream fedora which might disguise his bald head but I'd never taken to hats and mine was on the floor.

As well as our small cases containing a change of shirts, socks and underwear Saul had already handed me a black brief case which contained documents for the embassies in Lisbon and Madrid. Willie had been entrusted with a battered Gladstone bag which contained gold coins along with a sizeable quantity of industrial and commercial diamonds and two Browning High Power 9mm automatic pistols with spare clips and holsters. Saul had also acquired two Shanghai fighting knives with scabbards which we'd trained with in Scotland and these were in Willie's bag. These were diplomatic bags and couldn't be searched. We were assured that another sealed diplomatic bag containing some of Willie's favourite toys along with a rather special leather suitcase had already been delivered to Lisbon and would be waiting for us in the embassy. My courier passport was made out for Mr Jack Aubin Renouf though Willie was now Mr William Green. Both would have to be surrendered with our "despatches" and new ones issued on behalf of His Britannic Majesty by the minister in Madrid if we got that far. At present, there were no women in evidence which clearly disappointed Willie until a very shapely air hostess appeared to check tickets and take the first group outside to the jetty and the waiting tender. It ploughed a furrow out to the flying boat and we watched them helped aboard.

Saul consulted his watch again. 'They'll be closing the flight soon. You'll have to go out with the next group. Whoever Philby's sending is going to miss it.'

Another equally attractive hostess approached our short queue and asked for tickets. Willie doffed his hat and started flirting with her while Saul looked anxiously about before dashing off to the entrance. He returned at a trot. 'They've just arrived but…shit… this is going to be difficult. I don't think you should acknowledge them. Pretend you've never met. There are several neutrals on this flight and their tongues might wag.'

'What the hell are you talking about…' But the words died in my mouth as Nicolai and Masha appeared. She was wearing a plain black dress with a cream overcoat draped around her shoulders. There was no sign of the medal. Nicolai looked uncomfortable in a black serge suit; his massive neck in danger of being throttled by a very tight shirt collar. They must have been briefed by someone less excitable than Saul as Masha smiled a fleeting hello before sweeping to the head of the queue. Nicolai trailed her carrying two bags and favoured me with a brief smirk as he nudged my shoulder in passing.

Willie whistled softly. 'Do you know her?'

I nodded; trying to control my pulse.

'Good. Well, bugger Marcks; I'll be looking for an introduction as soon as we're aboard.'

36

From the outside the Boeing looked rather like a floating whale but inside it was more like a luxury hotel. This one still bore an American registration, NC-16604 and was named *Atlantic Clipper*. Underneath the pilots' cockpit, which towered above us as we boarded over the lower set of sea wings, was a very large painted American flag which might persuade Luftwaffe pilots not to press their firing buttons.

We were the last to board and had to traipse through a passenger section, a large dining/lounge area, Number Two compartment, then squeeze between a galley on the port side and the gentlemen's rest room on the starboard before we reached our allocated seats in the most forward Number One compartment. Our stewardess opened a door beyond that to show us the anchor and gear section which was also an emergency exit. As this was a daytime flight she told us she wouldn't need to demonstrate how to turn our compartment into sleeping quarters. Each area seemed to have its own individual paint scheme and ours was a mixture of light blue and purple with cream seating.

Our port side window seats, which were facing each other, were separated from two rows of three by an aisle. Before I settled I examined the rest room, peeked into the empty galley then opened the end door and walked into the nose area. There was a short ladder leading up to a nose hatch and a longer one up to the flight deck. Another door on the port side looked like it folded outwards to provide an access platform for boats. A stewardess wearing enough makeup for all the women in a small English village politely barred my way, informed me that this was for crew only, and asked me to return to my seat for take-off. I guessed one of the perks of flying to neutral countries was the absence of rationing and presence of luxuries. Perhaps this journey would be fun after all. As she guided me back to my seat I asked if it would be possible to visit the flight deck once we were cruising. She pointed out the spiral staircase alongside the galley and said she'd ask the captain but did assure me that I'd have the freedom of the rest of the clipper once we had reached our cruising altitude.

I hadn't spotted Masha but realised there were compartments further aft to search later. When I returned, Willie was chatting to a group of four Americans who were already seated. I slumped into mine and buckled up as Willie passed me a glossy card with the flying boat's layout and other information to read. One by one the engines growled into life as we manoeuvred out to our runway. As we didn't have any brakes the pilot couldn't hold us while he built up revs so we gained speed quite slowly at first until the airframe was shaking with the combined 6,400 horse power of the four giant engines. Through the intense spray I could just about make out Brownsea Island as the nose finally lifted and the clipper unglued itself — immediately turning from a wallowing whale into a labouring goose.

There was little to see from the port side though Guernsey would be about eighty miles to our south. I listened to the Americans discussing what they could see as we climbed steadily passing Weymouth then Plymouth before altering course to the south-west. Somewhere off to my right was Helford and I wondered if Joe was causing Dot any more problems. Eventually the engines were throttled back and we settled into a cruise at about 15,000 feet. Below the sea seemed corrugated as the westerly wind caught the tide retreating down the channel.

The American across the aisle, who had introduced himself as Brian Avery but I could call him Buster if I wished, seemed upset as I excused myself and started to explore. After I'd reached the entry point where Masha must have turned right the hull sloped up towards the tail and there were three more levels accessed by stairs. One of these contained the ladies rest room and a small passenger section. Beyond that was the final compartment with a locked door. I asked another stewardess, most English women would have killed for her lipstick and stockings, what was in there. She smiled and told me it was the De Luxe compartment sometimes known as the "Bridal Suite" but usually reserved for the exceptionally wealthy or VIPs. I knew there weren't any named celebrities on the manifest but I asked if there were genuine honeymooners or film stars in there. She found that very amusing and confided that on this voyage it was being used by a Russian diplomat and her aide who had paid the purser an extortionate amount for the upgrade on boarding.

I asked if it was possible to speak with them but she explained very firmly that it was the privacy they had paid for and not the sumptuous leather seats. Thwarted, I returned to Willie and whispered the news. Perhaps Masha would emerge for lunch later on so I turned to Buster and introduced myself. Before long the six of us were playing poker using stake money so thoughtfully provided by Saul while I tried to casually extract as much information as I could about our destination from our garrulous American friends.

The dining room held sixteen comfortably around four tables and there were two sittings. I followed our new American friends in and fiddled about waiting to see if Masha would appear. As she didn't, I made an excuse and returned to our compartment where I'd left Willie to guard our bags. This gave us the opportunity to compare notes on the information the Yanks had provided. They'd seemed particularly excited because today was Thanksgiving though they explained it was a bit odd as normally it was the last Thursday in November. However, their Democrat president had decided to bring it forward a week to allow more time for Christmas shopping stateside. This wasn't universally popular and sixteen states had decided to celebrate on the traditional day and call it the Republican Thanksgiving. The others, including embassies abroad, were going to push out the boat tonight and they'd invited us to join them at the Avenida Hotel which was close to the British Embassy where we'd told them we were staying. Apparently the entire diplomatic community would be enjoying the festivities — even the Germans and Italians. I hoped that included the Russians as well.

When our turn came we took our diplomatic bags into the dining room and found seats with two Portuguese businessmen who spoke excellent English. The food was a real treat though I declined the wine. I got the sense from these two that, even though their leader Salazar maintained strict neutrality, the 600 years which marked Portugal as our oldest ally meant that we were more welcome than most in his country. As Masha didn't appear I assumed she was either thinking of her figure or eating in her "bridal suite".

Our American friends were dozing when we returned so Willie pulled his fedora over his eyes and joined them. We were halfway across the Bay of Biscay with nothing apart from scudding clouds and distant sea below so I decided to re-read some of Kitty's book. I was examining some of her footnotes when the stewardess who had been outside the "bridal suite" brushed past me, trailed by Masha. She opened the emergency door and showed her inside but didn't enter. They were chattering in Spanish as they returned through our compartment. When they reached the foot of the spiral stairs Masha half-turned and flicked a hand at me. I looked around but there was no sign of Nicolai. Perhaps he'd enjoyed a lot of liquid with his lunch.

Careful not to wake Willie I got up and followed. Halfway up the stairs the stewardess noticed me and held up her hand. 'I'm sorry, sir, but I don't have permission for you to go any further at this stage.'

'Oh, that's a shame but what about this lady?'

Sensing a problem she interposed herself between me and Masha. 'Please return to your seat, sir. I will try to arrange a visit later.'

Masha touched her arm and leant up to whisper in her ear. Even through the makeup I could see a blush form on the stewardess's cheeks as she pursed her lips and hurried up the stairs.

'Why have you been avoiding me?' I asked.

'Our uncles. Mine because he is cautious for me and yours because he is cautious of me.' She laughed.

'Where's Nicolai?'

'Asleep, I hope.'

We stared at each other. She was two steps higher and I had to look up. 'We can't really talk here and there's no privacy in this plane.'

'Why do you need privacy, Jack? What is it you want to say to me that can't be overheard?' Her tone was teasing, almost flirtatious and I felt some crimson tickling my cheeks now and I didn't have makeup to hide it.

I decided to play her game. 'Apart from our intimacy which is not really appropriate in these surroundings...' I pointed up the open stairs, 'I'd love to know why you are here and if it's to help or hinder our mission.'

She stepped down until our heads were level — her eyes sparkled with mischief as I felt her warm, sweet breath on my face. 'You're on a mission with that rather attractive man, are you? Is he also a soldier?'

This was going to be difficult. 'We're here to find Hélène. What are you up to?'

'Why, the same of course.'

'So why can't we work together?'

She looked to be considering the value of a lie versus the truth when the stewardess glided down the thickly carpeted staircase and told us she'd arranged for me to visit the flight deck now. I took Masha's arm, probing its softness gently and was about to lead her up the stairs when I felt a rough hand on my shoulder. It was Nicolai.

Masha spewed a string of Russian at him but he kept his grip on me. I'd tried to avoid this but it seemed he'd left me with no option. His hand was on my left shoulder so I released her and prepared to pivot towards him then drive off my left foot and bury my right elbow in his neck. Starting to swivel, my eyes locked onto Masha's and the fear in them made me pause.

I heard another string of Russian but from a male voice which I recognised immediately. Nicolai turned away from me and looked over his shoulder. He had no chance now and, drink befuddled or not, he realised that and released his grip.

'Jack, aren't you going to introduce me to your friends,' Willie asked in his most innocent tone.

Social training took over and we all shuffled down to floor level. 'Mrs Mariya Dobruskina, Comrade Nicolai ... this is my companion, Mr William Green.'

Masha laughed at me then offered Willie her hand before addressing him in Russian. He responded in the same language, bowed and clicked his heels. Nicolai looked embarrassed and muttered something while the stewardess retreated up the stairs and disappeared; probably to call someone from the flight crew.

'I suggest that we return to our seats but not all at once. We don't know who's been observing us and we shouldn't be seen together. Masha, you go up to the flight deck with Nicolai. We'll wait a few moments and—'

'Yes — that make's sense, Jack. We'll find some time to talk, perhaps this evening. I'll explain to Nicolai that my uncle's instructions don't need to be taken too literally... *poka*.'

'What's *poka*?' I asked Willie as we took our seats.

'It's very informal... between friends. He smiled at me. 'It almost holds a promise...but, Jack — she is far too grown up for you!'

37

Lisbon :Tagus River docks 15:30

Some enterprising American car salesman had done a good deal here. As we arrived in the terminal and queued for customs I spotted a veritable forecourt of Buicks waiting outside. They seemed almost identical though the one bearing the Union flag was the least highly polished. Alarmingly, the one next to it bore a swastika on its bonnet and, on the other side, stood a gleaming specimen sporting the Spanish flag. There were others, though the American embassy car was a brand new Packard with massive white-wall tyres.

Masha and Nicolai were met by two brutish looking specimens and hurried to a dusty old Ford sedan which disappeared in a cloud of acrid blue smoke. From what we'd been told the Soviets hadn't had diplomatic relations with the Portuguese for some time but there were business connections. I didn't know where they were going but I was interested to discover which of our passengers would be collected by the German embassy. To my horror it was the two Portuguese "businessmen" with whom we'd enjoyed lunch.

Willie prodded me. 'A lesson there I believe. Trust no one on this little holiday!'

That also extended to Saul as His Britannic Majesty's representative wasn't expecting us and sped off with two uniformed naval officers. Eventually, we realised that we'd have to join the queue for taxis. We'd just reached its head and were preparing to explain our needs to a grinning fellow in a rusty old Citroën Berline when Buster called out to us from the driver's window of a cream Packard, which wasn't bearing a flag, and offered a lift. The journey to the British Embassy was very short. Buster told us that nearly all the embassies were in Lapa on the hill leading down to the harbour.

Ours had a rosy hue and appeared to be blushing as the sinking sun shone along its length highlighting at least fifteen wrought iron balconies projecting into the road from the arched first floor windows with LVSITANIA picked out in black above the central entrance. I hoped the Germans weren't planning to torpedo it while we were staying. Before he drove off he reminded us of the Thanksgiving party and hoped we'd join him.

'Out of the question!' The cultural attaché to whom we'd presented our credentials was adamant. 'Everybody will be there. You don't know the game yet. It would be quite unsafe for you to attend. Goodness me, Jerry would love to catch a couple of innocents abroad, don't you know.' His plummy accent was beginning to irritate and, before Willie could frighten his socks off with some explosive German, I asked to be shown to our rooms. 'Rooms? Do you think this is a bloody hotel? You're lucky the ambassador is in Madrid at the moment. He'd be most offended.'

'So where are we staying?'

He consulted a file and scratched his ear. 'It would seem that you've been booked into the Avenida. You'd better leave your diplomatic bags here though. There are all sorts of thieves and agents in that place.'

Willie unlocked his Gladstone bag, extracted the two Brownings, holsters and our knives and dropped them on the attaché's desk. 'We'll take these with us then — just in case.'

The man spluttered, turned puce and thumped the desk. 'No you bloody won't. You can't start a war here. The Portuguese would lock you up and throw away the key and we would disown you. This is a neutral country.' He smirked. 'After the PVDE had amused themselves with you there wouldn't be much left to lock up anyway.'

'Who are they?'

'My point, exactly — you don't know what's going on here. They're the secret police and they've been keeping Salazar's regime in power for even longer than the Gestapo have been torturing Hitler's opponents.' He sighed. 'Look, I don't know why you're here.' He waved the file. 'There's precious little information and—'

'I can enlighten you if —'

He held up his hand. 'The less I know the better. I've seen this before. Some upstart in London has a brilliant idea and sends untrained personnel out to dig around. Don't they realise that this place is crawling with professionals? You two look like exactly what you are — soldiers seeking for a bit of excitement — impossible for you to blend in.'

I shrugged out of my jacket, picked up a holster, slipped it around my chest then inserted one of the Brownings under my right armpit. I did the same with the knife holster and wriggled it under the opposite side. Willie copied me and when we were both equipped we put our jackets on, checked for bulges and glared at the civil servant. 'Thank you,' I read his nameplate, 'Mr Johnson. We'll be sure to include you in our report to those upstarts in London when we get back.'

'There's no need to take that tone with me, young man!'

Willie leant over the desk until their noses were almost touching and, in his best Fleming impression, said. 'I say, old chap, next time we meet it would be wise of you to make sure your socks are freshly laundered.'

After depositing our diplomatic bags in the strong room we carried our personal kit around the corner to the Hotel Avenida which looked like a palace and was truly regal inside. The same couldn't be said for our room which was on the fifth floor with a view of very little at all. Fortunately, it had two single beds which were comfortable enough. We discussed the situation and, once Willie had tired of teasing me about Masha, agreed that we should accept the American's invitation and attend the party which would be held on the ground floor later. Even with the restricted view it was obvious that we had entered a different world as lights were blazing everywhere. War? What war?

Lisbon was an interesting mix of the spectacular and the downright odd. Winding roads led up to a hillside dominated by a multi-turreted castle. Trams clattered about everywhere punctuating the evening bar chatter with their clanging bells. We passed a corner shop with two large brightly lit windows proclaiming ALEMANHA above one and DEUTSCHLAND above the other.

Willie translated the posters and laughed at what he described as infantile propaganda. I suspected that he was tempted to find a brick and institute his own Kristallnacht so moved him on until we found a comfortable bar. The Americans had extolled the virtues of Thanksgiving and competed with each other to list the likely ingredients of a typical feast so we didn't feel the need for any food.

No one seemed interested in us and we didn't detect any one following but as Mr Johnson had explained we weren't professionals — at least not in the dark arts of spying. We decided that, in the morning, we would hire a car and travel north to the border town of Vila Real where we had an address to check. Until then neither of us could think of a good reason not to have some fun with our American friends.

Willie picked the lock of the door which led up to the roof above our room and we wrapped our automatics and knives in pillow cases and hid them in four separate places. They should be safer there than in our bedroom.

After a good soak we each changed our shirts and essentials, polished our shoes, put on our suits and got ready to party. Buster had promised dancing and I was looking forward to some floor-based action hopefully with Masha.

No one asked for tickets or invitations and we were soon tucking into a spread as spectacular as the Americans had promised. I had no idea how they had conjured up hot roast turkey and Brussel sprouts let alone chestnut stuffing and that was only the centre piece as the supporting tables were laden with everything one could wish for in an exotic buffet. War? What war?

Buster and company found us and insisted that we sit and drink with them while feeding our faces. They'd acquired a group of young women who smiled and nodded a lot but seemed to have a poor grasp of English. They were pretty enough for it not to be a concern and everywhere I looked there appeared to be more than enough young ladies to ensure an interesting if not exciting evening. Sadly, there was no sign of Masha.

Everyone seemed to be enjoying themselves and had wisely chosen to forgo uniforms for the evening though the room resounded to merriment in several languages. The mystery of the food was solved when a group of musicians wearing American naval uniform trooped in and set up on stage. Buster pointed out that they were from a cruiser paying a courtesy visit which was moored around the bend from the flying boat terminal.

Once the band got into its rhythm the sprung floor started to bounce then heave with couples of all nationalities gyrating to the captivating swing of American music. As time slipped by without Masha and the atmosphere thickened with smoke and became more raucous I felt morose and resisted the imprecations of my new chums to get up and "cut the rug". Willie wasn't so restrained and must have danced with a dozen women while I sipped slowly at my wine. I kept looking at my watch and as the time crept towards midnight without any sign of the revellers' intensity slackening I decided to slip away to our room and try to resolve a few puzzles.

I was stretching across to shake Buster's hand and give my apologies when I spotted Masha dancing with Nicolai. I'd missed her entrance but she was making herself obvious now as the pair of them carved their way through the uncoordinated mass and created space with an energetic jive.

Willie returned from his latest foray and downed a beer before belching and slapping me on the shoulder. 'What are you waiting for? Go and excuse the bear and show her what you're made of. Hey, if you won't, I will.' He pushed me onto the floor but it would be like diving into a whirlpool until the music changed to something slower. I hung back and watched her intently through the swirling dancers as she sparkled in the light.

After another wild number the band switched the pace and slipped into a slow foxtrot. Many took the opportunity to return to their tables to rehydrate themselves though others grabbed the chance to get up close to their partners. Nicolai seemed unsure so I hurried forward, tapped him on the shoulder and said. 'Excuse me.'

He bridled and glared at me but Masha released herself from his hold and said something quietly in Russian. For all I knew she might have asked him to get some drinks or even go and boil his head but he went.

I took her in hold and spun away before she could change her mind. My mood had changed in an instant and now we sparkled together. Her hair was loose and whipped around as we dipped and turned in the corners. She seemed so relaxed, so happy that my heart was fit to burst and it wasn't from the exercise.

Through the crowd I occasionally spotted Nicolai sulking at a table peering at one drink and knocking back another so I kept us on the fringe of the floor furthest from his lair as the music changed again into a waltz. It was relatively quiet in this corner so I leant in to make a suggestion that we find somewhere quiet for a drink when I felt a tap on my shoulder. Was it Willie trying to pounce? If it was I was not going to yield. I turned my head to suggest what he do with his when the world froze over and I stumbled to a halt.

'Renouf; what a pleasure. I do hope you are going to be reasonable this time. No fisticuffs please.'

My nemesis stood there; a cynical smile etched into his handsome face. His nose just begging for my fist but Masha must have sensed something for she held my hands and dragged them to my sides. 'Aren't you going to introduce me to your friend, Jack?'

My limbs were encased in ice and my voice lost somewhere beyond my reach yet I heard one which sounded like mine say. 'This is no friend. This is Standartenführer Rudolph Kempler of the *SS*. Unless he leaves immediately, I am going to kill him. '

38

'Renouf, how delightfully melodramatic. Look around you, dear boy; is this really your first choice of a place to die?'

Of course he wouldn't be alone and a quick scan showed that four thuggish looking men were spread across the only entrance and staring in our direction. There was no limit to his arrogance but I was fairly sure he didn't plan to strike the first blow. He didn't want to dance either so why had he bothered to confront me rather than have me knifed in the back when my guard was down?

I was trembling with suppressed adrenaline but our training had sought to teach self-preservation rather than suicide and there were a lot of people depending on me. I pulled Masha off the floor and onto the carpet. 'You're right, Kempler. It would be unseemly in front of our hosts though if the PVDE arrest us I do hope they stick us in the same cell.'

He laughed. 'You're quite new to this aren't you? I believe you have an English expression — he who pays the piper calls the tune — best heed that in Portugal and…Spain.'

'What do you want?'

'Why, to dance with the lovely lady of course — if you can remember your manners and introduce her.'

Masha studied his face then said something in German which wiped the smile from it.

He scowled. 'She is very rude but then you always had a poor taste in girls.' He reached out for her arm. 'Nothing that a few turns around the floor can't cure though.'

'No, Rudi. Why don't you dance with me?' I stuck my right thumb between the thumb and forefinger of his left hand in a move I'd practised so many times, seized his left elbow, stepped forward and turned so that we were facing the same direction. I forced his left forearm up across his chest and towards his left shoulder by pulling his elbow over my right forearm then jerking it upwards. He was strong but not fast and I soon had him up on his toes by bending his fingers downwards. He stifled a scream as I whispered in his ear. 'I'm going to release you and let you return to your men but stay out of my way or I will finish you — whatever the consequences.'

I forced him to bow to Masha then twisted and shoved him loose onto the floor. This was not the first time we'd tangled. On that occasion, during a water polo match, I'd knocked him unconscious with an elbow, on the second I'd been drunk and broken his nose with a punch. Later, foolishly, I'd saved him from drowning only to find myself inches from death as he jabbed a knife at my throat before I'd reversed the position and only been stopped from killing him by Caroline. The last time, we hadn't touched, but he'd dragged Caroline from my grasp. And now he held my parents hostage and, short of killing him, there was nothing I could do to protect them.

His eyes were afire and I was enveloped in a red mist of my own. My gun was on the roof but given enough time I could strangle him with my bare hands. We stood like two demented bulls then he grinned, turned his back and I saw his right shoulder move as he reached for something under his jacket. I knew what it was and I had enough space but would there be sufficient time to disarm him when he turned?

I prepared to pounce but two large shapes brushed past me on either side and seized Kempler under his arm pits, lifted him off his feet, carried him across the room and dumped him in front of his men. Willie and Nicolai stood guard over him while he shook himself down, straightened his hair then left the room.

It felt like an eternity but the whole business from thumb grab to his exit had taken less than thirty seconds. Most of the revellers hadn't noticed and the band segued into a quickstep which filled the floor again. Willie and Nicolai joined us and we found a table in the corner of the room well away from the entrance. Willie signalled a waiter and ordered a bottle of champagne while Masha looked at me expectantly waiting for an explanation.

First I spoke to Willie. 'Did he recognise you?'

He shrugged. 'I doubt it. We haven't met since 1936 and we never trained together. I knew him though from the moment he crossed the room which is why I enlisted Nicolai's help.'

The giant Russian grinned. 'Is good, no? We show Nazi pig.'

'Did he have a gun?'

Willie shook his head. 'No, he was reaching for his cigarette case, trying to appear calm and in control. I don't think his friends were armed either. We haven't seen the last of him though.'

Masha asked. 'Is this wise; the four of us sitting together? '

'I don't think it will make a great deal of difference after that little altercation. I'm sure all the agents are aware of our presence — they just don't know why we're here.' I answered.

'So, perhaps this would be a good time to discuss what we are doing and how we're going to do it.' She replied.

After the second bottle of bubbly we'd been as open and honest with each other as could be expected from two sides on what would turn out to be very different missions but united in a single purpose — to find Hélène.

The more he drank the more trusting Nicolai seemed to become and when Willie suggested they find some ladies to dance with he joined him without any stern glances in my direction.

Masha moved her chair closer to mine, took my hand in hers and kissed my cheek. 'You need to tell me all about Caroline and Rachel and this Nazi creature then I'll know if it's right to let you take me to bed.'

39

I told her everything but somewhere during my description of my last meeting with Caroline I sensed I was losing her…and myself…so I asked her about her husband and gradually we both realised that becoming lovers was not the answer to either of our problems. That didn't stop us going to bed together though just for a cuddle. But such is the nature of agreed platonic encounters, where each is seeking human solace, that close contact of flesh usually triumphs over best intentions and I learned that, deep beyond mere physical pleasure, lies something unselfish and heartening which blesses those who find it.

Of course we agreed that this was wrong and we promised not to do it again…twice. Her room was on the first floor, much larger than mine and lavishly furnished so I would have opted for the sofa if she'd let me. Before dawn she suggested it would be sensible if I returned to mine to avoid any embarrassment with Nicolai. As I'd last seen him and Willie heading in the direction of the bedrooms with their arms around very attractive and seemingly willing young ladies I thought he might be the one wishing to avoid embarrassment of his own. It was possible but I doubted that Kempler and his thugs had followed and attacked them. The PVDE wouldn't tolerate such behaviour and were probably watching all of us. I wasn't aware of any prying eyes on my journey through the hotel but I put my ear to the door and listened before inserting the key into the lock. Nothing — no snoring, creaking springs or other human noises, so I opened the door carefully easing my fingers along the frame to test the hair we'd stuck there as a warning about any secret search. It was intact. Willie had not returned.

Alarmed now, I searched the room but nothing seemed to have been disturbed. Hiding our weapons on the roof had been an excellent idea but, without Willie's skill with a pick, I couldn't get up there without smashing the door lock to the stairway. I freshened up then locked the door and returned to Masha's. She'd told me Nicolai had the room next to hers. There was still no sign of staff so I rested my ear against the wooden door and strained to listen. Faint at first then growing in volume was the distinctive sound of snoring — in harmony. They must both be in there. Then I heard female giggling. They weren't alone but the footsteps were approaching. I turned tail and hurried around the far corner until I heard a door close. I knelt to peer around at floor level — another training trick — and spotted two curvaceous behinds swinging down the corridor away from me. It wasn't even six o'clock so I might be able to steal some sleep before breakfast or…I returned to my room and opted for the sleep.

Willie stumbling over the chair I'd placed as a trap behind the door woke me up and I took some glee in asking where he'd spent the night. That was short lived as a battalion of infantry started marching around in my head. Sleep is best avoided when one's body is preparing for the torture of a first class hangover induced by consuming too much cheap sparkling wine masquerading as Champagne. Attempting to drown the throbbing with pint upon pint of water creates a new problem but experience has taught that there are few shortcuts though we'd had the sense to bring one of them and I swallowed half a dozen Aspirin tablets to kick start the healing process.

Willie didn't ask any questions but kept smiling at me as we accessed the roof to retrieve our weapons then went down for something to soak up the poison coursing through our bloodstreams. But this wasn't England and breakfast lacked sufficient greasy protein though the coffee was real and rich and, by the time Masha and Nicolai appeared, my mouth had stopped tasting like the inside of a stoker's glove. They were wearing hiking boots and heavy weave trousers tucked into thick woollen socks.

'Are you going mountaineering?' I asked.

'No, but the address you have is a long way from the city and civilisation is only skin deep in this country.' Masha looked at our feet. 'Fine for dancing and promenading around the cafes, but little else.'

We also needed to return to the embassy to retrieve more items from our diplomatic bags including letters for Hélène from my uncle and Fleming. They had to arrange a car and driver so we agreed to meet at 09:00 where the Avenida de Liberdade joined the top of Rossio Square.

Our friend, Mr Johnson, was less than delighted to see us and kept us standing in front of his uncluttered desk while he made a call. I tried to speak but he held up his hand then covered his ears looking like all three of the wise monkeys at the same time. Minutes later another civilian with a distinct military bearing strode in and placed a file on Johnson's immaculate desk.

He addressed us with a strong Scottish accent. 'I'm the commercial attaché and—'

'Do you have a name to go with the title?' I asked.

'No.' He glared at Johnson, who scurried out; then he settled into his place and indicated we should sit.

He opened his file. 'Renouf, you appear to have established relations with most of the city's agents already. Dropped outside our embassy by Brian Avery of the US State Department, lunching with two Portuguese businessmen who were picked up by a German embassy car, attacking the representative of the Reichsbank and,' he shook his head in mock despair, 'sleeping with a Communist agent. Green seems to have enjoyed a night sharing the company of two of Franco's more attractive female agents with another Communist and now, I understand, you are planning to cause mischief near the Spanish border.' He closed the folder and considered us. 'While we sit here, I imagine my counterparts in the American, German, Spanish and Italian embassies are discussing your exploits. I've already had a call from Captain Menendez of the PVDE about you and he's offered a small wager that we'll be repatriating you in coffins before the week is over. Those will go by ship and not flying boat so whoever was insane enough to send you two clowns over here will have to wait a while before they can count the bullet and knife wounds you sustained in the course of fucking up whatever it was you thought was your duty.' He placed his elbows on the table, rested his chin on his hands and blinked at us. 'Now, is there anything you wish to tell me that I might not already know or provide any reason why I shouldn't accept his bet?'

Philby's briefing had been quite precise and the description accurate. 'Tell me, Major Friedman, are you familiar with this Latin phrase *fide nemini praeter ipsum*?'

He snapped upright. 'Where did you get that name?'

The code was in the name and not the phrase so I responded. 'I think you know the answer to that so you will have to *trust someone other than yourself.* Now we have some questions don't we, Mr Green?'

Willie nodded. 'Do you know why that bastard Kempler is here?'

'It's his first visit but we understand he is meeting with government officials to discuss trade relations which basically means new ways of smuggling wolfram through Spain and greasing palms. You may have noticed lots of new Buick cars in the short time you've been here. We believe that the dealership in the city is a major conduit for Nazi gold which is used to buy influence though Salazar pretends to be above that sort of corruption.'

'Aren't we up to the same tricks ourselves?' I asked.

He sighed. 'Naturally, but the Germans seem to have more gold than us —'

Willie leant forward. 'Would removing Kempler be helpful do you think?'

'It might have been if two British agents hadn't already been seen fighting with him!' He shook his head. 'No, that could provide Hitler with the excuse he needs to invade Portugal and there is bugger all we can do to stop him. For all our sakes, leave Kempler alone and if he decides to attack you then just run and hide.' He scratched his chin. 'How do you know him, anyway?'

I answered. 'It's a long story. I will kill him one day but not while we're in Portugal—'

Willie cut me off. 'That's if I don't get there first.'

'If it's not to kill him then what are you really here for?'

'We can't tell you that but it's nothing directly to do with the Germans or the Portuguese or even the Spanish. It's a favour for someone we want on our side.'

'The Americans?'

'I've said enough. All I can tell you is that we are heading for somewhere called Vila Real—'

'Do you have any idea what is up there?' He studied my face. 'Thought not. On me!' He pushed back from Johnson's chair and marched out of the room. We followed until he opened a door and ushered us into what looked like a conference room and led us to the far wall on which was pinned a large map of Portugal.

He lifted a long wooden pointer from an umbrella stand and tapped the middle of the map. 'Vila Real is in the mountains about 2,000 feet above sea level and—'

'Enough of the geography — what's so special about it?' Willie interrupted.

'The whole area is controlled by the Communists and even the PVDE won't venture there. He moved the pointer to the right. Here are a couple of wolfram mines in the Vale das Gatas. One is under British ownership and the other is controlled by the Nazis. We ship the ore to the west coast and the Germans ship theirs to the Spanish border. The Communists ambush the German shipments and sell them to us for gold—'

'What, Capitalist Communists? How does the Party reconcile that?' I asked.

'The PCP — Portuguese Communist Party — was expelled from Comintern for disobedience so they don't care. Their real beef is with Salazar and the gold allows them to buy armaments from us and influence from the Portuguese. They dislike us but they hate the fascists.'

'How do they view Russian Communists then?'

He smiled. 'You mean your Soviet paramour? With deep suspicion but, at heart, all commies are united by their desire to bring about the workers revolution and end Capitalism though I don't suppose dialectical Marxism was part of your pillow talk.'

Willie shrugged. 'At least these Reds are doing more than talking.'

The major tapped the map again this time further to the south-east. 'Guarda — that's the centre of the smuggling into Spain but the Germans have their own security there. We have some at Vale das Gatas but there is an understanding that we don't attack each other — neutral country and all. We let the gold do the fighting for us.'

'Just gold?' I asked.

'No — uncut diamonds are acceptable — anything other than paper currency which would be worthless if either side lost the war. We used to exchange wolfram for, coal, oil, cotton, wheat, munitions, fertilizer… but we can't supply those anymore because of the U-boats in the Bay of Biscay. The Germans send coal but the commies aren't interested in that.'

Diamonds? I'd tuned out the rest. Could this be Fleming's real plan within the plan — using Hélène's horde to purchase wolfram for Britain? But if she was trying to use the diamonds to gain her husband's release by buying wolfram to send to Spain and then Germany then this could become very uncomfortable for us little piggies in the middle. And what was Masha's part in this? It was all too byzantine for my sleep deprived brain but I resolved to keep the information I had about Hélène to myself until I could make more sense of the mess into which Fleming had flown us.

Friedman was tracing a route from Vila Real back to Lisbon and commenting on the roads when I refocused on him. 'Well, good luck — you're going to need it.' He pulled a black notebook from his jacket pocket and flicked through its pages then extracted a Parker pen and scrawled something on a sheet of paper. He handed it to me. 'Here's the telephone number of Antonio Velosa, the manager at our mine. He's Portuguese British and might help if you get stuck — don't expect him to summon up the cavalry though as this is strictly Indian country and he's not going to leave his fort.'

'Telephones? In this wilderness?' Willie sounded incredulous.

'Oh, yes — electricity as well. The mining areas are booming — bars, brothels, luxury goods, but the roads to the capital are atrocious and they seem to like it that way. Anything else?'

'You don't communicate with Mr Velosa by telephone do you? I asked.

'Don't be stupid. The Portuguese secret police bug the external phones of all foreign embassies. We only communicate via radio using Morse and that is in secure code.'

'Is Velosa's telephone tapped as well?' Willie enquired.

Friedman shrugged. 'Probably not for local calls but the exchanges are very tiny up there and who knows what the telephonists pass on. Best be cryptic and speak in English if you do need to call him.'

I shook my head. 'We need access to the diplomatic bags you're holding for us. One of them contains a suitcase radio transceiver — one supplied by your mob at MI6 I believe. It's a bit cumbersome but I'm told S.O.E is working on something a lot smaller. Let us have your frequencies and we'll agree a one-time code then we can avoid using the telephone. Don't worry we'll keep it short but, if you don't hear from us or we don't return in five days, please let London know and hope that the PVDE find enough of our remains for you to identify and settle your bet. Oh, one other thing. There's a black tin in the bag — do be careful with it.' I looked at Willie. 'Any questions, Mr Green?'

'Just one,' he smiled at Friedman, 'are you wearing clean socks?'

40

Pot holes and poverty was a good summary of our journey into the interior. We'd spent enough time in the Scottish wilderness to pack the right footwear and clothing so, appropriately dressed, we had met Masha and Nicolai and loaded our backpacks and other equipment into a dusty but almost new Chrysler Imperial with mud-splattered number plates. Perhaps the Buick man didn't want to deal with Communists but this was a massive vehicle. The boot was packed with spare parts; tools, inner tubes, cans of oil, four 20 litre jerrycans of petrol and two of water plus several tins of paint. There was a spare wheel underneath the false floor and another stashed on its side but there was still enough room for our kit though Willie clung on to his.

Masha introduced the tiny driver as Severino **Pereira do Sameiro** emphasising the surname as if I should know him. His grey eyes held what I sensed was a cynical humour as he brushed his extravagant moustache and nodded but didn't speak. Nicolai climbed in alongside him. I opened the near-side rear door and ushered Willie in. Masha went next to make a very pleasant sandwich between us. As this model had a floating rear axle there was no intrusive transmission hump so the middle passenger had plenty of leg room. The seats were like armchairs and individually sprung so, if the roads had been in even slightly better condition, I might have been able to snooze though, as Severino worked the car like a Parisian taxi driver, it would have been difficult. Willie once again demonstrated his ability to sleep anywhere anytime as he pulled his fedora down over his eyes, rested his head against his haversack and appeared to nod off. It might just have been his form of diplomacy as Masha snuggled into me leaving her left hand in a place guaranteed to keep me awake.

Having left a trail a blind man could follow we didn't bother to check the split rear windows for the first few miles. It was very dry and the dust thrown up by our tortured tyres obscured everything behind us anyway. Intrigued by Severino's handling skills I leant over the middle of the front bench seat and watched him working the synchro gear box with nonchalance. From the surge as he swapped ratios it was also clear that this straight eight cylinder engine had been fettled and was thumping out far more horse power than standard. This was a sophisticated but heavy car with cutting edge engineering but he controlled it like an expert and I realised where I had heard the name before. Sameiro had been a famous international racing driver but I thought his first name was Vasco. Perhaps Severino was a relation but no matter because, despite the treacherous roads, I felt safe enough in his cultured hands to sink back into my luxuriously upholstered seat and giggle with infantile pleasure.

Masha wanted to know what had amused me so I told her adding the fact that I'd just remembered Vasco's nick name — "**O Rei de Villa Real**". I'd already told Masha that Vila Real was the name of the town where we hoped to find the first contact and that we'd have to travel through Vila de Rei to get there though I'd kept the actual address to myself.

The first forty or so kilometres to Carregado were uneventful though the Chrysler's hydraulic shock absorbers were being tested to their design limits in places as Severino found the racing line on every corner. The next stage, north-east fifteen km to Azambuja, along the fertile plains bordering the Tagus River was less bumpy though fraught with the hazards of horse-drawn farm vehicles. We made better time through to Santarem and reached Abrantes just after midday. We'd already decided to stop to check the tyres and suspension at Vila De Rei which was another thirty-five km along the route. The roads might have been ancient but the telephone lines ran straight and true and Masha had arranged a similar car to ours to act as a decoy. It pulled out behind us at a junction two kilometres short of the town and we speeded up while it tried to create as much dust as possible before veering off to the north-west. We climbed the hill, negotiated some dilapidated buildings and hid in a high walled courtyard then stretched our legs and enjoyed a picnic under the warm sun.

The first 185 kilometres had taken four hours and we still had another 270 to travel. Friedman had estimated that it would take over twelve hours to complete our journey at an average speed of less than forty kph. This little devil at the wheel was going to knock a big chunk of time off that if we didn't become airborne too often. However, the suspension had taken some pounding so it wasn't surprising that a few kilometres out of Belmonte we had to pull off the road with our first puncture. I guessed we were close to 2,000 feet high now but views in all directions were blocked by pine trees.

While Severino supervised Nicolai and Willie changing the wheel Masha and I wandered through the overpowering scent of pine and up the winding track. When we were out of sight, we kissed and hugged. I felt light headed. Was I confusing euphoria with sleep deprivation? It was hardly oxygen depletion at this height. We were canoodling when I heard a sharp whistle from below. Reluctantly we trudged back but stopped when we heard an automobile engine labouring up the steep gradient. Had our followers tracked us down or was this just a local vehicle? We'd seen hardly any cars on our journey so far. In confirmation of Friedman's information, Masha had told me that Guarda, which was on our route to Vila Real, was the centre of a wolfram smuggling operation and the locals used anything they could find to shift the stone closer to the border where they employed mules and donkeys to transport it into Spain. Half of it went in the other direction towards the Atlantic coast where the British paid roughly the same price as the Germans for the tungsten. The Portuguese police were greased by both sides but occasionally there were disputes; some of which led to gunfights.

We ducked down as we approached the bend and peered through the branches of a young tree. A Buick was slowing down and I heard another engine straining not too far behind. Perhaps they were stopping to help. Perhaps not? I still had the Browning in a holster under my jacket as well as the knife. I grabbed Masha's arm and pulled her close to me so I could whisper instructions in her ear. She listened then nodded and crept across the track for a different view. I waited until she was in position. We heard doors slamming and she held up three fingers and pointed below. Willie and Nicolai could handle three men though I had no idea about Severino's fighting skills. They should have had enough warning to grab their own weapons even if they had been struggling with the wheel but the second car was a worry. If only I could get behind them. Masha must have read my thoughts because she raised her arm again and pointed up the track, made a curve shape and circled her hand in the air.

I crawled over to her and gave her my gun warning her that it was in the "made ready" or what the Yanks called "cocked and locked" position with the hammer pulled back, a round in the chamber and safety catch on. She released the catch then ushered me away. As I stepped lightly over the dead pine needles through the trees I could hear voices. I couldn't make out the words but they didn't seem to be speaking Portuguese. Eventually I reached the side of the road and could see the rear of a Buick and the roof line of another stopped several yards in front. Now I could hear Willie's voice and he was speaking in Spanish. I slipped out of the trees and crept towards the Buick.

The driver was still in his seat but I could now see six men surrounding our car. The voices were still calm. None of them was looking behind so I peeked through the rear window and saw that our Chrysler was back on its four wheels and Nicolai was balancing the punctured wheel on the lip of the boot. Did we really want a shoot out here in daylight?

As I was contemplating that, the drivers of both Buicks left their vehicles to join in the conversation. I had no idea what line Willie was shooting but doubted he could keep it up for much longer. I withdrew my knife and sliced into both rear tyres. I doubted they would be carrying two spares but they were identical cars so they could salvage one if they had sufficient tyres. I crept around to the front and despatched those as well. The voices disguised the faint hissing from the deflating tyres but I'd made the first move and there were only two possible outcomes now. Slowly I crept forward to the first Buick and sliced its two rear tyres. I couldn't get to the front ones without revealing myself so, if they had two spares in each boot, they'd still be able to get one car going if we managed to escape intact. I needed a gun. I sidled back to the second Buick and eased the boot open a couple of feet. Praise be — there were two MP38 sub machine guns lying on sacking with magazines attached. I extracted both, slung one over my shoulder then released the bolt on the other and cocked it. These were automatic only weapons but quite slow firing so it was possible to get off single shots if I was careful with the trigger.

I'd experiment on the tyres first. As quietly as I could I lifted the false floor and slashed the single spare tyre, closed the boot and crept forwards until I was shielded by the bonnet of the first car. Willie was looking in my direction and must have seen me as he changed from Spanish to German and barked some commands. In the confusion I stepped forward and loosed two shots into the front tyres then one into the ground behind the eight men. Masha charged down the path pointing the Browning while Willie and Nicolai grabbed the two closest men, twisted them into strangleholds and used their bodies as shields. Severino scooted off to the driver's seat and started the Chrysler's engine. One of our ambushers reached inside his jacket and I shot him in the foot. Unfortunately my finger was a bit too firm and three rounds ricocheted off the road surface and hit two of the others in their legs. Willie shouted something else and those still standing threw themselves to the earth. I stepped over and covered them while Willie removed a pistol from his human shield before chopping him to the ground. Nicolai did the same then they both searched our prisoners for weapons.

I handed my machine pistol to Nicolai and walked over to Masha. She looked calm enough but I took her out of earshot. 'This is awkward. We don't want to give the Germans an excuse to punish Portugal. Any ideas?'

She thought for a moment. 'There's strong opposition to Salazar in these mountains. How can we make it look like bandits?'

'Would they kill the Germans?'

'Not unless…' she looked back at the scene, 'they would humiliate them though. Cars are no use to them so they'd probably wreck them and…'

'Would the Communists get the blame?'

'Yes; but they get blamed for everything and Salazar doesn't have the military strength to fight them up here but…I wonder how they found us so quickly.'

'I don't know but there is a way of finding out if you're not too squeamish.'

She gave me an appraising look. 'After what these fascists did in Spain I have no feelings for them. Do what you must.'

We walked back and I took Willie aside and whispered in his ear. He smiled then marched over to one of the men and hauled him off the ground. Extracting his own knife from its holster he dragged him up the track. Apart from one agonising shriek we didn't hear anything more until the German emerged, stark-naked carrying his clothes but with his socks stuffed in his mouth. The terror was in his eyes as Willie shoved him forward and spoke more quietly this time to our prisoners. Almost immediately they got up and began to undress until they were standing in their birthday suits lined up between the lead Buick and our car. It was tempting to laugh at their discomfort but I managed to keep a straight face even when Masha decided to inspect their small arms with the point of Willie's knife. It made me queasy to watch so I took Willie aside and asked him in French what he'd discovered.

He told me that a special order had been issued by an SS officer that an Englishman had to be captured and brought to him for interrogation in Lisbon. Our decoy car had broken down and been intercepted. From information extracted from the driver the general direction of our travel had been calculated and groups activated along our anticipated route. This one had been posted on the outskirts of Serta and had spotted us as we passed through. If we hadn't stopped for that picnic they wouldn't have had time to set their trap.

I mentioned my discussion with Masha and how important it was to make this look like a Communist ambush and I believed we shouldn't kill the Germans. Even though they had our descriptions and would know who had attacked them would they be prepared to admit it to their superiors? If they did wouldn't they appear to be hopelessly incompetent and a laughing stock?

He told me I was being soft again and that dead men tell no tales but I explained that a massacre would give Hitler a perfect excuse. Even if we buried the bodies, we wouldn't be able to move the cars and once they were found it wouldn't be long before our hurriedly constructed graves would be discovered. Reluctantly he agreed that humiliation would be a safer option and that getting Portugal invaded wouldn't be of much help to our cause. He did remind me that this was now the third time I'd stopped him reducing the Nazi population and he was becoming rather tired of my misguided interference. So he could take his frustration out on something I opened the Buicks' bonnets and let him savage the electrical wiring with his knife while I removed the distributor caps from the straight eight engines and threw them into the trees. After her inspection Masha barked at the Germans and they all snapped to attention. She launched into what sounded like a lecture then pumped her fist in the air and shouted '*Avante!*'

Severino had been busy with a pot of white paint and daubed the same word on the two sad looking Buicks before slapping a broad streak down each of the German's shivering backs.

I asked Willie what she'd said and he told me she had been quite clever. As well as threatening to cut off their cocks and make them eat them if they entered her territory again she gave them a speech straight from the Communist manifesto and claimed this as a victory against Salazar and his *Estado Novo*. She also used the slogan of the PCP.

If I was the German in charge trying to explain myself to Kempler would I tell him that I'd been defeated by an old Portuguese, three men and a woman or would I let him believe I'd been surrounded by Communist terrorists armed to the teeth? After we'd driven for another kilometre or so we started to throw the Germans' clothing out of the windows until Willie remembered that we'd left them with one pair of socks and almost split his sides with laughter.

41

More mini adventures followed, including a loss of traction as the brakes struggled to hold the heavy car on the steep descent into Viseu. Finally, we crawled up an endless hill into Vila Real in the moonlight wrapped in a cloud of steam from an overheating engine. Oil pressure was minimal, the valves were clattering, ignition timing was out causing backfires in an area where trigger fingers were probably quite itchy and the nearside rear shock absorber was buggered. We'd need a garage or at least a barn with some lights where I could get to work.

In the morning I expected the view to be spectacular in all directions. There was some electricity but I doubted Friedman had ventured this far out of the capital as this town didn't look as though it had been touched by the mining boom. The terraced buildings were plastered and whitewashed and clustered along steep cobbled tracks barely wide enough for a horse and cart let alone a car built for American highways but we bumped along until we discovered an inn with sufficient space outside to park.

Severino ventured inside and, moments later, reappeared with a broad smile and ushered us in. Not only was there a bar but several tables in what seemed to be a family restaurant. We'd been surprised at how quiet it seemed as we drove through the town and the owner appeared very pleased to see us and launched into a long speech which I assumed detailed the delicacies he had on offer. Severino appeared to be negotiating on our behalf and very soon we were sipping some robust but tasty wine while unusual smells wafted over us from a kitchen beyond whitewashed walls decorated with hanging agricultural implements. Severino chatted to him and told us that the town was quiet because during busy periods at the mine most of the men stayed at Vale das Gatas about twenty km away over the mountains. Their wives wouldn't frequent the inn without them.

Hunger satisfied by some very fatty garlic impregnated stew produced from a mystery animal and sponged up by crusty bread I asked Masha to find out, through Severino, if there was a garage in the town. There were two but the owner could only recommend one which we later discovered was run by his wife's second cousin, Carlos. "Garage" was perhaps a misleading description though it did have a roughly hewn inspection pit and an old Weaver tyre changing machine. Carlos moved the cart that he was working on to make room for our massive car.

Conveniently, Carlos' first cousin ran a boarding house which he could recommend most highly and was only a few doors away. Miraculously it had sufficient rooms for all of us though Masha thought it would be insensitive for us to share a room unless we were to pretend to be married. I took the hint as we all needed sleep before setting out again in the morning. She was also anxious for me to take her to the address I had so we could enquire about Hélène but I wanted to fix the car first so she had to sit on her thumbs while I played the mechanic.

Willie and Nicolai used the tyre spreader to replace the inner tube on our punctured tyre and inspected the others for damage. I changed the oil, fixed the timing, adjusted the valves and was delighted to discover that we carried two spare shock absorbers. That was the most difficult job but, with Carlos' help, much knuckle bruising and cursing in several languages, I managed to swap the exhausted one. The leaking radiator was more of a problem but Carlos demonstrated his engineering skills by chewing some American gum until it was soft enough then plugged the holes with the sticky mess. I couldn't issue a guarantee but reckoned the Chrysler was good for another day's adventure in the mountains.

After I'd degreased myself and freshened up I walked Masha back to the inn and finally shared the address Rachel had reluctantly provided. The owner offered to show us to the property himself but Masha declined. Instead we followed his directions down the steep and dimly lit streets until we reached a stone footbridge over a fast flowing stream and crossed into what seemed, from the rugged stonework, like a less prosperous part of town. It was just after nine o'clock but disconcertingly quiet, though yellowish light flickered through a few windows. I wondered how the inn could make a living if everyone stayed at home during the evening. Perhaps, some would venture out later. We'd brought a torch each but still had to be careful because of the haphazard construction of these basic buildings. I played the beam around but couldn't see any telephone or electricity cables on this side of the bridge and no house which matched the inn keeper's description. We retraced our steps and carried on further downstream until we stumbled onto a much smaller wooden bridge where the water hissed and tumbled over a steep drop. My torch revealed electrical and telephone cables strung from poles onto the other side though I could only pick out one detached property. It was much larger than others we'd passed and its front door looked more substantial. There was even a knocker and the upstairs windows which must enjoy a good view over the stream glowed with golden light. Masha lifted the knocker but I pulled her aside and told her we should check the place for exits first. My training was kicking in and it had been stressed enough times that front doors could be death traps.

Shielding our torches, we crept around and found a terraced garden dropping several feet towards what sounded like a waterfall. Hugging the walls we discovered two shuttered windows each side of another solid door. On the final wall there was a barred window which was so low it must serve a basement area. I tried to peer in but, behind the bars, was a thick wooden sheet and no glass. A secure area for goods and weapons I suspected. The back door was locked so I tried to lever it open with the edge of my knife. Willie would have opened it in a trice but all I managed was a few scratch marks in the unusually hard wood. It would probably have been sensible to go back and get Willie and Nicolai but I was hoping for some more time alone with Masha so, confident now that I had a reasonable idea of the layout, I led her back to the front door and the knocker.

An attractive woman wearing a heavy skirt, high collared blouse and a thick cardigan answered our knock but, unless she'd changed her hair colour as well as her perfume, it wasn't Hélène. Masha's Portuguese was quite basic but, compared to mine, she was a linguistic virtuoso and, if the woman was shocked by her enquiry, she hid it well. We were invited in and followed her up a flight of stone steps to a large wooden floored room well lit with electric table lamps. A fire spat and crackled with pine logs and she asked us to sit by it and offered us coffee. Even though I wasn't thirsty it would have been rude not to accept her hospitality and, while she disappeared down the stairs to brew it, I spoke softly to Masha and asked her what else the woman had said.

She whispered back. 'She's good, didn't show surprise but I don't think she's Portuguese – possibly French. I think we were expected — be on your guard.'

The Browning was in its holster so I unbuttoned my jacket, eased off the safety, stood up and looked around. There were two doors leading off this room and both were closed. Rugs were scattered around but I wondered if the floorboards would squeak if I tried to investigate further. They didn't but the doors were locked. I moved quietly down the stairs and listened while the woman fiddled about in the kitchen. I noted the telephone on a table near the front door and the passageway leading to the rear of the house. There was a door opposite the kitchen, also locked and one which I guessed led to the basement. I tried it but with no success. My nerves were jangling trying to convince me that there were people behind these locked doors. I tiptoed back upstairs past the noise of coffee preparation anxious now that I'd left Masha alone.

The lights were out. I drew my gun and peered into complete darkness punctured only by a flickering red glow of alarm. My eyes registered the movement but my body was too slow to react as the house fell on me and even the fire was gone.

42

It was either the inhuman scream or the cold water that restored the fire and light but the burning was in my shoulders. As my eyes adjusted I realised my arms were spread-eagled and pinioned to a stone wall by ropes secured to hooks. Hammers cracked inside by head which was just a bell of pain but I hadn't screamed. I fought the agony in my neck to search out the source. It was coming from a naked man hanging by ropes tied to his wrists which were secured behind his back and strung to hooks high above him. His shoulders must have been dislocated but the scream had been provoked by an iron bar swung into his stomach.

The perpetrator dropped the bar which bounced and clanged on the stone floor then mopped his brow on a towel before picking up a cup and sipping from it. Low wattage electric bulbs illuminated patches of the room and cast shadows as two other men moved around. Briefly, I caught a glimpse of the woman who had brewed the coffee and the callous smile on her face. On the opposite wall underneath a large square of wood hung the body of what had once been a man. It had been butchered which accounted for the nauseating smell soaking this charnel house.

Water dripped from my head into my eyes and I blinked desperately searching for Masha. She was resting against the fourth wall looking towards another woman lying in a large puddle on the flagstones, naked, bleeding and soaking wet — her lungs heaving for breath. Her blonde hair clung to her face but there was no doubt it was Hélène. I tried to speak but my mouth was full of what tasted like a urine impregnated rag.

I focused on the man next to me who must have been the screamer. Although battered and bloody I recognised his face. I'd fought with him when trying to rescue Rachel from Hélène...his name was Georges...and he'd saved me from a German. From the source of my pain I thought someone had hit my neck with a weighted cosh. I hoped it hadn't been Masha for now there was no doubt whose side she was on.

Someone had thrown water over me. He approached now and ripped the rag from my mouth. He lifted my head, examined my eyes, pursed his lips, turned away and picked up another cup. I tried to work it out. These three could either be fascists or real Communists. Either way, it made little difference as their purpose would be the same. They would want the diamonds. Judging from the state of Hélène, they hadn't found them yet. The dead one was probably her bodyguard and Georges looked to be joining him soon. But what would they want from me? What, apart from the address, had I kept from Masha? How had they found Hélène? Who else had Rachel told? It couldn't be Saul for, if it was, there was little point in living anyway. Surely Uncle Fred wouldn't betray me? What about Fleming? But why? Who else knew? Philby? But he was in charge of the whole area. If he had betrayed us we had no hope. What about Nicolai? Would he have attacked Willie? And Severino and the inn keeper and Carlos?

My head was already spinning in one direction from the cosh and now my mind gyrated on an opposite bearing but I mustn't let confusion lead to paralysis. As far as I could judge I hadn't suffered muscular or skeletal damage yet. Instead of praying for divine intervention I had to rely on my training and observe them closely in the hope that I could exploit any potential weaknesses in their organisation and control of their prisoners.

The "barman" finished his drink. The slaughter house stench was so overpowering I couldn't tell if it was the coffee the woman had prepared for her guests or something stronger to fortify him for his strenuous work. He put it down and prodded Hélène with his foot and spoke — in French.

He asked her if she was ready for another swim but, before she could answer, he and another man dragged her to her knees and propelled her towards a large wooden tub of what looked like water. She struggled in vain as they each grabbed an arm and forced it up beyond shoulder height and dunked her head over its lip and into the water. Morbidly, I counted the seconds. After forty they jerked it out and let her slump to the floor. I couldn't see if she had struggled but water exploded from her mouth and they laughed.

Our training had been merciless and we'd been prepared for German torture. We'd been warned about the Gestapo's fondness for this dunking method and been tested up to a point. The consensus of our trainers was, that if our interrogators used it correctly, our best option was to try to drown ourselves as quickly as possible. Correct use against strong well trained soldiers involved leverage and the use of wooden poles to control their arms. Just using hands might work on a weaker woman but would not be sensible on a man who should have his hands tied securely behind his back.

Where's there's life there should be hope and I clung to one that was totally dependent on the amateurish approach they had displayed with Hélène. That's if they decided to subject me to the same torture. If they used knives, iron bars or flame there was nothing I could do. Even if they did make a mistake there were three of them and two women who didn't seem in the slightest bit squeamish. Was this really the Masha…but I stopped the thought. I needed to stay strong.

The one who had ripped away my gag returned and prodded me with a rubber truncheon. He spoke to me in French though I detected some underlying Spanish intonation. He asked me if I could help Hélène remember where she had hidden the diamonds.

'Speak in English as I have no fucking idea what you're talking about!'

He laughed then ran the tip of the truncheon down my belly until it rested on my privates. 'Mr Renouf, we know everything there is to know about you including some things which are not worth putting in a report.' He turned to Masha, 'Isn't that so, Mariya?'

She looked up but avoided my eyes. 'Tell them what you know, Jack. I can only promise a quick end if you do.'

'From what you told us that's all he can manage anyway.'

This bastard's English was perfect and almost without accent and once again I marvelled at the Russians' training.

'Well, as I've told her everything I know, perhaps you should try drowning her to find out!'

The older looking one who appeared to be the leader finished his drink, wandered over and spoke in French telling me that he had all the time in the world and that I shouldn't expect any help from my Jew friends as they'd been eliminated. There was no answer to that but it did strike me that these three didn't have the bearing of soldiers or even look particularly athletic but perhaps they didn't need much strength to torture women and hogtied men.

Hélène muttered something and he returned to kneel alongside her. He picked up her head and listened then beckoned to Masha and said something in Russian. Masha walked over and stooped down. She'd told me she'd met Hélène when they were both looking for information on their missing husbands in Spain. Fred had confirmed that. Perhaps there might be some sisterly love left in her soul after all.

Hélène raised her head and whispered something to Masha. She knew we were all watching and showed no reaction but I sensed that what it was had struck home. Instead she slapped Hélène's face and stood up.

'Trotskyite bitch. She deserves whatever is coming to her.' She looked over at me for a long time. 'She might drown first though. Perhaps we need to test her with some fresh meat. I know she is fond of this young man. Let's see how strong her stomach is.'

"Barman" nodded enthusiastically, picked up his implement of choice, approached me and lined up a swing at my lower legs. He spoke in French. 'I'll start down here and work my way up. Hold her up so she can see…and hear.'

'Wait. I have a better idea. He's told me he's always been frightened of drowning. Let's see if we can cure him of that first.' Masha walked over and stared into my eyes. 'Would you like that, Jack?'

What game was she playing? In one of those quiet moments when random thoughts are exchanged on pillows, she'd asked me how I rated Willie's skills against mine and I'd told her that he could beat me in strength, unarmed combat, cunning and deception and that we were even on the surface of the water but underneath he had no chance. I'd even told her how long I could hold my breath. I wanted to spit in her face but decided to play along and tried to paste fear on mine instead.

She laughed and pointed to my mouth. 'See, he's dying for a swim.'

The other two men picked Hélène up and tied her to another hook in the wall then closed on me. They might not have mastered certain techniques but they weren't stupid. The leader pulled out a gun and pointed it at my head. "Barman" untied my right wrist and folded my arm behind my back. The other one did the same for my left. With the barrel of my own Browning inches from my head and both arms gripped firmly now wasn't the time chance my luck. "Gunman" stepped to the side keeping it pointed at me while the other two moved outside his arc of fire, manoeuvred me to the tub and forced me to my knees. I struggled but was careful not to break their grip. I had to suffer pain and persuade them I was helpless before I took my one and only chance.

They used the same method they had on Hélène only this time "gunman" stood behind with the business end of the Browning pressed into my neck. He spoke softly. 'Whatever you may believe when you are under there, lungs bursting and praying for death, we will not allow you to drown. Eventually, when it is time and we do kill you, it will only be after we have heard you beg for hours and you can't do that underwater can you?'

I didn't need to simulate trembling as my knees were shaking of their own volition. Slowly they levered my arms upwards and forced my shoulders down and where they went my head followed. The water was cold and before my nose disappeared under it I was aware of the stink of blood mixed with urine. I sucked in a mouthful and held it in my cheeks then started to count. After sixty I started to struggle even though I had plenty of breath left. There is no trick to this but an understanding of what is happening is vital to prevent panic. I surrendered to the "diving reflex" like I'd been trained and felt my pulse slow as my metabolism began to reduce the need for oxygen and conserve energy in the cold liquid. They held me down for another fifteen seconds then hauled me out and let me collapse to the floor like a stranded fish. I thrashed about and spewed out the water aware that the gun was still trained on me.

Dimly, I heard the leader ask Hélène if she had anything to say. Her answer couldn't have been to his liking because I was dragged up again and thrust back into the tub. I could have broken free but with the gun still commanding the situation it would have been the iron bar and a gradual destruction of my body so I kept up the pretence and allowed them to hold me down. This time I struggled after fifty seconds but they held me down for a further forty before dragging me up and dumping me on the floor. I writhed and spewed trying to release some of the carbon dioxide which had been trapped in my body, burning its way into my lungs. I needed to prepare myself for the next dunking which would test my training to the limit when my diaphragm would spasm as my blood acidified and I might very well drown if they held me down too long. Under normal conditions I could hold my breath underwater for well over three minutes but this wasn't an exercise and several lives depended on how well I could manage the next immersion.

Before they thrust me under Masha knelt down and spoke in English. 'I think you might be ready after this, don't you Jack?'

I managed a brief nod then they shoved me under. Perhaps they'd had enough and didn't have the energy to batter me with iron bars but they kept me down ignoring my writhing. There would be worse ways of dying so I struggled harder which used up oxygen and reduced my reserves. After two minutes of counting I felt the first spasms and my lungs seemed to be on fire. I struggled helplessly for another fifteen seconds then relaxed and tried to become limp. Staying still was harder than fighting and deceiving my body almost impossible but after another twenty seconds I felt their grip loosening and sensed them standing back. Everything now depended on how correctly or incorrectly I had understood Masha's question.

A hand tugged at my hair and I felt my head lifting into the air but I didn't take a breath and it dropped me again and my neck hit the side of the tub leaving one ear out of the water. I could hold on for another thirty seconds but no more before my body forced me to breathe.

After twenty and on the point of fainting and surrendering to my innate reflex for survival I heard Masha's voice followed by a crash and a startled shout. I rose from the tub and smashed my right elbow into the nearest body part I could find. As I'd started from a kneeling position and my nearest torturer was standing that was his testicles. Before he could collapse onto me I rolled away and kicked out at the other man's knees. They folded and, using the heavy tub for purchase, I smashed my left elbow into his temple. Still moving, I spotted Masha slicing open the leader's throat then turning sharply to stab the coffee maker in the chest. The two who had been drowning me were in distress on the floor. Realising we might need some information I broke the neck of the one holding his testicles but slammed the other's head against the tub until he went limp in my hands.

When he came round I'd see how long he could hold his breath but my immediate concern was Masha and how far I could trust her. After that I'd need to turn my mind to Willie and Nicolai but for now I had a question.

I inspected Hélène. She was in considerable pain but her eyes were focused and there seemed to be a slight smile on her battered face. I spoke to her in English. 'What did you say to Masha?'

She grimaced, swallowed then whispered. 'I told her that they've been lying to her and that her husband wasn't killed. He's alive and being held hostage with mine. I promised her you'd help us find them.'

43

These Communists were a wonder to behold but there wasn't time for discussion. I cut her down and placed her as gently as I could on the floor. She was in shock and needed warmth and nursing but she begged me to help Georges. With Masha's help I untied him but he was barely conscious. His wounds were horrific and as I lowered his broken body to the ground I felt an anger so consuming that I wanted to lash out at both Masha and the venomous torturer now helpless at my feet. She must have sensed my fury and she stepped back.

'You're right. I haven't been completely honest with you and probably deserve whatever punishment you are planning but…' she sank to her knees, '…help me save my Anatoliy first.'

I didn't have time for this melodramatic nonsense and shoved her aside. 'Now is not the time. We'll talk later. Do something useful. Help Hélène over here. She wants to talk to her…friend.' I almost choked on the last word but held myself in check long enough to bring them together.

Hélène stroked Georges' face with her blood encrusted hands and whispered in French to him. I couldn't catch the words but the meaning was clear enough. His undamaged eye flickered open and a rictus of a smile crossed his battered face as it focused on me. His lips moved and he mouthed the word "*merci*" before his neck jerked and his head collapsed onto Hélène's hand. His body gave one last violent spasm as his spirit fought its way free and Hélène cried out in despair.

As Masha lifted her up and helped her towards the stairs, I noticed that the "barman" had regained consciousness and was trying to crawl away. I fought the almost overwhelming desire to smash him to pieces with the iron bar he had so cruelly used to demolish his prisoners but I wanted him alive for a while. He had things he needed to tell me. Almost indifferently, I watched him sliver into the pool of gore surrounding the woman Masha had so coolly despatched then I grabbed the bloodied rope which we'd untied from Georges and hogtied the bastard until he was immobile. Moving quickly now to use up the destructive energy foaming in me, I cut down Hélène's other brutally used friend and dragged his corpse over to lie next to Georges.

Now for the task which Willie would have relished but the prospect of which turned what bile was left in my stomach to acid. I grabbed his hair and dragged him towards the tub. I'd tied rope around his ankles which pulled his legs backwards until they almost met the similarly restrained arms behind his back. I tightened the knots then rolled him onto his side, picked up the iron bar and prodded his face.

Trying to control my voice to eliminate any doubt in his mind of my determination I spoke to him in French and explained that he had a choice. If he answered my questions promptly and honestly I would allow him a quick end but if he lied or failed to cooperate I would use the bar on him as he had on the others and leave him to an agonising death in the dark. His eyes betrayed his fear and something else. For all the Communist clap trap, he was just another sadist, empowered by a ruthless state apparatus, who truly enjoyed carrying out his orders. Not someone who was prepared to sell his life for a noble cause.

Soon I knew all about how they'd found Hélène though he didn't know who had made the phone call which set them on their journey through France. I even got confirmation of the hatred Stalinists had for anyone they believed was deviant — especially those who might have followed Trotsky before he was assassinated months before. He told me about their route in and where they had hidden their car. I asked him about Masha and he said they'd been surprised to find her here but she was known to the leader who believed she was there for the same reason and could be trusted. Because of her relationship with Ambassador Mayskiy, he believed she was still true to the cause despite her husband. He didn't know much about him other than the fact that he was on a very long list of undesirables who were still alive and out of the State's reach. It seemed that Stalin distrusted anyone who had been foolish enough to be captured in the Spanish war. The name Nicolai meant nothing to him but that didn't relieve my worry about Willie and what might have happened since we left him in the garage.

Finally, I asked him what they'd learnt from their prolonged and inhuman torture of Hélène and her two men. "Nothing", he said and then started to beg and whine and… but one glance around the bloody dungeon removed the final vestige of pity from my heart. I dropped the iron bar and, while it clattered into silence, I dragged him to the tub then tipped him in head first. I looked away until I guessed that both three minutes and the vicious brute had expired.

Masha had pulled up a sofa, wrapped Hélène in a blanket and settled her upstairs by the fire. She'd washed the blood from her face which seemed relatively unmarked and was dabbing iodine on cigarette burns on her breasts. Hélène pulled the edge of the blanket up to her neck as I grabbed the bottle of brandy. I took a good swig to cleanse my mouth then spat it out onto the hearth where it sizzled like the adrenaline now flooding my body. I took another mouthful but swallowed it this time letting the alcohol warm me from inside.

Hélène released her hand from the blanket and seized mine. It was only a few months since I'd last seen her but she looked ten years older. Yet, underneath the tang of the iodine and the stench of the brutality to which she'd been subjected, was still a trace of *Vol du Nuit*. She didn't speak, just gripped my fingers and took deep breaths. Masha told me to look after her while she found some clothes. Soon, she returned from the bedroom area having found something else — another body. She broke the news and tears dripped from Hélène's cheeks. I tipped the bottle to her lips and let some of the fiery liquid do its work. By my count we now had seven bodies in the house, three of whom must have been close to Hélène. The others would have families as well but, if we did what was now necessary, they wouldn't discover their well-deserved fate for years if at all.

The brandy must have loosened Hélène's tongue because she spoke in a hoarse whisper to me in English tinged with her faint French accent. 'I once told you that you've never be Jewish but…I now think you would make a fine Communist.'

Masha laughed but I'd lost my sense of humour. 'What? Like one of those Stalinist thugs? I think I'd rather be—'

Masha interrupted. 'They're not Stalinists; they're not really Communists — just criminals. They—'

'But—'

Hélène squeezed my hand. 'How much are those diamonds worth?'

'Last year…the Germans were prepared to pay over nine million pounds for them though they were illegally purchased for less than half a million. I suppose they wouldn't pay so much now after capturing Holland but—'

'In our system I only pass information upwards to one man. He told me to keep the diamonds safe until he got an answer from higher up about what to do with them...I don't think he...' She swallowed and tried to catch her breath.

'So when he discovered that you wanted to use them to buy your husband's freedom he panicked and sent these monsters to find you and extract their location...by whatever means?'

She nodded.

I looked at Masha. 'So; that I can understand — but what about you? Why didn't they tie you up?'

She sighed. 'They thought they could persuade me that Hélène was a traitor and, as my uncle is—'

'But how did they know you?'

'You've seen the medal I wear — Stalin made me a celebrity, sent me around the embassies and—'

'Now, your husband's still alive will he want it back?'

Hélène answered. 'Worse. He distrusts everyone but those who have been captured and are famous he fears the most. Masha's husband may be alive but to Stalin he is dead!'

I slumped onto the sofa and studied the two women's faces looking for...deceit? Guilt? After a minute or so I was none the wiser. Could I trust my instincts?

'Where did you learn to fight like that?' I asked Masha.

She smiled. 'We have a different view of a woman's role in our system. We know we will never be as strong as men — with the exception of Yuliya of course — but there is little discrimination. We make excellent snipers and tank drivers and with a little training can wield a knife just as mercilessly as any English gentleman—'

'Untroubled by conscience no doubt—'

'Yes, and we won't have to explain ourselves to St Peter outside your bloody pearly gates either!'

Touché so I changed the subject. 'Where are the diamonds now?'

Hélène took another sip of brandy then answered. 'Twenty-one crates are in Brittany near the coast. Georges and I emptied the other one and divided them into ten packets of about two kilos each. We brought them over with us. They're in the garden.'

It hurt my pounding brain but I managed the calculation. 'The Germans might pay up to £40,000 for each of those packets but they were virtually worthless to us. Saul tells me we have over twenty-five million carats sitting in vaults in London. I'm guessing you have a Spanish contact who'll give you a fraction of the price and then sell them to the Nazis. Am I right?'

She nodded.

'And for this he's promised to bring your husbands to you?'

'No. He can't do that.'

'So, what's your plan?'

She swallowed again. 'He can help them escape but he can't get them over the border...' She looked at Masha, 'that's why we need you.'

44

That wasn't my immediate concern. Willie was outnumbered and I had to find if Nicolai and the other commies had turned on him. Masha assured me that they wouldn't have but I needed to see for myself. I couldn't leave her with Hélène so grabbed her hand and dragged her out of the house. I frisked her none too gently for any hidden weapons then pushed her up the hill ahead of me. There were few certainties here but one did stand out — Hélène would never reveal the location of the bulk of the diamonds unless we helped her recover Juan. The Gestapo's most inventive torturer might destroy her body but even he would be defeated by the strength of her mind. Willie and his socks would just make her laugh.

Just as he was amusing the others when we found them in the bar playing his favourite game of Skat with, what he always assured me was, an unmarked deck of cards. I didn't want to alarm them so when Willie asked if we'd discovered anything I lied and told him we'd found our friends and had been invited to stay with them. I asked Masha to explain this to the Portuguese, thank them for their help and pay them for the lost income from the guest house. Willie yawned before insisting we all have another drink then catch some sleep. We joined them and I kept between Masha and Nicolai so they couldn't converse in Russian as we downed something fiery called *aguardente*. After, we excused ourselves and wandered back to the boarding house to collect our bags before setting off down the hill again not speaking until we reached the house.

Once inside I let her give Nicolai the news about her husband. At first he was incredulous then exploded with joy, swirled her round, kissed her cheeks and shook everyone's hands to express his gratitude and delight. When he had calmed down I explained what had happened and showed them the mess. Willie had lots of questions but I insisted we clean up first. I removed the brute from the tub and untied him. There were only a few superficial bruises and from a casual inspection it would appear that he had drowned. The one whose neck I'd broken could also pass as a similar victim. The one with the slit throat and the woman with the knife in her chest would be more difficult. Georges and the one destroyed by "barman" would need to be buried as would, Dolores, Hélène's Spanish friend whom we'd found upstairs but would Carlos and his relations be inquisitive enough to search the property after we left? If so, what would they do if they found graves?

We had a discussion and came to the conclusion that, as we needed the house as a base, we'd have to take that chance. In the morning we would look for a suitable location. As this whole area was littered with old mine workings it shouldn't be too difficult to find a shaft for the two with visible wounds while the other two could be dumped into the gorge where the fast running water would take them miles downstream. Police presence in this area was minimal and, according to Masha's interpretation of Severino's comments, easily bribed into silence. In the fragments of moonlight we dug three graves in deep soil near the edge of the garden. It was private in that corner and in the morning I felt sure that Hélène would want to say goodbye to Georges, Dolores and, what remained of Miguel, properly.

After our exertions we sat around the fire talking quietly over a map with Hélène trying to work out how best to rescue two prisoners who had been incarcerated by Franco's thugs for nearly three years. According to her they were both working as slave labour in the Barruecopardo mine over the border in Spain. It was nearly one hundred km away as the crow flies over mountainous terrain and there were no proper roads. The big problem was the Duero River which defined the border in this area. The only road crossing was at Vilar Formoso where the Germans had the guards in their pockets. However, other enterprising Portuguese had established their own smuggling routes using mules and there must be a narrow part of the river where a crossing could be made by raft or other means. Severino volunteered to find out what he could though he warned us that for most of the route the sides of the Duero were steep cliffs and impassable without ropes. Willie and I had sufficient bruises from our training in Scotland to see that as not too difficult an obstacle. We'd need ropes though and hauling men weakened by years of hard labour and beatings up vertical cliffs wouldn't be easy or contribute much to their chances of recovery.

Before she fell asleep Hélène made us promise that we'd do everything we could to save their husbands. Masha stared at me as I agreed and I accepted the naked challenge in her eyes. There were three bedrooms. Severino agreed to stay with Hélène and sleep on the second sofa. Willie and Nicolai took a bedroom each once Hélène was asleep, I suggested Masha share a room with me. We both realised that the only activity would be talking but that was far more important than anything else.

As she talked I practised a new skill of uninterrupted listening. At times she was almost manic in her intensity. I learnt more than I needed to know about Captain Anatoliy Dobruskina and their brief time together before he "volunteered" to help the Republicans in Spain. They'd been friends for many years before they fell in love, had been especially trained in foreign languages and other essential skills for those selected to serve the cause abroad. By turns she was excited at the prospect of seeing him again, disbelieving that he had survived, guilty that she had betrayed him with me and desperate to assuage that with her life if necessary. A picture emerged of a young man only twenty-three when he was shot down with a wry sense of humour and an absolute dedication to turning the world order on its head. I found this difficult to reconcile and wondered if she was exaggerating either his humour or his dedication to a cause I found so alien. I supposed that if the State had total control of your upbringing and education it was almost certain to steal your soul. If you resisted then the same State which had invested so much time and energy in indoctrination would dispose of you without mercy. To that extent it wasn't so different from the Catholic Church in the middle ages. But, fighting the urge to debate, I continued to listen and discovered so much more about Masha. By the time she'd talked herself to sleep she'd stolen even more of me and provoked such an intense jealousy that I didn't really want to save this superman of hers.

45

Drinking cheap brandy on top of a coshing probably isn't the most sensible way of treating a headache and it felt as though a brigade of miners was excavating wolfram from my skull with pickaxes when Willie shook me awake. I needed his help to stagger from the floor and down the stairs and allowed him to alleviate my symptoms with streams of cold water splashed over my head from an old long-handled garden pump.

Spicy chorizo sausage and stale bread passed for breakfast before we assembled at the foot of the garden to pay our last respects to Hélène's friends. She looked far better than I felt and managed a few words in French to thank them before we lowered them into the graves and shovelled the rich earth over their bodies which we'd shrouded in a mixture of sheets and curtains. We did our best to disguise the freshly dug earth with rocks and stones as well as replanting some shrubs over them. I wondered if we should mark their graves with small crosses but held my tongue in respect as I didn't think she'd want their journey to Communist heaven to be compromised by any Christian symbols. As I shivered in the early morning cold I was heartened by the spectacular views across the valley and thought this as good a spot as any to be laid to rest. Hélène interrupted my musing to hand me a shovel and took me to the spot where she'd hidden the diamonds. Soon I had swapped them for the bodies which seemed a bitterly unfair exchange and slumped to the moist earth dizzy from more than shortage of blood circulating in my befuddled brain.

Willie dragged me back inside, inspected my eyes and waved a finger in my face. I followed it wondering where the digit was going next but he withdrew it and pronounced me fit enough to continue. We needed to contact Velosa at the mine in Vale das Gatas but I was reluctant to risk the telephone. Willie was better trained than me in wireless communications so I suggested he get the suitcase transceiver from the Chrysler and set it up in the highest part of the house. When he returned it took a few minutes to string the aerial along the roof line and then we had to wait for the valves to warm up. This gave me time to code a short message asking if we could visit the mine the following morning and mentioned Friedman's name. When the set was ready and the correct frequency selected Willie took my message and tapped out the coded call sign we'd asked Friedman to forward to Velosa. Philby had told us that apart from the weight and underpowered battery the other problem with this set was the lack of side tone which meant Willie couldn't hear his own message on air and had to rely on the clicks of the Morse key which were difficult to hear through the headphones. I could just about follow as his hand was much faster than mine but had to watch his face to see if he was getting a response. He shook his head then tried again. Another minute passed without reply and I was about to give up and risk the telephone when he gave me the thumbs up and started keying the coded message. He waited impatiently rolling his eyes at me in frustration then he started writing down a series of letters. I decoded as he wrote and it appeared that Friedman had done as promised. Velosa would receive us after 09:30. All his miners would have returned home for the weekend by then. I'd already coded a few possible responses and gave Willie the one confirming with an ETA of 10:30 that morning.

That settled, I gave Willie the directions to find the car our departed enemies had hidden nearby. While he and Severino were away, Nicolai and I carried the bodies of the unfortunate pair who were about to experience an accidental fall several hundred metres into the gorge below the garden. Judging from the speed of the cascading water anyone finding them would be hard pressed to determine the actual scene of the accident.

As we returned from our task Severino appeared and ushered us out onto the track to display his new find — an oddly elegant if dented and dusty Peugeot 402 with its headlights behind the heart shaped radiator grill. While he fiddled around with the engine and checked the tyres, Willie and Nicolai carried out the two who wouldn't pass as drowning victims and squeezed them into the boot. They sped off to the nearby old Roman mine workings to find a suitable shaft for their disposal. We'd discussed the possibility that the three bodies we'd buried might be discovered but Hélène was adamant that they shouldn't be thrown down a shaft or tossed into the river so perhaps there was some hope for her after all.

By the time Severino returned with the Peugeot I had retrieved the Chrysler from Carlos and had half of our belongings and equipment loaded in its boot. We put the rest into the Peugeot, locked up, and finally just before 09:30, Masha and Hélène joined me and we set off for Vale das Gatas. Hélène had been there before and as we negotiated the twisting track which rose up to the mine we had to pull over for an ancient bus which was probably carrying the weekday miners home to put a smile on our inn keeper's face.

Antonio Velosa would have passed as an English gentleman though, because of his dark skin, might not have easily gained admission to one of the more snobbish London clubs. He was charming and seemed pleased to see us though I sensed some alarm in his deep-set brown eyes as we trooped into his office. I suspected that Friedman had been in touch as he offered any reasonable service he could for His Majesty's representatives. As I was the closest to an Englishman in our motley group I thanked him on the King's behalf.

He produced some excellent coffee and told us a bit about the mine including the location of the staff especially the armed guards who remained for the weekend. There'd been an increasing amount of banditry as the value of wolfram had shot up dramatically. While the main German owned mines were further south around Guarda the one across the valley had suffered some losses recently. Though he didn't confess I got the impression that he had been paying some of these bandits to relieve the Germans of several tonnes of the hard rock which he mixed in with his own before sending it to the coast for shipment to England. He apologised but informed us that because of the possibility of the Germans being tempted to play the same game he couldn't spare any of his guards for whatever scheme we had in mind but would offer advice and any other practical help that was feasible.

We discussed the plan we'd hatched but he was very sceptical about crossing the river as he explained that, though the Duero levelled out from its source at over 2000 metres high in Spain on its 900 kilometre journey to Porto on the coast, in this area around the border, it fell 500 metres over a relatively short distance. There were some places where it might be crossed in summer; but this time of the year the midstream currents ran faster than a galloping horse.

I explained that two of us were trained to swim across such currents and he suggested that we carry out an inspection of the least treacherous spot before we decided. Although we'd discussed inserting Willie and me into Spain in this manner I wasn't that keen to swim against such rapid currents in cold water especially as we'd have to do it in the dark. However, it did provide the shortest route to the Barruecoparedo mine where Juan and Anatoliy were slaving away digging out Spanish wolfram. We'd studied the Michelin road map and our more detailed War Office General Staff Geographical Section sheets and thought we could swim the 900 or so metres across the current towing our clothes and boots on floats behind us. Covering the nine kilometres from the river to the farm when Hélène's agent was planning to hide the two men would be simple enough if there was sufficient moonlight. We'd then protect them until the transport arrived.

The alternative was to put all our eggs into the two baskets we planned to hijack. We'd need the two trucks to extract everyone though it was possible that we could manage with one and a car. Velosa had told us about the regular Sunday shipment from the German mine on the eastern side of Vale da Gatas which drove down to Vila Formosa and crossed over the bridge into Spain. This involved border guards and customs officials on both sides but the Germans had paid them off and they were usually happy just to collect their presents without inspection and wave the trucks through. They didn't even bother to stop them on the return journey but, as with all corrupt bureaucracies, there were times when changes of personnel, inspections or sudden loss of memory caused problems.

As we had time to spare and would have to spend the night here anyway I suggested that Severino drove Masha and myself to the river side near Freixo de Espada à Cinta and Willie and Nicolai carry out a reconnaissance of the German mine while Hélène gathered her strength.

It was a pleasant enough day and the scenery, once we'd left the desolation of the mine workings, was majestic but, after an hour bumping along, I began to regret the decision as sleeping would have been a more profitable use of my time. Masha curled up on the back seat like a cat and managed to rest but by the time we reached our destination I'd gone off the whole idea. When we scrambled down to the river's edge I accepted that Velosa was right. Even a boat with a powerful outboard would have difficulty getting across the surging torrent in the middle of the river. If we started about five kilometres up stream we might just struggle across the flow and land in our intended spot but it could take hours in water which felt very cold indeed.

We'd have to take our chances with bluff and Sunday sleepy guards in both directions. Velosa estimated that the return journey would take at least fifteen hours and, as we had to time it to ambush the two trucks shortly after they left their mine at 08:00, we wouldn't be back until well after dark. These trucks had an established routine and if we returned too early for the bridge crossing the guards, however well bribed or sleepy, would be suspicious on either or both sides. I swapped places with Masha for the three hour return journey from our abortive mission but couldn't get comfortable enough to sleep especially when I reflected on something else I had learned from Velosa.

Hélène had asked him why the Germans were shipping wolfram from one mine to another and not sending it straight to Germany. He'd told her that he didn't know the answer but I'd read something in his eyes which suggested he might be lying and had asked him again when she'd left the room. He explained that everything was driven by money — especially in the case of the poverty stricken Spanish — greed and graft. From his information he believed that Spanish mines had been set quotas for wolfram production and severe punishment would be meted out to their managers, who were paid a pittance, if they weren't met. Franco's secret police, who controlled the prison camps, provided labour and a per capita allowance for feeding the "slaves". The guards kept much of this for themselves and the prisoners worked on the brink of starvation. Mortality was high and productivity suffered as the local miners couldn't make up the difference so a deal was done with the corrupt border officials to divert some shipments from Portugal to Spanish mines to make up the shortfall and provide a bonus for the mine's managers. The Germans were aware of this but they had quotas to meet as well and were paying in stolen gold so didn't make a fuss. He hadn't mentioned this in front of Hélène or Masha as he didn't want to add to their obvious distress. He also advised me to stay well away from the mine unless I had a particular wish to witness a new form of Hell.

Willie was sanguine about our chances of successfully ambushing the two trucks and was keen for some action. Hélène's only means of contacting her man across the border was by telephone. We debated driving back to Vila Real to make the call from the house but none of us really wanted to see that place again so we decided to take the risk and use Velosa's phone. She spoke Portuguese to the local operator then Spanish once she was linked to the exchange in Spain and waited for the call to be answered. It rang for a long time and she was about to give up when someone picked up. Willie told me after that it sounded like an innocuous family conversation with some times thrown in along with an agreement about green rather than blue curtains. She seemed confident that the coded message had been understood and marked the time and location on our map.

The best Velosa could offer us was a bunk room with a curtain strung between the ladies and gentlemen's sleeping areas. His cook provided something quite palatable and I was pleased to note that we all refrained from alcohol though Masha used some on Hélène's cuts and re-bandaged her wounds.

46

Overnight, a weather front had moved in and by the time we set off the following morning visibility was about as good as it would have been trying to swim across the river at night. Velosa didn't think it would stop the German shipment and believed it might keep the border guards in their huts. We were in position by 08:00 about ten km south of the mine with the Chrysler blocking the road about fifty metres over the top of the steep hill leading up to the ruins of an old fort. I donned an oilskin cape and hat provided by Velosa and fought my way through the freezing rain to keep a lookout around the final bend.

I had to wait twenty minutes before I sensed movement in the valley below then, as two dark shapes pushed the rain aside in their struggle up the incline, I hurried back to alert the others. We heard the straining engines before the first truck, which looked like a fairly new Ford V8 with double rear wheels, appeared over the crest. Its brakes screeched in protest as the driver spotted the obstruction. It skidded, wriggled and then slithered to a halt all six tyres hissing and squealing before it stopped, feet short of the Chrysler. Willie and Nicolai were crouched down just over the ridge and waited until the second truck performed a similar dance on the uneven and slippery surface.

Masha emerged from our car and waved her arms at the first truck while I slipped alongside the passenger side of the cab hidden by the load bay from the vehicle behind. I waited for Masha to get close enough to call out to the driver then yanked the passenger door open and dragged the guard out. He tried to draw his pistol as he flew from his seat but was far too slow. I smacked him in the temple with the butt of my Browning then jumped up onto the running board and pointed it at the driver. We needed him alive.

I listened while Nicolai and Willie dealt with the second truck but, apart from two distinct thuds, only heard the rain bouncing off the canvas. I handed my pistol to Masha and she made herself comfortable alongside the shocked driver. I helped Severino transfer our equipment from the Chrysler's boot to the rear of the canvas covered truck then hopped in to check the contents. It was almost full of coal sacks and I hefted one to gauge its weight. Years of lifting sacks and barrels of potatoes suggested that it was slightly over one hundred pounds. Digging inside I extracted what looked like lumps of coal but felt much heavier. Mainly a shiny black, they were inlaid with a mixture of gold and silver streaks. Some were smooth like pebbles, some crusty and flecked with white but most were rough with edges jagged from pickaxes when they'd been won from the narrow mine shafts. So this was wolframite for which, according to Velosa, the Germans would pay about £7,000 per tonne. Twenty of these sacks would weigh about that so each would be worth at least £350 — more profitable than our Jersey new potatoes then! Severino joined me and, for such a small man, showed surprising strength as he helped me create a space behind the sacks to store our equipment.

I called Willie over and asked him to relieve Masha before Severino and Nicolai rearranged the furniture in the second truck where they created an aisle through the sacks and set one up as a door to close from inside should any nosey guard want a peek at our cargo. Once we got closer to the crossing point the women would join Nicolai in there. Hélène drove the Peugeot out from the fort and waited while we transferred our equipment to the second truck. Masha swapped with Severino and manoeuvred the Chrysler down the hill and turned left along a track then parked and locked it under a copse of pine trees. Hélène followed her and the two of them waited for us to mount the trucks.

I checked with Willie and was pleased to see that the driver was still breathing though it looked as though all the blood had drained from his face. I checked the prostrate passenger but he was beyond help so I dragged him to Nicolai and between us we loaded the three corpses into the back of the second truck while Severino climbed into the still warm driver's seat. Nicolai clambered into the back and made himself comfortable on the pile of blankets we'd brought from the bunk house.

He'd have some unresponsive company until we found a suitable spot to dispose of them. We picked up Hélène who sat alongside Willie and Masha who slid in between Severino and me. It hadn't taken long but we were all soaked. Fortunately, the two Fords had heaters and, at the risk of misting up the windscreens, we turned them on full. Willie had the map so we followed his truck as he persuaded the driver to continue his journey.

It took longer than expected to reach Sabrosa but we sloshed through the rain then settled for the longer stint to Torre de

Moncorvo. Willie pulled his truck off the road a few kilometres later and I went forward for a quick conference. Because of the cold and rain we agreed to keep the women up front until we were almost in Vila Formoso. We spoke in French and Willie told me that Hélène had been calming the driver with promises of freedom if he followed our instructions precisely and kept his nerve at the border crossing. He confirmed that he'd travelled this route several times before and was known to the guards on both sides but that the other driver, who we told him was tied up along with their two guards in the truck behind, would be released once we had finished out business. Hope springs eternal but Willie had his alternative plan ready sharpened in its sheaf under his arm.

We made better time on the long run in to Vila Formoso but we took an even narrower road to avoid Guarda which was a major hub for the Germans though Velosa had assured us that they didn't operate on Sundays. After we'd passed through Castelo Rodrigo we encountered a massive pine forest on our right. Willie must have read my thoughts as he slowed down and pulled into the side just after a junction with a track leading up through the trees. I jumped down and approached, checking the driver's mirrors to make sure he couldn't see us, then waved Severino onto the track before re-joining him in the cab. He drove up until we found a small clearing where he would be able to turn and I helped Nicolai carry the corpses into the trees and dump them. Within minutes we were nosing up behind Willie's truck and we started off again.

On the outskirts of the border town we pulled off the road again and the women took their places on the blankets with Nicolai. If it looked like the guards wanted to inspect our vehicle on the Portuguese side Severino would reverse it, swing around and race off back to Val das Gatas. If this happened on the Spanish side we would have to fight our way back into Portugal and hope for the best. While confident that we could overcome both sets of guards we knew that once the alarm was raised we'd need to drive away as fast as possible and had agreed to meet up at the crossroads just short of Almeida.

Vila Formoso was much larger than I expected and seemed quite busy for a very wet Sunday in late November. We passed the railway yards and station where Velosa had told us wolfram and other strategic minerals were shipped into Spain for onward transport through France to Germany under a strict cloak of secrecy. The first obstacle was the concrete Guarda Nacional Republicana building on our side of the road. There were two battered old Ford saloons and an ancient Dodge truck queuing outside. The GNR men seemed reluctant to venture out into the rain from their cosy interior as each was waved through after a brief inspection of their papers. We watched anxiously as Willie's truck nosed alongside. An arm clad in a waterproof sleeve stretched out and Severino relayed what was happening. He saw our lead driver hand a parcel over and we waited on tenterhooks until the arm reappeared and waved him through. As we drew alongside the guard nodded at us then returned to his newspaper.

The customs official in his wooden Alfândega hut didn't even bother to hang out a begging arm and soon we were over the border and approaching corruption in another language. It was guards first this time and another parcel was handed through the driver's window and both vehicles waved through. The customs officer didn't open his window and soon we drove past a bleak group of hovels which purported to be the village of Fuentes de Oñoro. After an hour following a road, which was the equal of the ones we had endured in Portugal, we reached the largish town of Ciudad Rodrigo, crossed over the Rio Águeda and turned north towards our rendezvous in Saldeana another sixty-five km away.

While the women would no doubt have appreciated riding up front I thought it best to keep them hidden. Spain was run by a dictator even more deluded than Salazar and he had probably issued a decree that women should be in their hovels cooking for the men on a Sunday after attending church and not travelling in trucks on what passed for a highway.

From the infrequent signs of life even though the rain had eased I guessed that Sunday was a day for rest for the men as well. Shortly after three p.m. we rolled through Saldeana but, instead of taking the right turning onto the track that should lead up to the farmyard where Hélène's contact should be waiting with good news, we carried on for another few hundred metres before finding a sheltered spot to deal with our driver and check for ourselves.

47

Willie tied him up and borrowed his socks then bundled him into the back of his truck. He might come in useful for the return over the border. We left Severino in charge of the second truck and brought Hélène out of the back to sit with him. I asked Nicolai to look after the first but he refused until Masha persuaded him with some soothing words in Russian. She wanted to come with Willie and me to recce the farm though I suspected she really wanted to get the first glimpse of her husband if indeed he had been rescued. We were still over 2,000 feet up in the mountains and it was cold and miserable but I shed my oilskin as it might ruin a silent approach. Masha didn't complain as we forced our way through another copse of sticky pine trees then scrambled over terrain that would need explosives before it was ever ready for the plough. Perhaps *farm* had a different meaning for the Spanish.

Soon we spotted the entrance to a lane which fitted the description she had. A wooden gate set back about ten yards from the narrow road was secured with a chain but no padlock. We waited patiently but didn't see anyone keeping a lookout. We crept across the broken surface and into a ditch to the north of the gate. An avenue of evergreen trees which I didn't think were pines led from the gate to some stone buildings with grey tiled roofs about two hundred yards down the lane. I whispered to Willie and he slipped back over the road and set off to explore the lane from the south. Masha and I continued up a slope still shielded by the trees until we were several metres above the property and able to see into the large yard surrounded by stone buildings. An old Chevy truck which might once have been red was parked in front of a barn-like structure with one door slightly ajar. I checked the windows in the main house again but still didn't see any movement. Leaving Masha on over-watch with one of the MP38s we'd captured from the guards I crawled down the reverse slope and worked my way closer to the yard. For the final few metres of open ground I drew my Browning then sneaked over to the truck and felt its bonnet. It was warm and I could hear metallic ticking as the engine cooled. Willie would be on the other side now so I decided to gamble and hurried over to the open door and peeked into the barn. Two men were drinking something hot and talking quietly in Spanish. Behind them I thought I could see two human shapes huddled in the corner with hoods over their heads.

If these were the husbands we could steal them from under their guards' noses, after breaking them of course, and spirit them away without payment. We could even take the precious wolfram back over the border and save it from the Germans. We could keep the diamonds as well. It was only a brief thought as to escape without raising any alarm we'd probably need to kill more people and I'd had enough of that for one day. I'd stick to the plan so I shuffled back around the barn and hurried up to Masha to discover Willie already there. He hadn't seen anyone but when I reported my find I had to restrain Masha from rushing into the barn. Between us we persuaded her that it would be too dangerous not just for us but for whoever was under those hoods. Reluctantly she agreed and scooted off to our trucks to make a frontal approach while Willie and I guarded the rear.

Before the trucks arrived we split up again. I circled the barn looking for another entrance while Willie went to explore the house. The barn didn't have a back door and I crept around the side so that I could observe the track from behind a stack of empty barrels which smelled of raw alcohol and explained the *farming* element in the description of this cluster of buildings. I listened for movement from inside but also cocked an ear in the direction of the road. I must have heard the engines first as the two men were still chatting when the distinctive note of the V8s began to resound in the yard. They stopped talking and I heard the click of rifle bolts and footsteps as they approached the opening.

I couldn't see around the corner but could hear the tyres as our two trucks ground to a halt though both engines were kept running. I heard a truck door squeak open and then Hélène's voice calling out in Spanish. The two men separated, only by the wooden wall of the barn, were no more than ten metres away from me but neither answered. She called out again and this time I heard an answer from the other side of the yard. I left the cover of the barrels, already feeling lightheaded from the fumes, and crept to the corner of the barn where I could see Hélène's back as she approached a thickset man standing in the doorway of the house. He held out his arms and she hurried forward to hug him but I wasn't going to reveal myself until she gave me the all clear.

If no one else was in the house Willie would have sneaked upstairs and have the yard covered by now so I just had to wait but Masha couldn't. All discipline lost in her excitement, she jumped down from the second lorry grabbed Nicolai's hand and pulled him towards the barn shouting out in Russian though I could only make out her husband's name. Hélène's new friend shouted something in Spanish and the barn door slammed shut.

I suppose there was a natural order to these things when money or goods were exchanged for human life and we weren't really in a position to alter that but had to trust Hélène. She spat something at Masha in French and she stopped and pulled Nicolai back. I didn't want to intervene unless either of the two men made a move towards her but I suspected they had their rifles pressed into the hoods of the two hostages at the moment.

Hélène spoke to her contact again — more calmly this time — then called out to Nicolai in English that he should bring the packages. I suspected that was for my benefit as he didn't understand French and that was the only other language she and I shared. The next voice was in German as Willie appeared behind the Spaniard's back holding his Browning in his hand.

Matters were quickly resolved after that and while Severino helped the Spaniards unload the wolfram sacks and Hélène's new friend counted his diamonds the two women and Nicolai rushed into the barn for their reunion. Heart pounding for reasons I really didn't understand I left them to their privacy and went to help the others.

Our host, who introduced himself as Marcel, invited us into the farmhouse for some refreshment after we'd emptied the trucks of their contraband. Our driver was still hooded and tied up but in a moment of weakness I took him a tumbler full of the decent brandy we'd been offered. I didn't know what we were going to do with him yet but if it seemed the gentlemanly thing to do. He was pathetically grateful and, even though I didn't understand his questions in Spanish and German, I did when he broke into English and begged for the lives of his comrades. I nodded but didn't reply as I tied him up again almost envying the distance a sniper, an artillery man or a bomber pilot could put between himself and his victims.

Unable to constrain myself any longer I walked into the barn.

48

Any misgivings I might have been harbouring about forgiving my enemy evaporated in an instant as I was introduced to Juan and Anatoliy. They were brutalised skeletons — yet in Juan's one remaining eye sparked a brightness of spirit which was humbling to see. Anatoliy still had both of his but his spirit had faded to a mere flicker of hope. His lungs struggled to suck in air and he could only whisper. They were both dressed in rags and their feet were lumps of raw meat. I wanted to rush over to the farmhouse and flagellate the Spaniards who had not even bothered to treat their injuries but Hélène must have sensed my intent and grabbed my arm.

'No, Jack. Please, without them I wouldn't have seen my husband again. It is what it is. They took enormous risks. Just help us get them back over the border.'

I nodded, not sure what to say but worried that they might not survive the journey. Anatoliy looked as though he needed immediate hospital attention just to get through the next few hours.

Hélène interrupted my thoughts. 'Juan was…is a doctor. I brought some medical supplies with me — there's Pervitin and morphine sulphate. Get them from my backpack in the lorry. We'll do what we can for Anatoliy before moving him.'

Masha looked at me. Her eyes were wide with shock and something else which I couldn't fathom. She added "please" to Hélène's words then turned back to her broken husband. Any jealousy or envy I'd felt was banished in that moment; replaced by something dark and dangerous and I hoped for his sake that Hélène's pack was nowhere near our helpless driver. I found it on the front seat of the first truck so spared the driver for the moment. Hélène discussed what to do with Juan and asked Nicolai and me to leave them for the moment.

Marcel was examining the diamonds on the table when we returned to the kitchen. She'd given him five packets in exchange for the prisoners which worked out at over £200,000 plus the £14,000 worth of wolfram. Neither had cost us anything but I felt bitter that they would end up with the Germans. Marcel called his two associates over and poured diamonds into their hands. The greed in their faces started a fire in my belly which I knew would consume me unless we left soon. I was about to return to the barn when an animal scream pierced the air.

Nicolai reacted first and sprinted out of the door. I caught up with him as he crashed into the barn. Masha was hugging her husband rending the air with screeches of pure anguish. While Nicolai rushed to her I looked at Hélène. She shook her head sadly and Juan bowed his. Something inside me dissolved into acid and I knelt beside the doctor and questioned him in French. He told me that Marcel and his two associates were guards at the camp who had dragged them away the previous evening. They hadn't been fed or offered water and when he'd protested they kicked and punched him into silence. I asked him how many prisoners were still in the camp. He answered that nearly 500 from one of Franco's punishment battalions had arrived three months before to work the mine. There were fewer than one hundred left and only twenty fascists remained to guard them. The regular Spanish miners didn't work on Sundays and had gone home for the day. He couldn't tell me much about the guards' disposition or routine but grabbed my arm as I stood up and begged me not to let Hélène administer any morphine to him until, as he put it, "matters were resolved".

I nodded assent, released my arm, pulled Nicolai to his feet and told him that whatever happened we needed one of these *pigs* alive. He followed me into the kitchen to find Willie and Severino covering Marcel and his men with their pistols. I told them about Anatoliy, who these creatures were and how they had treated their hostages. I took Willie aside and listed the questions to which we needed answers. He smiled and shoved Marcel out of the kitchen and into a room across the corridor. Nicolai pushed the two men out into the yard and I made them reload the wolfram sacks into the trucks in the same arrangement as before trying to ignore the obscene noises emanating from the house. When the men slackened and started to protest Severino pulled out his knife and prodded them back into action. Long before they'd finished loading all noises from the house had ceased. I didn't think Willie had bothered with socks this time and when I looked in I discovered that he'd used some of Marcel's expensively gained diamonds instead.

He had answers to all my questions and some I hadn't thought of as well. We returned to the yard as the final sack was being loaded. Willie stopped the man, wiped his knife on the sack and slit it open. He extracted a handful of wolfram, kicked the man to the ground, rammed it into his mouth and stood on him as he struggled to breathe. Nicolai didn't have that much patience and snapped the other's neck in one swift movement.

There was a well in the yard and we picked up the three bodies then dropped them one at a time to the bottom. It took five seconds for the first splash which, by my calculations, made it at least 350 feet deep. Out of sight so out of mind and mine was churning so violently that I was about to throw the driver after them when I remembered we'd need him to get back over the border.

Hélène came out of the barn and demanded to know why I didn't want her to administer morphine to her husband. I told her and explained that she shouldn't sedate Masha either. I followed her back in and made Masha a promise I desperately hoped I would be able to keep.

We locked the barn and farm house and drove up the tree-lined track, turned left and then right at the junction but, instead of heading back to the border, started the long climb up the potholed road to the mine where this wolfram shipment was expected by those guards who were not part of Marcel's greedy scheme. I'd released our own driver, who Willie told me was called Kurt, and now he drove the first truck with Willie and myself sharing the bench seat. I hadn't studied Kurt before but I was struck by his incongruous appearance. A shock of blonde hair framed typical Portuguese features. His eyes were pale blue and shone with a strange innocence from his tanned face. He looked even younger than me. But, as he was dispensable, I didn't really want to discover any more about him.

We'd debated placing Juan in the rear of the second truck with Hélène to attend to him but he'd wanted to see the countryside and the cushioned front seat would be more comfortable so he sat between his wife and the desolate Nicolai. Severino, driving Marcel's old Chevy, brought up the rear with Masha in the passenger seat. Anatoliy had no need for comfort but we'd tried our best to provide dignity and he was wrapped in the best linen we could find in the house and laid out, supported by blankets, behind the wolfram sacks in our truck.

We didn't need to recce the camp. We knew from Willie's questioning that all the prisoners were locked up for the day without food or water, the money for which the guards had shared out amongst themselves as their usual Sunday bonus. There would be two on the main gate and the rest would be playing cards or sleeping in their barracks. The two on duty peered through the light rain and seemed to recognise our driver as he pulled up at the gate. They waved and I forced him to return their greeting before one of them lifted the barrier. They must have noticed Marcel's truck and wondered what he was doing but, before they could ask any questions, Willie and I had slipped out and silenced them. Kurt sat in his seat trembling with fear until I pointed my knife at him and indicated he should turn the truck to face down the hill. As he complied, Nicolai and Masha dismounted from theirs, unslung their MP38s and joined us. We waited for Hélène to help Juan towards us then set out for the barracks. Nicolai took the rear and Willie and I burst in through the front door waving our pistols. He shouted in Spanish and German and quickly eighteen guards in various stages of undress were formed up outside. Some recognised Juan as he was helped forward and started muttering and giving each other fearful looks. One tried to break away but Willie shot him in the leg. Others helped him up and Willie barked at them to march around the corner of the barracks to the long side.

There, nailed to the wall, we discovered two naked corpses. Both had been whipped to death and their spines were exposed. Juan limped over to them and turned their heads to look at their faces. He said a few words in Spanish then walked back to us with grim determination and relieved Nicolai of his machine pistol. His voice trembled as he spoke to the guards but not as much as these brutes who shivered under his pitiless gaze. Slowly they shuffled into a line and stood against the wall. Some turned their backs but Juan raised his voice and they faced him again. He invited Masha to join him then made a short speech in Spanish. I wanted to add something in English about my uncle and Malita but it would need translating so I stood there and thought it instead. One of the guards moved forwards but Masha started firing, followed by Juan, who broke his Hippocratic Oath eighteen times as he emptied his magazine into the bastards who had tortured and abused him and his fellow prisoners.

The air was still ringing with the sound of automatic fire when Hélène passed him another machine pistol with a loaded magazine but it wasn't needed as Masha had borrowed my pistol and delivered the coup de grace to any still twitching. It had been conceived in anger and executed swiftly. It wouldn't bring Anatoliy back or relieve the suffering of the thousands persecuted and methodicly stripped of their humanity by this fascist creed and I could only speak for myself but, for a few moments the burden of anger I had carried since my uncle had described Malita's torture, lifted from my shoulders.

In the strange silence we all stared at the jumble of broken bodies. I looked at Willie. 'What the hell have we done here?'

He shrugged. 'Balanced your famous British scales of justice? I don't know, but don't feel bad about it. You'll see far worse before this war is over…at least you've given me hope that you have what it takes to see it through.'

'What about the prisoners? Should we release them?' Hélène asked.

Juan shook his head. 'To do what? Most of them are in as bad a state as Anatoliy was. They'll only wander around until they're recaptured and you don't want to imagine how that will end or—'

'But couldn't we take the fittest with us?' Masha interrupted. 'We could dump the wolframite and get at least thirty in the three trucks.'

'And where would we take them?'

'Over the border and release them—'

'Into the tender care of the Portuguese? Remember most of them are Communists and you know what happens to those if the PVDE get their hands on them—'

'But they haven't got any papers so how would the PVDE know that?' I asked.

Willie pointed at the execution site. 'I think that's your conscience talking, Jack. You must be more realistic. I believe Juan will agree that there is nothing we can do other than leave them locked up so they are not blamed.'

I turned to Juan. 'If you were locked in there what would you wish us to do?'

He thought for a while. 'If you don't mind, I will ask…but don't worry, I won't tell them anything about you though I will mention Anatoliy. Do you have time for me to do this?'

We all nodded and watched as Hélène helped him across to the hut and he spoke through the wooden wall. I heard his Spanish but couldn't make out any replies. As he returned he shrugged off her arm and limped towards us his face impossible to read but I noticed tears on his cheek.

'They were worried about us. They are sad about Anatoliy but happy for me. They give you their thanks for killing the guards and wish you to escape and kill many more fascists. For themselves they ask only for water and food and a way of escaping from their prison once we are gone. In an hour or so after they have eaten and drunk their fill they will break out. We must leave the guards' weapons and ammunition and they will wait for the Spanish to come tomorrow. Then they will kill as many as they can until they are dead themselves. They will not let anyone be taken alive. This they wish above all else.' He reached for Hélène's hand and faced her. 'Were it not for your sacrifice I would stay with them…they ask also that we find their records and take them with us so that one day their families will know how and for what they died.'

'We can do more than this. We will take all the records, of the guards, the managers — everyone involved in this…and make sure the whole world knows.' My voice sounded hollow as I fought back tears for these brave men.

Willie snorted. 'He still has much to learn about the world and how little it cares. But, time is not on our side. Let's find the food and water then prepare the weapons for them. Juan, you and the women go and get the files from the office. If Kurt wants to live, he'll come with me as there's another message I want to leave here.'

Severino, Nicolai and I scavenged through the barracks and kitchens then carried the spoils to the prisoners' hut and unlocked the main door. They stood back while we passed the supplies in deliberately avoiding looking at us. They asked us to close the door again but leave it unlocked. We hurried back to the barracks and removed all the old German bolt action rifles checked they were clean and loaded their magazines from the ammunition boxes kept in the store. Next we broke into the armoury and removed three cases of Soviet stick grenades and two Italian Breda strip fed 8mm light machine guns with several boxes of ammo. We laid all the weapons including two of our German machine pistols out in the barracks. There was sufficient killing power there to last the prisoners a couple of hours and, in honour of their final request, we placed all twenty Russian Tokarev automatic pistols and ammo we'd found for them to ensure a quick and merciful ending.

As I left the barracks, I spotted Willie and Kurt manhandling a wooden cart down towards a tunnel leading deep into the hillside. It was loaded with cases of dynamite, blasting caps, electrical cable and two detonator boxes. Willie was planning to make a big bang. I knew that the nearest habitation was nearly four kilometres away to the north. Given that the wind was blowing from that direction it was unlikely that the sound of small arms fire would have carried that far.

The shock wave rumble of underground explosions might and, as blasting didn't normally take place on Sundays, there was a risk someone might take the trouble to investigate.

I suggested that he use the standard PE charge and fuses we'd brought with us so that the explosion would occur well after we'd left but it might be useful to set up other charges for the prisoners with which to surprise their attackers when they arrived the following morning. He agreed and when he returned with a backpack and torches I followed him down the first gallery until we reached a crossroads of shafts leading down at a variety of angles. Kurt had little option and nervously carried bundles of dynamite sticks for us. Willie cut up three of the one and half pound blocks of plastic explosive into smaller chunks and tied them to the dynamite before lashing cable around each of the dangerous packs.

He extracted a flat tin which looked like it might hold slim cigars and pulled out some No 10 switches. We called these "time pencils" because of their shape. Each container held five of these and along with a No 8 detonator could be used to set off the explosive for anything from ten minutes to twenty-four hours. He chose the one with the yellow safety strip which would detonate in twelve hours depending on air temperature. It was cold here so it might take thirty minutes longer. Before he stuck the pencil into a block of PE he squeezed the copper tube which broke the glass ampoule containing the steel wire which was restraining the striker. He then gave the pencil a good shake to ensure the liquid made good contact with the wire and removed the safety strip. Until he inserted it into the explosive the worst that could happen now was a sharp crack as the detonator fired but once in the heart of the block if it fired prematurely we would be eviscerated and become one with the mine. Carefully, he lowered the whole bundle into a shaft then we repeated the procedure for three more before retiring from the main gallery. He wanted to find some more galleries but I was conscious of time ticking away and insisted he use it to set up dynamite bombs at the main entrance for the prisoners to use. There was sufficient cable to cover the one hundred metres or so and within ten minutes he'd buried two large charges and wired them back to a detonator box placed behind the prisoners' hut.

I found Masha and Hélène stuffing records of everything they could break out of the filing cabinets into kitbags they'd pinched from the barracks. Willie popped in to have a look and stuck his last block of PE into one of the drawers complete with a detonator before removing the blue safety strip which would blow in twenty-four hours.

While the women loaded their haul into the first truck, Nicolai and I went around sabotaging the engines and electrics of the motorised excavator and shovel and smashing the control mechanism for the crushing plant before slicing through the telegraph and telephone wires leading into the mine.

Satisfied but feeling empty I waited while Juan returned to the prisoners to explain what we had done and warn them to stay well away from the main gallery and the administration office. His face was blank as he returned and let Hélène help him into the back of the truck. Minutes later our sad little convoy trundled out of the miserable hole which would soon become yet another graveyard of hope for men stripped of humanity by perverted politics and greed.

49

We pulled off the road just before Lumbrales and found a secluded spot to refuel from our spare Jerrycans. Before we abandoned it, Severino siphoned the petrol from the Chevy into one of the now empty cans and put it in the rear of the lead truck. We rearranged ourselves so that Willie sat with Kurt again and I joined Severino in the second Ford. Nicolai and Hélène took up station in the rear but Masha insisted on riding with Anatoliy's body behind us. It was four p.m. when we restarted and the sun was setting over the mountains ahead of us as we rolled up to the customs post. It was empty but the sole guard on the Spanish side showed little interest and waved us through. Portuguese customs was also unmanned — Sunday evenings would be a good time for smugglers.

The GNR post was manned and Kurt was waved through but a guard stepped out to wave us down. Packages weren't normally offered on the return journey but this one looked hungry. He fired some questions at Severino in Portuguese, shook his head at the answers and started moving towards the rear. Willie's truck had pulled up to wait for us. Kurt hopped out and called out to the guard who stopped and walked towards him. We waited while they exchanged a few sentences but Severino didn't seem perturbed by what they were saying. He whispered to me that Kurt was reminding the guard that arrangements had been made with his *chefe* and he would be unwise to interfere. Velosa had estimated that the chief customs officer, whose monthly salary was only 1,000 escudos, received over three million in bribes a year from this one route alone

What were we going to do with Kurt? It would be no good asking the others as they'd expect me to make the decision. We'd killed his comrades out of necessity but he'd done nothing to sign his own death sentence. Willie had told me he was Portuguese German which was an unusual combination especially as he suspected he might be Jewish as well. The guard shrugged in dismissal and returned to his concrete bunker. Graft seemed to be the key to this benighted country which gave me an idea about how I might resolve the issue.

Twilight disappeared long before we trundled through Torre de Moncorvo and we had to slow down as more heavy rain rattled on our canvases. We'd been lucky with tyres so far but, as we started the long climb up to Vale das Gatas, Severino had to fight the wheel as one of our double rears split its sides. He flashed his headlights at the leading truck and pulled off the road so we could inspect the damage. Fortunately it was the outside of the pair so we could change it if necessary but, as we were only a few kilometres short of where we'd left our cars, I decided we'd carry on and hope.

It held until we reached the old fort but I didn't want to risk the steep descent and had to disturb Nicolai, Juan and Hélène to extract the spare. As we were going to take the trucks to the English mine to unload the wolfram and Willie would need to stay with Kurt, Nicolai and I would have to drive a car each. Severino helped us but the screw jack struggled to lift the weight of the loaded truck. I didn't want to unload in the rain so dragged Willie and Kurt out into the elements to help. Nicolai placed his massive hands underneath the load bay, bent his back and lifted that side off the ground. Willie joined him and between them they held it up while I twirled the brace and removed the wheel nuts. Kurt detached the punctured wheel and I presented the spare and tightened the nuts. Without Nicolai's enormous strength and Willie's steady hands it would have been almost impossible without unloading. Hélène gave us a clap but Masha was still with her dead husband in the back of the first truck and wasn't able to admire her protector's feat.

I knew what Velosa would do with the wolfram but wasn't sure how he'd view the trucks. He wouldn't want the Germans to discover them so perhaps I was presenting him with two very unwelcome gifts. His workforce would be returning in the morning so we'd have to resolve it before then. I explained the problem to Willie who shrugged and said the answer was simple and returned to his cab. I passed the keys for the Peugeot to Nicolai. He led Juan and Hélène to it and helped them into the rear where it would be a lot more comfortable than the back of the truck. I opened the Chrysler ready to follow the trucks but, before I could start the engine, Masha slipped over the tailboard of the Ford, hurried over to my car, slid in beside me burrowed into my shoulder and sobbed until I thought my heart would break for her.

I waited for her to speak but she just tugged my arm and pointed forwards, urging me to follow the others while still clinging to my right arm which made gear changing very challenging. It was a difficult twelve kilometres not because of the darkness, the sweeping changes in elevation or treacherous track but, for every metre, I was fighting an overpowering urge to stop and comfort her.

As agreed, we skirted to the south of the German mine and pulled off the road about five kilometres short of Velosa's. It was raining heavily again as I hopped out to confer with Willie. We didn't want to risk driving in to the mine with the Fords but needed to unload the wolfram and find some shelter for Juan and Hélène. We weren't too keen on trekking through the rain either, so Willie brought the suitcase radio to my car, strung the aerial over the roof, and we set it up on the back seat. We soon established a link with Velosa and sent a coded message informing him of our cargo and requesting permission to bring it in. The response was some time in arriving and I wondered if he'd contacted Friedman before answering. Eventually, he replied that we were welcome but must be gone before dawn.

He met us at the gates and led the two lorries into a shed. While Nicolai, Willie and the increasingly helpful Kurt were unloading the sacks he took Hélène and Juan into his own private quarters and installed them in the guest bedroom. He ordered food for everybody and while that was being prepared he took me into his office.

'I apologise for the delay in letting you in but, as you might have expected, I had to contact Friedman who sends his regards and mentioned something about a wager which he wanted you to know wasn't complete yet. Anyway, he needs you to return to Lisbon as soon as possible as London has issued new orders.'

'That's fine with us but I don't think we should travel back on the same route. We have another problem; two actually. Masha's husband didn't make it and we have his body in one of the trucks—'

'Do you want to bury him here?' There was a trace of alarm in his voice which made my response rather sharp.

'No. Masha would like to bury him somewhere he is actually wanted.'

'My apologies. So you want to take him with you to Lisbon.'

'No. We need to get him to England along with Hélène and Juan and I hope you will be able to help us with shipping.' Before he could interrupt I continued. 'You told us that you use Portuguese vessels from the Leixoes docks in Porto to ship out your wolfram. With this cargo of about two tonnes we've liberated from the Germans perhaps you could add some of your own and make an early shipment?'

He consulted a ledger on his desk then pulled out a notebook from a drawer. 'There is such a possibility. We were planning a convoy next week but with your extra load we could set off tomorrow. There is an understanding with the Companhia Colonial De Navegaçao, the owners of the SS *Cassequel*, that we sometimes need cargo space at short notice. There will be paper work of course and,' he rubbed his fingers together, 'arrangements to be made but—'

'This should help.' I'd anticipated this requirement and pulled out two bags from my backpack and dropped them on his desk.

He hefted them then opened the heaviest and examined the gold coins. He was a bit more sceptical about the diamonds but took them over to his safe anyway. 'It seems you understand how business is conducted here.' He moved to the large wall map and traced a line from the mine to the coast. 'My workers will return in the morning and you must be gone before they see you. I can spare two guards who will drive our two Bedford OL lorries which can carry four tonnes each plus your…friends… into the docks. Before I have the wolfram loaded you will need to dispose of your Fords. You will follow in your two cars but when you reach here,' he tapped the map, 'at the Dom Luís I Bridge you must cross the Douro and head south – you will find the roads…marginally more comfortable. You will leave the other arrangements to my men.' He looked up at me. 'Is this acceptable?'

It was a risk for Hélène and Juan but taking them to Lisbon might be even more dangerous. 'When will the *Cassequel* leave and how long will she take to get to England?'

He consulted his note book again. 'She is due to leave tomorrow on the tide at 20:00 and will cross the Bay of Biscay on her way to Liverpool with a mixed cargo of sardines, olive oil, cork, blankets and some agricultural machinery. She's not the fastest but should reach Liverpool in about three and a half days.'

'What's the risk of submarines or the Luftwaffe attacking her?'

He shrugged. 'Quite low. The ship is painted white and is well lit at night. There are very few German or British patrols on this route and, so far, there have been few incidents with neutral ships.' He smiled. 'It is safer than flying.'

50

Severino and Willie drove the two Fords a few kilometres east while I followed in the Chrysler. We found the spot Velosa had recommended, pushed the trucks off the road and listened while they hissed through the rain, tumbling and crashing into the ravine 300 metres below. On the way back I asked Willie about Kurt. The boy had told him that his father was German and his mother a Portuguese Jewess. They had lived in Germany until 1935 when his father, who was worried about the Nazis, arranged for his wife to return to Portugal with their thirteen year old son promising to join them a few months later. He never arrived but they'd lived in hope until she was killed in a hit and run accident in 1939. Her relatives had shut their doors to him and in desperation he had asked for help at the German legation. They had found work for him at the mine but he hated some of his German co-workers who bullied him because of his mixed race. Fortunately, they hadn't discovered he was half-Jewish as well.

It sounded like a carefully constructed tale to win sympathy to me but Willie was adamant that, if nothing else, the boy was Jewish and he felt we should take him with us and get him to England. He was sure that someone who spoke fluent German, Portuguese and Spanish and who had demonstrated cool initiative would be very useful once trained. I didn't argue with him but couldn't see how we could spirit him away with no papers unless we paid for his transport on the ship.

Back at the mine Velosa explained that he'd found a bed for Masha in his quarters and that Nicolai and Kurt were waiting for us in the accommodation block. Part of me hoped that Nicolai had resolved the problem for us but we found them drinking *aguardente velha* and playing chess with a set they'd discovered. Velosa would wake us at 05:00 so that we could help the guards load the wolfram into the two Bedford lorries. I wasn't convinced by Kurt so I insisted we tie him up to his bunk bed while we tried to sleep. Nicolai, Willie and Severino were soon snoring but I couldn't clear my mind and my head still throbbed from the coshing so I got up and moved quietly over to Kurt. He was awake and, in the dim light of a shaded lamp, I looked into his eyes to help me make a judgement. He thanked me so I probed him with more questions but couldn't find a weakness in his increasingly sad story. I bid him goodnight and returned to my bunk only to find that solving the problem of Kurt had only been my mind suppressing the much larger one of Masha.

I was still awake when morning twilight seeped into the room followed by Velosa who thought it amusing to bang a saucepan with a large spoon as an alarm. At least he'd arranged some hot breakfast which we demolished quickly before hurrying through the cold to warm ourselves up with some heavy lifting. Velosa's two men were also Anglo Portuguese and seemed keen for the day's work. We placed all the kit we would need for Lisbon in the Peugeot as the German spies might be on the lookout for the Chrysler which Severino would drive to Porto and abandon in the dock area before catching a train back to the capital. Hélène and Juan would be his passengers. Nicolai would drive the Peugeot with Masha up front with Kurt and me in the rear. Willie would sit alongside the driver in the first Bedford. Once we were all settled our little convoy moved out heading south to avoid the returning workers.

It was about 120 km to Porto so we planned to keep moving unless there was a breakdown or puncture. Willie told the drivers I was an expert on Bedford lorries so not to worry if bits started falling off. I told them that Willie was a clown who didn't know a wheel brace from a foot pump and to only wake me up if one of their engines fell out of its bay. I knew my chances of sleep were slender especially as I was still trying to resolve the Masha problem which pummelled my brain every time our eyes met. For the moment she was out of sight but we'd be together for the much longer drive to Lisbon so I begged my conscious mind to give it a rest for a while.

I woke briefly as we rumbled through the cobbled streets of Amarante then again when we stopped at a road junction in Parades. Two hours of sleep was better than nothing but as we grew closer to Porto it became elusive again. The lead truck stopped short of the bridge we were meant to cross but I told Willie to drive on to Leixoes which was another ten km through the city as I wanted to see this ship for myself. No one objected so we trundled on until we reached the south side of the dock and assembled by the lead truck. The driver jumped down, stretched his legs, yawned then pointed out the ancient tramp steamer tied up on the other side of the harbour. She had a tall single stack behind the bridge. I guessed she was about 5,000 tonnes and had indeed been painted white at some stage though this was now streaked with rust. CASSEQUEL –

PORTUGAL was painted in massive yellow letters on a black background along the port side which was facing us. I assumed the same was on the starboard side as well. Even a half blind U-boat commander could see she was a neutral ship which was a great relief.

It was time to say goodbye. I shook hands with Juan, whose face now had a bit more colour, then embraced Hélène. As we parted I handed her a slip of paper on which I'd written Fleming's contact number. She accepted it but I suspected she would make her own arrangements when they arrived in Liverpool which had no shortage of comrades manning the docks. I didn't really care if she revealed the location of the diamonds or not. I was still debating what to do about Kurt when Nicolai removed his and Masha's bags from the Peugeot and transferred them to the Chrysler.

'What are you doing? We're going to Lisbon in the Peugeot.'

Masha moved into me, wrapped her arms around my neck, kissed my cheek and whispered in my ear. 'You are but we're going on the ship to help Hélène and Juan.'

'But what about—'

'Don't worry; Mr Velosa has made the arrangements. You must know it is safer for us this way and you as well.'

Her soft words raked my insides sending a hot shiver up my spine. I stepped back and stared into her eyes looking for any hint of amusement at a clever joke but there was none. She was deadly serious. So be it. 'In that case, you won't mind taking Kurt with you — will you?'

'Of course not. Willie and Hélène have already arranged that. It's the best solution to your problem isn't it?'

I nodded dumbly. It was but it hadn't solved the other. There was nothing more to be said but I was going to fill Willie's ear with some Anglo Saxon words he had not yet heard on the journey south. I shook hands with Severino and thanked him profusely then clapped Kurt on the shoulder and wished him well. Nicolai advanced for a bear hug but I side slipped and shook his hand instead getting my thumb in the right position so he couldn't fracture any bones. Willie did the rounds after me but didn't flinch from Nicolai's embrace. I desperately wanted to hug Masha but that would only prolong the agony so I turned away, grabbed Willie's arm and shoved him towards the Peugeot.

As we drove away I couldn't resist twisting my head to look in my wing mirror. They had all climbed back into their various vehicles apart from Masha who stood beside hers and lifted her arm, started to wave then turned it into a clenched-fist salute. If I'd known a bit more about Communism and hadn't been watching her in a mirror that salute would have told me something about her that might have saved me from considerable future pain.

51

The coast road along the Atlantic was sure to provide a quicker, more comfortable route to Lisbon. It would be flatter, have fewer potholes and, though there might be heavier traffic, it shouldn't take more than ten hours even if we only averaged thirty-five kph. Severino would have known the best roads and crossings but our Michelin map lacked detail and the military grid sheet for this section was missing. After a fruitless search for a vehicle ferry along the north bank of the Rio Mondego we'd had to go as far as Coimbra to find a bridge. We refuelled the Peugeot and our stomachs there but neither of us could summon enough energy to start a conversation which might end in a shouting match. It had been a long and silent journey so far with just the occasional comment on the route and the lack of infrastructure in this poor country. Just before dusk we climbed up into the hills again before heading to the coast and south to **Nazaré** where I set up the radio, made contact with the embassy and gave them an ETA of just after midnight. I also asked for accommodation and a garage for our car. We still had weapons, explosives and various items which might cause embarrassment should we have an accident or be pulled over by the police. You can't tell much about tone from decoding radio messages but I got the sense that whoever had responded on behalf of the ambassador would prefer it if we kept going until we were in the middle of the Tagus river.

One wheel change later and we only had just over one hundred kilometres left before Lisbon. We'd shared the driving but it was my turn as we made the final run into the city. Perhaps it was the bright lights or just tiredness but I misjudged a turn on the north edge of the Praça Dom Pedro, braked too sharply, skidded on the wet cobbles, missed a tram by inches and embraced the backside of a taxi. This drew a crowd of interested spectators from the nearby cafes. They enjoyed the sound and fury of the taxi driver whose tirade was both dramatic and melodic at the same time.

While I inspected the minimal damage and kept a wary eye open for any policemen, Willie engaged the driver in a vocal duel which, judging from the crowd's reaction, he had little chance of winning. Satisfied that there was no real damage I called out to him in French that it was time to leave but Willie does not like losing any contest so he turned on the victim of our vehicular abuse and fired a fusillade of German at him. That silenced the crowd but I sensed that it also incensed them and dragged him away before they abandoned their neutrality and declared war on us.

We escaped intact then sped off across the square and headed for Lapa and the British Embassy. I parked on the pavement outside the double doors which led into the courtyard while Willie assaulted the front door with his fist. Both doors opened quickly and we were ushered inside. Minutes later we were in Johnson's office receiving a tongue lashing.

I waited until he seemed to have run out of steam. 'I say, old chap, a nice cup of tea would be most welcome. Any chance?'

'No, you imbecile and there is no accommodation either. You can keep your vehicle here overnight and unload anything which might be incriminating and make your beds in it.'

'Is Major Friedman still here? We have some things to tell him.' I asked.

'Never heard of anyone of that name. You will report to me at 08:30 in this office and I'll give you your new orders.'

'Will we be flying to Madrid tomorrow because—'

'Madrid? Embarrassing us in Spain as well? If I had my way we'd be nailing you in a crate and shipping you home on a very slow boat. Now get out of my sight before I have you both arrested'

Willie sighed heavily, rested his hands on the desk and spoke softly.
'Are you the only one on duty tonight?'
'Why?'
'Do you have accommodation here?'
'Why?'
'Do you have a wife, girlfriend or boyfriend sharing it with you?'
'What are you talking about, you oaf?'
'Take us to your rooms.'
'Don't be absurd. I'll do no such thing!'
'Are you wearing clean socks?'
'What? Get—'

Willie moved very quickly and, five minutes later, we were comfortably ensconced in Johnson's bachelor accommodation at the rear of the embassy. He was less comfy, tied to a chair, with his socks where you would expect them to be if you had taken the risk of irritating someone as intolerant of pompous bureaucrats as Wilhelm Karl von Gersdoff.

52

Comfort is relative and I suppose a couple of sacks on a stone floor are better than the back seat of a car as you can at least stretch your legs. Someone must have missed Mr Johnson's quacking or they'd heard him fall off his perch as we had been roused at silly o'clock by a quartet of Royal Marines who escorted us to new quarters for the remainder of the night. We had no particular beef with them but they weren't inclined to answer our questions or ask any of their own so, without the benefit of a menu, we were served with tepid porridge on enamel plates as breakfast. It might have been lunch as our watches had been removed along with our belts and boots and there were no outside windows in this basement storeroom. Willie was of the opinion that we'd slept through and it might even be our tea time treat.

With no sharp objects, bludgeons, heavy boots or buckled belts to hand, I judged it safe to now raise the issue of his collusion with Velosa and Hélène to deceive me over Kurt. To my great surprise he apologised and explained that, as I seemed so befuddled with Masha, he thought it best to make the decision himself and get me away as soon as he could before I did something really embarrassing for everyone. I had a short rant but my heart wasn't in it as I realised that he was right and lapsed into silence again. Apart from a faint ticking from the low wattage light bulb and the occasional sound of water gushing down a drain there was nothing else to be heard.

It was pointless speculating about what Mr Johnson and his colleagues were planning for us so we relaxed on the sacking replenishing our batteries which had taken some beating over the past few days. I was thinking about Masha when the door was thrown open and two marines marched in holding bowls of stew. Willie asked the time and was told to shut his before they thrust the bowls at us. The two guards behind them stepped forward and dropped wooden spoons on the floor then stood back almost inviting us to start a fight. It must be quite dull guarding an embassy and I guessed that we'd provided the only excitement for some time. They were big, strong guys with hobnailed boots and batons ready to hand. We had two wooden spoons and I sensed that even Willie could see little profit in brawling so I asked politely if they could tell us the time.

'Time for Johnny Johnson to wash his socks.' The cockney chuckled then winked as they all withdrew carefully. I heard one ask the other the time in a loud voice when they were outside. It was 18:05 so this steaming mess was our evening meal. It was tastier than it looked and was quickly demolished.

Willie got up and banged on the door demanding the use of a lavatory.

'There's a bucket in the corner, mate. Or use your socks!'

I could only hear two voices chortling outside so they must have a rotating guard and feed us on change over. If they relaxed that routine I felt sure Willie would do something unpleasant with the smelly bucket and their socks should they venture inside without backup. We slept some more but when the door opened again I wasn't feeling hungry so guessed it was only early evening.

'Oot ah my way, bampots!' Friedman's voice exploded into the room. 'Smells like a Glasgow cludgie in here. Get these two cleaned up and in ma office afore I squeeze ya tackle.' He pulled his greatcoat collar up to his face then exited holding his nose.

It had been a few days but I wasn't sure it merited a hosing down with freezing water but I did feel refreshed as I towelled down in the yard after. We both needed a shave and brush up but the marines hurried us along. I noted that the Peugeot had disappeared. Correctly attired in our uniforms, which had been retrieved from the baggage we'd left behind, we were marched into Friedman who was now wearing full regalia including medals — one of which I recognised as the Military Cross.

'Sit and listen.'

We both saluted and complied.

Rough Scots accent dropped now, he continued. 'You two monkeys seem to have been very busy. We're picking up reports from all over Portugal and even Spain about unusual incidents on which you might like to comment.' He eyed me first. 'Renouf, what do you know about a group of naked Germans found wandering about around Belmonte?'

'Nudists, sir? I know the Germans are very fond of nature.'

'I see. It's going to be like that is it?' He reached for his telephone. 'Shall I call the marines to return you to the stores so that you have more time to come up with better answers?'

I sighed. There had to be a sensible limit to our bravado. 'That won't be necessary, sir. They were tailing us. We thought we'd lost them by setting up a diversion but it failed and they caught up with us while we were changing a wheel. We had little option but to neutralise them. I'm pleased to report we did that without killing anyone. There were eight of them so I thought they'd be reluctant to broadcast their failure to capture four men and a woman and would blame Communist bandits.'

'I see, so that's why someone daubed *Avante* over their wrecked cars.' He nodded. 'Quick thinking. It might have fooled the Germans but it's cost me another wad of Escudos with Captain Menendez of the PVDE. I'll have to tell him, of course. Now, let's turn to Vila Real. The police have found two corpses floating down the Rio Corgo. They appear to have drowned but someone forgot to remove all their ID and Menendez now has a name of a Frenchman he's anxious to trace. Any ideas about that?'

We'd already decided that the episode in Vila Real was deniable so I shook my head. 'Sounds like an accident to me, sir.'

He snorted. 'Moving on. Acting on information received the PVDE visited a house on the outskirts of that town which had been rented by a woman bearing a striking resemblance to this Hélène you were sent to meet. It seems that she might have been running a butcher's shop from the basement. Any comment on that?'

'I'm no expert in Portuguese meat but I suppose there might be a small profit to be made somewhere along the supply chain. When I was farming sometimes we butchered our own—'

He held up his hand. 'Enough. Velosa has told me about the house. Don't you think it was rather stupid to bury the bodies in the garden though?'

Willie spoke before I could. 'Let us stop beating about this very British bush, Major. Those bodies were colleagues of Hélène's. They were all Jewish and, as *you* very well know, we bury our dead within twenty-four hours. They were all tortured to death by three men and one woman who were trying to extract the location of the diamonds from Hélène. They had come from Paris and were acting independently of Comintern. They saw a chance to make some money and failed. Two of them went for a swim. The other two wouldn't have looked like drowning victims so went mining instead. The car they drove from Paris was in your courtyard last night. You have either given it a new identity now or donated it the foundations of a new bridge which is so badly needed across the Tagus.'

It was a long speech for Willie and he hadn't barked any of it. Friedman heard him out then looked at me invitingly. 'Tell me about Spain.'

'Nothing much to tell really, sir. We intercepted a convoy of wolfram, took it over the border along with some diamonds to pay for Hélène's husband's release, discovered that the men who had him captive were undesirable and treacherous human beings and disposed of them down a well, then—'

'That's enough. I don't need to know and shouldn't be told any more about your cross-border incursion. Suffice to say, you returned with the wolfram and the diamonds which are now on their way to Liverpool. There's also the matter of an odd crate which is on the ship's manifest. Can you confirm that it holds the remains of Captain Anatoliy Dobruskina?'

'It does, sir and his widow is travelling with it to ensure an appropriate burial in the UK.'

'I assume that Anatoliy isn't Jewish then?'

I looked at Willie. He shook his head. 'Not as far as I know, sir.'

'There is something else. A young man called Kurt Behring has taken passage along with Mrs Guzman, Mrs Dobruskina and Nicolai Vorolov. What's his story?'

Willie responded first. 'He was working for the Germans without them realising he was half-Jewish. We saved him before they found out.'

That was a reasonable approximation to the truth so I didn't add anything.

Friedman stared at us for a while. 'Anything to tell me about your journey from Porto before Menendez does?'

'Apart from our Peugeot attempting to copulate with a Mercedes taxi in Lisbon, not much really, sir. Can I ask you something?'

'Of course, but only on the understanding that my answer might not be quite as honest and truthful as yours.'

'What's the news from Spain?'

He smiled. 'Heavy showers, cold winds, unexplained thunderstorms and considerable unhappiness in Madrid particularly at the German embassy. The PVDE are somewhat amused that their counterparts don't seem as competent at managing their political prisoners as they are. I'm sure more details will emerge but don't expect them to spread any further than those charged with guarding the secrets of either country. And, before you ask, the German mine at Vale das Gatas appears to have mislaid a couple of new Ford trucks along with their drivers and guards. The border crossing at Vilar Formoso has been closed while investigations are carried out on both sides.'

'And the SS *Cassequel*, sir?'

'Left Porto last night and is on the way to Liverpool.'

'Are we still going to Madrid for Commander Fleming, sir?'

He sat back in his chair and steepled his fingers. 'No, you have new orders. I rather fancy that your boss is planning a trip there himself. He's due to arrive here in a few days but you will be long gone.'

'Doesn't he want to see us?'

'Not particularly and that might be for the best. He wants you to take a bit of a break then bring him complete details of where those blessed diamonds are hidden so that he can have them extracted.' He opened a file on his desk and pulled out a sheet of paper. 'Accordingly you have been booked on the *Cymric* departing Lisbon for Liverpool tomorrow at 08:00. She's Irish and will be carrying a mixed cargo of fertilizer and agricultural machinery from America. Gods of war and weather permitting you should arrive within hours of the *Cassequel*. To avoid any further incidents and to placate Menendez you will remain here until you are delivered to the docks in a closed van.' He stood up, walked around his desk and shook our hands. 'If you stayed here much longer I fear that you might create sufficient mayhem to set all the dictators at each other's throats and start an Iberian war all by yourselves…and that is not in the interests of His Britannic Majesty's government…at present…*entrez-nous* and not for repetition in London, Menendez did say that if Britain could field more lunatics like you two the war should soon be over.'

He chuckled as he led us to the door. 'You will excuse me but I have to return to a function at the American legation and pay him a small fortune in bets. We'll be going to the casino in Estoril after the speeches so I'll probably win it back. Have to change out of this rig first though — not acceptable to flash one's uniform in front of our enemies. The Yanks love it of course but…never mind. Oh…one final thing. You will be sharing the voyage with Mr Johnson who is being repatriated as he is suffering from a nervous condition which precludes him working here any longer. Please don't interfere with his socks.'

53

I suppose the role of an SIS officer in a neutral country demanded a range of social as well as espionage related skills but Friedman also seemed to be blessed with a vindictive sense of humour. On first sight we had no transport waiting for us as we stumbled out of the blacked out van but, as my eyes adjusted to the bright morning light, I realised that there were various definitions of cargo vessel and this one didn't match any I'd imagined. It was painted white and CYMRIC - EIRE was displayed in large lettering on its flank but it didn't have a funnel or even a bridge structure. It was a sailing vessel with three masts and wasn't much more than twice the length of *Étoile de Jacob*. Nestled against the harbour wall it was dwarfed by the dockside crane which towered over it as its main jib swung landward; loading apparently complete.

Friedman had told us this little vessel would reach Liverpool about the same time as the *Cassequel* which had left Porto at least twelve hours earlier. Saul would have calculated the speeds in an instant but it took me over a minute to realise that if the old tramp steamer cruised at about ten knots this schooner would have to fly at nearly fifteen to catch up. That would not make for a comfortable journey across the Bay of Biscay. Willie managed one word in German which I imagined was not one of appreciation for the vessel's sleek appearance.

'Top of the morning to you.' A squat seaman, whose face was framed by an impressive beard, called out to us in a soft Irish accent. 'Take it easy on the gangplank. Need a hand with your luggage?'

The thought of lying in a bunk canted at an acute angle as *Cymric* battled the waves for over three days was not enticing. Sea air would be cleansing but this deck was strewn with a multitude of cables and I expected that passengers would be confined below deck. The only way to survive this was to insist on helping the crew and that would involve a white lie. As soon as we'd deposited our bags in the surprisingly spacious double-bunked cabin I asked to see the captain.

Dermot McConnell looked more Breton than Irish with deep brown eyes glinting with mischief in a nut brown face. But he was Irish and I knew they had no love for the English so I introduced myself as a Jerseyman fighting to free my island from a foreign invader. Willie picked up on my cue and told McConnell that he was a refugee who'd fled from the Nazis. The captain gave us a long stare then laughed and laughed until the tears ran down his cheeks and disappeared into his whiskers. 'I couldn't give a rat's arse who you are, or claim to be. To me, you're just cargo so I'll ask no questions and you'll tell me no lies — agreed.'

We nodded as he opened a drawer and extracted an unlabelled bottle of something he called poteen and assured us was Ireland's answer to vodka, polished three glasses on his sleeve and offered two to us. 'Now we'll drink a dram or two of this filthy stuff as a toast to a safe journey before I batten you down in your cabin.'

'We'll drink to that but we'd like to help your crew. We're both experienced sailors and want to work our passage.'

He seemed surprised. 'That'll be a first for *Cymric* — useful passengers.' He knocked back his drink. 'Well, we're normally eleven crew, including me, but we lost one in Guinea on the last trip. Well, not quite lost if you understand my meaning. His body's in number two hold.'

'I'm sorry. What happened?'

'Drink as usual then Flynn caught something terminal.'

'I suppose disease must be a problem in West Africa.'

'It might have been but we'll never know…' he lowered his voice, 'you see, he was messing with a pretty Balanta lass and the thing he caught was a machete in the back of the neck from her husband!' He roared with laughter having hooked and landed me like a gullible fish. 'So if you two can keep your hands off the galley maid we can probably find something for you topsides but if your hands wander, or you get in our way, we'll make you walk the plank. Now drink up and follow me.'

We ducked and weaved around the schooner trailing in his wake. He knocked on a cabin door and got a muffled reply. 'It's our other passenger, Mr Johnson. He's seasick already and we're still tied up. You could help by nursing him if he gets dehydrated from vomiting. Would you do that if asked?'

'I think we'd prefer to lash ourselves to the main mast. We know him and, shall we say, his health might suffer from our presence.'

'I see. I met him briefly and he doesn't elicit the milk of human kindness.' He peered into my face. 'I guess that you two are probably more experienced in dispensing death than medicine. So, you'd like to play in the shrouds would you?'

Not quite sure what he meant, I nodded. He hurried back on deck and beckoned us to follow him up the narrowing rope ladder which I remembered was what proper sailors called a shroud. He was quick despite his bulk but we didn't disgrace ourselves as we scurried after him. When the tour was over he took us to the foredeck and down into the crew's quarters. We'd met several on our journey already but there were half a dozen resting or playing cards. He introduced us and explained that we wanted to help. This caused some amusement and one suggested that, if we wanted to be useful, we should move in with them and join in their watches. I suspected that we were being played but agreed that this would be a sensible move. He didn't wait but picked up his kit, tapped a mate on the shoulder and informed us that they'd be off to exchange their luxurious bunks for our cramped quarters.

Well, we had to laugh with them and join in the mutual back slapping especially when the captain introduced us to Dermot, the "galley maid", who was the bulkiest of his crew by a considerable margin but the only one without a beard. After he'd chased me around the cabin a couple of times trying to plant a kiss on my cheek, McConnell called a halt to the festivities, picked out the two most piratical looking crew members and detailed them to look after us. They seemed a jolly crowd and perhaps we might learn something and have a brief working holiday before we discovered what Fleming had in store for us. Managing sails and booms and all the paraphernalia needed to control a bucking bronco at sea should take my mind of Masha for a while at least — even if the "galley maid" didn't.

Cymric lived up to her looks and was as swift as a greyhound — albeit one which specialised in running on two legs because, on the long stretch up the Portuguese coast, her starboard stanchions were barely a foot above the waves as we sliced through a following sea heeling over under full sail. At one stage the captain claimed the trailing speed log showed over twenty-two knots. While it was exhilarating it couldn't last as the wind shifted then dropped and our hissing hull became a heaving iron tub at the mercy of the growling sea. *Cymric* had an auxiliary diesel engine much smaller than *Étoile's* though it had sufficient power to manoeuvre us into position for a different reach and we were off again. We passed Porto just as nautical twilight faded away towards the west and settled into the long run along the northern coast of Spain and into the Bay of

Biscay. Lit up like a Christmas tree we began to catch the full force of the rollers sweeping in from the vast reaches of the cold Atlantic Ocean. We shortened sail and settled into a night running routine. Willie and I were allocated the morning watch from 04:00 to 08:00 and fell into our bunks amongst the snoring Irishmen and were asleep within seconds.

I'd seen dawn over the sea many times but not one where the sun's rays were dragged down through tautly stretched sails spread from wooden masts towering a hundred feet above me. It was breath taking but chill as the speeding air pressed my eyes into sprouting tears but these were natural and not reactions to self-inflicted emotional confusion. As the last vestige of land disappeared over our stern, time seemed to slow and my mind began to fill with possibilities for this amazing vessel. She had two large holds with the potential for secret compartments, three generous cabins, room for a dozen or so crew and neutral status. The engine would need upgrading though the passage from Cornwall to Brittany would be best navigated under sail. Frenchman's creek on the Helford wasn't named by accident as the secluded river, overhung in so many places by mature oak trees, had been the haunt of smugglers for centuries. Instead of brandy and tea slipping in under the noses of the customs officers we would be taking a very different and far more lethal cargo in the opposite direction.

Willie and I might be able to hijack *Cymric* and sail her up the Helford but that might cause unnecessary friction with the Irish as she was an impressive sight in daylight and difficult to hide. McConnell was in this business for his pocket and not his health. He'd told me the schooner was part of a fleet based in Arklow on the east coast of Southern Ireland midway between Wexford and Dublin. She was owned by a Mrs Hall who was taking advantage of Eire's neutral status to run a five-legged trade route over several thousand miles with good profit on each leg. But it was hard won profit with great risk. She might be seduced by a simpler route and persuaded to run her ship for Holdsworth on the occasional charter basis. I'd put the idea to him when I returned to Cornwall. It might even appeal to Fleming as *Cymric* or one of her sisters would make better bait for an E-boat than a captured bomber crash landing in uncertain seas. Perhaps I was just being fanciful but believed I might need something to offer next time I was in the "headmaster's" study.

Aching all over from muscles I didn't know existed I leapt and crawled all over the ship, furling and unfurling sails, fighting wet canvas and trying not to get in anyone's way. Back in the crew's quarters or joking around the dinner table as we caught our food before it disappeared over our shoulders I grew very fond of our ever cheerful and rugged shipmates. I sensed they were a trifle suspicious of Willie even though he did his best to fit in but he wasn't a Celt and, despite my Norman heritage, I'd always felt I was.

Dermot attended to Johnson who had asked to be lashed to his bunk and could only manage water. The crew laughed about his distress but the general opinion was that they'd seen worse and he'd survive. McConnell informed us that he had to as a dead body or absence of one would slice a big chunk off everyone's bonus. I wondered if Friedman had realised what a hellish voyage this would be in late November for a man so obviously unsuited to such a primitive and violent type of travel.

Another day and night passed and we were still only half way across the notorious bay. Our average speed had dropped and it was now doubtful we would arrive on the same day let alone within hours of the *Cassequel* but there was nothing to be done and so I surrendered to the rhythm of the sea and, when not on watch or eating and drinking, slept soundly in my cramped bunk.

As Saturday dawned we made landfall off St Mary's in the Scillies many miles off course and half a day behind my calculated schedule. McConnell brought us round to a more north-easterly line as we headed to St George's Channel on the final run in past the captain's home in Wexford and around the Welsh coast to Liverpool. For the first time in days I began to focus on Masha again convinced now that the *Cassequel* would have deposited its cargo and passengers and that I was unlikely to see her for some time as she was sucked back into the comradely embrace of her Soviet masters.

54

Despite making excellent progress up the channel in the steady south-westerly wind we had to slow to a crawl when we encountered fog about ten miles short of the Mersey. So, just before midnight, we dropped sea anchors and rode gently in the relative calm of Liverpool Bay. We might be neutral and well lit but, even though we couldn't see it, we knew the coast line was blacked out. A smell I recognised from St Nazaire suffused the whole area penetrating the enveloping fog as acrid smoke stretched its tentacles out to us. The Luftwaffe had paid a call. McConnell spoke with the port authorities on the RT and his face was heavy with despair when he relayed the news. Apparently waves of bombers had dropped hundreds of tons of HE, incendiaries and mines on the city and docks for over eight hours on Wednesday from seven in the evening until three o'clock the following morning. Another short raid had taken place over night on Friday and the docks weren't accepting shipping until the Mersey had been cleared of mines.

Had *Cassequel* been caught in the raid? McConnell explained that specifics wouldn't be revealed on an open radio channel but he would work his contacts to discover what he could after we had docked. I spent a restless night until my watch at 04:00 worrying that, after all they'd been through, Hélène and her husband might have been injured or worse by a random bomb or mine.

Everyone, apart from Johnson, was on deck as we motored up the Mersey following a naval tug through what we hoped was a newly cleared channel. Apart from the gut-wrenching smell and wreathes of curling smoke from the bonfire of people's homes and lives there was little destruction to see. We covered our noses as we slid past the towering hulls of cargo ships; crane jibs spinning as goods were snatched from their holds. McConnell expressed surprise that the union had allowed the dockers to work on Sunday but assumed a special price had been negotiated. What better time to hold the Capitalist pigs to ransom than during a war? I thought he was being ironic as Irish Catholics didn't usually make good Communist bedfellows.

Eventually we found our spot against Canning dock, tied up and waited for a crane to attend to us. I was anxious to get ashore to find out about the *Cassequel* and get in touch with London where I was sure the Naval Intelligence Division wouldn't be following the orders of union bosses. I also wanted to leave before Johnson appeared and started asking questions. McConnell told us that, assuming it was still standing, we could get breakfast in the Sailors Home which was only a short walk away at the junction of Park Lane and Canning Place. He said there was a telephone box outside and he was kind enough to give me a fistful of coins. Earlier I had sounded him out about charter work for the Royal Navy but he'd been very reluctant until I'd mentioned gold. He said he'd discuss the matter with his owner when he saw her the following day in Arklow. I couldn't tell him anything about the sort of work, or even if his services would be required, but gave him Saul's details and a contact telephone number. I was sure that Fleming would be attracted to the idea of using a sympathetic neutral and wouldn't be too worried about the cost. In return, McConnell gave me his owner's address. Ireland sounded an attractive proposition for a short break especially as he had told us about the abundance of food, drink and the great craic we would enjoy in Wexford.

Many handshakes and back slaps later we shuffled down the gangplank carrying our luggage, spent a few moments regaining our balance on a surface which stubbornly refused to shift under our feet, then picked our way over crane lines and set off south towards Canning Place. We had to pass Salthouse Dock on our right and I stopped to see if I could spot an old tramp steamer with a white hull but McConnell had warned me that if I started looking for *Cassequel* I could be in the docks for days as they were spread all along the Mersey on both sides of the river and she might already have left anyway.

One large rust bucket was unloading pallets of cardboard cases which we were close enough to read contained canned foodstuffs from America. As the crane's jib swung away I thought I recognised, through a gap between two warehouses, a funnel in the next seaward dock. It was white but the Portuguese flag was painted around the smoke stack. I was carrying the suitcase radio in one hand and my personal kit in the other. My haversack containing weapons and other items was on my back. I asked Willie to fish out the binoculars and hand them to me. While he fiddled around I sensed several dockers staring at us. I realised that we were both looking rather scruffy in our well-worn working clothes and hoped that Willie wouldn't take umbrage and shout at them in German.

Once I'd focused the lenses I forgot about our suspicious appearance as it was clear that the ship was the *Cassequel*. I put on my best officer's accent and issued an order to Willie to follow me. On reflection, speaking in the voice of a class enemy might not have been the wisest thing I'd done in the past few days as two of the dockers stopped what they were doing and called out to us. I didn't understand what they said but it didn't sound polite. Other voices responded to the call and we were soon surrounded by a gang of swarthy men wielding wooden-handled hooks and poles.

Of course a German spy might very well have tried to mimic a British officer and my slightly foreign look and Willie's bald head would have looked suspicious to locals probably desperate for revenge after the recent bombing. Between us we had sufficient skills and weaponry to deal with the situation but these docks were teaming with men who wouldn't think twice about wading in and, once we were down, they'd rip us apart then ask questions afterwards. Willie sensed the danger, shrugged out of his backpack and readied himself. I did the same then extracted my ID card from my jacket rather than the knife or gun I sensed Willie was gripping in his bag.

I stepped forward to confront the man who had initially called out. 'Good morning, we're British soldiers, just disembarked from the *Cymric* out of Portugal. I just confirmed that the *Cassequel*, also out of Portugal, is docked over there and we're just going over to speak to her skipper. So please—'

'Oooh, listen to Mr Lardy Da.' His accent seemed a mixture of Irish without the soft lilt and something much more guttural and harsh. I'd heard it before and realised it was called scouse but it didn't make it any easier to understand though the menace in his tone was clear.

'Is there a problem?' I asked

'No. Not for us, mate. Big one for you though. You're fucking Jerry spies aren't you? Trying to sneak in after your bombers. Thought we wouldn't be working on a Sunday didn't ya? Well, we are and we're going to unload youse two.' He brandished his hook while the gang growled their approval.

I held out my ID which he snatched and passed to someone alongside him while he continued to stare into my face.

His mate laughed. 'Sub-Lieutenant Renouf, it says here He's only Wavy Navy and taking the piss, Ron. Even if he's not a fucking Nazi he deserves a good hiding for showing his officer's mush down here.' He threw the card back at me.

As I bent to pick it up, I realised that we were now in the manure up to our necks. Our only hope was a standoff until someone in authority or the police arrived. If these dockers discovered the radio in the suitcase their suspicions would be confirmed and we'd have to use weapons.

'I suggest you send for the police to confirm our identities. Please don't do anything foolish.' I spoke slowly and calmly just in case they found my accent as difficult to follow as I found theirs.

'Threatening us, are you?' Ron stepped closer and spat. 'In our docks? You fucking vermin I'm going to teach—'

Actions always speak louder than words and his were swallowed in a blur of movement as Willie whipped the hook from his hand, twirled him round into a half nelson and placed the sharp end under his chin. It was so quick that the gang were stunned for long enough for me to extract the Browning from my bag and chamber a round with a loud click.

'Easy now, all of you. We're not just British soldiers — we're fully trained commandos — returning from a secret mission in Europe where we've been killing more Jerries than you've seen in your entire lives! Now, back off and wait for the authorities.'

That had confused them so I followed up. 'Threatening to kill a British officer is a capital offence and if you don't return to work immediately I will have you all arrested. Do you understand?'

The one thing they must have recognised was the voice of hated authority and they glanced at each other before nodding and lowering their weapons. I still wanted to visit the *Cassequel* but could I trust them once I turned my back or lowered my gun? I'd start with a peace offering. 'Let him go, sergeant.'

That was Willie's equivalent rank in the Foreign Legion though he was still a private in our army and he smiled at the promotion then pushed Ron away and tossed his hook after him. The sullen band of dockers still didn't look convinced and stood there glaring at us. I was aware of more men closing in from the south but there still wasn't any sign of the police. Perhaps they allowed the dockers to manage their own laws in this part of the world. I glanced over my shoulder trying to measure the distance to the *Cassequel*. It was a good 400 yards and we'd have to negotiate cranes, rail tracks and all the detritus of a working quay to get there. We'd also have to put on our packs and pick up our luggage. *Buggeration*; this was a mess.

Ron was made of sterner stuff than his followers and as soon as he was back in their ranks he started to rally them again. Only this time, instead of ten or so, there were nearly fifty tough looking dockers to contend with. Willie had realised this as well and had removed his Browning and a Mills grenade from his pack. He tossed the grenade to me and I caught in in my left hand. This provoked shouts of alarm from the growing gang. I tucked the Browning under my left arm, removed the safety pin from the grenade with my right hand and depressed the striker lever. We'd fused these in Portugal and they were still live. If the dockers had the courage to attack we could chuck the grenades over their heads leaving us with three seconds to duck before they exploded and blasted shrapnel into their backs. I felt queasy at the prospect but it was them or us. I just hoped they had more belief in my resolve than I did.

Willie had prepared his own grenade and we stood side by side for over a minute while we waited for Ron and his men to make their decision. A growl grew from the rear of the ranks and quickly spread to the front. They'd worked out the odds and were going to have a go. I pulled my left hand back ready to toss the grenade underhand into their ranks and sensed Willie do the same. If we weren't killed we'd probably hang or spend the rest of our lives in prison for this but there was no way we were going to surrender to this mob.

They weren't stupid and slowly they began to spread out to the sides trying to surround us. If we let them succeed we'd be lost. I had to make the first move so I pointed my gun at Ron. 'Call them off or I will put my first bullet through your skull.'

He glared back at me. 'Go on then, you brave fucker. Shoot an unarmed man and my friends will rip your guts out and fry them in front of you!'

Bravado or genuine courage in the face of what he believed was the enemy. He'd never know. I started to squeeze the trigger.

'Jack, what the fuck's going on here?' McConnell's wonderful Irish brogue shattered the silence.

'Ask them, Dermot — they think we're Jerries!' I shouted.

'Is that you, Ron?' McConnell walked between us and stood in front of the bristling docker. 'What would your missus say? Bejesus, would you stop this nonsense. These two aren't Germans; one's a

Jerseyman and the other's French — though, after our trip from Lisbon, we just made them honorary Irishmen.'

Relief flooded through me as it must have through the whole crowd.

'Thank Christ for that, Dermot — if we'd known they were fucking Irish we'd have left well alone!' Ron reached out to shake McConnell's hand. 'Okay, lads back to work.'

There were lots of sheepish grins as they dispersed. They couldn't fight Germans thousands of feet up in the sky and, because of their reserved jobs, wouldn't have been allowed to join the services to fight them close up so this had been the only opportunity they were likely to see unless the Nazis invaded. I was shaking and trying desperately to control it. Killing the enemy was one thing but destroying your own side to preserve your life was quite another. Between us we might have wreaked as much devastation on one hundred or so Liverpool families as a squadron of German bombers.

After they'd gone we retrieved the safety pins and carefully pushed them back into the grenades. McConnell shook his head in disbelief. 'Leave you alone for ten minutes and you're starting a war with your own side.'

'Lucky you turned up then as I would have shouted "Long live Ireland" as I tossed this bugger at them.'

'That's not even funny, you silly shite!'

'Sorry, but why did you follow us?'

'Ah, we got a message. A car's coming to collect you and Johnson in an hour. So you'd better come back.'

Double buggeration. 'Do you know where it's taking us?'

He shook his head. 'No; but judging from what I've just seen, probably to the nearest mental asylum!'

'An hour you say? So that gives us time to have a word with *Cassequel's* skipper. Do you know him?'

'Mario Oliveira? Yes, we've met a few times. He's a bit slippery but—'

'Would you come with us? I really don't want to shoot anyone today.'

He shrugged. 'Make it quick. I have to get back to supervise the loading and tidy Johnson up so it doesn't look like we've been mistreating him.'

Cassequel was the only ship in the Albert Dock and, with McConnell in the lead, we were soon aboard and sipping *bicas* of the ultra-strong coffee favoured in Lisbon with Oliveira. His English was fractured but McConnell was almost fluent in Portuguese and between them I had answers to my questions. An unusually large limousine and covered lorry had collected the passengers and the crate the previous afternoon and driven off. He had no idea where they had gone but, apart from the one in the crate, all were healthy when they left. The wolfram cargo had been unloaded and they were soon to take on coal and other mixed goods for the return journey. He had been well paid by the man who collected them whom he believed was Russian.

55

Johnson was shouting the odds when we returned, complaining bitterly about the rudeness of the crew, the lack of respect for his person and the very poor accommodation he'd been offered. Considering he had been almost comatose for three days and only kept alive by crewmen helping him drink and cleaning up his vomit I thought that was a bit rich and was surprised the recipients of his pompous diatribe hadn't turfed him overboard. We dumped our kit and followed McConnell up the gangplank. When Johnson spotted us his voice dried up and he started to shake. McConnell caught him as he collapsed, lowered him to deck gently then propped him up against one of the capstans.

He turned to us with a pleading look. 'Take him away with you please and straighten out any…difficulties…if you catch my drift.'

Willie grinned. 'It will be a pleasure, captain. Is that his luggage there?' Willie pointed to three expensive looking leather cases.

'Yes, that's *all* he brought with him.'

Willie knelt down and opened the largest and rummaged through it. Pulling something out, he held it behind his back as he approached the stricken diplomat. 'Now, Johnny, you're going to be a good boy, aren't you?'

Johnson spluttered something uncomplimentary so Willie brought his arm out and, opening his hand, revealed a pair of neatly folded socks which he dangled in front of the silly man's face. 'You can sit there patiently and thank the captain for his hospitality politely before you leave or I can put these on for you again. It is your choice.'

Those members of the crew who had been observing the little scene with some amusement now burst into laughter as Johnson nodded quickly and shuffled away from Willie. Before I could add any words of advice we were startled by a car horn honking from the quayside. I turned to see a khaki painted Humber draw up at the foot of the gangplank. It was driven by a pretty WRAF corporal who alighted quickly before hurrying around to the passenger door to open it with due ceremony. A dishevelled figure in naval uniform emerged and waved.

'Saul, you…' but I *was* pleased to see him and stifled my intended insult, 'are a sight for sore eyes and most welcome.'

'*Kwas*, are you alright, Jack or have you suffered such a blow to your head that you have turned into a polite gentleman?'

'No fear of that — just load our bags will you and introduce Willie to the corporal.' I turned to shake hands with McConnell then stooped to lift Johnson to his feet and drag him off the schooner. A couple of the crew helped Willie with the diplomat's bags and we soon had him settled on the back seat. The boot wasn't big enough for all our kit so Willie had to assist the corporal to heave Johnson's bags onto the roof rack and tie them down. The pair of them seemed to be enjoying themselves so I took Saul aside.

'This Johnson creature is a real pest and needs a long holiday somewhere quiet where no one will listen to any complaints he might have. He could be a security risk. Where are you taking us by the way?'

'London; Fleming wants to see you before he skedaddles off on his holiday to Portugal and Spain.'

'In this car?'

'No, silly; Speke aerodrome is only seven miles away along the Mersey. We're flying down. We can take this Johnson with us but I don't know what to do with him. Someone might miss him.'

'I doubt it but you probably have somewhere you can stash him. He needs to be made aware of his obligations.'

'We'll find somewhere. Now get in the car and tell me all about your adventures.'

'Not in front of him. You'll have to wait until we're in the air. By the looks of things it's going to be a struggle to tear Willie away from your driver!'

And it was but, after she'd helped him load all the kit into the luggage compartment of the DC3 which was waiting for us, he got her name and contact telephone number and promised to call in on her next time he was in the vicinity. I thought he might need a parachute for that.

The aircraft was camouflaged, bore RAF rondels and was kitted out as a passenger transport with reasonably comfortable seats and rows of square windows. Once we had boarded I pushed Johnson up the steep aisle to the front of the compartment and belted him in. We settled down several rows back and Saul started his barrage of questions. But I wanted to know about Masha before I would answer. He hadn't seen her or any of the others and told us that, apart from Kurt Behring who was being debriefed by MI5, they were staying in the Russian Embassy. After Fleming had finished with us I was to present myself to Ambassador Mayskiy.

After an hour of Saul's incessant questioning, I'd had enough and told him to wait until he read the report if he was that desperate for information. I heard some new Afrikaans swear words as he explained that he was the one who had to write the *bliksem* thing. I handed him over to Willie who answered two questions before squeezing Saul's knee until he shut up and let us rest. I tried to doze but couldn't banish Masha from intruding as the aircraft lumbered through scattered clouds towards Hendon.

My meeting with Fleming was brief as he was in a hurry. He didn't seem interested in our adventures as, apart from a couple of tons of wolfram, we had nothing to show for them. My idea of chartering the Irish schooner was dismissed as soon as I'd uttered it. He was very disappointed that I hadn't secured the location of the diamonds but told me that, if I didn't want to be posted to the Outer Hebrides on a permanent basis to guard the sheep from German paratroops, I'd make sure Hélène passed over the information when I met her later that day. As a parting thrust he told me that until the diamonds were in our hands he wouldn't be sending me to the Royal Naval College in Greenwich to complete my officer training. He would RTU me along with my private's scratchy khaki uniform.

Saul had listened to this in silence but as Fleming scurried away from his desk towards the exit and Horse Guards Parade he called out. 'Do we have your authority to carry out a raid then, sir?'

The Commander stopped, swivelled, marched back to Saul and poked him in the chest several times. 'Of course you bloody do, Marcks, but don't bother to come back without them!'

Our reception at the embassy was, by contrast, almost effusive. Before I could ask about Masha, we were both ushered into the conservatory where Mayskiy was finishing lunch with a group of well-groomed men, two of whom I thought I recognised as government ministers. He excused himself and led us into an ante room where he offered cigars and vodka. While I declined Saul took both and was soon puffing and sipping away. Mayskiy took me by the elbow and pulled me towards a door. Saul started to follow but he was waved away.

As soon as we were alone in what seemed like a store room Mayskiy wrapped his arms around me and kissed me on both cheeks.

His eyes seemed moist as he thanked me profusely on behalf of the Soviet Union for the safe return of his niece and the body of her hero husband. He was also immensely grateful for my rescue of Hélène and Doctor Guzman. He apologised for not being able to congratulate me in public but assured me that the time would come when he would be able to make a more tangible recognition of my bravery. Rather flummoxed by this I tried to retreat into modesty but he wasn't having any of it. He told me that Nicolai had provided a full report which had been confirmed by the others and that my name would be recorded and passed to the appropriate Soviet ministry. Though I was sure my uncle would be delighted I wasn't convinced this would be in my best interests but there was nothing I could do about it.

He said he would have to excuse himself to return to his guests but that Saul and I along with my comrade Wilhelm were invited to the private funeral for Hero of the Soviet Union, Captain Anatoliy Dobruskina to be held later that afternoon in the grounds of the embassy and he wished for us to attend the reception in his honour that evening. He hoped we would wear our uniforms and medals. With that he led me back to Saul and returned to his guests. Nicolai's sister, Yuliya, appeared and led us to the front door. I tried to ask her about Masha but she didn't reply but, as our taxi drew up, she winked at me.

56

Saturday 7th December 1940: Six nautical miles south-west of Concarneau in Brittany

Étoile de Jacob had a new name — *Loup de Mer*. I'd thought it up as, after our Portuguese mining expedition, *Sea Wolf* seemed appropriate and Daniel, our skipper, believed it might amuse the other fishermen when we tried to mingle in with them. We'd also repainted her in new patterns of the blue and orange favoured by Concarneau tunny fishermen and she bore a new port number of CC 4051.

We'd been travelling since leaving Helford at midday; transiting the Channel until we were level with Ushant off the coast of Brittany having stayed well out to sea until dark. Daniel knew these waters intimately and had conceived a plan for extracting the diamonds from Quimper now that Hélène had given me the location. Torture hadn't been required though she'd spent a lot of time inhaling Mayskiy's pungent cigar smoke and having to keep up with his vodka elbow. She was with us now as there was no other way to get the boxes released unless we were prepared to fight our way into the secret store. We were primed for other battles though and had even brought a Boys anti-tank rifle with us in case we had to disable the engines of any pursuing vessels. Accurate to 500 metres, this infantry weapon was over five feet long and fired a .55 inch steel-cored bullet which could pierce 20mm of armour plate at that range. It also had ferocious shoulder recoil with a kick as powerful as Victor's, our family bull. Joe had nabbed it for himself though he hadn't faced any real competition for the prize.

Daniel's plan was to slip through on the tide at very low revs until we were about one kilometre short of a secluded beach near the hamlet of Lanadan. Unlike other beaches around Concarneau, this one funnelled inland for a hundred metres or so and was overhung with evergreen bushes. We would carry our inflatable boat over the sand and hide it before ascending the hillside and finding the road which wound its way into the outskirts of Concarneau about two kilometres to the south-east. Hélène was still sore from her injuries but was determined that she could keep up with Daniel and myself.

Juan had hoped to stay with his wife but had collapsed after the funeral and was being nursed in the Soviet Embassy. I'd felt like collapsing myself as it had been so poignant especially as Masha had spoken so lovingly about her murdered husband. I'd hoped she would come with us but Mayskiy had decided she needed to get away and had flown her via neutral Sweden then Germany to join the embassy staff in Paris. When we'd stolen a few moments together she'd seemed excited at the prospect but, as ever, full of contradictions, confided that she would also be desolate that we would not be able to cement our relationship. Women were so much more adept at delivering the brush off than men.

I guessed that her main task would be to gather intelligence about the Nazi's plans by mixing with all those eligible young German officers and diplomats. Stalin still seemed convinced that he had secured a lasting deal with Hitler but his minions didn't seem so sure. I also suspected that she was going to be looking for the man who had made the phone call to send the torturers to find Hélène in Portugal. If Masha found him I doubted there would be much left for the fish when his remains were dumped in the Seine. She had taken Nicolai and his sister with her so there was nothing left in Kensington Gardens for me anymore.

We'd brought along two more not so secret weapons but they wouldn't be needed until the following night if all went to plan. When they'd crossed the Meuse during the blitzkrieg which defeated France in a matter of weeks the Germans had used inflatable rubber boats large enough to accommodate a fully armed section of twelve men. Some of these had been captured and Holdsworth had purloined two for the flotilla's use. His tame shipwright had created wooden transoms for them so that outboards could be attached. Normally these were too noisy for clandestine operations but he'd visited the Marston factory at Hamworthy in Dorset and persuaded them to fit additional noise suppression to a batch of their twin cylinder Seagull engines. We'd tested them in the creek and, even on a still night, they were virtually silent. Part of Daniel's plan was to use both to transfer the crates of diamonds from shore to *Loup*. Our trials showed there was little risk of capsizing as they stacked well on the wooden planks we'd made up as temporary decking. If the Germans started shooting at the inflatables the sea floor in this section of the Baie de la Foret could become, for the Germans at least, the most valuable part of the whole region.

The low rumble from *Loup's* muffled engines puttered into near silence as Saul turned her around 180 degrees. Once her head was into the flooding tide, he opened the throttle slightly to maintain our position. Joe and Willie lowered the small inflatable into the water on our starboard side and held it steady with fore and aft ropes while I helped Hélène into it. Daniel followed and I handed him the two oars we would use to pull us into the shore less than one kilometre away. The moon was obscured by the clouds and little light reflected off the relatively calm sea as, this close to shore, we were well protected by the coast on every side but the south.

While I'd been in Portugal Daniel had made two trips to this area; one to Douarnenez, eighty-five nautical miles away to the north around the Île de Sein but only thirty-five kilometres by road, and the second to Concarneau where he'd used one of the flotilla's other disguised French fishing boats to join up with the tunny fleet and get the latest information on German procedures and guard routines. He was sure that the *Boche* had focused their forces in the town and port and left the coastline thinly patrolled, if at all. That didn't guarantee we would be unmolested but it did reduce the risk. In other parts of Occupied France we might have to contend with French police and fascist irregulars but Brittany had always been a law unto itself and its people had little time for authority beyond the region's borders.

Joe leant over the side and hissed. 'Saul wants to know if you're ready.'

I put my hand in the sea to test the temperature then splashed a handful up at Joe. 'We are now. Same time tomorrow unless you hear otherwise. *À bétôt; bouonne cache, man l'anmîn man.*'

'Never mind that *Jèrriais* country nonsense — you take care now.'

'Wait, ' Willie's tone was soft but urgent, 'you've forgotten the radio.'

'*Merde.* Hand it down will you.' Had we forgotten anything else? I checked the floor boards. Our three backpacks, containing weapons and other essentials were there but leaving the suitcase radio behind would have been foolish in the extreme. Some in the flotilla were carrying these as standard now as more agents were inserted into the region though this would be the first for this area. If the diamond extraction was successful Hélène was going to stay in Brittany for a while to try to rebuild her network. Even though the Germans weren't actively pursuing Communists there were plenty of French patriots who were but she had been insistent that Stalin's honeymoon with Hitler wouldn't last for much longer and she had to prepare.

I checked everything again then asked Daniel and Hélène to cast off the ropes as I manoeuvred an oar across the boat so that I could push off from *Loup*. Without Hélène we would probably have used our frogmen's suits and swum in but from the tingling in my hand from its brief immersion I wasn't too displeased that we hadn't. Daniel and I were wearing traditional blue canvas smocks and orange trousers as it seemed the local fisherman were a colourful lot. Hélène was also dressed in practical trousers and a thick high-collared sweater under a waxed overcoat. Her blonde hair was bundled up under a woollen hat which covered her ears.

Loup burbled away as I settled on the centre thwart and began to row with the tide. Daniel steered and Hélène perched in the bow searching for rocks as I pulled steadily for what I hoped was a sandy landing. Our first indication of the shore was when the bottom of the dinghy began to undulate as we reached the point where waves were forming. I'd surfed boats ashore so wasn't too perturbed but these rollers were larger than expected and soon we were hanging on as they caught us and we accelerated. I hoped Daniel had got us into the right position for the run in as this cove was only about sixty metres wide and guarded on both sides by granite outcrops. Fortunately for us, the moon broke through just as a wave picked us up and revealed fingers of rock only yards from our starboard side. I hauled in the opposite oar and so it wouldn't catch, released the other from its rowlock and held it out ready to fend us off if we got any closer. It was touch and "no go" now, but the next surge swept us past the grasping fingers and we bounced onto the shore as the tide pushed us up the beach.

Daniel and I disembarked and hauled the boat far enough up so that Hélène could step out. We grabbed our equipment, shrugged into our back packs and, while Hélène carried the suitcase, Daniel and I lifted the inflatable and hurried with it up the beach to its narrowest point and pushed it under some overhanging bushes. We unrolled the canvas cover and secured it over the boat and oars then shovelled sand over it until it could pass for a dune. I extracted a shaded torch from my backpack and checked our sand castle building skills. It was difficult to be certain but once we had swept our footprints away down to the high tide line I felt it would be extreme misfortune if the boat was discovered during the day. In summer this was a favourite spot for swimming but even the French weren't that fanatical about fitness to play in the surf in December.

Daniel took the torch and guided us up the steep pathway which had been trampled out of the hillside by summer swimmers. Canvas is quite effective at brushing off persistent prickly undergrowth and soon we were trudging along a sunken road towards a T-junction. Turning right would take us along the main road which led into the town but Daniel hurried us across and into barren fields until we came to a thick band of oak trees. Stripped of their leaves they would provide little cover so he led on until we found ourselves in a strand of firs and he stopped.

'I will leave you here while I find my friend's house. It may take an hour or so but I will return before dawn. The Germans do not patrol this area but they do march through the town every hour. You can hear their jackboots from hundreds of metres away so there is no problem. You are okay?'

Hélène was sitting on her backpack and spoke softly. 'I will be when Jack gets his flask out and pours me some coffee.'

He patted me on the shoulder. *'Au revoir.'* And he disappeared.

It was the first time I'd been alone with Hélène for some time and I wanted to ask her about Masha but as soon as I'd provided her with the warming drink and started to speak she shushed me. 'Listen to the silence, Jack. Voices carry a long way. We'll talk on the way to Quimper. You can ask about Masha then…and Rachel as well if you wish…or you could always tell me about Caroline.'

Oops — not a sympathetic ear then. I sipped my coffee and listened to the forest.

Hélène was right; sound does carry and I heard Daniel squeezing through the trees long before he appeared. We followed him through more thickets, sunken roads and over fields until he led us across a yard and into a house nestled in a depression. Judging from the animal smells and noises we were on a farm. I wondered if they'd want any help with the milking. They didn't but we did get served a hearty breakfast if you like grilled sardines and crusty bread.

At about nine o'clock we clambered aboard a Citroen truck loaded with potatoes in barrels and Daniel drove us out through a network of minor roads onto one which he told us would eventually lead to Quimper. Hélène gave him an address and he calculated it would take about forty minutes to get there. On the way he chatted about his life in Concarneau before the *Boche* arrived and what he hoped to do with it when they left. In the meantime he was happy to assist the British in reducing the number of German soldiers in any way he could. His stories solved my problem of having a private discussion with Hélène as I wasn't sure I needed any more advice about my relationships. Instead, I listened and watched the road as we clattered through the French countryside noting the activity or lack of it in the fields and the sombre atmosphere as we drove through the little villages on the way.

Unlike the English, the French had retained their road signs — they were already defeated and occupied so there was little point in trying to confuse the invaders. According to the sign we were four km from the centre of Quimper when Hélène instructed Daniel to turn left off the road and follow a track that wound through the bare trees. After about a kilometre of bouncing about we pulled into a farm yard. Daniel drove into a large barn and turned off the engine. I got out first and sucked up the familiar smells of a working farm. I'd spotted some chestnut-brown pied Normande cows in the fields. They were almost twice the size of my pretty and docile little Jerseys though their milk was nowhere near as rich. Even though the Normande bulls were far larger than Victor none could compete with him or any Jersey bull, for aggression. I was debating whether to poke around a bit more when Daniel called me over. He was standing next to a very pretty woman of about my age who was hugging Hélène.

'Jack, allow me to introduce, Analena.'

I offered my hand but she moved in close and kissed me on both cheeks. From the strong cow smell and manure on her boots I guessed she had recently finished the milking. Her eyes were darkly speckled rather like the Normande cows though her face was far from white. Either she'd retained a healthy tan from summer or there was some Mediterranean in her genes. Her name had a Spanish flavour to it as well. She was about Rachel's height and build but her face was open and unchallenging though her eyes probed mine when she stood back.

Hélène sighed theatrically and said something in Spanish which caused Analena to glance at me and laugh. After that we spoke in French and I discovered that she was the daughter of one of Juan's cousins. Her grandparents owned the farm and she and her younger brother helped them with the herd. I wondered what had happened to her parents but sensed that it would not be appropriate to pry unless information was volunteered.

She led us into the farmhouse where her elderly grandparents offered us some warm croissants and cups of rather bitter coffee. There was general discussion about the *Boche* and their growing intrusion into everyday life especially their interference into farming affairs which sounded familiar. I told them a bit about Jersey and our farm then we got down to the real business of the day.

Sebastien, her strapping younger brother, was sent for and we set about unloading the Citroen. Bringing potatoes to a farm was a bit odd but they provided a good cover story and would help disguise any other cargo we took back with us. Once the lorry was empty Daniel drove it down a short track to a dilapidated store with crumbling stone walls. It was deceptive from the outside as, from within, the roof looked well maintained and weather proof. The earthen floor was strewn with old straw but, once we'd moved a few barrels and scraped away the surface, Sebastien bent down and pulled up a large metal cover. He shone a torch into the void and revealed a basement. Analena lifted a sturdy ladder from behind more barrels and poked it through the opening. She invited me to follow though I thought it would be more interesting following her up the ladder rather than down. The basement was much larger than I expected and, once more barrels were removed, I could see a tarpaulin tied down over a stack of angular shapes.

With Sebastien's help she released and rolled it back. I'd only ever seen four of these cases in Caroline's cellar well over a year before but I recognised them immediately. Each was about two feet long, eighteen inches high and the same in depth. "Forminiére" and the initials "SGB" were stencilled on each top. There were metal carrying handles on each long end and a locking clasp with a padlock in the middle of the front. The crates were made of some tropical hardwood; probably Sapele from Africa from where they'd originated. With their contents, each weighed about eighty lbs — not too difficult for farm boys to lift and nicely shaped for storage.

Hélène had joined us and I asked her if she had stored the keys as well. She shook her head and Sebastien pulled a short crowbar from his overalls then waited. She nodded and he levered off the first padlock. I lifted the lid to reveal a blanket of black cloth. I peeled it back and was almost blinded as this layer caught the torchlight and, like sparklers on bonfire night, dazzled the eye. Even though these didn't look like typical diamonds, their yellow to brown hue was just as bright. There were thousands of these tiny stones and, if our calculations had been correct, these remaining twenty-one cases held nearly three million carats or twelve million individual stones — enough to supply German arms factories for three months. I heard the gasps from Sebastien and Analena while Daniel whistled almost in disbelief.

Hélène spoke first. 'Is it better to take them out of the cases and put them in barrels?'

'I'm not so sure. These are easy to transport but do look suspicious if we're stopped and searched. Each of these cases weighs about twelve pounds empty and contains about sixty-eight pounds of diamonds. We could get them into far fewer barrels but they'd be too heavy to manoeuvre and we have to get them down to the beach. The cases would be easier. I suppose we could burn off the markings—'

Daniel interrupted. 'I agree with Jack. Leave them in their cases and we'll take our chance. The big question is do we move them in daylight or wait until dark?'

Analena answered. 'The Germans sometimes have road blocks during the day but most of the time they don't. There doesn't seem to be a pattern. But driving at night is forbidden and you will be heard.'

That settled it and for the next thirty minutes we lifted, shoved and carted the crates up the ladder — though I never managed to get behind Analena — and stored them in the truck. We drove back to the barn and reloaded two rows of barrels to hide the haul of diamonds. Hélène and I were taken up to the attic where I helped her set up the suitcase radio. Between us we coded a message and she tapped it out in Morse to inform Saul on *Loup* that stage one was complete and to expect us at the arranged time. Shortly a coded acknowledgement was received. We decided to wait until the last possible moment to set off before the curfew was imposed so that we'd have some cover of dusk and catch any Germans manning temporary road blocks at the end of their duty period.

Alone at last with Analena, I discovered that she was indeed the same age as me and had been studying Law at the University of Brittany in Rennes until her parents and elder brother were killed during the Blitzkrieg. It was a difficult moment so, in empathy, I told her of my own brother's death at the hands of the Luftwaffe. We were both silent for a while but, as the emotion of our mutual loss gripped us, we hugged each other. I felt wetness on her cheek as I blinked furiously to control my own despair. Eventually we pulled apart and she tried very hard to smile as she wiped her cheeks and dabbed her eyes with a rag she extracted from her overalls. I forced a smile as well then asked her what Hélène had said earlier about me which had made her laugh.

She giggled as she answered. 'She told me not to be fooled by your charm. That you are kind and considerate but completely incapable of romantic commitment. She said I would find it easier nailing butter to a wall than ever feeling secure with you.'

No surprise there. 'Did she say that I was just a foolish boy then?'

'No! Not at all. Quite the opposite. She—'

'Jack, it's time to go and Hélène needs Analena for something.' Daniel tried not to sound too pleased but failed.

As Sebastien and I herded the cows into the milking parlour Hélène took Analena aside and spoke to her at length. They didn't look in my direction so I assumed I wasn't the topic of conversation. Daniel and I secured the tailgate of the truck and checked that the boxes were sufficiently hidden then waited for the women to approach us to say goodbye. They came side by side and hugs were exchanged before Hélène beckoned me over for a private word.

'If all goes according to plan someone, possibly you, will extract me in six weeks. If it is you and you have to come here *please* don't get involved with Analena. She has suffered enough. I'm not sure what drives you, Jack, but it's probably beyond your control. You have to understand that vulnerable young women like Rachel and Masha and Analena are not right for you. I've never met Caroline but I believe she is. You need to think of that before you let your eyes or hands wander in any new direction. You—'

'But Caroline is beyond my reach. Do you suggest I become a monk?'

She laughed. 'No, of course not — there are plenty of party girls available. Just leave the nuns alone. Now, off with you!'

I wanted to snap back but she'd waited for the man she loved, had risked everything she had to free him and lost close friends in the process.

Suddenly I realised something which I should have recognised long before. Hélène was an older wiser more grown up Caroline.

57

When planning you have to allow for the unexpected but that can fall into several categories from the expected unexpected through to the totally unexpected expected. When I was playing Shylock in the trial scene from the *Merchant of Venice* in one of our school performances two of the minor characters had got us stuck in a dialogue loop. As the *nasty* Jew on trial for his life I could only answer the questions posed and had to wait until they either heard the prompter or sorted themselves out. This crucial and dramatic part of the play was about to descend into farce until Saul, playing the merchant Antonio, rescued it by inventing a line of his own which he directed to me. I needed him now because the unexpected expected had happened and we'd suffered two punctures in less than three kilometres. The first, to the near-side rear had taken a few minutes to replace as the jack was up to the task. The second to the right front tyre was a major problem as we didn't have another spare wheel. With time and the right tools we would have been able to repair the inner tube but we were running out of light and the curfew was approaching. And now, a German motorcycle combination had pulled up alongside and none of the three soldiers seemed to speak or understand French. Saul would have manufactured some excellent excuse in German but we seemed to be stuck in a language loop as Daniel and I tried to explain through mime what we needed to get us going again.

The German sergeant exasperated by these two French peasants resorted to the fundamentals and demanded our papers. Daniel's would pass scrutiny but my ID card was a forgery. Using his torch the German inspected mine closely and seemed less than convinced. He muttered something to the soldier manning the machine gun in the sidecar and he clambered out. Distracted by his movement I didn't notice the sergeant's Luger until it was in his hand and pointing at me. I protested in French hoping the prompter or my fellow actor would come to the rescue. Fortunately, there was no audience to disappoint just a few crows squawking from the telephone line above. Then I twigged. If the Germans couldn't understand us we could make use of that and organise a defence. Still complaining vociferously in French, I shouted some instructions to Daniel who screeched back that he understood. As the dismounted soldier took his torch to the rear of the Citroen and unlatched the tailboard I raised my hands and stepped slowly towards the sergeant. He backed away and shouted at me then gestured that I should turn around and face the truck.

This suited me as this was a situation we had trained for extensively. Disarming someone from the front depended on speed and decisive movement and, if the man holding the pistol didn't read your intentions, stood a reasonable chance of success. Trying the same when your back was turned depended on surprise and total commitment. It was my favourite move and reminiscent of my special skill as a water polo centre-forward where the danger was usually from behind. I waited for the sergeant to move closer to check me for weapons then, as soon as I felt the pistol on my spine, spun inwards towards him, passing my left arm over and around his right forearm close to his wrist. It was now impossible for him to shoot me or release his arm. Before he could make a decision I kneed him in the groin and straight-armed jabbed his chin with my right palm. He should have released the pistol but, even though he was slow and clearly not trained in unarmed combat, he was strong and held on. Keeping my palm on his chin I stretched my fingers into his eyes. He cursed and dropped the gun, feverishly trying to free his right hand to fight back. Two more blows later and he was unconscious at where my feet would have been had I not jumped onto the pillion seat and put a stranglehold on the rider. I'd left the pistol for Daniel and heard a thud as he introduced it to the soldier with the torch.

Now, we had a three-wheeled lorry loaded with a fortune in diamonds, a three-wheeled motorcycle and three unconscious Germans on our hands and we were more than three kilometres from the beach below the little hamlet of Lanadan. We had a quick conference and concluded that one of us would have to ride the motorcycle combination to Concarneau to obtain a suitable wheel or another lorry. We'd already pulled the Citroen off the tree-lined main road into a small clearing before the Germans arrived. If we could manoeuvre it further in it would be hidden in the rapidly fading light unless a passing vehicle spotted it and stopped to investigate. I couldn't be bothered with socks but, after stripping them of their uniforms, we tied the Germans' hands behind their backs using their belts then dragged them further into the woods. Between us we unloaded three of the potato barrels and carried them to the semiconscious soldiers. We tipped the potatoes over them then, using the Citroen's tow rope, lashed the barrels around the trunk of a sturdy pine tree. Into each barrel we planted a near naked German head first then packed the space with potatoes. They might suffocate but we didn't want them wriggling free. After all they weren't invited guests so we didn't need to be polite or show them much in the way of hospitality. At least we'd given them a chance to survive and they wouldn't starve.

I inspected the combination and discovered it wasn't the usual BMW but the superior Zundapp KS750. This wasn't an easily detachable sidecar as its wheel was driven by the bike's engine. Daniel confessed that he'd never ridden a motorcycle which caused a problem as I didn't know how to get to his friend's house and this combination would be tricky for a novice rider. I had considerable experience on motorcycles which were a lot more powerful than this model so had few qualms about riding it even with the unusual gearbox. Ideally, one of us should have stayed with the truck but, under the circumstances we'd have to abandon it. We'd also have to wear German uniforms just in case we were spotted. I rather hoped that this was the only German unit allocated to the road that evening and it had a free hand to patrol until the end of its shift but, as neither of us spoke German, we wouldn't be able to tease that information out of our potato plants.

Daniel did know how to operate the MG34 drum fed machine gun so he dressed in the private's uniform and I donned the sergeant's. This bike could cruise at sixty kph and reach about eighty if needed but the headlight was too feeble to take chances and it took us fifteen minutes to reach the farm where we'd acquired the Citroen. We didn't encounter any other traffic on the journey but edged carefully into the yard. We would have been heard and were conscious that weapons might already be covering us so Daniel called out in French before we dismounted. There wasn't another lorry available but we found a spare wheel in the barn and pumped up the tyre. It was from a different model Citroen but Daniel's friend was sure it would fit.

    We secured it to the bucket seat, covered it with a piece of tarpaulin and Daniel hopped onto the pillion saddle. We were back at the scene of the crime in ten minutes and changed the wheel without further difficulty. Our potato plants were still alive as their feet were kicking so we left them to enjoy their break. Daniel led the way in the truck and I followed up with the Zundapp. Either the French were very obedient or the Germans very complacent because we had the road to ourselves and within minutes we had hidden both vehicles in the bushes above the beach. Now we had to wait for at least five hours for *Loup* to arrive at the rendezvous point. That gave us time to lug the boxes down to the beach in preparation for loading confident that, even if our German plants were discovered, they wouldn't know where to look for us.

At 02:30 I helped Daniel launch the dinghy and pushed him through the small waves and out into the bay. He was confident that he could navigate to the correct spot so that he could guide the two large inflatables to the shore. We decided that I should stay in case he did miss them as they would attempt to land anyway and someone needed to be on the beach to receive them. I stood for what seemed like ages on the beach trying to listen for muffled engines over the sounds of the increasing surf pushing in with the tide. As agreed at 03:00 and at one minute intervals I blinked the torch on a compass heading of 180 degrees. After five attempts I was rewarded with a double flash from the right direction. A few minutes later I could just make out the muted sound of the outboard engines as the inflatables crested the surf and rolled onto the beach. Joe and Willie jumped out dragging lines with them and rammed spikes into the sand to hold them. Daniel followed in the small inflatable and, with four of us working as quickly as we could, we soon had both of the larger boats loaded. There wasn't much we could do to disguise the signs of our activities and the vehicles would be discovered in the morning. The Citroen was stolen and had false number plates so Daniel's friends were confident it wouldn't be traced to them. It was a risk they were prepared to take though they had little idea and didn't want to know why they'd been asked.

The return to *Loup* was more difficult against the tide but, with Daniel navigating and the small inflatable in tow, we found her within thirty minutes. There were still over two hours left before nautical twilight but we had to cover about nine nautical miles to the uninhabited reef to the north-west of the Ile Saint-Nicolas and skulk about there waiting to join up with the fishing fleet from Concarneau when they arrived about an hour after dawn.

Everything was stowed away in our false hold before the first boat appeared. Daniel had warned us that the Germans placed soldiers on different boats each time and usually accompanied the fleet with an armed trawler and sometimes two. They employed a system of flags to identify fleet members so we ran a white one for that day up our mast and streamed some long fishing lines as we drifted towards them. Daniel had discovered that the planned fishing for the day was to be centred on the Ile Saint-Nicolas where the relatively shallow ground, while potentially treacherous, yielded good quality catches. As the fleet passed us, Saul started up the engines at their lowest sensible revs and we merged in with the other boats most of them quite a lot smaller than ours. Unless the Germans were half-asleep this was going to be a problem though Daniel assured us that the Germans on the fishing boats had no radios and had to rely on flag signals or Morse code lamps to the armed trawler if there were concerns.

If just our German potatoes had been discovered there was no reason for the authorities to suspect the fishing fleet but if the motorcycle combination and the Citroen truck had been found along with footprints and evidence of boat loading then even the most complacent German would be suspicious and alert those in the harbour. Our original plan had been to stay with the fleet all day and slip away when the boats returned to Concarneau but as the morning slipped by I began to feel increasingly uneasy. Short of boarding the armed trawler I couldn't see a way to improve our position and prayed for some deterioration in the weather to hasten the fleet's return to harbour. Sadly, the sea state mocked me by becoming even calmer until Saul started whistling and pointed to the west. What had been a clean horizon now appeared somewhat fuzzy. I grabbed his binoculars and focused them on the distance. Mist — had my prayers been answered? It would seem so as the air took on the distinct chill of impending fog. Daniel called out and I turned to see that most of the fleet were turning about and heading north-east. Perfect! I rubbed my hands in relief and was about to order Saul to increase speed and head into the approaching fog bank when Willie hurried past and disappeared below quickly followed by Joe. A light blinked at us and I turned the binoculars on its source. An armed trawler similar in size to *Loup* but with its 20mm canon uncovered and pointing in our direction was picking up speed. Daniel interpreted the Morse and warned me that we were being ordered to heave to and wait.

'Should we try and bluff them?' I asked.

He shook his head. 'They have a radio and will send our details to their HQ in the harbour. It will take them a while to find the harbour master and check his records but they will discover that our number is false and we don't belong to the fleet.'

Willie appeared again carrying a Lee Enfield sniper rifle followed by Joe with the anti-tank weapon. 'How far away are they?'

I focused the binoculars again. 'About 700 yards and closing rapidly. They're clearing the canon for action.'

'What about the fog?'

I looked in the opposite direction. 'A couple of miles perhaps and moving slowly.'

He handed me the rifle. 'Five pounds you can't hit their helmsman before they start shooting.'

A .303 bullet versus a 20mm canon shell? We were still stationery which was good as I'd have a steady platform. The German boat was travelling at speed so their gun layer wouldn't. I scrambled up onto the wheelhouse roof and assumed a prone position. It was the only flat surface and I would have had to kneel over the gunwale anywhere else on deck. The Aldis telescopic scope was already fitted and had been zeroed during our trip down so I felt comfortable that my shooting would be accurate enough. There was some horizontal movement but little correction to be made for wind speed. As I settled I called down to Willie. 'You're on but make it ten shillings!'

I was aware that Joe was kneeling over the prow with the Boys rifle but he needed to hit the trawler side on to penetrate the engine. Saul was calling out to him where to aim. The Germans could hardly miss our preparations so it was time to start shooting. My first attempt was high but hit the radio mast which was probably a good result. The second ploughed into the wheelhouse but there was no deviation in their course. The third went through the window and the trawler suddenly veered to port and swung its hull broadsides. It was less than 500 yards away now and the canon barrel was tracking towards us. I fired again — at the gun crew this time and smiled in grim satisfaction as one of them slammed backwards and disappeared over the side. A .303 round at this range packed one hell of a punch. I worked the bolt again and this time the round ricocheted off the canon's magazine.

Lights twinkled from the trawler as two of its crew opened fire with sub-machine guns. Some of their rounds smacked into our hull but most whizzed harmlessly past us. At this range their retaliation was more of an irritant than a threat but I had to keep their canon suppressed. I'd used one five round clip from the magazine and had five left. I shouted to Joe. 'Now would be a good time to use that pop gun!'

Seconds later the crack of the .55 inch armour piercing round travelling at over twice the speed of sound echoed over the water. Through my scope I spotted a large hole appear in the trawler's hull but suspected it was too far aft and too high. 'More central and lower with that elephant gun!'

While he adjusted I loosed off two more rounds at the canon to keep its crew's heads down. Joe's next shot was about where I expected the engine to be but it didn't seem to have any effect. We could stay here shooting blind at the engine or bugger off into the fog while we had the chance. Willie anticipated my order and shouted to Saul to open the throttles. This was a heavy boat and acceleration wasn't instant so I was able to empty my clip before the wheelhouse started to shudder and roll as we gained speed.

Luck had been on our side so far. We just needed a clear passage out of the bay and the fog to increase in density and keep the Luftwaffe grounded. I lowered myself to the deck and entered the wheelhouse. 'How much fuel do we have?'

Saul looked at me. 'Depends on our speed.'

'Okay, be difficult if you want. Assume we go flat out to the south-west for let's say one hundred miles then turn north-west for the same distance. How far would it be to Helford?'

He didn't need to look at the chart. 'Another 150 but, before you ask, we'd have to crawl along for the last one hundred even using our reserve cans.'

'Would they expect us to go north-west immediately?'

He sighed. 'They don't know for certain where we've come from or where we're going but let's assume they've guessed that we're heading for England. This mist could be just thirty feet above us or it could be a couple of hundred. It might stretch for a few miles or it might disappear at any moment. I think you're right about heading out into the Atlantic though. It leaves us short of fuel but it's our best chance.'

'What's the most you can squeeze out of the engine?'

He shrugged. 'Theoretically, about twenty-two knots but that is assuming the sea state doesn't deteriorate. At that speed it will take about five hours before we need to turn. It will be dark by then and we should be safe but we'll have to slow to cruising speed which makes us an easy target for a submarine.'

'If they spot us. Why would the Germans bother? They have no idea what we have on board. They probably think we're running agents or arms. Hardly worth a sub, surely?'

Willie chimed in. 'You're right. They wouldn't waste a U-boat even if they had one in the vicinity. Our main threat is the Luftwaffe unless there's an E-boat or a destroyer close by.' He pointed out of the window. 'It really depends on what happens to that mist. Saul and I will pray to our God. You should try and contact yours.'

I suspected I had used up all my credit with the mist and from the evidence of the last few years I was fairly sure that their God had already given up on his followers. So, instead of praying I went below, brought up the Bren guns and had them attached to their stands. Then I went below and talked to the engine in English, a language I was sure it understood.

Five hours later we crossed the continental shelf and left the relative safety of having only 600 feet beneath our keel to over 12,000. It was academic anyway but it was now dark and the Luftwaffe was no longer a threat. Saul brought us round onto a new heading which would take us just under ninety miles west of Ushant before we turned north-east for home. We still had about nine hours of darkness left and though we would have to reduce speed for the final leg we should be well into the Celtic Sea before dawn. As *Loup de Mer* chugged on, Willie thought it amusing to point out that we'd rescued the diamonds for the *wolf.*

EPILOGUE

Sunday, 22nd June 1941
Royal Naval College, Greenwich, London

'*Eto krasivo.*'
  '*Da, eto ochen' bol"shoy,* ' I replied.
  Rachel laughed and threw a handful of grass over me then continued in French. 'You need to work on your vocabulary unless you were describing the college. I meant the whole vista. You can see for miles and miles from here.'
  We were lying on the grass on our discarded uniform jackets near the Royal Observatory two hundred feet further up Greenwich Park from Sir Christopher Wren's magnificent early Eighteenth Century buildings where we'd been in training for the past twelve weeks. Rachel had grasped the difficult Russian language much more easily than me and she wasn't going to let me forget it. She continued. 'The word you should have used was "*neveroyatno*" because it is incredible—.'
  'What, with those bloody barrage balloons everywhere?'
  'If nothing else I thought you would have appreciated the allotments we had to tip toe through to get up here.'
  'We did get some strange looks though.'
  'You should have let go of my hand then.'
  'You asked me to hold it when we left the dining room, didn't you.'
  'You know why that was and it doesn't mean anything so don't start getting ideas.'
  I threw some grass back at her. 'Don't worry. I know my role for this evening is to discourage any of my colleagues from trying to get too close to you but you might have to dance with some of them.'
  She sat up and frowned. 'That wasn't the arrangement. I suppose *you* want to try your luck with some of my WRNS classmates.'
  'I might. Hélène told me I should keep away from nuns and prey instead on party girls or didn't she mention that after you extracted her?'
  'Of course; Hélène told me everything she thought I needed to know about you — it took one short sentence!'
  I slumped back and stared at the cloudless sky. This was not only the longest day of the year but the hottest by far. The shade

thermometer had read eighty-six degrees as we started to climb through what had been the lower reaches of Greenwich Park before they had been commandeered as part of the Dig for Victory campaign. Rachel was right; from this height we could see the muddy Thames winding its way around the Isle of Dogs and the eastern reaches of Dockland. When we'd started our courses the cables dangling from the barrage balloons would have been competing with multiple columns of smoke from the bomb damage in the East End. We were all surprised and thankful that the Luftwaffe had been on holiday for well over a month now and hadn't popped across the channel to pay us any unwelcome visits.

One of the reasons Rachel had dragged me up the steep incline was to walk off the substantial lunch we'd been forced to endure after the joint passing out parades for newly commissioned RNVR sub-lieutenants. Ours were the only two jackets to bear single bright green wavy stripes below the gold of mine and the light blue of her rank. Like Saul and Fleming, who had enrolled us, these signified our particular expertise. Unlike the majority of other officers who were going to sea either in Executive or Engineering, we were consigned to the Special Branch.

We'd had to attend the whole range of seamanship lectures and take the relevant tests but every evening Rachel and I had been privately instructed in the Russian language by a crusty old professor dragged in from Kings College's School of Slavonic and East European Studies. Whatever the weather or entertainment programme provided by the Luftwaffe, he had been driven from Bloomsbury half-way across London and he let us know in all of the six languages in which he was fluent of his absolute *delight* about the arrangement. Unfortunately, as Rachel had been an attentive and charming student, most of his ire was directed at me. Whatever Fleming had planned for us next I suspected that I was in for more Slavic torture.

Still speaking French — we'd been forbidden by Fleming from using English when we were together — she interrupted my thoughts. 'It's a bit like home isn't it?'

I rolled over and tickled her until she screeched for mercy — in French of course. 'In what way could this possibly be like home?'

She wriggled away, crouched then launched herself at me like an enraged cat. I absorbed the attack and lay back while she squirmed onto me, hitched her long skirt up and sat astride my thighs. I let her pin my arms down and waited for whatever she planned next. She bared her teeth then bent over until she could nibble my ear.

She lapsed into English. 'Sometimes, I hate you Jack Renouf.'

'And the other times?' I enquired.

She collapsed onto my chest; her tie fell across my mouth. We lay quietly feeling our hearts beating in rhythm, expelling shallow breaths. Despite regulations, she was wearing a subtle yet heady perfume I didn't recognise. It was a magical moment but one I couldn't prevent myself from ruining as my *little* brain decided that this was more than a sign of friendship and started to make his presence felt.

She bit my earlobe and rolled off me. 'Your self-control hasn't improved then?'

'Sorry. I didn't mean—'

'I know. I was silly. Still friends?'

'Of course and for Taynia's sake we must always be friends which is why I'm not going to let anyone else dance with you this evening!'

'Spoil sport!'

'Do you think we'll be allowed to visit her soon?' Saul had wangled a twenty-four hour leave for us for Taynia's first birthday soon after we started the course and what a delight that had been. Kitty was there and Malita had laid on a wonderful party for our lively little princess. She'd tottered towards us when we'd first arrived then stopped not sure which one to hug first. I'd helped by standing back so that Rachel absorbed the impact as Taynia launched herself.

'Saul might be able to tell us something this evening. I do hope he remembers to bring your new dress uniform. I'm not going to dance with a scruff…and of course you will allow me to dance with him. He's such a better lead than you.' She propped herself up on her left elbow and stared into my face. 'Do you remember that awful dance on the terrace when that German bastard…'

And we were off; reminiscing about our first encounter with Kempler and our almost innocent adventure that summer two years before. Yes, we'd always be friends unless…but that was a dreadful thought.

She must have sensed it as she reached out and touched my arm. 'Caroline will survive, don't worry. She promised to let me make the wedding dress, you know. I could even be the bridesmaid. Wouldn't that be fun?'

I didn't want to answer that. Of the three of us Caroline was probably the most likely to come through the war. Rachel would almost certainly be sent to help the growing resistance in France and I'd be catapulted into whatever nightmare scheme Fleming devised next. Even though we were now fully commissioned officers in the King's navy we couldn't wear ID tags on our secret missions into Europe so, if caught, we'd be executed after...but I didn't want to think about that on such a beautiful afternoon. Instead, I reached out and touched her long lustrous hair which she'd unpinned before we lay down. I studied her face and, though her eyes were in shadow, I could sense their keen appraisal as she stared back. A bead of sweat had formed on her upper lip and I flicked it away with my finger.

She smiled and tweaked my nose. 'What's the time?'

I glanced at my watch. '17:05.'

'What's that in real money?'

'Time you remembered the twenty-four hour clock Third Officer Vibert! Five minutes past five.'

'Gosh. We'd better get back. I've got to prettify myself for all those gorgeous young officers who will be shoving you out of the way to get to me.'

'Careful you don't overdo it because your Wren sisters will claw your eyes out.' In truth, she was the most attractive newly minted Wren officer by a mile.

She stood up, brushed the grass off her skirt then started to re-pin her hair so that it could be squeezed under her new navy-blue cap. Without a mirror it wasn't going well but I refrained from comment. Finally, she gave up and plonked it on letting the reluctant strands fall where they wanted. I helped her into her jacket then brushed the grass off her back with firm yet kindly strokes. She retaliated by seizing my tie and pulling me towards her. She stood on tiptoe and rubbed her nose against mine. I thought she was going to kiss me but she looked down. 'Oh dear, we are a messy eater. What are those stains on your tie?'

I fell for it and looked at the offending article which was clean of course but gave her the chance to flick my nose. Laughing, I finished dressing, set my cap at a jaunty angle and hand in hand we ambled down the hill towards the Queen's House which had recently been converted into the National Maritime Museum. Beyond that, in the West Wing of the College, lay King William Court which contained the famous Painted Hall. To avoid any blackout problems the ball would finish before the end of nautical twilight at 22:30. After lunch we'd peeked into what we'd been told was both the finest dining hall in Europe and England's version of the Sistine Chapel. With hundreds of candles it would certainly be dramatic — even more so if the Luftwaffe had received an invite as well.

One of my many weaknesses, according to my detractors, was my seemingly total lack of awareness and disregard for the way my attitude, comments and appearance were viewed by others. I'd secretly thought that a strength but that very conceit probably demonstrated how much of a weakness it really was. Wandering down the hill in such an intimate manner with a beautiful young woman, I tried to imagine how others might be seeing us. It wasn't necessarily against naval regulations as we were both officers though it would be frowned upon. But I was feeling happy for once and looking forward to a glittering evening in the company of the woman who was so much more than my closest friend.

Of course, this dance wasn't being staged just for the benefit of the 120 or so newly commissioned RNVR course members. It was the Mid-Summer Ball and the top brass would be out in force. It wouldn't have surprised me if Fleming graced us with his presence though I rather doubted that Admiral Godfrey could be persuaded to exchange his desk for a dancing partner. I didn't share my thoughts but kept a firm grasp of her hand wondering which of us would break hold first — determined it wouldn't be me. It wasn't.

Rachel stopped and withdrew her hand to raise it to her forehead and shield her eyes from the sun. 'That's Saul isn't it?'

I did the same and there, emerging from the porticoed columns of the Queen's House, was his shambolic figure shuffling towards us in what for him would pass as a sprint.

'Oh, bugger. I hate it when he runs. It usually means Fleming has set fire to his tail and he's been sent to find me with unwelcome news.'

'Don't be so mean. I'll race you to see who can hug him first.'

'That's a race I don't mind losing.'

By the time I reached them Saul was gasping for breath and trying to tug a packet of cigarettes out of his pocket while Rachel fussed over him like an owner of a long lost pet.

He extracted a du Maurier and offered her the packet but she waved it aside and pulled out one of the Gauloises Caporal unfiltered coffin nails she'd adopted as part of her French disguise. Apparently they were essential equipment on the S.O.E course she'd completed in what she jokingly called one of the "Stately 'Omes of England" before Fleming despatched her to Greenwich.

I made my expected disparaging comments but, as usual they were ignored as Saul sucked in the smoke probably believing it would somehow compensate for the oxygen he had expended in his gentle jog up the hill towards us. From experience I knew I had to wait for him to recover and after his first explosive coughing fit I asked. 'Why are you here so early?'

'Something's happened.' Cough, splutter, and wheeze, 'Fleming wants you back in Whitehall immediately.'

'Buggeration. No ball for us then. I was really looking forward to that.'

'Never mind the dancing. What's this *something*, Saul?' Rachel sounded anxious.

He looked around. 'Not here. I'll tell you in the car.' Fortified by the nicotine boost he led us through the columns towards the road which ran along the south side of the College.

'How did you find us?' I asked.

He exhaled another cloud. 'Easy enough. You two seem to have created so much gossip that I saw a captain observing you through his binoculars!' He herded us towards a khaki painted Vauxhall Ten.

'Where's the driver?'

'There isn't one. I drove it here.'

'My God. Who let you loose on the roads? You haven't got a licence and you certainly haven't passed the test.'

'No need. Tests are suspended for the duration and I do have a licence — issued in South Africa.'

'Best say our prayers now, Rachel.'

'Shut up and get in.' She pulled the front passenger door open and slid along the bench seat as Saul got in the driver's side.

I squeezed in and shoved her up along leaving little space for him to make gear changes but plenty of room for embarrassment. I wanted to be up front in case he failed to spot any stray elephants. Several missed gears later we emerged onto the main road which led to a choice of bridges to cross the Thames.

'So what's the emergency and what are we going to do about our kit?' I asked.

'That'll be sent on. Now listen. The War Cabinet has been meeting since early this morning. Churchill will address the nation at 21:00.

Some of us aren't surprised but I suppose you two have been so busy learning the difference between a reef knot and a bowline that you have no idea.'

'About what?'

He grinned in his superior way when he knew something I didn't. 'At 03:15 this morning Hitler unleashed over 130 divisions on three fronts against the Soviet Union. Over four million men, 3,500 tanks and nearly 3,000 aircraft caught Stalin with his pants down. Early reports suggest that the Soviet air force was destroyed on the ground and that their front has crumbled already. It's the Blitzkrieg all over again. Total shambles for the commies. We've known about it for ages and been trying to warn Stalin but he wouldn't listen. Even when we obtained the German Order of Battle and the full plans for what Hitler's calling "Barbarossa" but we've known as Fuhrer Directive 21 for months—'

'How?' Rachel asked.

'I can't tell you that but it's general knowledge in the intelligence community.' He glanced at our sleeves. 'And there you are in the Special Branch of the Naval *Ignorance* Division . "Need to know and all that", as Fleming would say. Stalin has brought it upon himself and he's probably hiding under a table somewhere in Moscow needing a change of trousers. '

'But why wouldn't he listen. He knows he's on Hitler's shit list or didn't he read *Mein Kampf*?'

'He knows but didn't want to believe that the house painter would attack them until he'd finished us off. He thought it was just a Capitalist plot to drive a wedge between him and the Fuhrer. If it wasn't so sad it would be funny. Anyway, Fleming thinks that, like Napoleon before him, Hitler's left it too late.'

'What do you mean? If he's broken through and destroyed the Russian air force how can he be too late?'

'Russia's a vast country. Moscow is a long way from Poland but it's less than a third of the way into the Soviet Union. The campaign was meant to start nearly six weeks ago but was put on hold because Hitler had to rescue Mussolini's nuts from the fire when the Greeks kicked the Italian ice cream vendors back over their border. Now, there are German divisions stuck in the Balkans when they should already have captured Moscow. Anyway that's Fleming's view and he's an expert on Russia.'

'So why does he need us? What can we do? Please don't tell me he wants us to deliver diamonds to Stalin.'

Saul laughed. 'No — and best not to mention diamonds when you see him. He's still aggrieved that Salazar and Franco weren't interested. All they wanted was gold or American dollars. He was there in February, you know, trying to bribe their advisers into remaining neutral or even joining us. Fat lot of good it did him though he claims he paid for the trip by winning big in the casino in Estoril. The only countries who need industrial diamonds are Germany, Italy and Japan. If we used them to bribe the Spanish or Portuguese they'd only sell them to the Germans who'd use them to make more planes to drop bombs on us. Mussolini would probably turn them into earrings for his mistress and, if we sold them to the Japs, our American cousins would definitely bomb us. Things aren't looking too good in the Pacific at the moment especially now Roosevelt is trying to starve Japan of oil and other strategic materials. Mark my words — this is going to turn into a proper world war soon.'

'Where are the diamonds then?'

'In a safe place; along with our other reserves. You know, Fleming suggested scattering them with our bombs over Germany as a psychological ploy. Air Marshall Harris, Deputy Chief of the Air Staff, was not amused and threatened to drop him over Germany if he darkened his doorstep again.'

'Right — so what *does* he want us for?'

Saul shrugged which put too much input into the steering and we veered across the road and nearly collided with a lamp post before recovering and bouncing over the pavement like something out of a Charlie Chaplin comedy. 'I don't really know. He's just come back from America with the Admiral. They were trying to set up some joint intelligence initiative with the FBI but Hoover showed them the door. It seems that once again our Yank friends aren't ready to help out yet. It took them three years last time to wake up and realise that, if Europe is lost to democracy, America might soon follow.'

'So what's your best guess?'

'Ambassador Mayskiy requested a meeting with Churchill this afternoon. Fleming thinks he's going to ask for help. We believe that Russian embassy staff in both Berlin and Paris have sought refuge in the Swedish embassies. Even though Stalin refused to sign the Geneva Convention, the Swedes are the "protecting power" for diplomats from both countries. Anyone who got to the embassies in time will eventually be returned to Russia via Sweden.'

He peered around Rachel and spoke to me. 'The Gestapo have seized both embassies. You can work out what that means—'

'Documents and details of their spy networks?'

'And a lot else; unless they've managed to burn them but, as their air force was wiped out on the ground, what are the odds that they weren't prepared for this either?'

'Shit. Where's Hélène?'

'With Masha somewhere in Brittany but Mayskiy should know more. I think he's going to ask us to rescue them if they haven't been able to get protection from the Swedes.'

'So we're going to France?'

He sighed. 'One of you is. The other is going to the American Embassy. Someone called Brian Avery wants to see you, Jack.'

Bollocks and double buggeration.

Rachel turned her head and placed her hand on my arm. She looked sad and worried. I just felt hollow and drained. I'd hoped we'd be sent to France together where I might be able to look after her but what could the Americans possibly want with a French speaking, Russian mumbling, Wavy Navy. Emerald green, Special Branch non-executive officer who had precious little intelligence about anything?

**Principal characters in order of appearance.
Fictional, unless otherwise stated.**

Jack Renouf : Private (Hampshire Regiment), Jersey, 20
Saul Marcks : Acting Sub-Lieutenant, RNVR (SB), South African Jew, 20
Nicolai Vorolov (Boris): Starshina, Russian, Soviet Diplomatic Service, 28
Miss Yuliya Vorolov (Doris): Russian, Soviet Diplomatic Service , 25
Ian Fleming : Lt-Commander, RNVR (SB), English, 32, **(Historical)**
Alice Philby (Litzi): Hungarian Jew, 30, **(Historical)**
Harold (Kim) Philby: English, (Head of Iberian Desk), 28, **(Historical)**
Mrs. Maryia Dobruskina (Masha), Russian, diplomat, 23
Ivan Mayskiy: Russian, 56, Soviet Ambassador **(Historical)**
Peter Cassons: Flight Lieutenant, RAF, English, 25
Willie Grun : Legionnaire (French Foreign Legion), German Jew, 24
Joe Buesnal : Private, (Hampshire Regiment), Jersey, 20
Daniel Lagadec: Breton, fisherman, 28
Miss Rachel Vibert: Jersey, 20
Mrs. Mary Renouf: Jersey, (nee Le Brun), 49
Mr Aubin Renouf: Jersey, farmer, 50
George Le Bihan: Jersey, fisherman, 18
Brian Le Masurier: Jersey, fisherman, 18
Miss Caroline Hayden-Brown: English, 20
Miss Dorothy Collins (Dot), Cornish, 21
Frederick Le Brun (Red Fred), Jersey, 52
Senora Malita Perez (Lita), Spanish, 36
Katherine Stewart-Murray, Duchess of Atholl (Kitty), 66, (Historical)
Mr Brian Avery (Buster), American, diplomat, 26
Mr Derek Johnson, (Johnny), English, diplomat, 40
Rudolph Kempler, (Rudi), Standartenführer SS, German, 25
Joseph Friedman, Major, MI6, Scottish Jew, 36
Severino Pereira do Sameiro, Communist agent, Portuguese, 33
Madame Hélène Guzman, Communist agent, French Jew, 35
Senor Antonio Velosa, Anglo-Portuguese, Mine manager, 45
Doctor Juan Guzman, Communist agent, Spanish Jew, 39
Dermot McConnell, sea captain, Irish, 39

Separating Fact from Fiction

Operation Ruthless (October 1940)
The plan was that the German bomber would follow on behind aircraft returning from a night bombing raid. When crossing the middle of the English Channel, it would cut one engine and lose height with smoke pouring from a 'candle' in the tail, send out a SOS distress signal and then ditch in the sea. The crew would then take to a rubber dinghy, having ensured that the bomber sank before the Germans could identify it, and wait to be rescued by a German naval vessel. When on board the 'survivors' would then kill the German crew, and hijack the ship, thus obtaining the new month's codes to help Alan Turing with Enigma decryption at Bletchley Park

A Heinkel 111 was available for this operation. The aircraft, Werk Nr. 6853, had been captured in airworthy condition after being operated by the German bomber unit, Kampfgeschwader 26. On 9th February 1940, it had made a forced landing after being damaged by a Spitfire over the Firth of Forth. It was subsequently assigned the Royal Air Force serial number AW177 and flown by the RAF's Air Fighting Development Unit and 1426 Flight.

Fleming had proposed himself as one of the crew but, as someone who knew about Bletchley Park, he could not be placed at risk of being captured. The aircraft was prepared with an aircrew of German-speaking Englishmen.

Fleming took his team to Dover to await the next suitable bombing raid, but aerial reconnaissance and Wireless telegraphy monitoring failed to find any suitable German vessels. Wiser heads also decided that it would take the bomber too long to sink thus exposing its crew to discovery so the operation was called off. Alan Turing was very unhappy at this outcome and challenged the decision.

Lieutenant-Commander RNVR Ian Fleming (1908-1964)
Details of his activities at the heart of the British war effort only emerged in the late 1990s long after he became famous as the author of the James Bond series. He played a significant role in clandestine operations throughout the war and many of his plans, such as Ruthless, were as imaginative as those he concocted for Mr Bond. Along with Alan Turing, whose decoding exploits helped win the war, he was also a supreme athlete though neither were team players.

Soviet Embassy in London
Like many of his colleagues Ambassador Mayskiy was stunned by Stalin's pact with Hitler but they all knew better than to challenge it! Stalin and Molotov, his Foreign Minister, had spent considerable time and effort trying to persuade Britain and France to join them in a pact but the Western Democracies dragged their feet to such an extent that he turned instead to Hitler to guarantee his borders while he continued to terrorise his own people.

Mayskiy and Churchill met on several occasions in the embassy in Kensington Palace Gardens before Hitler reneged on his pact. The British had acquired highly detailed plans of Hitler's planned invasion (Operation Barbarossa) but Stalin refused to believe they were genuine and he was still authorising rail shipments of strategic materials to Germany one hour before the surprise attack began at 03:15 on 22nd June 1941.

After their invasion the Germans sacked the Soviet Embassies in Berlin and Paris and discovered a veritable chamber of horrors in the basements. Sound-proofed rooms had been set up by the Soviets as torture chambers along with acid baths and incinerators for the disposal of those they had interrogated. Even the Gestapo were surprised at the efficiency of their Russian counterparts in dealing with dissidents. As Britain never had cause to break into the Embassy we'll never know what "facilities" had been constructed in its basement in the heart of Kensington.

Harold (Kim) Philby (1912-1988)
A Communist spy and traitor, he passed highly secret information to his handlers throughout the war. He continued to do so after hostilities were over and was responsible for exposing many Allied agents to his Soviet spymasters. Many of these were captured and tortured in other basements before being executed. After his defection to Russia in 1963 he was granted political asylum, Soviet citizenship, a pension and several medals for his services to the Revolution.

Café de Paris
This wasn't quite as bomb proof as its clients believed. During a raid on the night of 8th March 1941, one 50kg bomb fell down a ventilation shaft and exploded in front of the stage. Snake Hips' head was blown off and thirty-three others were killed. Another eighty or

so were severely injured. Fortunately, this occurred at 21:15 while the Café was less than half-full. Had the bomb exploded an hour later the death toll would have been that much greater. This was the heaviest raid for some time and Buckingham Palace was also hit by five bombs and seriously damaged that evening.

S.O.E. & Setting Europe Ablaze
Churchill set up the Special Operations Executive in July 1940 to strike back at the German occupiers in Europe. Fleming, in his role as Deputy Director of the Naval Intelligence Division, was closely involved. S.O.E. was also known as: "Churchill's Secret Army" or the "Ministry of Ungentlemanly Warfare".

Helford Inshore Patrol Flotilla
The Helford River had been a smuggler's haven in the past and was perfect for the task of inserting agents into France. At its height the Flotilla employed more than a dozen vessels, mainly adapted French fishing boats. As it grew in size the splendid three-masted schooner Sunbeam II was moored up Port Navas creek and provided a floating base and accommodation for other ranks. Ridifarne continued to be used as the officer's HQ. S.O.E. had a separate base close by at Pedn-Billy in Bar Road.

Occupation of the Channel Islands
The Germans occupied the islands from 1st July 1940 until 9th May 1945. There were many attempts, mostly unsuccessful, to insert commandos and other raiding parties onto Jersey. After the D-Day landings the islands were cut off from France and their populations, including the occupiers, suffered considerable deprivation until they were liberated nearly one year later. During the period of this novel, the Germans are consolidating their positions though serious fortification didn't start until after the invasion of Russia when Hitler decided that he would defend to the last man the only British possessions he ever managed to conquer.

Katherine Stewart-Murray, Duchess of Atholl (1874-1960)
Kitty was a fascinating character and along with Churchill a political outcast during the period leading up to the war as both fought against the popular consensus that "peace was possible in our time". She'd seen the results of the Nazi's activities in Spain and, though she was a Conservative politician, challenged the orthodoxy that Communism was more dangerous to Western Democracy than Hitler's brand of fascism.

Boeing 314 Clipper flying boats
Only twelve of these were built but they were magnificent aircraft and the first to provide regular trans- Atlantic and trans-Pacific services in the late 1930s. A one-way ticket on one of these luxurious floating/flying hotels would cost the equivalent of a small house. Three of them were purchased by the newly created B.O.A.C. (British Overseas Aircraft Corporation) and used on the routes described in the novel. One was named Berwick and flew Churchill to various locations during the war. The Yankee Clipper, crashed and sank in River Tagus near Lisbon, Portugal on February 22, 1943

Foynes Flying Boat museum in County Limerick in Ireland, where both the Boeing Clippers and the Short Sunderland Empire Boats plied their European and trans-Atlantic trade, is worth a visit as a full-sized replica of the Yankee Clipper is moored there and can be examined in all its former glory.

Portugal & Spain
The continued neutrality of the two fascist dictatorships of Spain and Portugal was essential to Britain as there weren't the resources to counter any German invasion should Hitler decide Salazar and Franco were not being sufficiently helpful. Consequently there was much secret movement of gold from Britain and Germany to bribe both dictators. In one attempt to persuade the Spanish to resist Hitler's attempts to move German troops through their country to seize Gibraltar and effectively seal off the Mediterranean, Fleming even made the journey to Madrid himself. Travelling as a civilian wearing a dark-blue suit and Old Etonian tie, he carried a commando fighting-knife and a fountain pen with a cyanide cartridge. He christened this operation "Goldeneye"!

Wolfram & Industrial Diamonds
If you have read **Against The Tide** will be familiar with the role industrial diamonds played in the war and the exorbitant price the Germans were prepared to pay for them. The same applies to wolframite which was so named by German miners in the Eighteenth Century as, in its natural form, it is black and hairy like a wolf. Contemporary accounts are quite descriptive with one claiming it "tears away the tin and devours it like a wolf devours a sheep". It was so important to the Germans that its price soared from just over $1,100 in 1940 to over $20,000 per ton by late 1941. Portugal, under the fascist dictatorship of Dr. Antonio Salazar, reaped enormous profit from this even though much of it was creamed off through corruption before it reached his coffers.

Neutral trade
Sweden, Switzerland, Eire, Portugal and Spain remained neutral throughout the war and continued to supply strategic materials to the combatants. Ships were brightly painted and well lit at night. Considering the overall tonnage shipped there were very few attacks made on them by either side.

Apart from the Clippers and other flying boats, normal land-based aircraft kept regular services going throughout the war. Initially, the Germans respected the flights from Whitchurch in England to Lisbon in Portugal but as the war progressed there were several attacks. B.O.A.C. flight 777, a Douglas DC-3, was shot down over the Bay of Biscay by eight Luftwaffe fighters on 1st June 1943. All seventeen passengers and crew were killed. Among them was the famous film actor, Leslie Howard. It is believed the Germans suspected that Winston Churchill might have been on-board.

Jack Renouf — Book One

**It's July 1939
you're 18 and in love
your father hates you
your uncle is a Communist
your best friend is Jewish
now a Dutchman is
drowning you
in front of 500 witnesses
you're Jack Renouf and
it's time to start swimming**

against the tide

John F. Hanley

Jack Renouf — Book Two

**It's June 1940
you're 19 and still in love
your father still hates you
your uncle is still a Communist
your best friend is still Jewish
Caroline and Rachel are ignoring you
now a German is
dropping bombs on you
you're Jack Renouf
and you're aboard**

the last boat

from the author of 'Against the Tide'
John F. Hanley

Printed in Great Britain
by Amazon.co.uk, Ltd.,
Marston Gate.